A Black Rose
For
The Angels' Share

A BLACK ROSE
FOR
THE ANGELS' SHARE

STEVI JAMES

To order additional copies of this book, contact:
Xlibris Corporation
1-800-618-969
www.Xlibris.com.au
Orders@Xlibris.com.au
501305

To those who live on.

"God made his world green,
And a fool with a knife made it red.
I stand with my Dark Rosaleen
Counting the graves of our dead;"
-from Dark Rosaleen by David McKee Wright

Irish Gaelic Pronunciation and Meanings

Aisling	*ash-leeng*	vision
A ghrá mo chroí	*ah gra moh kree*	love of my heart
Bean Sidhe	*ban-shee*	female faëry, omen of death, wails
Cill Rónáin	*kill ronan*	main town on the island of Inis Mór
Codladh sámh	*cullah sovh*	sleep well
Craic	*crack*	good conversation
Geansaí	*gan-zee*	jumper/sweater
Geis	*gaysh*	a curse or a prophecy
Inis Mór	*Inishmore*	one of the Aran Islands
Roísín Dubh	*Rohsheen Dove*	dark rose / spirit of Ireland
Sláinte	*slawnt chah*	cheers (to health)

PROLOGUE

It was his earliest memory. He was on the beach at Cill Rónáin on the island of Inis Mór, sitting around the fire with his family and their closest friends. They had been fishing all day and the woollen geansaí that Ruairi's Ma had knit him itched at his collarbone fiercely. Rosaleen Jameson had knelt down in front of him and slowly slipped her tiny hand beneath the rolled collar. He gasped as her cold skin touched his chest. She looked up at him and smiled.

"Is that better then?" she asked, her dark hair shimmering in the firelight.

He could only nod.

She removed her hand but he could still feel the icy grip she had on his heart. She turned, leaning up against his legs and resting her head on his knee.

The fire spit handfuls of blazing confetti into the air and Ruairi watched it fade away over the water. Little Maggie Monroe began to dance around the flames. She started off slowly, circling and weaving in intricate patterns. Her red hair streamed out behind her as she twirled.

She sang as she danced; a song from the past. She sang in the old tongue of Ireland. It was the song of Roísín Dubh. Everyone listened and was haunted by the little girl's cries for her country.

When the song was over, she stopped dancing. Her green eyes sparked in the firelight as she stared at Ruairi through the flames. In her emerald eyes he could see Ireland and she was a black rose; she was a raven haired maiden.

"You will die for her," Maggie said softly. Then she began a new dance.

CHAPTER 1

The stars had already gone out as Gracie stepped from the motorcar and waved her goodbyes to the last few sleepy occupants. The haze from the rising sun rippled; a golden extension of the early morning Atlantic.

She longed for her bed linens. The previous night's mixture of champagne and martinis were threatening to render her unconscious. She quickened her pace as she approached the driveway but something in the stillness caused her to pause for a moment at the steel and brick gates of her family home. She leaned her back against the cold bars which still bore hints of the morning's dew and she shuddered as the water slid down between her shoulder blades, slowing as it curved out from the small of her back. She tipped her head back and inhaled.

The air was moist and salty. Fresh, not like the oppressive air of London. The sea-side moisture of Charlottetown had become intoxicating to Gracie. For the first time in her life, it wasn't hard to breathe.

It wasn't just the air in Charlottetown, it was the people. Although a fair few of the family friends were from the old country, Prince Edward Island was full of new faces, new ideas and new money. Not that Gracie mixed with the 'new' often but it was there; shiny and bright.

She shivered. June mornings held a subtle winter reminder in them. Her hands were cold. She flexed her fingers and glanced down at her left hand. A new diamond glittered audaciously. She smiled at the memory of Johnny Bexley kneeling down and asking her to be his wife. It had happened only two weeks before and tonight he would announce it to the world at their engagement soirée.

She exhaled. Her body relaxed and her eyes closed heavily. She didn't particularly want to be home. She opened her eyes and fixed them to glare at the house before her. It was impressive, of course, with two stories and columns that supported an upper level balcony wrapped around the entire house. It was white like most of the homes on the Brighton Road and it boasted a high level of grandeur. It went with the neighbourhood. An abundance of wealth was evidenced by a lack of colour and vice versa. All of the houses around the harbour were slatted and painted fabulous shades of primaries and yet their inhabitants lived in the grey state of the lower class.

The only clever feature about Gracie's house was a pair of crimson doors set above large granite steps. She often wondered where that splash of colour was reflected in her family life.

Soon the draperies would be drawn aside and breakfast would be served. The nurses would come to tend to her father while her mother sat outside on the back veranda with her coffee and cigarettes. Her older brother, Billy, would be headed out on his morning run, a habit he had picked up during his army training. Gracie would be due to practice her French with the Québécois chamber maid, much to her Parisian mother's chagrin of course, for she didn't want her accent muddled. There would be no time for sleep. With a frustrated sigh she steadied herself against the gate as she slipped her feet out of the black patent heels that she wore. Leaning down, she picked them up and, with barely a glance back at the house; she pressed forward from the steel and walked back down the street towards the piers.

In less than an hour the dock workers would be out starting their day and then the factories would open and Gracie would no longer be alone. She wanted to take advantage of the peace that the dawn afforded her. She made her way towards the privately owned boats. Family friends' of theirs had a small yacht there, *The Diplomat*, which Gracie thought was an awfully boring name for a boat. Name aside, however, it had a relaxing lounge chair on the deck that was perfect for napping in. As she neared where the boat should have been moored, she was annoyed to find another boat in its place. A low-slung cutter called *The Phoenix* bobbed lazily in front of her. She groaned again, wondering where now she would get some sleep, and was about to turn around when she noticed a heap of white sails at the bow of the boat. They had been tossed carelessly and had floated down into an alabaster bed of canvas.

Gracie looked around and smiled to herself. She could bed down in the sails for an hour's relax and then make her way home past the bakery. It would be the perfect start to a day that had been designed to be flawless. She threw her shoes onto the boat's deck and bent down to hold onto the side of the pier as she stuck one bare foot out and onto the polished wooden deck of *The Phoenix*.

A few streets back from the harbour two men sat on a park bench facing the water's direction. Their backs faced the archways of Province House. It seemed the perfect backdrop for the business of the day.

"He's late." Karl, seated on the right, looked at his watch for emphasis.

Stavros, on the left, reached into the breast pocket of his tan leisure suit and fingered his money clip. "Look, Karl, I'll make you a deal," he started.

Karl glared at him from under the brim of his black fedora. "I don't want to make a deal. I just want my money."

"You don't even know what the deal is yet," Stavros complained.

"I know it's more of a deal for you than it will be for me," Karl argued back.

"No, no, listen," Stavros went on, "I've got this friend, a lobster man of sorts."

"Of sorts?" Karl snorted.

"Well," Stavros splayed his hands and shrugged his shoulders, "You know what I mean. He says he can get me some real cheap lobster. Top quality, though," he assured Karl vigorously, "maybe you could plan tonight's menu around it. Lobster makes great hors d'oeuvres."

"I already have a lobster man," Karl was less than enthusiastic.

"Yeah, well, if you call that lobster . . ." Stavros trailed off.

"You don't like my lobster?" Karl asked in a stiff voice.

"Well, it's not really as fresh as I like it," Stavros finished his sentence and had to duck as Karl's palm swatted at the back of his head.

"How much lobster do I have to buy to get you off of my back?" Karl got straight to the point.

"A couple hundred pounds," Stavros said quickly, wincing noticeably.

"Two hundred pounds? How am I going to get rid of two hundred pounds of lobster?"

"Soup?" Stavros had to duck again. This time he was too slow and Karl's palm collided with his skull. "Ow!"

"It better be a bloody good deal."

"I'm sure it was," an Irish voice laughed from behind them. "Cause there's no bloody way Stavros would be stupid enough to have used any of my cut to purchase it."

"You already bought it?" Karl's voice was beginning to have a manic edge to it.

"It'll be delivered to the Club by ten'ish." Stavros wouldn't look Karl in the eye.

"Tell me you have some good news, Ruairi," Karl had his head in his hands. "There's a big race on this week and I got a good tip. I need the cash to put on it."

Ruairi grinned down at him, "I do have news. I've been in contact with Bill McCoy."

"The American?" Stavros was impressed. Bill McCoy was quickly becoming notorious as the most reputable rum-runner in the business. He would only deal in uncut alcohol giving him the nickname 'The Real McCoy'.

"Aye, the American," Ruairi smiled, "And he has agreed to try our last batch. We have a big rendezvous this afternoon. Thomas loaded *The Phoenix* up in the middle of the night and I'm headed straight down to the docks to take her out on a little fishing trip." He looked down at Stavros and playfully wrapped his fingers around the back of the little Greek man's thick neck. "That is unless I have to get rid of a body first."

Stavros reached into his pocket and pulled out the money clip which held a tight fold of cash. "Don't be so hasty, Ruairi. You should think this idea through. I could give you some investment advice, you know."

Karl scowled at him, "Investment advice or bankruptcy advice?"

Ruairi leaned down and snatched the roll from Stavros' hand while flipping the money clip back to him. "It's grand of you to offer, Stavros, but I think I've got this money thing sorted out," he winked at them both and laughed. "I'll see you both tonight with another good take."

With that, he jogged off towards the water. He turned back when he hit the edge of the gardens and chuckled to himself. It was like looking at an oil painting by an artist with a dirty sense of humour. In the background stood an imposing symbol of the unity of immigrants who had become countrymen; in the foreground, two petulant models bickering over money. His chuckle faded as he was passed by two factory workers, witnessing the same tableau but with expressions of suspicion. Suddenly, Ruairi just hoped Karl and Stavros would call a truce before anyone else noticed the two well dressed immigrants at too early of an hour to be discussing the beginning of an honest day's work.

The Gainsborough household was slowly waking up as the sun thrust its rays through every eastern facing window. Nurse Betty rapped softly on the double doors of the master bedroom. They were opened by Lady Genevieve Gainsborough, the title being an acquisition from her English father's estate. Her estranged brother had inherited the estate but had continued to pay the generous living that her father had bestowed on her. They had grown up separated by querulous parents. Her French mother had left her father when she was only four and taken her to Paris, allowing her to only return to England for Christmas. Genevieve was stripped of the lifestyle she would have enjoyed by a Bohemian mother who refused to conform to any of the social conventions that ruled the English upper classes. She insisted that Genevieve relinquish her English title as it would serve her no purpose in Paris. Genevieve had only reclaimed it when she married; her new husband being more than happy to exchange his surname for a titled one. But some of her mother's ideologies had stuck with her and she often found her return to English life stuffy and pretentious. She was regularly shocking society members with her radical thoughts and always insisted that friends call her only by her Christian name.

She had already bathed this morning and was wrapped in a gorgeous saxe satin shift. She was tall and willowy with bobbed auburn hair. The most recent fashions had yet to reach Charlottetown and many in the little harbour town thought that the way she presented herself was a silly physical representation of the dramatic feminist upheaval that was grinding away the solid foundations of tradition. For Genevieve, it was much more than that. She had served her time alongside her husband and son as a nurse with the Red Cross. No hairdo or dress was going to make her feel any more justified. She was Parisian, she was confidant and she was tired of corsets.

Nurse Betty nodded her head and scooted past Genevieve to tend to General Gainsborough. William Gainsborough had been a highly decorated General in the British Army and had served his country through the entire war. His military career had started a few years before the Boer campaign in South Africa. He had worked his way up the ranks quite quickly through his resourcefulness and tenacity. He met Genevieve as a young officer who had yet to experience war first hand. He was boyishly handsome and full of charm and wit. So much so that even without attractive prospects and against the wishes of her family, Genevieve agreed to marry him.

The Boer War gave William an opportunity to prove himself to his country and to his new young family. He returned from South Africa with a focussed intensity that drew the attention and admiration of the upper echelons of the British military and gave his wife and children extreme pride. He was commanding but not overwhelming.

The promotion to General came in the tense months before the assassination of the Archduke Franz Ferdinand. As the ferocity of the conflict increased however, William's intensity became less about the protection of his home and family and more about the protection of his King and his flag. He was away for long stretches and when he obtained leave he would come home quiet and aloof.

Genevieve had seen the effects that war was having on the young men she treated in the hospitals but whatever it was that was changing William was something altogether different. Instead of night terrors and shell shock, he suffered rages and delusions of grandeur.

He was sent to Dublin first in 1916 to put down the rebellion and then returned to Ireland after the war as the British tried desperately to regain control of the tiny country. He became very secretive about his work and refused to talk about Ireland or the almost fatal wound that he acquired there.

Genevieve had tried on many occasions to enter his private thoughts but he kept her out firmly; sometimes with a look, sometimes with more. She bore it graciously at first but the war had taken a toll on her as well and she had become weary.

The move to Charlottetown two years earlier had been abrupt. The bullet wound had begun to plague him and infection had set in. He resigned his post and was offered a prestigious position in Canada working alongside the Lieutenant Governor Murdock MacKinnon. He was thriving in the political environment.

"I'm going downstairs, Will, to have my breakfast. Shall I send some up for you or do you think you will be able to fetch it yourself this morning?" Genevieve called to him.

"You make it sound like I'm some sort of dog," he grunted.

"Well, Darling, I'm sure that's not what I intended," she cooed.

"Don't worry, Genevieve, I'll *fetch* my own breakfast," he scowled.

"Wonderful Darling," She smiled sweetly at him and disappeared through the bedroom doors.

When Genevieve appeared at the breakfast parlour, the kitchen help was still scurrying around laying out the croissants and fruit platters. Although she had been pleasant to every person under her employment, every one of them had witnessed her icy demeanour towards her husband and they were all on edge, biding their time until she directed it at one of them.

"I beg your pardon, Madame," one of the younger servers said quietly, "The rolls were a bit finicky this morning."

"Don't apologize, Dear, I need a cigarette." Her smile was genuine and disarming. The fidgeting maid seemed to almost relax. Genevieve walked out onto the veranda and stared out across the lawns towards the water. She lit her cigarette and inhaled heavily. With a flick of her wrist she put out the match and then dropped it carelessly at her feet. It was only about a hundred feet to the embankment and she felt the sudden desire to take her corgi, Marie Antoinette, for a walk along the beach.

"Elsie!" she called for the nanny who appeared by her side almost immediately. "Good morning, Elsie."

"Good morning, Lady Gainsborough."

"Elsie, I feel like taking a walk before breakfast. Could you please have Marie Antoinette brought out on her lead?"

"Yes, Madame." She stared down at the walnut stained boards that made box patterns across the expanse of the veranda, waiting to be dismissed.

"Elsie?"

"Yes, Lady Gainsborough?"

"Have you seen Gracie yet this morning?"

"No, Madame." She wondered if she should tell the Lady that Gracie hadn't come home at all but she decided to play it safe and only answer the direct question.

"Hmm, well then, that will be all."

Elsie nodded and returned to the house.

Marie Antoinette was brought to the veranda by yet another maid, a luxury the Gainsborough's never seemed to be without, and Genevieve removed her shoes to walk barefoot. The lawns were squishy with moisture and Marie Antoinette kept her nose close to the grass so that she could lick dew drops if she felt the need. Genevieve laughed loudly and reached down to pat the dog's head lovingly. Marie Antoinette was always able to make her smile.

As they picked their way down the embankment, Genevieve could see her eldest son Billy running towards her. He was gleaming with sweat in the early morning sunlight and Genevieve smiled to herself as she thought about the looks on the faces of the women at the Club the first time he had been introduced. His dark brown hair was cut close to his head and he had deep blue eyes and a strong jaw. He was fit and loved to challenge himself physically. After the war, he began to study law but returned to active duty in Ireland within a few months. His conscience refused to let him read while more young men died. He put on his uniform and went back to war.

He had been offered several jobs upon the family's arrival in Canada but had been easily persuaded to work for Lucas Bexley, whose cousins owned the estate neighbouring the Gainsborough estate in England.

"Good morning, Lady Gainsborough," Billy took his mother's hand impulsively and kissed it.

His playfulness made her blush, "Stop it!" She swatted at him. "You know I hate that title! Call me Madame or Maman, s'il vous plaît."

Billy leaned down and rubbed Marie Antoinette's ears, causing her to roll over and wriggle excitedly. "And what about you, Marie Antoinette?"

"I think she would prefer the title 'princess' or even 'queen'!" Genevieve laughed again.

"And where is the *other* princess this morning?" Billy asked, referring to his sister, Gracie. The whole day was set to revolve around her but she hadn't been in her bed when he had checked before his run.

"I'm not sure that she came home last night. I think she spent the night with Norah and the girls," Genevieve said quietly, looking off across the water again. She suddenly felt the urge for another cigarette. She inhaled heavily and closed her eyes, silently pleading for the relaxation that would wash over her. Gracie was becoming extremely independent of late. She was a young woman now.

"Maman, tell me what it is that makes you against her marrying Johnny. From what you've told me of our histories, the Bexley estate and the Gainsborough estate have always been keen to have a marriage unite them."

Genevieve exhaled slowly. She tried to choose her words carefully, a skill she always found tough to master. "That's exactly why I'm worried, Billy. Gracie hasn't really chosen Johnny. He was sort of forced upon her by our incessant need to blend families."

"Fortunately though, she seems to love him. Maybe you chose the best for her."

"Maybe we didn't. I'm almost hoping that something goes wrong," she sighed and another long stream of smoke floated away on the breeze. "Oh, Billy, it's hard for me to explain. I just want your sister to have more. Anyone can give you a lifestyle. I want her to have the life."

"He'll give her the same kind of life that the old General in there gave you," Billy argued.

Genevieve noticed how 'the old General' replaced 'Father'. She hadn't the heart to open that wound just yet. "That's what I'm worried about," she said softly.

Billy looked down and kicked at the sand with his tennis shoe. He had found himself numb when he left Ireland; numb to life and numb to death. He recognized the opposite defenses in his mother. She seemed tired of her propriety and was taking cautious steps towards recklessness. He felt every conversation was a tango with her and he was lost on the turns. His thoughts were momentarily distracted and he chuckled. "You better get going or Marie Antoinette's going to gnaw through that lead!"

Genevieve had been so focussed on her estrangement from her husband and the engagement of her daughter that she hadn't noticed Marie Antoinette tugging in annoyance and growling softly. Her mood slipped away easily and she laughed again. Her laughter was infectious and Billy joined in while Marie Antoinette bounded up and down making it impossible for them to stop.

Ruairi made it down to the docks and looked around a few times to make sure he wasn't being followed by anybody. He smiled and said hello to a young boy who skipped by him and jumped onto a waiting fishing boat. It was going to be a warm day and Ruairi was happy he had put a vest on beneath the geansaí that his ma had knit for him. It would protect him from the itching. She had used the cable stitch for the wool to keep him safe. She had always been superstitious like that.

He had dressed down today to pass as a leisurely fisherman. His tan trousers would keep him relatively cool but he had laughed into the mirror. He was reminded of the day when he had enlisted for the War. He was just eighteen when the war had begun but he had thought himself a man then, ready for action and adventure. He was not yet political and paid no mind to those who refused to die for a foreign king. It was the first time he had been dressed in gentleman's clothes and he had felt completely out of place. He was more comfortable when that first smudge of dirt had appeared on his uniform.

He glanced around casually before leaning down to untie the heavy ropes that held *The Phoenix* fast; first one rope, then the next, then the last. As he tossed them over the edge of the boat and leaped forward, he struggled to keep his balance. He was startled to find himself staring at the body of a young woman, nestled into the pile of sails that he had tossed over the trapdoor. He watched her closely to make sure she was still breathing. When he was sure, he moved towards her to wake her. He would have to pull back up to the dock and offload her. He stared down at her. She was beautiful and aroused his spirit. He swallowed hard and shook his head. He reached towards her. Instead of waking her though, he gently dragged his fingers down her arm. He pulled his hand back, disgusted with himself. He shook his head again trying to clear it and think sensibly. He couldn't. And he found himself drifting further and further away from the dock.

CHAPTER 2

He tried not to stare at her. He had quite a few hours until McCoy would show up on the horizon line and he knew that she would wake in that time. He had picked up his fishing rod about five or six times. Each time he passed it hand to hand, slowly, letting the weight of it pull at his wrists. Then he'd quietly put it back down, convincing himself that he should keep as still as possible to avoid waking her. But why had he taken her in the first place? He closed his eyes and groaned. She shifted. His eyes flew open.

He waited. She didn't move again. He exhaled. She was beautiful, to be sure, but he spent his time with many gorgeous women. He looked at her mouth. There was something vaguely familiar about the way the bow of her lips was exaggerated. His mind wandered from the familiar to the unknown. He was noticing the moisture, the pinkness, the sensuality of her lips.

It had been years since he had actually stopped to enjoy the female body. His only love had been his best friend, Rosaleen. But as romantic counterparts, they were much too volatile to survive. They loved each other passionately and fought each other violently. It made for an impossible love affair but the best of friendships.

She understood him completely, and that, he felt, was a very difficult task. She had stood by him when he had enlisted with the British in the war, when so many others had called him a traitor. He had no understanding of the political rhetoric; he saw the war as a reprieve from the thousand years of unrest between the Irish and the English. They could fight as brothers. His naïveté was soon shattered and after a year and a half of mutilated bodies, bloodshed and terror, he realized how dirty defending nationhood could be. When his father was killed in the early months of 1916 during a protest back in Ireland, he knew that if he gave his life for any country, it was going to be his own. While on leave for the funeral, he heard the rumbles of an upcoming rising. Ruairi's younger brother Thomas had been enrolled at St. Edna's School and had become enraptured by its headmaster, Pádraig Pearse, a man who believed in poetry and freedom. Thomas implored Ruairi to meet with him and so with Rosaleen by his side, they made the journey to St. Edna's and were quickly won over by the revolutionary teacher and his proclamation of Irish independence.

Ruairi fought valiantly with the Irish Volunteers that Easter to bring Ireland her Republic but it wasn't until the British fired the shots of execution into Pádraig Pearse that his heart was hardened to the cause.

Ruairi would never return to fight in their war. He joined Michael Collin's until the treaty, but the partition of Ireland broke his heart. He knew that not even one of the battles he had fought in had prepared him for the Civil War that followed. His loyalty was to Ireland and so he left Collin's Free State Army and followed Eamon de Valera into the depths of the Irish Republican Army. He would continue to fight until he won; or they lost; whatever that meant.

He looked at the strange girl again.

Gracie's eyelids fluttered slowly. She could feel the sun warming her skin and she sank back into the sails. The canvas was warm and comfortable and no matter how hard she tried, she couldn't pull herself from the hypnotic state she had entered. She lazily opened her eyes and stared up at the cloudless sky. Her head was still a bit fuzzy and her throat was dry. She licked her lips. The day had broken out in glossy sunshine and Gracie could feel the promise that floated around her. She stretched out her arms and sighed deliciously.

Ruairi tensed. Any second, she would realize she was no longer tied to the dock. He hadn't prepared anything to say to her. He wasn't even sure what had made him continue out of the harbour other than he had liked to look at her. He had no excuse; he had no way of saying he didn't see her. She had been in plain view on a very small boat.

And yet, he had taken her.

Karl sat behind his massive maple desk and drummed his fingers against the polished surface. He was a brooding man, always lost in the deepest archives of his own mind. He owned the Club in Charlottetown on Prince Edward Island and it was well known that he had kept the liquor flowing freely when the rest of the province had gone dry. Prohibition had come to the island in 1901 and the rest of Canada and the United States followed soon after the war. In an attempt to bring moral respectability to the masses, the governments had inadvertently introduced a prosperous criminal enterprise; rum-running.

In Charlottetown, Karl relied on smugglers to bring him the finest that the Caribbean had to offer. It was well known that Karl had connections three miles off the Atlantic coast at the Rum Line where national laws ceased and criminal law reigned. What wasn't known was how he kept the authorities off of the Club premises. Although every church affiliated temperance group on the island had tried to shut him down, the Club had never once been raided by the police.

Tonight would be no exception. Karl had spent the last week making sure the tiniest details of this event were not overlooked. Eleanor Bexley was adamant that only the best French champagne was to be served alongside a selection of top quality spirits and wines. Ruairi had taken care of this for him last week, taking *The Phoenix* out to Rum Row and picking up a shipment from Miquelon, a French island off the coast of Newfoundland. Karl smiled to himself. He had unpacked the shipment himself and marvelled at the fortune he would make off a supply such as that. Some of the labels that sat in his cellar were even rare in Europe since the war.

Karl traced his thoughts back to Eleanor Bexley's other requests. She was convinced that the dress code for the evening's service had to be stepped up. Tonight, no one would be allowed through the doors without black tie attire. The servers would be in tails and the polished silver trays would be balanced atop gloved fingers.

The thought of Stavros' swarthy little body in tails made Karl laugh out loud. His thoughts went from Stavros in tails to lobster tails. Dinner service had been suspended in favour of fancy hors d'oeuvres. Of course, Stavros' lobster would become a main feature.

There would be lobster puffs, lobster cakes, lobster pâtés, and still, Karl would have pounds of lobster left over. He could hear Stavros' voice in his head and he cringed. He would have to have the kitchen make soup.

There was a knock on his door. He stopped drumming his fingers and sat back in his chair.

"Come in," he called out.

The door opened and in strode the long legs of Rosaleen Jameson. Karl stiffened. Very few men could claim being at ease in her presence. There was something enticing about the way she looked and yet something so cold in the way she moved.

"Good afternoon, Rosaleen." His voice was muffled by his hand, which he had nervously moved over his mouth.

She had an amused look on her face. "Anything I can do to help?" she asked lightly.

"No, no. Everything's taken care of," he said dismissively.

"Did you get the mother of the groom off your back?"

"No, but it's been about . . ." Karl looked at his pocket watch and clucked his tongue, "well, almost twenty-five minutes since her last call so we're making progress." He watched her as she slowly walked around the room. She was a cat prowling; waiting; toying. Karl was her mouse. "Is there anything I can do for you?" he asked, hoping she wouldn't keep him in uncomfortable silence for too long.

"Well, yes, actually there is, Karl," she turned and faced him, the amused expression was gone. Karl felt his pulse quicken. "I want you to make sure that we get a table on the patio, near the steps. I don't want to be stuck at a table inside."

"The patio is for guests of the engagement party," he said slowly.

"Then put me on the guest list," she instructed, her tone was persuasive.

"May I ask why?"

She just looked at him, expressionless.

"Of course," he acquiesced, aware that she was not accustomed to being questioned. "Of course, I'll let the host know."

"Grand."

Business now over with she asked about Ruairi's whereabouts. Karl hadn't known the two of them long enough to figure out how the relationship worked, but the two of them seemed to share the same soul. What confused him is why they didn't share their bodies.

"He isn't back from his rendezvous with McCoy."

"Well," she smiled, "goodbye Karl."

With that, she turned and left Karl to the sudden cramping in his groin.

Gracie finally felt the urge to prop herself up on her elbows and take in the day. She felt well rested but figured she couldn't have been asleep for too long as there was very little noise around her. Even the gulls were quiet. Her eyes focussed on the wide expanse of water and Ruairi watched closely as the realization of where she was, or rather, where she wasn't, registered on her face. She still hadn't noticed him. She was up on her knees, and then her feet as she slowly looked around. Ruairi couldn't tell whether she looked like she was going to be sick or cry. He was surprised she hadn't screamed.

Suddenly, she locked eyes with him and her eyes widened and her face went very white. He tried to smile to show her that he didn't mean her harm. She screamed.

"Dammit," he muttered. "I knew it." He stood up and started to walk towards her. Without warning, she flung herself overboard. Ruairi ran to the rail.

"What are you doing?" he yelled at her. The boat was quite low so she was still within reach. She was trying to swim away but she wasn't moving very far. He reached down and grabbed the edge of her dress but she swatted him away with her foot.

Gracie rolled onto her back. The freezing water had shocked her back to her senses and she realized the futility of her decision. But she didn't want to admit it to whomever it was that was standing at the edge of the boat staring down at her. She gasped as the crushing cold made her chest feel as though it would collapse.

He was offering a hand to her but she kicked it away. She wanted to yell something at him but she didn't know what. Finally she sputtered, "Who are you?" in her distinct London accent. His cringe was noticeable.

"Who am I?" he asked, strengthening his own Irish brogue in defiance, "Who the hell are you?"

"Who am I?" she screamed back at him, "You must be aware of who I am! You stole me!"

"I didn't steal you! You got on my boat!"

"For a sleep! Not to go sailing the Atlantic!" she was treading water now and her teeth were chattering. Her pink lips had turned purplish almost instantaneously.

"Let me help you up," he offered his hand to her again. She glared at him fiercely, challenging him to try to fish her out. He stared back at her as if she were an idiot. It was warm on the boat but the water would be icy. The North Atlantic was not the ideal swimming hole. It would be at least a month before the water would be even somewhat comfortable and only close to the beach.

"Fine, freeze to death, if that is what you want." He turned to walk away.

"Just tell me why you took me!" she yelled at his back.

"Would it matter right now?" he asked. "It's not like you don't have a better chance of surviving if you trust me. Do you really think you're going to make it back to shore? Do you even know which direction shore is?"

He had a point. She reached up to him. He smirked at her. She splashed him and pulled away.

"Are you always this much of a handful?" he asked, annoyed. He thought about how perfect she had looked while she was asleep. She was a whole different kettle of fish when awake. He should have known. She was a woman and an English one at that.

When he finally pulled her up and onto the deck, she was too busy shivering to put up much of an argument. He wrapped her in the only blanket he could find and then sat her down and piled the sails around her.

Although cold and scared, she couldn't help but notice his features. He was handsome, in a rugged sort of way. He had a strong jaw and rich honey coloured eyes. She flinched and tried to pull her hand away when he reached out and checked her pulse. "Are you some kind of doctor?" she asked. Her tone had an edge of sarcasm and one perfectly manicured eyebrow arched sceptically.

"And are you some kind of diver?" he matched her.

"Well, what do you expect?" she snapped." I wake up to find some lunatic has kidnapped me and taken me out to sea."

"So, you jumped overboard and hoped for the best, did you?" He looked at her like she was a foolish child.

The look angered her. "Well, you could be some kind of maniac, or worse, a murderer."

Ruairi felt the sting of the last word. He had been called that many times before. He looked her straight in the eye. "I'm not a murderer, possibly a maniac though," he added with a wink.

His smile was harmless and she didn't have that knotted feeling in her stomach that usually signalled something was wrong. "So you'll take me back to the harbour?"

"Well, yes, but not yet. I have an appointment."

"Out here?" Little wrinkles formed between her eyes as she looked around, confused. "Do you need me for this appointment?"

"I don't need you but I can't really take you back now," his accent thickened again.

She looked at him, expecting more of an explanation. When it didn't come she continued her questioning through chattering teeth. "What are we doing out here and why do you have all of these extra sails?"

"They need to be mended. I was hoping I'd have some time today."

"You come all the way out here to mend sails and have appointments?"

"Is it really any of your business?"

"Well, seeing as you stole me, I think it is."

"I didn't steal you." There was an arrogance about her that irritated him. It also strangely excited him.

"Well, what would you call it then?" she asked. There was something so familiar in the way she watched his every move.

Ruairi had been trying to figure out the end to this conversation all morning. He shrugged his shoulders at her. "I'm not quite sure. I guess I just wanted the company," he smiled. He needed to keep her as calm as possible while he figured out what to do now that she was awake and English.

She didn't accept his answer easily. "That's ridiculous! Don't you agree? What kind of man sails out of the harbour with a strange woman asleep on his boat?"

"What kind of a lady sleeps out in the open on a stranger's boat?" he growled. She was provoking him. He really didn't need this disturbance today. This was why he stayed away from women. Nothing was simple with them. They couldn't understand simple things. They were always trying to make something more complex than it was. He didn't have a reason. He just did it. She should be satisfied with that. But she wasn't.

He thought it best to turn the questions on her. "What is your name?"

"Lady Gracie Gainsborough," she responded.

Ruairi felt as though his heart had stopped. He drew a deep breath and waited for the next beat. If she hadn't been so concerned with adjusting the blanket, she would have noticed the look of shock that broke his composure. He stared at the water and clenched his jaw to regain his cool.

He cleared his throat. "And you're from London are you, Lady Gracie?"

"Please, just call me Gracie, and yes, how did you know?" She looked up at him from where she was sitting. She looked vulnerable and small huddled beneath the now soaked blanket. He could feel the blood in his veins. It made him eerily conscious of his mortality.

"The accent gave you away."

"By your accent, I would guess you are Irish. Not a good mix in a small boat!" She spoke without thinking. When she realized what she had said she bit her bottom lip and looked away.

He didn't trust himself in this conversation and so he remained quiet.

"And what is your name?" she asked, in a tone too pressed for politeness.

"Ruairi."

"Just Ruairi?" she tried to smile at him.

He swallowed and looked away. "Just Ruairi."

"You seem very mysterious, *Ruairi*," she exaggerated his name slyly.

He laughed in spite of himself. He decided the only safe thing to do would be to change the subject. "That blanket isn't doing much good anymore. Why don't you take it off and I'll give you my jumper. It will be much warmer." Without hesitation he pulled the geansaí up over his head, revealing very muscular arms and a tattoo across his back that was impossible to read because of the interruption of a cotton vest after the third letter. All she could make out was "ROI" on his left shoulder blade. He turned slightly and Gracie caught a glimpse of the other side of the tattoo peeking out near his right shoulder blade. It was the letters "BH" which left her with quite a puzzle.

Gracie found herself unable to take her eyes off of him. She knew that a lady should be repulsed by the vulgarities of the lower classes but she had always had a strange fascination with the idea of a handsome young nobody.

"What does your tattoo say?" she asked, her teeth chattering.

"Róisín Dubh," he said, the Irish soft and lyrical, "It means 'dark rose'."

"And why do you have it tattooed on yourself?"

"For a friend," he said.

That explanation meant nothing to Gracie but he didn't seem to be forthcoming with any more of a story.

Ruairi leaned down to help her unwrap herself from the mass of sails and the blanket. Most of the moisture had been soaked up by the blanket but her damp dress still clung to every curve as she slowly stood up.

She tried to take the jumper from him but her hands were shaking.

"You must be really cold. I'm afraid that if I don't take you back immediately, you will catch pneumonia." Ruairi knew it would be risky to go back to the harbour this late in the morning and then sneak back out without arousing suspicion but it may be worth risking imprisonment to get the Gainsborough girl off his boat.

"I thought you had an appointment?" she was surprised to find herself a bit disappointed. Even if he was Irish, he was easy to look at.

He looked at the sun and sighed, "I do." He had told McCoy to be there by three. He wouldn't normally rendezvous that early. The Coast Guard was an ever present threat in the daytime but Rosaleen had told him she needed him at the Club tonight.

"The sun is warm, I'm sure I won't catch pneumonia," she argued. "But I will have to insist that you have me back by two or three o'clock. I have to start getting ready for tonight." She was still staring at him, her arms stuffed into his sleeves but she hadn't been able to break her gaze to put her head through.

He was amused by her demands. "What's so important about tonight that you have to start getting ready this afternoon?"

"My family is throwing an engagement party for me and my new fiancé at the Club."

Ruairi closed his eyes and groaned to himself, "Well, congratulations." It all made sense. The blood in his veins was suddenly hotter. Rosaleen needed him at the Club because she knew whose party they would be spoiling. He silently cursed her. He wondered what else she had failed to mention.

"Yes, and everybody's going to be wondering where I am! What a funny story this will be!" She giggled to herself. She was no longer scared. The Irishman was harmless and definitely attractive. This little wrong turn had actually improved her already perfect day.

He shook his head. His luck couldn't have gotten worse. His day had started out so well.

"I'm not sure this is the type of story you should be telling many people," he cautioned, his tone a bit acidic.

Gracie looked genuinely confused. "Why not? I've done nothing wrong."

Ruairi raised an eyebrow. "I'm not sure that matters much to your kind when a young woman is caught with a young man who is not her betrothed."

A sudden tension materialized in the air.

"My kind?" Gracie's tone was frosty. The difference in their status had been apparent from the beginning but to bring attention to it was, in her opinion, just bad manners.

Ruairi hesitated. His choice of words was poor. "The English aristocracy," he clarified.

"Are you telling me that the lower classes of the Irish have no such rules?" Gracie knew she was risking being a snob but he had angered her.

Ruairi narrowed his eyes. The question had the pretence of innocence but he knew he was being led into an age-old trap of English civility and superiority. "Oh, the Irish have their morals, mi'lady. We are all Catholic after all."

Gracie looked away from him, feigning thoughtfulness, "It's interesting, really isn't it? How vastly different *our kinds* are and yet geographically, so close. Sometimes I wonder if keeping Ireland as part of the kingdom is really worth it." When she looked back at him she knew she had salted a wound.

Ruairi was snarling at the ocean. "I believe I may be able to find the time to take you back to the docks."

"I think that may be best," Gracie said tightly. She suddenly wanted off of the boat as quickly as possible.

Ruairi turned the boat and kept his back to Gracie. He put his hands on his hips and let out a frustrated sigh. His decision, or lack of one, had gone from bad to worse. He stared out at the horizon, hoping McCoy would be late.

As the morning progressed, Billy became more and more agitated by his sister's absence. When Norah, Johnny's sister, showed up at eleven o'clock saying that Gracie should have been home by half past five in the morning, the Gainsborough house began to panic.

"Where could she be?" William was noticeably ruffled. "Should I telephone the police?"

Norah was trying to remember what Gracie had said when they had dropped her off at the gates but her mind had been foggy from her consumption of gin martinis. Her head was still busy reminding her of them.

"Give me an hour before you do something that drastic. I'll check the bakery and the harbour-side first. She may have just decided to go for a walk or some breakfast. You know how she can be sometimes when she gets excited." Billy took Norah with him and headed to the docks.

"This is what happens when you let her think she is an adult and allow her out until all hours of the morning," William growled at Genevieve as the door closed behind Billy.

"She's about to get married, William. She is an adult," Genevieve hissed. "How do you intend to keep her locked up once she has a home of her own?"

"It will be Johnny's job to keep her locked up and I can assure you, that boy knows how to behave properly." William stormed by her and into his study.

Genevieve let her voice carry so that he could hear her, "I didn't think new money was all that interested in propriety."

"They have an English name and English blood in their veins no matter where they were born!" William shouted back, slamming the door to keep his wife out.

Almost ten minutes had passed with neither of them speaking to each other. Ruairi paced up and down the deck, silently stewing over life's latest injustice. He couldn't believe he had just sailed out of the harbour with General William Gainsborough's daughter as his unsuspecting passenger. He was also struggling with the knowledge that his best friend may have betrayed him; for the second time.

When he turned back around, she was looking at him. He met her eyes and took a deep breath.

"How are you? Are you still cold?"

"I'm fine," she lied stiffly. She was unsure of who had been in the wrong and who should be the first to apologize and so she remained silent.

As the harbour neared, she felt a strange pang of regret. Some part of her wanted more time with this Irish fisherman. Her curiosity had been aroused and the uneasy silence between them was beginning to wear her down.

"Will you tell me about this appointment?" She finally broke her silence.

"No," he responded flatly.

She sighed and her bottom lip protruded the way it did whenever she wanted something from her father. She looked up at him to see if he had noticed but he was looking back out towards the horizon. It startled her when she felt the first hot tear slip between her eyelashes. She wiped it away quickly and turned her face from him so that he wouldn't see.

Billy and Norah wandered up and down the docks, searching for Gracie and asking every person they encountered if they had seen her.

"Hey, Jimmy!" Billy ran up to a boat on the main wharf where two fishermen he had recently met at an auction were unloading their morning's catch. "You didn't by chance see my sister this morning?"

"Sure did," Jimmy was in his forties and was married to his boat.

"Really? When? Where?"

"Whoa! Slow down, Billy! I saw her 'bout quarter to six, just as I was pulling out. She was getting into a boat. It didn't look like she was going anywhere though."

"What do you mean?"

The other fisherman, an older gentleman named Charlie took over the story. "She just laid down in it like she was going to sleep. No one was with her or anything," he added hastily.

"Do you know what boat?" Norah asked hopefully.

"I don't. Sorry."

"Do you know which dock it was moored in?" Billy was happy to hear she had been alone.

"Over in the private docks, by the Club."

"Thank-you!" Billy patted the side of the boat and took off down the wharf. Norah followed as quickly as she could in heels.

Jimmy and Charlie looked at each other awkwardly.

"You think we should have told him it was *The Phoenix*?" Charlie asked.

Jimmy shook his head. "Ain't nobody I'd cross that Ruairi O'Neill for. Not even Billy's pretty little sister."

As *The Phoenix* slowly glided towards the dock, Ruairi took stock of the greeting party that awaited them. There were two people. One of them looked relieved. The other was Billy Gainsborough. His lips were tight and his eyes were narrow slits. His expression didn't change much when Gracie stepped onto the dock and threw her arms around him.

"Oh! You must have been dreadfully worried. I'm so sorry." She looked up at her brother and then nuzzled into his chest. She could feel the heat from Ruairi's gaze and she felt a bit weak. He had refused any attempt at conversation the rest of the way into the harbour. When he did break the silence it was only to tell her to avoid napping on other people's boats in the future.

"What the hell are you doing here with my sister?" Billy's tone was extremely aggressive.

"It's all right, it was an honest misunderstanding." Gracie was touched by her brother's protectiveness. At least one man was making a fuss over her, even if it was just her brother.

"What did you do to her?" Billy was pulling Gracie around behind him to shield her from the Irishman. Norah instinctively moved behind him as well and put her arms around Gracie.

Ruairi stood squarely on the boat. "I saved her from drowning and hypothermia," a dark shadow settled on his face, "I think that was enough for our first meeting."

Billy took a step forward and glared down at him from the edge of the dock, "Listen here, if you laid a finger on her, I'll . . ."

Ruairi was off the boat in a second, standing close to intimidate Billy. "You'll what? What are you going to do?" The smile on his face was cruel. He challenged Billy with his eyes.

Gracie was terrified by Ruairi's sudden ferocity. Norah noticed how rigid her friend became and she tried to lead her away. "You're damp! Did you fall in? You must be chilled to the bone! Let's get you home and warm, darling."

Gracie reached for Billy's arm but he pulled it away. "Go with Norah, Gracie. I'll be along in a minute."

Gracie tried to argue but there was no point. Neither Billy nor Ruairi were paying any attention to her.

CHAPTER 3

Billy could taste the fear mixing with the bile at the back of his throat. It had been three years since he had seen Ruairi O'Neill. He could clearly remember that last morning in Dublin as Ruairi had walked him, with the gun grinding into his back, past St. Stephen's Green, past the GPO, past the burned out buildings and bullet holes. He had never expected to be let go. He thought he would be the one to pay for his father's transgressions. But the shred of humanity left in the eyes of the mad had won out. Now, staring into those same deeply troubled eyes, witnessing the same cold grip on sanity, the courage he had found to confront this demonized saint withered. There had been too much history between the two of them even though their acquaintance had been short lived.

It was 1920 and Michael Collins was making the British Intelligence look like a contradiction of terms. Ireland was in the throes of a war against English domination and the Irish Republican Army was perfecting a style of warfare that was stretching the British military beyond their limits. Guerrilla assaults had struck terror into the core of the military operation and the British government was pressuring them to somehow get the situation under control. Billy's father, General William Gainsborough had been targeted by the enemy for assassination. One by one, British Officers and politicians were being picked off and the General's time had come.

The British Army had received word that the orders were coming from one of Collin's men; a rogue disciple and incredibly unpredictable, his name was Ruairi O'Neill. He had proven more elusive than Collins' himself but they had one vital piece of information that kept them on the hunt. Ruairi O'Neill had been a soldier in the British Army. He had gone on leave in 1916 and never returned. If caught, he would be tried and shot for desertion and treason.

The Irish firesides had come alive with tales of Ruairi brazenly kidnapping the General's son and waiting for an onslaught. When the British sent men in, Ruairi and his men took out an entire brigade, leaving only the General standing, barely. But that was just how the story went. The truth was far more complicated.

Billy remembered being ordered to stand and salute in front of his father. He thought he would be shot in the back of the head. Instead, he was made to listen to his father's confessions. It was a worse punishment. Billy had wished for that bullet on so many occasions since, that chance to bring back the innocence of paternal adoration. He could remember his hand slowly returning to his side, his head lowering in shame.

Ruairi had laughed. Not a laugh of amusement, a laugh of disembodied understanding. It haunted Billy.

And now he was face to face with him once again, gazing into those lurid eyes. It made him shiver.

He looked around to make sure his sister was gone. "It's been a long time, Ruairi," Billy said softly, "and you are a long way from home."

"We both are," Ruairi agreed. "I never thought I'd be seeing you again." He held out his hand.

Billy shook it warily. "It is quite a shock, I must admit."

"It is indeed, Billy. It is indeed."

Rosaleen looked down at the little girl prancing around her bedroom in pearls and high heels. She was a pretty little thing, with incredibly pale skin and piercing blue eyes. Her features were exquisite, perfectly formed lips and high cheekbones. She was delicate like her mother and she had the same fiery temper. She may not have been purebred but she was Irish at the core.

She had never really felt like she was raising the girl on her own. Aisling was always there to give her a hand minding little Kathleen and the boys had taken to raising her as if she were their own.

Rosaleen's uncle, Michael Fitzgerald, had been like a Granddaddy, taking over for his deceased brother-in-law and spoiling Kathleen terribly. Ruairi's brother Thomas had tried to teach her to sing but that just meant that at three years old, Kathleen could rattle off every Irish pub song through the ages. Of course, everybody was astounded by the vocabulary of the child but her command of dirty words wasn't appreciated by most of the women with children of similar ages. Not that she was given much opportunity to play with other children. As the bastard child of a fallen woman, invitations of friendship were scarce for Rosaleen and her daughter. Ruairi had attempted the education part of the raising, and so, Kathleen could speak fluent Gaelic, recite Emmett's poignant speech from the docks, and name all thirty-two counties in Ireland.

This morning, she had been curiously prying Rosaleen about the importance of looking like a lady. She had stared wide-eyed as Rosaleen removed her dressing gown to reveal the thigh-high stockings and the lacy garter belt. In an attempt to avoid too much of an explanation, Rosaleen handed over the key to her wardrobe and allowed Kathleen to play dress up and learn about fashion on her own.

Without warning Aisling came scurrying in, breathless, and flopped on the settee in the middle of the room.

"Aunt Aisling, look!" squealed Kathleen, twirling around recklessly. "Don't I look like a movie star?"

"Oh! And aren't you a beauty! Look at those pearls!"

"Are you playing with me tonight while Mammy goes out? We could play dress-ups!" Kathleen pressed her face close to Aisling's to feel her warm breath on her cheeks. "Ew! You smell funny!" She pushed away from her and squiggled up her nose.

Rosaleen laughed as she watched Aisling try to smell her own breath. She answered Kathleen's question as gently as possible, knowing the girl would not be happy being left out of the fun that evening. "No, Darling, Auntie Aisling's coming with me tonight so you better run upstairs and put on your sundress. Peggy will be along any minute now. She's going to take you swimming at Valerie's and then stay with you this evening."

Kathleen dropped her lip and pouted. Peggy was an old fisherman's wife and her fingers smelled like cod fillets. "She smells funny."

"Oh, everybody smells funny to you, now run along and get ready!" Aisling jumped off the divan and pretended to chase the little girl towards her own bedroom. Her giggles could be heard echoing down the corridor.

The day was turning out to be a warm one. As Gracie walked home with Norah she tried desperately to tell herself that she was excited for the evening to come. She willed herself to picture Johnny, the man she loved.

"Have you ever been in love?" she suddenly asked Norah.

"Well, of course I have. I loved Henry. You know that." Henry had been Norah's betrothed but he had been killed in combat in 1917.

"What did it feel like when you looked at him?"

Norah furrowed her brow and looked thoughtful. "I don't know, I guess I just felt something . . . something I've never felt since," she smiled sadly, remembering. She stopped walking when she noticed the worried expression on Gracie's face. She put her arm through her friend's. "What's wrong?"

Tears glistened in the corners of Gracie's eyes. "I'm not sure," she whispered.

Norah turned and faced Gracie. "Darling, you are as pale as a ghost!"

"I feel ill," Gracie began to cry. Panic was making her shiver in spite of the sun baking her skin. In her head she could see the Irishman taking off his jumper and she felt nauseous. He had made her feel something; something that Johnny had never made her feel.

Norah reached out to steady her. "Is there something I can do? Gracie, you are scaring me."

Gracie wiped her eyes and shook her head. She couldn't reveal her thoughts. They were too scandalous, even for her best friend.

"You're just tired, Darling. You've had too much champagne, very little sleep and a very upsetting day, what with that boy and all," Norah shuttered. "We'll just get you home, and you'll feel better. I promise."

Gracie nodded but she wasn't convinced.

Ruairi looked over at the young Englishman. He was standing there, determined to say something of importance. Ruairi didn't have long to wait.

"Billy, it's been an unusual day and I'd love to hear what it is that you and yours are doing here, but . . ." he looked down at his watch for emphasis, "I'm wasting my day away and I'd like to catch some fish."

"I'll come with you," Billy said firmly.

Ruairi was half amused. "You want to go fishing?"

"Or rum-running, whatever you happen to be doing." Billy smiled nervously. "You know, you're taking a mighty big risk with those Coast Guard boys at this time of the day."

"And you're taking a mighty big risk coming near me," Ruairi baited him.

"Three years ago I wouldn't have trusted you." Billy bit his lip and thought for a moment.

"Nothing's changed." Ruairi narrowed his eyes.

"Everything's changed, Ruairi. I'm not a soldier anymore."

"You are still a Gainsborough," Ruairi pointed out.

"If that wasn't enough of a reason before, I doubt you'd kill me for it now." Billy could only hope his reasoning was logical.

"I don't think I should be trading bait with the likes of you." Ruairi switched tactics. It was more than just dangerous to have Billy this close.

The Englishman surprised him by jumping on *The Phoenix*. Looking back at Ruairi with a steely gaze he said, "Well, I think you should take me with you. And, if I get in your way, all you have to do is shoot me and dump me overboard. They'll never find the body."

Ruairi groaned. Outside of physical force, he couldn't think of a way to get Billy to go away. "What makes you think I'm armed?" he asked.

"I suppose it's just a feeling I get about you."

Ruairi frowned while he set about pointing the boat back out of the harbour. Fate was playing a trick on him. He had spent the morning with General Gainsborough's daughter and now would be spending the afternoon with his son.

"What are you thinking about?" Billy's question penetrated his thoughts.

"I'm just pondering life's little mysteries." Ruairi lit a cigarette and inhaled. He desperately wanted to know why the Gainsborough family was in Canada and how long they had been there but he bided his time. In a town the size of Charlottetown, it was a wonder they hadn't already crossed paths.

"Are you here to kill him?" Billy was sharing his thoughts.

"Don't flatter yourself." Ruairi exhaled a stream of smoke. The scent of it lingered against the smells of musty canvas and rotting seaweed. "If I wanted to kill him, he'd be dead. I wouldn't spend more than a bullet on him, never mind a few months of my life. I didn't even know he was here."

Billy snorted.

Ruairi glared at him. "I'm here for personal reasons. This had nothing to do with your Da."

Billy grimaced. He hated the smell of cigarettes. It reminded him of being stuck in the foxholes, shoulder to shoulder with twenty odd dirty, tired, and frightened men. "Raising money for the cause then?" he asked.

"Curious little bugger aren't you?" Ruairi coughed to mask the anger that was constricting his throat. Rosaleen had lied to him once again. He had so easily believed her reason for wanting to come to Canada over America. She had told him that she needed to go somewhere that her past was unknown. In New York, almost half of the population was Irish.

"Well, forgive me for being worried about the safety of my family with you in town."

"Forgiven," Ruairi said as he busied himself at the stern with some extra ropes that were knotted up. "Make yourself useful and hand me that fishing wire," he instructed, pointing to a reel lying on the deck.

Billy picked it up and handed it to him. He tried again to get Ruairi to talk. "I don't even know where to begin . . ."

"Then don't," Ruairi cut him off. "That war is over. I'm just a lad and you're just a lad and we're just fishing." Ruairi had a way of making himself understood.

Billy nodded. He couldn't take the chance of angering Ruairi too much. But he needed to know why Ruairi O'Neill was in Charlottetown. There was something believable in the way he had said he didn't know the Gainsborough's were in Canada. But Billy reckoned it hadn't truly been a coincidence. He would wait.

"So, where are we headed?" Billy asked, looking out towards the horizon.

"About five more kilometres northeast and then we'll cut the engine."

"And fish?" Billy winked.

"And fish!" Ruairi smirked.

"Who's buying the fish off you?" Billy was a bit curious.

"Better you don't know that, I think."

"You don't trust me," he said it more as a statement than a question. "Can you at least tell me what it is we are fishing for?"

"Whiskey. Uncut."

"How much?"

"A lot."

Billy looked around trying to guess where it would be hidden. Ruairi pointed underneath the sails.

"The hull is hollowed out," he stated simply.

"How long have you been doing this?"

"We sailed here almost a month ago and I started immediately. I arranged a bit of whiskey to get sent to Miquelon every so often after the Volstead Act went into effect in the United States. Prohibition has been a godsend for my pocket. My brother's been doing this for a few years in New York."

"So Gerry O'Neill is alive?"

Ruairi grinned proudly, "Gerry O'Neill is alive, alright. The Devil himself couldn't bring that lad down."

Billy scratched his forearm. The sun was beginning to burn his skin. "There were quite a few that tried," he paused. "The O'Neill boys have quite a myth surrounding them." He tapped the side of the boat. He had seen the little cutter's name when Ruairi had pulled up to the docks. It was very fitting.

Ruairi licked his lips and folded his arms as he leaned back. "My younger brother Thomas is somewhat of a poet," he said, in reference to the boat's christening. "He's rather fond of the allusion."

"Aren't you worried about getting caught?" Billy asked.

Ruairi flicked his cigarette into the water. "I've never worried about getting caught."

Billy gave a half-hearted chuckle, "The perfect criminal."

"I prefer rebel."

Billy pressed his lips together and sighed, "It's all just words, Ruairi."

"It's never been that simple, Billy."

"It was with us." Billy's mind went back to that night in Dublin. He remembered that face, staring down at him with those eyes. It had all been so disorientating. He had expected brutality at Ruairi's fingertips but found a safehouse.

"You're wrong. It was even more complicated with us." Ruairi stared at Billy.

Billy looked off over the water for a long while. The sun glinted off the silvery-blue waves. "You saved my life. I'd say that's pretty damn simple."

Ruairi rubbed his temples. "I would have killed you any other day."

Billy shut his eyes to stop the sun's spears from inducing the terrible memories. "Yes, you would have. And I would have captured you and ordered your execution any other day. It was a war. We were on opposite sides."

Ruairi raised one eyebrow and looked sideways at Billy. "You would have had me executed?"

"You deserted the British Army. Why do you think we were after you so badly?" he paused. "How could you fight beside our men in the trenches and then turn your back on them?" Billy wanted so desperately to know this strange creature; one part human, one part monster.

"Did you come with me because you wanted to understand the Irish?" Ruairi's face was calm but his eyes were gleaming. "I don't even understand the Irish."

"How do you desert your brothers?" Billy asked one more time.

"I ask myself that every night," Ruairi countered. "How could I have deserted my father, my brothers, my sister, my country, when it needed me most? So, I left your war and I went to fight our war."

"Why did you have to fight at all? And why, God help me, did you have to do it in the middle of the most destructive war this world has ever seen?"

"It was for that very reason, Billy. The British were distracted, vulnerable."

"And what if that would have cost us the war against Germany?"

Ruairi leaned forward, "I find it interesting that you don't see the hypocrisy in your question. You see our timing as a betrayal because it could have meant foreign domination in Britain."

"I see your timing as a betrayal because you were a soldier in the British Army."

"Don't be so naïve, Billy. I was never a soldier in the British Army. I was just a young lad out looking for adventure. The war made some soldiers. Mostly, it just made corpses." Ruairi threw his cigarette butt into the water.

Billy turned away from Ruairi. "It killed me a thousand times over."

Ruairi watched the young Englishman struggle with his conscience. "Why did you re-enlist and come to Ireland?"

"I believed it was my duty."

"You say 'believed' . . . do you not believe it anymore?" Ruairi asked. He wondered if the ideals had been smothered in the young Englishman.

"I don't know what I believe anymore," Billy sighed. He turned back to Ruairi and confronted him with his eyes. "Why did you leave me alive?"

Ruairi was silent for a moment. He would have to choose his words carefully. "Not every Englishman is the enemy."

"Every British officer is the enemy."

"It isn't that black and white for me. If you would have died in the lorry, it would have been part of the war. To shoot you after I had pulled you out . . ." he stopped himself.

"So why did you pull me to safety? I would have bled out quickly from that wound; you wouldn't have had to do anything." He didn't believe any other member of Ruairi's contingent would have left him alive.

Ruairi remained silent.

Billy wasn't satisfied. "Why didn't you kill my father?"

Ruairi sighed. "I tried, he escaped."

"All you had to do was fire another bullet into him."

Ruairi's temper began to flare. The Englishman was pushing for an answer Ruairi was unable to give him. "Don't mistake my conscience for an inability to pull the trigger."

Billy didn't make that mistake at all but he couldn't understand how Ruairi's conscience had prevented him from killing the General. It should have made the decision quite simple. "Did she want him dead?"

"Who? Rosaleen?" Ruairi's expression changed, if only by a flicker.

Billy was surprised by Ruairi's demeanour. He seemed bitter, not angry.

"Yes and no. It depended on what mood she was in when you asked her."

"Did you leave him alive for her sake?" Billy asked.

Ruairi stared at his hands. They were as steady as they always were. "You can make as many assumptions as you like."

Billy pleaded with him, "I need the truth."

Ruairi laughed softly, "There is no such thing as the truth, Billy. The sooner you learn that, the sooner things will make sense to you."

"He's unwell, you know. The wound got infected and it flares up on him every now and again."

"Hmm . . ." was all Ruairi would say.

Ruairi had shot General Gainsborough in the soft fleshy part between the shoulder and the heart. No one had understood why he hadn't shot him in the head.

"I heard that she had a little girl," Billy's eyes met Ruairi's.

"Her name is Kathleen." Ruairi watched him closely. "Rosaleen will be there tonight, Billy."

Billy's head snapped up. He suddenly believed Ruairi didn't know they were in Charlottetown. It was in his voice in that one sentence. He also realized that he may be in even more danger because of it. "What does she want from him?"

"I don't know. Women are a mystery to me. Maybe she just wants money for Kathleen," he paused and then said the words that they both were thinking, "or maybe she wants him dead."

"I never told anybody. Not Gracie, not my mother. I didn't want to ruin everybody else's life. I never thought they'd ever be able to find out. But now . . ." his voice trailed off.

Ruairi let a few moments pass before he spoke. "Kathleen has the same bow to her lips that your sister has."

"It's a Gainsborough trait."

"Hopefully it's the only trait that Kathleen's inherited."

"We're not all bad," Billy said quietly.

Ruairi raked a hand through his hair, "Well, Rosaleen was awfully fond of the Gainsboroughs."

"I thought you used to call her something else? Rosh . . ." Billy paused, trying to remember the name that Ruairi had used for her so many years ago.

"Róisín?" Ruairi conjured her in his mind, "Róisín Dubh; The Dark Rosaleen," he chuckled, "She was aptly named. In Irish it means 'black rose' and there are poems about her."

"She deserves poetry. She is a beautiful woman, you know."

"Too beautiful," he agreed.

"How did you never fall in love with her?" Billy asked, genuinely curious.

"I did. I still am. But like all fated lovers, we could never survive together."

Billy leaned back and smiled, "You're quite the tragic case, aren't you then?"

"The typical Irish martyr, I've been told." Ruairi smiled sardonically.

"So what role do you fill in her life, if not her lover?" Billy was fascinated by the boundaries Ruairi set around himself.

Ruairi hesitated. He wasn't quite sure how to answer that question. "Protector, I guess," he mused, "Friend, confidante . . ."

Billy raised his eyebrows and waited but Ruairi just laughed cheekily. "Has she ever cared for anyone else?"

Ruairi noticed Billy's growing agitation and was intrigued. "Do you mean your father?"

Billy ground his teeth, "Sure, my father."

Ruairi licked his lips slowly. "Aye, she cared for him. She must have cared for him enough to worry about you. She was the one who forced me to drag you from the vehicle."

"She was there?" Billy remembered her at the house but didn't realize she had been at the ambush.

Billy looked down and Ruairi watched his face colour with a hundred emotions. Ruairi allowed himself one moment of truth. "I would have left you to bleed to death."

The colour drained from Billy's face just as quickly. He looked fragile and sickly. "I made an important hostage."

"I didn't need a hostage," Ruairi growled, his face rigid and his eyes rocky.

"So then why am I not dead?" Billy looked straight into Ruairi's wild eyes. "I need to know."

"Then you'll have to ask her."

Billy was frustrated but he relented, "In case I never find out, thank you."

The look that Billy gave him was filled with a thousand years of apologies. Ruairi had to look away. Billy's eyes were too confronting.

Gracie stood in front of the mirror in her bedroom and smiled at herself. Her confidence had returned. A few deep breaths and a long bath had restored her composure and she was quite sure she was ready to be the future Mrs. Johnny Bexley.

She concentrated on her flawless reflection. Her diamond ring made for the perfect accessory.

Genevieve had designed the gown for her daughter and had made it quite daring. She had commissioned a Parisian couturier to sew it. It was a deep plum purple silk. The straps of the dress were very thin and set far apart on the shoulder blades. They curled around and set themselves high up on her ribcage.

Gracie's hair was smoothed and pinned in elegant curls at the base of her neck, a little bit to the right side of her head. Her lips were a scarlet pink and her cheeks rouged bronzy rose. But her eyes were dramatic, a smoky grey palette set above her icy blue eyes. In the center of her chest, a delicate pearl hung daintily from a strand of gold. It was a gift from her father.

Ruairi spent the next five minutes preparing Billy for the rendezvous with McCoy. This was the first big shipment of whiskey that McCoy would be taking from his crew and Ruairi didn't want to take any chances in how the transfer took place. He readied the boat and then leaned down to open up the trapdoor in the deck. A movement on the horizon caught his eye.

"Ah, shite," he cursed, dropping the trap and rearranging the sails.

Billy spun around from the stern where he was relieving himself over the rails. He quickly did up his trousers. "What?" he called up to Ruairi.

"We're not alone," Ruairi called back.

Billy followed Ruairi's line of sight and saw the boat approaching from the southeast. It was definitely the Coast Guard.

Ruairi stood up and stretched casually. "Don't make any sudden movements. They're watching us with binoculars. Go pick up a rod and start fishing. And remember, I'm armed so not a word," Ruairi warned.

Billy chuckled to himself. He picked up the rod and did as he was told. Within minutes, the Coast Guard had pulled up alongside *The Phoenix*.

"Ruairi O'Neill, eh?" The Captain shouted down, "And what are we doing out here today?"

Billy stood with his back to the patrol boat. He could hear the men snickering as they relished the thought of bringing in this already well-known rum-runner. He slowly turned around and addressed them.

"Captain Jackson! Nice to see you, Sir!" He gave a friendly wave. Out of the corner of his eye he could see Ruairi glaring at him. He had to bite his bottom lip to keep from laughing.

There was a look of utter shock on the Captain's face. "Billy Gainsborough? What are you doing with . . ." he stuttered, "With him?" he asked, pointing at Ruairi.

"Ruairi and I are mates from our war days! We're just out for a spot of fishing before my little sister's engagement party," he called up brightly.

Ruairi cleared his throat in agreement.

"Oh. Oh, I see," the Captain was at a loss. He wanted to seize the boat but he didn't want to risk accusing Billy Gainsborough of importing alcohol. His superiors would have his neck if he brought in such a prominent member of the British elite.

"Beautiful day for it, isn't it, Captain?" Billy continued his sprightly banter.

"Yes, it is." By now the crew was restless, wondering why they hadn't been ordered to board the smaller craft. "Well boys, you have yourselves a good day," he smiled faintly at a beaming Billy and then turned to glare at Ruairi. Ruairi winked at him cheekily.

The Captain turned once more to look at Billy. His confusion was evident and it was all Billy could do to smile and wave him on.

Both men held their breath until the patrol was well on its way. Then Ruairi walked over to him and slapped him on the back.

"Bloody brilliant, y'are!" he announced, impressed by the authority Billy carried.

"So you aren't going to shoot me then?" Billy teased him.

Ruairi cuffed him on the back and laughed, "Alright, let's switch fishing spots. The good Captain will still have us in his sights, waiting for any sign of action."

"So, we head where?"

Ruairi smiled crazily, "Out to the waves, able seaman! We'll have to meet McCoy as he rounds the eastern tip of Cape Breton."

Billy looked out at the inky black waves and frowned. It would be an early test for his sea legs.

Johnny Bexley took a mouthful of gin and grimaced. He was nervous. His confidence rarely waned but tonight's prospects had him feeling on edge. He sat alone in the enormous hallway, waiting for Billy to show up and calm him down. He stared at the grey and white marbled floor and rubbed his temples. He stood up. He walked to the parlour and sat in front of the empty fireplace.

He hated the thought of marrying a woman that he wasn't sure was going to satisfy him in the long term. Gracie Gainsborough was obviously the most beautiful woman around, and had all of the other qualities he was looking for; affluence, pedigree and style. But she wasn't exciting. She was rather stitched up compared with the girls he had been raised with. He wasn't sure she would keep him from wandering.

He rubbed his palms together and cringed at how sweaty they were. He sighed heavily and poured another tumbler of gin. The sun shot arrows of gold through the windows, dispersing a rainbow of colours onto the wall above the fireplace. Johnny twirled the cup in his hand and then held it up to read the inscription on the bottom. *Waterford Crystal*, he read.

Most of the married men that he knew had warned him of this. They had told him to make sure he knew what he was getting or else he would end up with a long line of mistresses. And precedence had now been set on divorce and infidelity with the wave of feminism that was stamping out all good sense.

He took another sip. Billy was late and Johnny had never been very patient. He checked the time and rang for the butler.

The Phoenix pulled up alongside a schooner named *Tomoka*. The late afternoon sun was casting shadows alongside shards of piercing gold. Billy hadn't noticed before that he was sweating.

Ruairi had the boats tethered quickly and was aboard the larger vessel shaking hands with the crew as if they were the best of friends. Billy was slower to disembark *The Phoenix* and nervously negotiated the gap between the two boats. He was immediately greeted by a tall, lanky man with a pleasant demeanour. Ruairi made the introductions.

"Pleasure to meet you, Billy," the infamous rum Captain, Bill McCoy, was relaxed and friendly, "You're looking a bit pale, son."

Billy swallowed as his stomach flipped. "It usually takes me a few voyages at the beginning of each season to master my stomach at sea."

Ruairi tried to hold back his laughter, "Are you going to be alright, lad?"

Billy tried to nod as the boat heaved over a large wave. His knees buckled but he caught himself on the rail.

Ruairi and McCoy shared an amused look as the Englishman vomited into the sea.

"We might give you some privacy and unload the cargo," McCoy patted Billy on the back.

Billy grunted his appreciation and waved them away with one hand.

"How did this batch turn out, Ruairi?" McCoy turned his attention to the whiskey.

Ruairi pulled a small flask from his pocket and handed it over.

McCoy tasted it and coughed, "I'm impressed. That's bloody good, son."

"It will get better," Ruairi promised.

"Good whiskey always does!" McCoy agreed, "Well, I'm happy for you to unload."

"Do you know where this shipment is going?" Ruairi asked. He was curious to know who would be drinking his first distillation.

"Florida," McCoy answered, "We're heading back down south to Bimini to pick up a rum shipment so we'll drop this off on the way down."

Ruairi grinned. "That will be grand! Will you let me know what the clientele think?" he asked as he hopped back down onto *The Phoenix*.

"Definitely; I'm pretty confident that it will be enjoyed, though. It's hard to get authentic Irish whiskey anymore and I won't sell anything else. You and yours have given me an edge in the market," McCoy assured him. Then he turned to check on Billy. "How are you now, son?"

Billy was wiping his mouth with his shirt cuff. "Better, thank-you," he inhaled the fresh sea air. His legs were feeling stronger. "Can I offer you some help?" he called down to Ruairi.

Ruairi glanced up at him and raised his eyebrows, "Do you think you can handle yourself? I'm not very good with another man's sick."

"I think I'll be alright, now. Just tell me what to do." He was embarrassed.

Ruairi began to pass him up crates, "Just don't drop them!" he advised.

The rest of the transfer went relatively quickly. The waves seemed to be growing in size but Billy became more confident as the work went on. He was amazed at the quantity of cargo that *The Phoenix* had been storing.

He felt McCoy behind him. "Are you going to be a regular on the contact boats now that you've got your sea legs back?" he asked.

Billy was quick to say no. "I'm a lawyer," he confided, "I don't think I'm much of a rum-runner."

McCoy appraised him with more respect, "A lawyer? We could use some of those too, my boy."

Billy was curious, "How so?"

He turned and leaned over the rail to speak to Ruairi. "He could be a mighty useful Baptist."

Ruairi sighed, "I think he might be too much of a Baptist."

"A friend of the angels, you reckon?"

Ruairi nodded.

"Bloody thieves, those angels!" McCoy laughed, slapping a firm hand on Billy's shoulder. "That's too bad. I liked you."

Billy was unsure of what the entire conversation had meant but he assumed that somehow, Ruairi had made it clear to McCoy that Billy wasn't one of them. He shook hands with the infamous rum runner and manoeuvred his way back to *The Phoenix*.

"Watch out for the Coast Guard," Ruairi called up to McCoy, "Especially if you are heading down to Halifax. They've been pretty sticky around there lately."

"We're headed up North here first," McCoy answered. "I wouldn't mind checking on a few of the operations in Miquelon now that we're up this far. I'm in no hurry and we're carrying an expensive load."

"I'll see you next month, then." Ruairi gave a wave.

McCoy grinned down at both boys. "I sure hope so."

As they cruised around the heads, Ruairi called Billy to his side. "I think we're both pretty clear on the need for secrecy about this afternoon.

Billy nodded, his hands on his hips. "I don't think I'll be risking my reputation just to tell the story."

Ruairi smiled. "I'd be more worried about my pride if I were you. I've never seen a lad as green as you. I thought we were going to lose you there for a moment."

Billy reddened slightly. "I was a bit shocking, wasn't I?"

Ruairi finished mooring the boat and reached out his hand. For the second time that day, Billy Gainsborough shook it. He pressed five hundred dollars into Billy's palm. "It was a good day's fishing," Ruairi smirked at him. "You've earned this."

"I couldn't possibly," Billy objected as he tried to hand the money back to Ruairi.

"I'm buying your silence, Billy. Take it and buy an engagement present for Gracie."

Billy nervously relented, "Stay away from my sister."

The mischievous smirk turned into a grin, "I'll be seeing you both tonight." With another impulsive wink, he turned and walked off down the pier.

CHAPTER 4

Headlights shone seductively from polished black Fords as the stream of Charlottetown's social elite made their way to the black and white marble steps of The Club. Valets in royal purple waistcoats performed a choreographed bow before parking the motorcars.

The lobby was lit by six crystal chandeliers and their illumination spilled out all of the way to the fountain in the center of the courtyard. Genevieve had gone ahead to meet with Eleanor Bexley and a few other ladies whose sole purpose in life was to attend teas and social events.

Genevieve was annoyed with the lack of decorum that Eleanor had showed in the organizing of the evening. There was not one single detail that hadn't been painstakingly planned by Eleanor and her team of busybodies.

Of course, William was in his element. He arrived with Lucas Bexley, freshly bathed after a round of golf. He was positively glowing as if the fresh air and exercise had done him good. They inspected the terraced patio, spoke with the barmen, and even went so far as to make the band play a few bars of a song to judge whether they were worthy to play at such an event. He had swaggered over to the young lady seated at the piano and whispered something in her ear. She had laughed and looked up at him with sultry eyes. He had a way with women.

Genevieve went into one of the powder rooms to make sure that her hair was perfect. She was dressed in a canary yellow satin shift. Her caramel skin set off the colour perfectly. She turned to the side, running one hand down her stomach and the other down her lower back, as she assessed her figure. She was flawless. As she stood in front of the mirror, studying herself, she saw the door open behind her and in slipped her husband.

She ignored him. He cleared his throat. She stared at him in the mirror and he moved towards her. He tried to put his arms around her from behind but she skilfully slid out of his reach. She turned to face him.

"You shouldn't be in here." Her eyes were dull when she looked at him.

"I just came to give you a kiss and tell you how lovely you look." He slowly moved towards her with his mouth. She turned her face away and his lips missed their mark, planting the kiss on her cheekbone instead. "Ah, Genevieve," he breathed, "Don't be like this."

Genevieve's stare was cold in the mirror. "I don't have time for this, William," she sniffed. "I have to go and make sure Eleanor isn't already setting the wedding date."

William grabbed her arm as she strode past and yanked her around to face him. "I will not allow you to ruin tonight for my daughter because of some daft notion that your mother put in your foolish head. You will show your support for this marriage," he threatened.

"Let go of me William, or so help me God, I will tell Gracie exactly what I think of marriage."

William raised his hand to her but was interrupted by the door swinging open and Eleanor Bexley poking her head in. "I thought I heard something," she chirped. "What are you two doing in the ladies' room?"

William cleared his throat and set about straightening his jacket. "We were just having a private conversation, Eleanor."

"Oh, I hope I haven't interrupted." She began to back away.

Genevieve turned away from her husband abruptly and smiled at Eleanor. "Not at all, we were just finishing." She was well versed in faking domestic bliss. "How about we go and check the taper heights for each table?"

Genevieve refused to acknowledge William as she disappeared through the door.

Norah and Gracie waited at the Gainsborough house for the boys to arrive. Billy and Johnny were to pick them up at seven o'clock. When the car pulled up, the girls climbed inside excitedly.

Norah was wearing a rather short, silvery grey sequined dress paired with two long strands of black pearls. Her legs were bare and her knees were rouged.

"Eleanor is going to be shocked, little Miss," Johnny warned his sister playfully. Since becoming part of fashionable society, Eleanor Bexley had become increasingly worried about what others would say about her or her family.

Norah rolled her eyes. "I don't care. I'm sick of worrying about Mother and her antiquated ideas. She'll have an even bigger fit when she finds out I've joined the local suffragists."

Johnny looked horrified. "You must be joking!" he exclaimed. "Why on earth would you do that? Isn't it enough that women can vote? Why would you want them in the Senate as well?"

"Possibly because I am a woman and I believe our opinions should be valued in this country." Norah looked at her brother as if he was ridiculous. "Honestly Johnny, women have only had the vote in this province for one year and there are still provinces in the Dominion that don't allow women to vote. It's 1923! The entire world is changing and if you are so worried about appearances, my dear brother, you will need to change with it."

Billy laughed at Norah's dig at her brother. She was an extremely clever girl.

Johnny ignored his sister and reached over to put his hand on Gracie's thigh. "At least I've found myself a sensible woman who's content to allow me to take care of the important things."

Billy was amused. "You're right there. The only thing Gracie would be interested in voting for is the annihilation of the colour peach."

"Well, it is a truly abhorrent colour. I don't know why anyone would want to wear it." Gracie stated, not realizing she was being made fun of. She had no interest in voting or politics but she knew her own mind and she had always taken comfort in that.

Norah and Billy shared a look and then burst into a fit of giggles.

Gracie made a face at them. "I can't believe you two are laughing at me after the horrible morning I had. Whatever happened with that boy from the boat anyway?"

Billy tried desperately to stop her before she finished her question but his protesting only confused her and she continued.

"What happened? He seemed really angry when I was leaving." Her look of concern prompted Johnny's curiosity.

"What's this? What man from the boat?" Johnny was looking between Gracie and Billy.

Gracie launched herself into the story of her morning while Billy silently reprimanded himself for not taking her aside when he had arrived at the house to tell her to keep the story quiet. He stared down at his hands waiting for the moment his name would come up. It didn't take long.

"Ruairi? That's Irish, isn't it? Must be one of those dockworkers," Johnny was sighing and shaking his head, disgusted. "It's so degrading when they try to socialize with us. This may be Canada but there is still certain standards that must be adhered to."

Gracie, Billy and Norah tried not to look as uncomfortable as they felt. Johnny's arrogance was one of his least favourable characteristics.

"Do you know this Ruairi, Billy? You've spent a lot of time down on the docks during the last sailing season," Johnny was still going.

"No, never seen him before," Billy lied, hoping their familiarity hadn't been noticed by the girls.

"Well, I don't want you to have anything to do with anyone Irish, Gracie. I don't think it's very acceptable in our circle," Johnny's tone always had an edge of control in it. "I also don't like to hear that you are spending time alone with other men."

"It was an accident, Johnny," Gracie protested.

"I know, just be careful in the future. I cannot tolerate those types of embarrassments."

The drive continued in silence. Billy watched his sister closely. She stared out the window at the setting sun deep in thought. Johnny had an annoyed look on his face as he unconsciously stroked her ring finger.

The motorcar pulled up in front of the Club. At the top of the stairs, both sets of parents awaited their children. Eleanor and Lucas Bexley stood off to the left, smiling giddy smiles and almost dragging the young couple up the steps through sheer force of their own excitement. To the right of them stood the Gainsborough's, a mixture of emotions written on their faces. William was indeed happy. He was proud of his daughter for attracting the most affluent of all of the young men she had met. Genevieve looked sad but she forced herself to smile at her daughter. She knew that from here on out, Gracie would need her more than ever as the reality of the life she was choosing was sure to sink in immediately after the honeymoon was over.

When Gracie had made it up the steps, the kisses and the hellos were all exchanged and Eleanor had a photographer take a picture.

Genevieve tried to summon the appropriate motherly response to the moment. "If this is what you really want, you know I'll be happy for you," she whispered in Gracie's ear.

Gracie looked up at her mother. Genevieve gave her a dazzling smile and then teared up, "And Darling, you look absolutely beautiful."

"Just like you, Maman." Gracie hugged her mother again.

Gracie turned and let Johnny lead her through the club, and out onto the terrace. She felt giddy, like a young girl on her first merry-go round ride. The stone patio was lit by hundreds of candles. William had also gone to the expense of renting strings of lights that were just becoming popular at Christmas time to decorate trees. He had them strung across the top of the patio. In the early dusk they looked like little stars, just out of reach of all of the guests. White lilies adorned table tops and tapers glowed around them. She couldn't wait for night to fall for the full effect.

There was already over a hundred people milling about. Waiters were walking by with tantalizing hors d'oeuvres and champagne in crystal coupes.

"Quite a party," Johnny remarked.

Gracie smiled demurely. "I suppose it had to be, what with my father and your mother presiding over it all."

Johnny chuckled, "Can you imagine the affair they will plan for the actual wedding?"

The crowd at the Club was made up of most of Charlottetown's privileged plus a handful of important guests who had made the journey from other parts of the country at the request of General and Lady Gainsborough. Some in the crowd were from England, over in the new world to make their mark away from the prying eyes of generations past. Others had been in either America or Canada for a little while now, quite comfortable in the ways of the young countries. Most of them had children old enough to give way to thoughts of an easy retirement.

A new generation had teethed on the rich red soil of the Maritimes. They were fresh and shiny and took on life with a vivaciousness that stunned their parents. They were surely capable of anything, as the times had proved.

The brightest in Charlottetown had been Lana Hamilton. She was the daughter of Peter and Juliet Hamilton, who had long held the title of Charlottetown's royalty. Peter was a shipping magnate and employed half of the East Coast of Canada. When the Gainsborough's had first moved to Charlottetown, William had gone to great lengths to ensure that Lana and Gracie became fast friends. At best, they tolerated each other civilly, but there was not much that resembled a true friendship. Gracie knew she needed to engage with the society girls of her new place of residence and Lana knew she needed to keep a close eye on her competition. It had taken Gracie just one promenade down the piers before all of the sailors in port were talking of her and Lana felt she had to be as close as possible to the girl that had dethroned her as socialite of the year. It also gave her the chance to be close to the delicious Johnny Bexley.

Ruairi dashed into the house and flew up the stairs to his bedroom. He heard Rosaleen call out to him but he didn't stop. He knew she would follow.

He had barely gotten out of his shirt when she came in. He glanced over at her and smiled. She was dressed in a very provocative black dress that pushed the recent shorter hemline trend to the limit. The heels that she wore made her incredibly long legs longer and instead of wearing stockings, she had left them bare, making it almost impossible for a man not to try to imagine where they ended.

"Where the hell have you been?" she asked, obviously annoyed that he was late.

"I got caught up."

"What happened?" She didn't turn away when he stripped off his trousers and his under shorts.

He wrapped a towel around himself and leaned against the door. He eyed her calmly and exhaled slowly. "Well, now that you ask, I had a very interesting day. I had the pleasure of bumping into Gracie and Billy Gainsborough."

Her eyes widened and she felt behind her for the bed. She sat down and waited for him to continue.

He levelled her with his eyes. "Rosaleen, this isn't a good situation for me to be in. I need to know what you're playing at or this is going to get very messy. Did you know they were here?"

She had tears in her eyes as she tried to nod. "Maggie sent me a telegram last year. He's been ill. I thought he might be dying," her voice was nothing more than a gasp. She felt the fear physically crushing her chest. He came over and knelt in front of her, taking her hands in his.

"Are you here to watch him die or have him killed?" Ruairi used a soft voice to ask a hard question.

"I'm . . . I'm, oh Ruairi, I don't know. I'm just scared that he's going to die and I won't feel as though I've resolved anything." Parts of this were true. She had felt this way so many times. There were moments that the desire to watch him die were so intense that every muscle in her body would knot up. She would channel all of her energy into her hatred and it would smoulder in her eyes.

Ruairi looked down at his hands clasped around hers. She was trembling violently and it scared him to see her like this. "Why am I here, Róisín? You must know that my first instinct would be to kill him."

She took a deep breath to steady herself. "I brought you here to protect me." She put their hands, still clasped, up to her face and her tears fell over them.

"Protect you from what?" Ruairi implored her.

Rosaleen was unsure of how to answer him. "I want to live here, in Charlottetown near Maggie. I need you here in case William won't allow me to."

"That may mean killing him, Love. He won't be happy to see either of us here."

She bit her lip. "I know but I hope it doesn't come to that."

"So why are we going to this engagement party tonight?" he asked.

"It's probably the best time to let him know we are in town. He won't be able to do too much damage with that many people around," Rosaleen reasoned. "Have I asked too much of you?"

Ruairi kissed her hands roughly. "I would do anything for you."

Rosaleen smiled down at him through her tears. "I know."

"Go fix your make-up, kiddo, you're dripping rouge." He watched her walk out of the bedroom and then sighed as she closed the door. He didn't know what it was about her that made him forgive her over and over again. She would get him killed one day, he was sure of it.

As the sun finally set over the harbour and Charlottetown was pitched into night, the Club twinkled incandescently. A husky voice was singing a soft love song. Jazz music was kind to lovers. Some had danced while others had snuggled in corners or off in the bushes. Most had sipped champagne and gossiped insidiously.

William and Eleanor had made their rounds, thanking everybody for coming and making the usual fusses over the engaged couple and the beautiful ring. Genevieve had been busy flagging down the champagne waiter in an attempt to blur the memories about to be made that night. Lucas was busy prepping his son for the big speech and Billy was being forced to chat to every available daughter by every eager mother.

Gracie stood in the center of the patio with Norah and the rest of the young ladies and looked around at the scene before her. She took a deep breath and tried to calm the butterflies in her stomach. A voice in her ear startled her and she whirled around to find herself facing a tall, wiry man in his early thirties.

"Are you Gracie Gainsborough?" he asked casually, a Scandinavian accent enriching the sound of her name.

"Yes, I am," she answered nervously.

"Karl," the man introduced himself and stuck out his hand. "I own the Club." He indicated to the building.

"Oh! How lovely to meet you, Karl." She put her hand in his.

With his other hand, he held out a box to her that had a white ribbon tied around it. "I was asked to personally deliver this to you."

"Who is it from?" Gracie loved presents.

"Not supposed to say," he shrugged.

Norah looked at Gracie and squealed. The other girls closed in around her.

Gracie looked at the little box and smiled. She slowly fingered the ribbon.

She untied the ribbon and lifted the lid off the box. Inside laid a stunning silver necklace with a large square emerald pendant surrounded by little diamonds. She lifted it out of the case and smiled. It was gorgeous.

With everybody's eyes on her, she felt she had to say something. She looked around until she spotted Johnny. He just shook his head and shrugged. "This wasn't you?" she asked shocked. He shook his head again. "Then who gave me this lovely necklace?"

She waited. Nobody said anything. She laughed, "Somebody gave it to me, so whoever it was, thank-you, I love it! I just wish you would come forward so I could thank you properly!"

Everybody smiled and then went back to their mingling. Billy walked over to her.

"That's a bit strange don't you think?" he said. It was an extravagant gift but Billy supposed it wouldn't have been too out of the ordinary as an engagement gift from any one of the wealthy couples in attendance.

"Look how beautiful it is! Here, help me take off the other necklace and put it on for me." She handed it to him and turned her back so that he could unlatch the pearl.

"William won't be very happy if you take off his pearl," Billy said to her.

"I bet you Papa bought it for me," she said happily.

"You're probably right. But if he did, I can't believe he didn't bask in the glory of your appreciation."

"He knows tonight is my night, Billy."

"I'm sorry sweetheart," he said as he slipped the other necklace around her neck and did up the clasp, "every night is his night. There, perfect."

He handed her the pearl necklace back and she slipped it into her pochette.

Billy saw Johnny walking towards them and he nudged his sister. "It's time for the announcement, I think." He kissed her on the temple and left her for her fiancé to claim.

Eleanor quickly shuffled people into seats as Johnny ushered Gracie back to their table at the far end of the patio. He held out her chair for her but remained standing. He looked around at all of the people gathered on the patio and felt a bit exposed.

He smiled nervously. "I'd like to thank you all for coming tonight to help me celebrate this lovely woman that has graciously agreed to be my lovely wife," he smiled down at Gracie. She smiled back. "If you will all indulge me this, I'd like to toast my bride-to-be."

Johnny raised his glass, "Gracie, I'm so privileged . . ."

"Oh, look boys!" a strong Irish accent rang out across the patio, interrupting Johnny mid-sentence. "We got here just in time to toast Gracie on her engagement!"

CHAPTER 5

For a moment, nobody dared breathe. Johnny looked confused and he opened and closed his mouth a few times without sound coming out.

He half turned his body and looked up at the gentleman who had interrupted him. "I'm sorry, do we know you?"

The man swaggered towards him confidently, with a broad grin on his face, "Gracie told me all about you this morning on our little boat ride, didn't you doll?" He nodded towards Gracie and stuck out his hand. "I'm Ruairi O'Neill."

Johnny narrowed his eyes. "The same Ruairi from this morning, I gather."

"I would assume so." Ruairi ran his eyes up and down Gracie.

Billy groaned. Beside him, an obviously shaken William was tugging at his bowtie and trying to remain calm. Everybody else was trying to figure out who the intruding party was.

"I'm sorry, am I missing something?" Gracie hissed, looking back and forth between Billy, Johnny, Ruairi and her father.

"Ah, the necklace looks beautiful, Love. I wasn't quite sure what was appropriate for an engagement gift since we barely know each other."

Gracie's eyes widened and her hand flew to her throat where the pendant rested, suddenly very heavily. "This was from you?" she stammered.

Johnny summoned the staff. "See this man and the rest of his party out, will you?" he asked sternly, indicating to Ruairi and the men and women that had come up the steps with him.

"That won't be necessary, will it General Gainsborough?" Ruairi directed his question to William, who was looking rather unwell. "I'm here with Rosaleen Jameson, I'm sure you remember her." His teeth flashed. "And anyway, Billy invited me himself this afternoon while we were out fishing."

Billy knew he had just been dangerously implicated as a co-conspirator. He raised his eyebrows at Ruairi, exasperated that he had been dragged into whatever game of chess they were now playing.

William tried to keep his face from betraying him but the accusing eyes that he turned on Billy revealed his fear. He had caught a glimpse of her as she had sashayed across the patio. She had sat, facing him, on the far end by the stairs. Now, he could feel her eyes on him and he began to sweat. He stuttered a few times before answering, "Of course you can stay. The Club is open to the public. But if you'll excuse us, we were just in the middle of something."

"Oh, not at all," Ruairi's smile was back. "I just came over to congratulate the bride-to-be!" He leaned over Johnny and grabbed Gracie by the hand. She was still terribly confused and it caught her off guard when he pulled her towards him and pressed his lips to hers. He held her for a moment longer than appropriate before he pulled away. "Congratulations, Love, I hope the evening was as perfect as you had planned," he whispered. Then he turned and strode back to his friends.

The instant that he was gone, the table erupted into chaotic questioning. They tried to keep their voices down to keep the tables surrounding them from hearing.

William glared at his son. "What is Ruairi O'Neill doing in Charlottetown, Billy?"

"Do you know this fellow, William?" Lucas asked.

"Unfortunately, yes. He is a member of the Irish Republican Army and played a very dangerous role in the Easter rising and the subsequent wars. We've had a long history, he and I."

"Did you know that when I was on the boat with him, Billy?" Gracie's eyes were wide with fright.

Billy nodded slowly. "Ruairi was responsible for holding up the lorry when I was injured."

Gracie's hand flew to her mouth and her skin went pale.

"Gracie was on a boat with him?" William roared.

Johnny practically lunged at Billy, "Gracie was in real danger!"

Billy buried his head in his hands. "She was in no danger. Ruairi isn't like that."

"All of the Irish are like that," Lucas offered his opinion.

Billy shot him a disgusted look. "What would you know about the Irish?" he challenged.

"Why have you invited him here, Billy?" William's voice was hard.

"I didn't invite him here," Billy hissed. "By some stroke of fate Gracie fell asleep on his boat. When I went looking for her, there they were, together. I had no idea he was here. And apparently, until this morning, he didn't know we were here either."

Eleanor turned on William. "What is your daughter doing alone with an Irishman? Do you realize how that looks?"

"Eleanor," Lucas admonished, "calm down!" He faked a smile. "Let's just take a deep breath and get back to what Johnny was saying."

"Do you really want your son engaged to a woman with loose morals?" Eleanor silenced her husband.

"Pardon me?" William stood up angrily. "How dare you imply that my daughter has loose morals?"

Gracie began to cry. Billy reached for his sister's hand.

Lucas shifted uncomfortably under the weight of William's glare. "I apologize for my wife's choice of words, William. They may have been too strong. But you must agree that the appearance is less than favourable."

"We can discuss this later, Father." Johnny could feel the eyes of the entire party on them.

Gracie felt very weak and reached for her water glass. Her hands trembled and she spilled the water. The glass rolled down onto the granite slabs and shattered. Everybody jumped up and the staff came running at the sound. Billy and Johnny tended to Gracie while Lucas, Eleanor and William directed the staff. Only Genevieve remained silent, sipping her champagne.

On the far side of the patio, Rosaleen smiled at Ruairi. "You've ruined the party."

"It's what I intended to do."

"Well, you sure as hell did it." His brother Thomas was at his side surveying the patio as it descended into disorder. "Now, where's the food?"

"On those bloody little trays," Stavros pointed at the waiters walking around with the platters. "Where's Karl? I want to know if he has anything decent to serve or if it's all that little bitty snobby stuff."

"Look around, Stavros," Thomas said motioning to the people on the patio, "It's all going to be snobby stuff."

Stavros made a face and then stood up. "Well, far be it from me to turn my nose up at free food, even if it is snobby stuff." He locked the nearest waiter in his sights and set off to relieve him of his tray. Thomas followed and they ambushed the poor young man, convincing him that Karl had sent for him and that they would circulate the tray in his absence. As soon as the kid turned his back, they carried the tray back to their table.

Aisling laughed when they set down the lobster puffs. "We can't just eat a whole tray of lobster puffs!" she exclaimed.

"Don't worry, my dear sister," Thomas grinned, "we'll be lightening the load of many a server tonight! I'm off to get the booze tray!" His loud voice attracted the attention of nearby dignitaries who gave the table a dirty look and moved on.

Mairtin Fitzgerald, a close friend of the O'Neill boys, made a rude gesture at them. The table laughed again.

Ruairi leaned in close to Rosaleen. "What's your plan, Love?" he asked gently.

"I don't have one," she said quietly. Ruairi looked at her. She stared straight at William. "Don't pity me."

Genevieve sat at the table. Somewhere in her head, she could hear the conversation going on around her but she was transfixed by the woman in the far corner. She was a beautiful woman; long, dark and sinewy. She wore a black dress and her lips were red. Genevieve was not so continental as to be ashamed of her own attraction to the girl. She couldn't even blame William for his indiscretion, not after seeing her. She reached for her champagne. She brought it to her mouth but it was empty. She put it down and broke her gaze away from the woman long enough to look for another tray of champagne. She saw one, a few feet away and rose to make her way towards it. She smiled blankly at the waiter as she lifted two glasses off the tray. She looked back at the girl as she put the champagne back to her lips. The bubbles tickled her mouth. She tipped her head back and drained the first glass.

"Would you like me to work on getting you a whole bottle?" a voice behind her asked.

Genevieve turned to find an unfamiliar gentleman standing near her. "I'm so embarrassed," she felt herself blush. "I didn't realize anyone was watching me."

"I couldn't help myself." He let his eyes travel the length of her. "A beautiful woman such as yourself is hard not to notice."

She was nervous under his gaze. She held out her hand to him. "Lady Genevieve Gainsborough. But please, just call me Genevieve."

He took her hand and turned it palm up. He gently kissed the inside of her wrist. "Lord Michael Fitzgerald," he said. "You can call me Mick, though."

She narrowed her eyes at him, mocking suspicion. "Are you really a Lord, *Mick*?" She gave his name an emphasis that he understood easily.

He narrowed his eyes back. "No, but what gave it away?"

"It might have been the 'call me Mick' part."

"Ah, too common is it?" He tried to look serious.

She laughed openly. He liked the way it made her eyes dance.

"Who are you here with, Mick?" she asked.

"Valerie Logan asked me to accompany her," he answered.

Genevieve was impressed. "You know Ms. Logan? I've heard so much about her but I haven't yet had the pleasure of actually meeting her. We never seem to attend the same events."

Valerie Logan was somewhat of a mythological creature in Charlottetown. There were many rumours about her and very little truth. The only thing that Genevieve knew for certain was that she was extremely wealthy, she was widowed and she was a feminist. For the last reason, William had forbidden Genevieve to attend any of her soirées, which were known to be the wildest on the island.

Genevieve was sure that Valerie hadn't been put on the guest list and was wondering why she would have come.

Mick was smiling at her. He had cloudy blue eyes. "You've never met Valerie? That surprises me. We'll have to remedy that. She's just over there," he pointed to the table where Rosaleen Jameson was perched.

Genevieve stiffened. "Let's not interrupt her. She looks like she's in the middle of something." She smiled at him. "It was lovely to make your acquaintance," she said as she turned to leave.

He caught her by the elbow. "Before you go," he released his grip and reached over to a passing champagne tray, taking two off the side and slightly unbalancing the tray. The waiter turned and looked disgruntled. Mick shrugged at him. He handed them to Genevieve. "You seem thirsty," he grinned cheekily.

Genevieve laughed in appreciation.

Gracie had pulled away from Johnny and excused herself to the Ladies' room. The large room was empty except for the long mirrors and overstuffed furniture and tall vases of flowers. She wasted no time locking herself in the tiny loo closet. She needed to be alone to breathe. Part of her was mortified and part of her was terrified. But there was also a part of her that was strangely excited by the prospect of the Irishman being there, buying her an expensive necklace, kissing her. She fingered the necklace as she sank back into the wall, breathing hard.

She opened her eyes when she heard Lana and the girls come stumbling in. Lana was the undisputed head of a group of heiresses that Norah liked to call the Peacock Brigade. She often said it was an insult to the actual birds.

The girls stood near the long row of mirrors. They were giggling and talking fast in their excitement but Gracie could hear every word that they said clearly.

"Well, I think it is safe to assume that Johnny Bexley is still available," Isabella Fontaine squealed with delight.

"Gracie Gainsborough is about to be thrown over. Won't that be a scandal?" Lana said into the mirror while reapplying her lipstick.

"Caught alone with an Irish rebel," Audrey Gilmour was re-pinning her hair, "what will they do with her?"

"And didn't General Gainsborough look like he'd seen a ghost?" Jessie Landry added.

"It's all very interesting, isn't it?" Lana smacked her lips together.

"I like dirty little secrets," Isabella mused.

"Well, what if I tell you that there is one more dirty little secret that wasn't quite exposed tonight but will be in the following days?" Lana stood tall in the mirror and gave the girls behind her a mischievous smile.

"Ooh, tell us!"

"Johnny Bexley had his suspicions about the suitability of Lady Gracie," she paused dramatically, "which is why he's been spending his free time with me."

"Lana!" Jessie gasped, "How could you keep that from us?"

"Oh, it's only been going on for a few days. I wanted to make sure there was actually a chance that he would leave her before I said anything. And just now, he sought me out to ask if he could see me later tonight."

"Oh my goodness, Lana! This is such wonderful news!" Audrey was clapping her hands.

"Well, we'll have to keep it quiet for the next few days but I just wanted you girls to be the first to know." Lana held a finger to her lips dramatically, sending the girls into high-pitched giggles as they filed back out of the powder room.

Gracie heard the door close behind them and the room went silent. She couldn't breathe. She felt dirty, hiding beside the toilet, clutching a pendant from an Irish rebel and wearing an engagement ring from a man who was being unfaithful to her.

Gracie felt her stomach begin to tighten. Her throat constricted and she thought she might vomit. She bent over the toilet but nothing came out.

"Are you all right in there?" an Irish voice asked her from the stall next to her.

Gracie was mortified. Somebody else had been in the ladies room. She took a ragged breath and tried to calm her stomach.

"I'll be fine," she called back, just loud enough to be heard.

She waited until she heard the other woman unlock her door and make her way to the vanity. When the noise finally dissipated and

Gracie was convinced she was alone, she opened her own door and went out to face the mirror.

Billy stood outside the restrooms, hoping to catch his sister. His father must have had the same intentions. When he saw Billy, his face darkened.

"What the hell is going on?" William charged.

"I told you everything that I know." Billy clenched his jaw and glared at his father.

"If this is some kind of revenge or . . ." William began to threaten.

Billy's voice was hollow, "You seem to forget that he wanted me dead too."

"I haven't forgotten anything," William growled, "All I know is that Ruairi O'Neill and Rosaleen Jameson have an army of Irish bastards at my daughter's engagement party."

"Well, maybe they just came to wish her well," Billy spit back at him. He turned on his heel and stormed off leaving William fuming with his hands on his hips.

Realizing he was suddenly vulnerable and alone, William quickly hurried off in the same direction.

The reflection wasn't pleasing. Gracie's hair had fallen loose and her skin was pale and clammy. Her makeup had run with her tears, leaving her face streaky and swollen.

She washed her face with shaky hands. She leaned over the vanity and wondered how she would make it out of the Club without being seen. She couldn't face anybody. Not now.

Another figure suddenly materialized in the mirror. Gracie looked around frantically, wanting to disappear. She watched as the figure floated closer. The girl was unmatched in beauty. She stared into the mirror at Gracie with dark eyes. Gracie looked away and tried to seem occupied with her lipstick application but her hands shook and she dropped the tube. The strain was proving too much, even for a girl well educated in keeping her emotions in check.

The dark girl was now beside her in the mirror. She turned Gracie towards her and stood no more than a foot away.

"It's not worth crying over, Love." The girl had the same accent as Ruairi. Her tone wasn't harsh but it wasn't sympathetic either.

Gracie felt her shoulders heave. She tried to breathe but the air caught repeatedly in her throat. The girl in front of her had a face of stone and Gracie fought to control herself as well as her counterpart.

The girl watched Gracie struggle for a moment, "You're better off without him."

Gracie found herself drowning in the dark eyes and her breathing slowed. "I'm sorry for making a scene," she sobbed quietly. She began to turn away but the girl stopped her with a strong hand.

"You're still wearing the necklace. I thought that would have been the first thing to come off." Rosaleen didn't like that Ruairi had given the English girl an expensive gift.

Gracie instinctively put her hand over it, as if by hiding it, the implication was hidden too.

"You must have made quite an impression on him for him to have given you an emerald. Anything that reminds him of home is sacred to him." Rosaleen's lips were tight.

"How do you know him so well?" Gracie's voice trembled.

"I've known him my whole life," Rosaleen said. Her tone was jealous.

Gracie put her hands to her face and began to sob again.

The girl watched on with pity. "It's been a rough night for you, Love," she sighed, "let's gets you out of here."

Ruairi looked around the patio at the flowers and the candles and shook his head. The party had gone on without the main event. Not many even seemed to care. Aisling had done a bit of reconnaissance and found out that most had expected the proposal to be a sham anyway. Juliet and Peter Hamilton had been subtly advocating for their daughter's suitability for such an advantageous match. Aisling had found their boldness mildly amusing. Ruairi actually found himself feeling a bit sorry for Gracie.

He looked up to see Billy coming towards him. He was well positioned to pull Billy away if the conversation got heated. He didn't need a public confrontation until he understood his own role in the situation.

He walked down the stairs and into the gardens. Billy followed. "What the hell are you doing here, Ruairi? I need to know!"

"Calm down, Billy boy."

"Don't call me that!" Billy snapped at him. He wasn't in the mood for Ruairi's sarcasm. "Gracie's night is ruined! Tell me how I'm supposed to calm down?"

"Have a cigarette," Ruairi suggested as he held one out to him.

"I don't smoke."

"You should. It would take the edge off," Ruairi said casually.

Billy was infuriated by him. "Do you know how many lives you've ruined?"

"Don't be so melodramatic. I didn't ruin your life." Ruairi took a long drag.

"Not mine!" Billy exploded, "Gracie's!"

"Gracie will be just fine."

"You can't imagine how she's feeling. She's been holed up in the ladies room ever since you're little disruption."

"She may have dodged a bullet there," Ruairi looked up to see the look on Billy's face. "Sorry, bad choice of words."

"Just leave Gracie alone. Please."

"I'm not doing Gracie any harm, Billy. This world you live in isn't going to protect her forever."

Billy started to walk away. He turned back and held up his hands. "You know, the sad thing is, you're right. She can't be protected forever. But I will do my damnedest to protect her for as long as I can."

"Sure you're angry right now, Billy, I understand," Ruairi called after him, "but you're angry with the wrong man. I'm not the one you need to protect your sister from."

Billy ignored him and kept on walking.

Gracie found herself tucked under the dark girl's arm and being led out some back corridor.

"I'm going to find your brother and tell him that I've sent you home. I'll make sure he meets you there so that you aren't alone," Rosaleen promised her.

She nodded. "Thank-you," she sniffed. Gracie looked down and saw the diamond sparkling on her finger as if nothing had happened. She stumbled over her heels.

Rosaleen caught her easily, despite her tiny frame and Gracie found herself staring into the dark eyes again. This time they seemed a bit softer. "You'll be alright, Love. This feeling won't last forever."

Gracie swallowed and nodded her head. "Who are you?" she asked timidly.

Rosaleen hesitated but knew it couldn't be avoided. "Rosaleen Jameson."

"Do you know my father from the war as well?" she asked.

Rosaleen looked away from the young girl, "How about we save that for another night and just concentrate on getting you home?"

When they turned the corner, Gracie found herself staring straight at her brother and Johnny. They were deep in conversation and didn't notice her at first. She took a step back, trying to melt back into the shadows but Rosaleen clamped down on her arm and dug her fingernails into Gracie's flesh.

Gracie yelped softly and looked at her with pleading eyes. But she stood her ground and held Gracie fast.

"I can't face him. Not here, it would be too humiliating," Gracie argued weakly.

"You've already been humiliated," Rosaleen assured her. Gracie looked like she would cry again but Rosaleen stopped her. "You're going to have to face this sometime and it might as well be now, when the hurt is fresh. You need to hurt him back."

Billy ran back up the steps and into the Club just as both sets of parents made their way out the front doors. Gracie faltered as she was shoved out of the shadows and it caught Johnny's attention. Johnny walked towards her with an outstretched arm.

"Gracie, sweetheart, I know nothing happened with that Irish cad. It was all just a bit of an embarrassment. We'll figure this out and we'll have some private time to talk it over. How does that sound?" He swept her into his arms. "Oh, my darling! Look at the tears! It's not so bad as all of this, surely!" he chuckled softly into her hair.

Gracie felt nothing but revulsion as his hands slid around her waist. She pushed him away from her and met his surprised eyes with her own suddenly fiery ones. "It is bad, Johnny, what you've done here to me is very bad! I don't want you anywhere near me." She looked over at her mother, whose shocked face registered nothing but confusion as her daughter spoke. "I need you to take me home, Maman. Now!" she demanded.

William tried to calm her down quickly. "Come here, Gracie girl," he soothed, "I know you're upset but none of this is Johnny's fault."

Eleanor exchanged a look with Lucas. "She's just embarrassed that she was caught with that Irishman."

Gracie felt the rage overtake her manners. She pulled the ring off of her finger and threw it at Johnny. "I have nothing to be embarrassed about! I would rather be seen with a hundred Irishmen than be seen with one man who sneaks around with other women while he is engaged!"

Johnny paled visibly as a silence fell over the protesting families. "Gracie, I'm not sure I understand what you mean," he trailed off.

"I'm sure Lana Hamilton can clarify it for you."

It only took Genevieve a second to gather her thoughts through the haze of champagne. "Get the car, William. I'm taking Gracie home," she snapped. She pushed past Johnny and cradled her daughter in her arms. Gracie finally broke down, the anger and the tears mingling in a hot bath of emotion.

"I'm sure this is all just a misunderstanding," Eleanor was saying to William.

William glared down at the young Bexley boy. "I think we may need to have a discussion, Johnny."

With all of the fuss, nobody noticed the dark beauty standing silently in the shadows.

Ruairi watched as the car door was closed behind Gracie. He hadn't been close enough to hear the exchange but he knew Rosaleen was within earshot. He could see her standing off near the corner. He watched her stare strangely at William and then she turned on her heel and disappeared into the night leaving the Gainsboroughs and the Bexleys sputtering in chaos. Ruairi put out his cigarette and walked back around to the patio, hoping to cut Rosaleen off on the other side. When he came out of the darkness he looked for her but couldn't find her at the table. He looked around at the slowly dispersing crowd but couldn't see her chatting with anyone. He waited for what seemed like an eternity until the Bexleys reappeared with Johnny and Billy. He gritted his teeth when William didn't return with them.

"Dammit," he mumbled to himself. He had a feeling that Rosaleen was planning something but he couldn't figure out what it was. He found the disorientation frightening. She had the ability to eclipse the sun and keep Ruairi's whole world dark. Tonight he could sense the shadows coming.

Rosaleen stood at the end of the pier, smoking a cigarette. She heard his footsteps coming up behind her. She bit the insides of her cheeks and willed herself to stay in control of the situation. She turned just as he got to her.

"Rosaleen," he said it softly, as he leaned in to kiss her cheek.

She let him kiss her. He was uneasy but trying hard to create a presence.

"Such a strange coincidence to see you here in Charlottetown," he started tentatively.

"I'd say it was rather fortuitous, wouldn't you?" her brogue was soft and sensual. "I've been waiting so long to have a chance to bury the past."

Her choice of words sent a chill through him. "Is that so? How do you mean?"

"I'm sure you remember all of that unpleasantness that passed right before we parted ways," she paused, her eyes burning into his. "I didn't want that to be your last memory of me. After all, my daughter is a Gainsborough."

William's cheeks inflamed and his pupils constricted. "Your child is a bastard!"

Rosaleen blew a cloud of smoke at him. Her movements were slow and deliberate but her eyes smouldered with recklessness, "That's such an ugly word, don't you think?"

William clenched his teeth and slowed his breathing. His muscles ached to slam her head into the dock and let the ocean take her body but he knew that tonight, she had the advantage. Ruairi O'Neill was only a few hundred feet away and no one would leave the party alive if his precious Rosaleen was harmed.

He ignored her question and posed his own, "How long are you in town for?"

"Indefinitely," she responded, the hint of a smirk pulled at the corners of her rouged lips.

"I see," William clipped his words inadvertently, "And why Charlottetown?"

"Unfinished business," she answered, allowing the smirk to come to the surface.

William pursed his lips and narrowed his eyes. "I see; and I take it I'm part of this unfinished business?"

"As I said before, I want to bury the past," Rosaleen steeled herself. "I want you . . ." She paused, taking advantage of his inability to figure out if she was serious and kissed him. He kissed back forcefully. He had never been a gentle lover. When the kiss broke, she searched his face for the look she knew; the look of power; the look of arrogance. It was there. So she finished her sentence, "dead."

William's nostrils flared. He pushed her backwards, away from him, and laughed sardonically. "So you're here to kill me, are you?"

Roasaleen smiled sweetly. She could see the fear and it made her blood pulse louder. "Oh, I'm not here to kill you, William. But if and when you are killed, I'll be waiting to celebrate your dance with the devil."

"I danced with the devil on more than one occasion. Or don't you remember those nights we spent together?"

"Do you really think I'm the devil?" she laughed at him.

William clenched his teeth. "Devil, prostitute, wench, whore; take your pick."

"I like the sound of all four." She smiled a defiant smile.

"What are you doing here, Rosaleen?" he growled.

"Don't worry, William this has nothing to do with you."

William narrowed his eyes at her, "I thought I made it very clear to you what would happen if you ever came after Billy," he warned her in a low voice.

"Your threats are empty this time, Love. I waited patiently for my time." She took a final drag on the cigarette. "Don't get in my way or Ruairi will kill you."

"Does Ruairi know the truth about you?"

But she didn't answer him. She turned and glided away from him, stamping out the cigarette beneath her heel at the end of the dock.

William watched her go. He needed to be clever not rash. He had made that mistake before and it had almost cost him his life and the life of his son.

He had become suspicious of Rosaleen when she had suddenly appeared at Dublin Castle, over a year after he had last seen her, telling him that she was ready to give him information on Ruairi's whereabouts if two conditions were met.

She wanted a guarantee that Ruairi wouldn't be executed if arrested. She was noticeably pregnant. William had initially assumed it was Ruairi's doing and that she was turning him in as some sort of attempt at protecting him. But her second condition made William uneasy. She asked that his son Billy be taken off rations duty the next morning. Her hand had travelled to her belly solicitously.

He had no intention of granting Ruairi a stay of execution. He convinced himself that pulling his son from duty may disrupt whatever Ruairi had planned for the next morning. He would have men nearby in case there was any trouble and he would have Ruairi picked up by the Black and Tans in Balbriggan.

He had waited for the news. Balbriggan was raided after a police officer was killed but Ruairi hadn't been among those arrested and three British soldiers were killed on the streets of Dublin in a shoot out. His son had been pulled from the rubble alive; by members of the IRA. Half a mile away from where William sat, Ruairi O'Neill had a gun to his son's head, but he hadn't pulled the trigger.

Why hadn't he pulled the trigger?

Tonight, William was willing to bet that Ruairi hadn't known.

He walked up the steps and saw Billy in the center of the patio, talking to some guests. He approached to see if he could have a private word when he saw Ruairi standing off to the left. William tightened his jaw and determined to face Ruairi. He strode towards him purposefully but was forced backwards when he saw Rosaleen approaching from the right.

Rosaleen strode right up to Billy, grabbed his necktie and pulled him towards her. She ran her free hand up his chest and then wrapped it around the back of his neck while she leaned in to kiss him.

Billy started to pull back but Rosaleen had a firm grip on the necktie. After the first contact, he couldn't help but soften into the kiss. Her mouth was warm and familiar and tasted like raw sugar. Her tongue flirted with his and she playfully bit his lower lip twice. When she finally let go of him he felt numb everywhere except his lips. They were tingling.

She smiled at him in a teasing way and then just walked away. It wasn't until he followed her path with his eyes that he saw who she deliberately strode towards. William stood at the top of the steps looking angrier than Billy could have ever imagined. Her eyes had hardened and her lips had locked into a cruel snarl. Whatever she said to William on her way past was lost to the night as she disappeared from the patio into the darkness beyond.

CHAPTER 6

Late that evening, Rosaleen tiptoed into Ruairi's room and crawled into his bed. She snuggled up against him and put her head on his chest to listen to his heart beat. It was beating quite quickly so she looked up at his face.

"You're awake," she whispered.

"Aye," he sighed.

"Are you drunk?" she asked.

"No. Didn't drink much tonight."

"Me neither. Should I go get the whiskey?"

He laughed, "No, I need to be up early in the morning. The last thing I need tomorrow is a headache."

She was quiet. He put an arm around her and rubbed her back. She was soothed by it. She knew he had been beside Billy when she had kissed him and she wanted to know what he was thinking.

"So, what kind of trouble are you getting me into?" he broke the silence first.

Rosaleen was quiet for a few moments. "Why do you assume I'm getting you into any trouble?"

Ruairi laughed, "Ah, Róisín Dubh, trouble follows you around and so do I. We both end up in the same room a lot of the time."

"Well, I don't think there will be too much trouble."

"Are you going to tell me why you kissed Billy Gainsborough?"

"There's nothing to tell."

"I doubt that, Rosaleen. I need to know what is going on with you and Billy if you want me to protect you from William."

She wondered whether he would forgive her when he found out the truth. She wasn't willing to risk it just yet. "You are the only man in my life, Love."

"I wish that were the truth," he said quietly, pulling her closer to him.

Tears started rolling down her cheeks and onto his chest. He had always loved her more than she deserved. "Why do you say things like that? You know that I would never be the only woman in your life. Ireland has always been your mistress."

"You are Ireland to me, Roísín."

"No, I'm not." She hated when he put that on her. "I am not Ireland."

He was tired of arguing that point with her. "Is there not room for Ireland and you, then?" Ruairi asked gently.

"No," she whispered truthfully. "I'm afraid she demands too much of you," her voice broke.

He gave her a few moments to compose herself. He stroked her hair. "Well, Love," he said finally, "you are my only mistress tonight."

She dragged her fingers through her hair and wiped her eyes. "Oh, Ruairi," she wailed softly, "would it be so wrong if I asked you to prove it to me?"

He smiled up at her. She was lying, practically on top of him in a silk nightgown and it had been so long. She leaned down and kissed his heart with cool lips, her raven hair feathering across his chest.

"I thought I had given you up," he groaned knowing that he would regret it in the morning.

Gracie lay in the dark clutching the pendant at her throat. She hadn't removed it when she had changed into her nightgown. She had been quiet for a long while, staring at herself in the full-length mirror. Then she had cried. When her sobbing finally subsided she was still again but for the movement of her thumb and forefinger as she rubbed the dark green stone. She closed her eyes briefly and saw his face, his strong features. She felt his hands on her and then his lips. Her eyes flew open and she gasped for breath. The tears came again only this time they were full of angry heat. She tore the necklace from her neck and threw it against the wall.

She would deal with him in the morning.

Genevieve stood outside her daughter's door, her head tilted, resting on the solid wood frame. She could taste her daughter's tears as her own. She too, had been deceived by love. It wasn't William's dalliance with the beautiful, dark Irish girl that had wounded her, however. She could have forgiven him that. It was his flirtation with the flag that had broken her heart. His oath of allegiance took precedence over his marriage vow and Genevieve was tired of the betrayal. She could no longer perjure herself by acting the dutiful wife and she would never willingly allow her daughter to endure the same fate.

The next morning, Ruairi was down at the docks before dawn making sure that he was ready for the trip to Halifax. He had a meeting with a few of the old boys later that day and he had a long trip ahead of him. He knew the hours would be spent parsing every second of the last twenty four hours to decipher the clues to Rosaleen's motivation. Deep down, she was a good girl but this morning he was concerned about what was going on just beneath the surface.

Last night, the pattern hadn't changed. She had made him believe that she was his in those brief moments that they were a part of each other but when he opened his eyes and looked into hers he knew what he had learned years ago; she belonged to someone else.

He returned to the task in front of him. Thomas and Mairtin were meeting him over in Halifax and they would all go out that night to a place owned by a friend. Ruairi had borrowed a fishing boat called *The Siren* owned by two older gentlemen named Jimmy and Charlie. They were easily persuaded. He was loading the last of his gear onto the deck when he saw a very upset young girl walking straight towards him. She was already dressed and groomed.

He put his hands on his hips, looked up at the morning sun breaking over the horizon and sighed. Then he cocked his head to the side and said, "You're up early, Gracie."

Gracie couldn't help herself. She had to blame somebody and he seemed the easiest victim. In her hand she held the necklace he had given to her.

"I came to return this," she said coldly.

"It was a gift." He refused to take it from her.

"I cannot accept it," she maintained, dangling it out in front of her.

"I want you to have it." Ruairi pushed it back towards her.

"I will not argue about this." She tried to make her voice sound authoritative but she only managed to raise its volume.

"Shush!" he held his finger to her lips, "People are still sleeping."

"I don't care!" She batted his arm away. "Take the necklace and stay away from me!" She threw the necklace at him. Her temper was threatening to get the better of her.

He caught it and slid it into his pocket, noticing the broken clasp. "Fine," he said simply and jumped up onto the deck of the fishing boat.

"Where are you going?" she asked, momentarily distracted by his sudden acquiescence.

"Away, just as you instructed." He couldn't afford to be late this morning.

"I'm not done speaking with you quite yet." She stared up at him, wringing her hands nervously in front of her. She had started out so confidently but now she was unsure of herself.

He saw the flickers of indecision in her eyes and was intrigued. "I apologize," he said, holding up his hands in mock surrender. He knelt down so that his face was close to hers. "Please, continue."

"I cannot associate with you. You need to stay away from me . . . and my family," she added.

"You already said that," he raised an eyebrow, teasing her.

"Let me finish," she said through gritted teeth.

"Look, Love," he said, his Irish accent soft, "I can't wait. I've got to go. Can we do this another time?"

"No, we cannot do this another time. I just finished telling you that I want nothing further to do with you."

Ruairi nodded and held out his hand. "Well, then, let's just say goodbye, shall we?"

She seemed uninterested in his hand. "Where are you off to in such a hurry this morning? Do you have another meeting?" she asked sarcastically.

"Actually, yes, I do."

"Well, then I'll just come along again. At least this time I'm awake and not being unwillingly kidnapped."

She startled him by kicking off her shoes and climbing onboard. The skirt of her dress was loose and revealed her knickers as she swung her legs over the side. Ruairi licked his lips and smiled.

"What?" she asked, glaring at him.

"Nothing." He tried to wipe the smile off his face but couldn't. "I don't have time to bring you all of the way back so it's really not a good idea for you to come on this trip."

"I will be fine. We need to talk and we're going to talk," her tone was almost threatening.

Ruairi tried not to look amused. "As interesting as it would be to give in to you, I feel I must make you aware of the fact that I don't intend on returning to Charlottetown until late tomorrow evening." He offered her his hand to help her back off the boat.

She refused it and stared off over the harbour, turning her back to him. It would be absolute madness to go with him. She inhaled sharply, "I suppose we'll have to think of something for me to tell my family then when I place a call to tell them that I won't be home this evening."

Ruairi cupped a hand over his mouth, pinching his lips together. Taking Gracie Gainsborough with him was ridiculously stupid. It was sure to mean trouble for him. It only took a minute for him to decide, "Alright, let's go."

Billy lay in bed staring at the ceiling. He hadn't been able to sleep all night. He couldn't stop thinking about Rosaleen Jameson. This time, she was more dangerous than Ruairi O'Neill.

She had revealed their affair without warning. It was a Judas kiss; a betrayal of the passion that they had shared.

Billy knew that there would be questions and he knew that one wrong answer would find him in a grave.

William sat across the desk from Lucas in the dark panelled study. It was a small room, insulated by shelves upon shelves of books ranging from classic literature to philosophical theses. He was a well read man.

Lucas looked into the eyes of his friend and saw fear. William was a confident man but he wasn't a stupid man. Ruairi O'Neill was a threat and he had to be dealt with.

"Are you sure that Billy doesn't know that he fathered the child?" Lucas asked.

"He wouldn't have left Ireland if he had known," William surmised, "but she's here to tell him. I have limited time to silence her."

"What did the Home Office have to say?"

"They told me to be bloody careful."

Out of the harbour, Gracie launched into a lecture. She told him that she was angry with him for ruining her party, for embarrassing her family and for kissing her. But mostly, she told him, she was angry because he had lied to her.

"When did I lie to you?" he asked.

"You didn't tell me that you knew my family when I met you on the boat."

"That's not lying, it's just not telling the truth. There is a difference." He smiled that disarming smile.

"No, there isn't," she crossed her arms in front of her and glared at him.

"I didn't mean to upset you," Ruairi said finally.

Her eyes softened and she shifted her weight. "Well, you did upset me. You upset me very much."

Ruairi held her gaze. "Well, show me then."

"Show you what?"

"Show me how upset you are. Yell at me or throw something at me or hit me or something."

"Pardon me?" she asked, slightly embarrassed.

"I said, get mad at me!" He watched her face for any sign of emotion. "You've barely raised your voice."

"That wouldn't be very lady-like," she protested.

He laughed, "Do you really think that I care about whether you are lady-like?"

She tried not to smile. She bit her lip and shook her head from side to side.

"How am I supposed to want to stay away from you if you are always so lovely?"

She blushed. They stared at each other for a few more moments.

"Come on," he encouraged her, "lose control. I promise I won't tell anybody." He winked at her.

She hesitated, but only slightly. She picked up the nearest thing to her and threw it at him. It was a box of fishing hooks and when they hit the ground about three feet to the left of Ruairi, they scattered across the deck.

He tried to contain his laughter, "That was pitiful!"

"I don't know what you want from me!" She was embarrassed and exasperated by him.

He threw up his hands. "I want the real Gracie! You have to be angry with me right now! I've ruined your engagement and I've humiliated you and your family. You should hate me!"

"I do hate you!" she said emphatically.

"Really? I don't believe you. I think you like me."

"I don't like you at all!" she denied quickly.

"Then why do you blush every time you look at me?"

Gracie flew at him with arms flailing, hitting him on the back and arms. He grabbed her arms and held her to him but it only made her wriggle more.

"I hate you I hate you I hate you," she sobbed.

"I know you do," he said softly into her hair. "You were born to."

She finally stopped struggling and collapsed into him. He gave her a moment and then gently pushed her backwards.

Without thinking, she reached up, and twining her hands around his neck she kissed him. Afterwards, her hands flew to her mouth and she ran away from him to the bow of the boat. The shock of the kiss wore off quickly when he heard her scream.

He groaned. She had stepped on one of the fish hooks with her bare foot and he could see the blood seeping out onto the deck.

She began to cry and her face went all white. He picked her up and carried her carefully away from the hooks. He sat her down against the cabin door and picked up her foot. The hook was stuck in pretty deep.

He looked at her face. She looked like she was going to faint. "Look, I'm going to have to take the hook out and it's going to hurt. I need you to look away, ok?"

She nodded. He held her ankle firmly in one hand and yanked the hook out with the other. She screamed again and her foot jerked in his hand.

"You still with me?" he asked, making sure she hadn't lost consciousness.

She cried louder in response.

"I need to clean the cut and then I'm going to wrap it so that we can stop the bleeding okay? It's actually not that bad, the hook came out pretty clean."

He reached over and took a bottle out of one of his bags. He took a deep breath before pouring half of it on her foot. She squealed again as the alcohol stung her. He took off his undervest, ripped it in half and soaked one half of it with the rest of the contents of the bottle. Then he gently cleaned out the wound. He used the other half to wrap her foot tightly.

"There we are, all patched up!" he tried to sound bright. "It's going to hurt but it really isn't as bad as I thought. Just a little hole! It's going to feel bruised and sore so you might want to sit still for a while."

"Thank-you," she said softly. She was still whimpering, "I'm sorry you had to ruin your undershirt."

"It's not the shirt I'm worried about. I just lost a bottle of Irish whiskey."

"Why did you help me?" she asked.

"What do you mean?"

"Well, I've been yelling at you and hitting you and then you saved my foot," she sniffed.

He chuckled, "Well, I couldn't just let you bleed everywhere, now could I? It's not my boat. And anyway, you forgot that after yelling at me and hitting me, you kissed me. It was a damn good kiss so I figured I owed you."

Gracie's tears began to flow again.

"What's all this?" he asked sitting next to her against the cabin. "Don't cry, Love."

"I'm completely ashamed of myself. I've behaved in a scandalous manner and I kissed you! And now I'm on a boat with you going God knows where!" Gracie couldn't contain her emotions.

"You shouldn't be so hard on yourself, Gracie. And I'm not going to tell anyone you kissed me, I promise." He held his hand over his heart. "I don't understand why you wanted to come with me and I have no idea why I agreed to bring you but I'm happy you're here, so let's try to enjoy ourselves, shall we?"

She looked over at him and sniffed. He smiled. He reached into his pocket and pulled out the necklace. "But only if you keep the necklace," he held it out to her.

She took it and smiled weakly, "I'll have to have the clasp fixed if I ever want to wear it again."

"I might be able to fix that for you after I pick up all of these hooks." With that he got up and went over to the scattered hooks. He knelt down carefully and one by one picked up the hooks and put them back into the box.

Gracie tried to struggle to her feet. "I should be doing that. I was the one that threw them."

Ruairi put one hand out to stop her. His fingers found her waist and their eyes met. "You need to stay seated . . . to rest your foot," he stammered.

She nodded and sat down quietly. "Where are we?" she asked.

"We're almost there."

"Almost where?"

He took a deep breath, "Pictou."

He could hear the panic in her voice. "Why are we going to Pictou?"

"That's where the car is."

"What car?"

"The car that will take us to Halifax."

"Halifax is a long way away from Charlottetown," Gracie began to fret.

"Not really."

"It is when no one knows where I am," Gracie's voice wavered.

"You'll be fine. You're with me."

"How do I know that I can trust you all the way out here?"

"Oh, Jesus, Mary and Joseph, have I harmed you yet?"

"You might just be waiting for the right moment."

Ruairi rolled his eyes and continued picking up the fishing hooks. "I'm not going to hurt you, Gracie. You are safe with me."

Gracie remained silent.

He set the box of hooks off to the side and sat down beside her. He reached for her hand. She tried to pull it away from him but he held it tight. "I need to check your foot and make sure you're going to be fine. When we get into Pictou, we'll find you a telephone and you can place a call to Billy and tell him where you are and that you are with me. I promise that if you want to have a good time here, you will. I'll make sure of it. But you have to play nice. And then I'll take you home nice and early tomorrow morning."

"I'm not usually this difficult," she tried to apologize.

He smiled, "I doubt that very much."

She stifled a giggle.

He moved down to her foot and unwrapped the shirt. He could see up her dress again and he tried desperately not to let on. He didn't want to risk upsetting her again. He undid the torn shirt and looked at it. Thankfully, it was fine. He was sure she'd be a bit sore but it would heal up nicely in a couple of days.

"Perfect," he said to her, putting her foot down again, "I'm going to get us into the harbour and then we'll be off."

Gracie grimaced as the pain throbbed up her leg. She felt absolutely ridiculous for her display of anger and emotion and couldn't even look at Ruairi for fear that she would see how silly she was reflected in his eyes. She groaned inwardly and her hands flew up to cover her face as she replayed the scene over in her head. *Why had she kissed him? Why had she gotten on the boat? Why had she even thought it wise to come down and see him?*

She knew why.

She finally found the courage to look up at him as he swung the boat around into its berth. He jumped over the side and quickly tied the knots to secure the boat to the dock. When he leapt back onboard, he glanced over at her. When he saw that she was looking back he smiled gently. She blushed and tried to look like she was busy standing up. It wasn't as graceful as she had planned and she felt his hands on her again as she straightened up.

"Thank-you but I don't need help. I'm fine." She brushed him off in an effort to be dignified.

"I know you're fine, Love, I'm just trying to be a gentleman. Isn't that what you're accustomed to?" He meant it to tease but he noticed how stiff she suddenly became.

"Don't try to be something you're not," she said tersely. "I'm much happier with you when you aren't like the gentlemen I know."

Ruairi laughed strangely. "I'm not sure how to take that."

He convinced her to go to breakfast with him before trying to find a telephone box. She was limping so he made her hold onto his arm for support. An old couple walked by, arm in arm, and smiled knowingly at them. Ruairi smiled back but Gracie jabbed him with her elbow.

"We are not a couple," she hissed at him.

"Then you better stop kissing me," he hissed back.

She glared at him, "You're not funny."

They found a tiny café and were seated in a corner booth. Breakfast was ordered and the two sat in awkward silence, sipping their coffee.

When the pancakes came, Ruairi devoured his. He looked over at her plate. She was slowly cutting them into tiny pieces, putting one piece in her mouth at a time and then chewing thoughtfully.

"Are you going to eat all of that?" he asked her, eyeing one that hadn't been meticulously cut up.

"Probably not, but it's not very polite to eat off of somebody else's plate," she said matter-of-factly.

"I don't care about polite. I'm hungry. There wasn't much food at your party last night," he said, reaching over to her plate with his fork.

She pulled her plate away. He glared at her. "Just give me the damn pancake. You said you weren't going to eat it."

"No. Wait until I'm finished with my plate. And watch your language. I'm a lady."

"You're an annoying lady," he said to her.

She put another piece into her mouth and chewed slowly. She had a mischievous glint in her eye.

Ruairi shook his head and started to laugh. Gracie put a hand over her mouth as she began to giggle too. They finally found themselves smiling at each other unselfconsciously. And he finally got her pancake.

After breakfast, Ruairi helped Gracie up the cobblestone street to a black automobile.

"Where are we going?" she asked.

"We will be driving to a hotel in Halifax. You can place a call from there and I can drop off my bag," he said.

Gracie looked a bit nervous. "We're going to a hotel?"

"Where did you think we were going to sleep tonight?" he asked.

She didn't answer.

"Don't worry," he continued, "I'll get separate rooms."

She smiled at him thinly.

A few hours later they arrived in front of the Waverley Inn on Barrington Street and Gracie's relief was audible as she exhaled.

"Did you think I was going to make you stay somewhere not worthy of a Gainsborough?" he asked her.

"Don't be cheeky," she said to him, "and yes, I did think I was in for a rough night. So, this is a rather nice surprise."

He helped her out of the back seat. "How's your foot?" he asked.

"Throbbing," she replied truthfully. "I need to call Billy," she reminded him as he began to turn away from the counter.

He nodded and asked the concierge to place the call.

The concierge dialled the operator and had the call put through to the Gainsborough house. Gracie asked for Billy and when she heard his voice on the line, she quickly explained to him where she was and how it had happened. When he tried to ask her any questions she handed the phone to Ruairi. She wasn't ready to talk.

The conversation between Billy and Ruairi was terse and the edge in Ruairi's voice made Gracie shiver. He did soften and promise to take care of Gracie before he handed the receiver back to the concierge. Then he asked for some ice to be sent up to her room.

At the door to her room, Gracie wanted to know what Billy had said.

"Apparently, there's a bit of gossip around town so it's probably best that you're here for the time being. Billy said he would cover for you and not to worry."

"What type of gossip?" Her face was rigid. The ice arrived and Ruairi came inside her room and made her lie back on the bed while he iced her foot. "What type of gossip?" she repeated. She wondered if everybody knew that she had been cheated on.

"I'm not sure, really. I didn't ask. Look, don't worry. It will all blow over. Somebody will sleep with somebody's wife and you'll be yesterday's news."

Her brow wrinkled and her eyes got teary. "Billy knows, doesn't he? And he told you, didn't he?"

"Told me what?" Ruairi looked at her like she had two heads. When he saw how close to tears she was he continued quickly. "Look, Gracie, he didn't tell me a thing," he assured her. "Is there anything you want to tell me?" he asked, concerned.

"No," she said quickly, still pouting.

"Alright. I've got to get to this meeting," he said, looking at his watch. "If you feel up to it, why don't you head down to the shops and pick yourself out a dress for tonight."

"Really?" Her face brightened.

"I'll take you out for dinner and then maybe we can find a place to dance or something." He took out his money clip and handed her a few large notes.

She smiled up at him. "You really are being nice, now."

He laughed. "I'm always nice, but bloody hell, you can be insufferable!"

Gracie had to bite her lip to keep from smiling. "Where did you get all of that money?" she asked, eyeing the money clip bursting with bills.

Ruairi smiled. "From my pocket . . . and that's all you need to know about that."

Gracie watched him with suspicious eyes as he slid out the door.

Billy sat in his room wondering whether he was going to regret the latest position he had been forced into. Norah had given him the perfect alibi for Gracie by deciding to go to a fox show in Summerside to look at furs. Billy had convinced his parents that Gracie had gone with Norah and would be fine for the evening. But he hadn't convinced himself. He had heard through his mother of Johnny's infidelity and had been furious. He knew how vulnerable Gracie would be and after the previous evening, he wasn't sure he could trust Ruairi O'Neill near her. Billy was doubtful that he would injure her but he wasn't sure that Gracie wouldn't injure herself in the state that she was in. She could break her own heart by falling in love with Ruairi.

Ruairi checked himself in the shop window as he strode past. He had changed back at the hotel and he now wore black trousers, a white dress shirt with a black tie, and a grey tweed vest matched to his newsboy cap. He had carefully hidden his loaded pistol into the back of his waistband and made sure that his vest was not cinched too tight. It was concealed perfectly. He checked his watch. He was already ten minutes late. He looked both ways before turning into the little alleyway and jogging down the steps to the basement door of a three storey building. He knocked lightly.

A large, bald man in his late thirties opened the door and gave Ruairi the once over with his eyes. Ruairi raised his eyebrows. The man nodded and moved aside, allowing just enough space for Ruairi to squeeze by. Then the door was pulled shut behind him.

"They're waiting for you on the first floor."

Ruairi walked up the stairs and into a large room that was furnished sparsely. There was a long bar at one end of the room and a few tables pushed up against a wall. Two men sat at a table that had been pulled into the center of the room. Ruairi walked over and shook hands with both men. They had stood when he had come up the stairs but no one had spoken. A few moments of silence passed and then one man, wearing a tan suit and a white collared shirt with a few buttons open, spoke up.

"You've quite the reputation, Ruairi; it's a pleasure to finally meet you," he said, coughing slightly. "My name is Angus and this is Richard."

Ruairi nodded. An uncomfortable silence passed again.

"Well, let's have a little chat about the whiskey, shall we?" Angus had a cigar in his mouth that wriggled every time he spoke. "How is the latest batch coming along?"

"Maggie has been tending to it mostly and she is the expert on distillation," Ruairi informed him, "but I'll taste the newest batches in a few days."

"And how is the distribution network coming together?" Richard was writing furiously in a beaten leather notebook.

"Over land we have had a few problems. Shorty has been rather slow on the payments but I'm taking care of him."

Richard raised an eyebrow, "He's always been fine in the past. I'm surprised you are finding him difficult to deal with."

Ruairi narrowed his eyes. "I think his loyalties have shifted slightly. He's less concerned with funding the rebuilding of the IRA than he is with funding his new luxurious lifestyle."

"Are you sure about this?" Angus asked.

Ruairi didn't blink. "It's nothing you really have to worry about anymore. As I said, I'm taking care of it."

Richard was concerned but he let the subject of Shorty drop. De Valera had warned them that Ruairi could be difficult and made it very clear that he was above taking orders from expatriates.

"How have the water transfers been going?"

"There's been absolutely no trouble with Billy McCoy. He's an easy fella to deal with."

Angus leaned back in his chair and smiled slowly. "I'm still confused as to how you were able to procure a meeting with him so quickly. He's become the King among rum runners."

"I could get an audience with the King of England if I chose to." Ruairi folded his arms over his chest.

Angus liked the lad's confidence but was wary of him. "I'd bet he would like that. He's got a lot of men out looking for you."

A shadow danced in Ruairi's eyes and he shrugged. "I haven't been hiding."

Richard and Angus shared a look and Ruairi could see that he hadn't only been summoned for an update on their fundraising project. He sat back and waited patiently. He would only answer questions. He had been taught well by Michael Collins to never give up information willingly. Although De Valera was his superior now, Ruairi found it difficult to take orders from a man who had escaped a British death penalty while his fellow countrymen had stood in front of the firing squad. Ruairi had grown up on the ideals of the Irish martyr and his love for Pádraig Pearse and the Proclamation of the Republic had been absolute.

Angus diverted to the news from home, "Dev's been . . ." he didn't get any further.

"I can read what Dev's been doing in the paper. I want to know what it is that you two are really interested in." Ruairi hated secret meetings. He wasn't the cloak and dagger type. He preferred to talk business over a pint while the fiddles wailed in the background and a man with a raggedy voice sang songs about Mother Ireland. Unfortunately, with Prohibition in full swing and the Canadian backdrop, there wasn't much possibility of that.

Both men looked uncomfortable. Angus licked his lips. "It has come to our attention that General William Gainsborough is living in Charlottetown."

Ruairi clenched his jaw. "Aye."

"Were you aware of it before you chose to come over?" Richard asked.

"No," Ruairi grimaced. He had no intention of implicating Rosaleen so he would have to be very careful. "I know it isn't ideal but it won't interfere with our plans."

"What if he alerts the British Army as to your whereabouts?" Angus asked.

"They won't come after me here. I'm outside of their reach," Ruairi spat out angrily.

"There aren't many places that their arm doesn't reach." Angus watched Ruairi carefully for a reaction. "General Gainsborough may be a little annoyed with how friendly you're becoming with his daughter."

Ruairi's face betrayed him and Richard smelled blood. "We've got a man on you, Ruairi."

Ruairi's temper flared. "Are you accusing me of something?"

"Not yet," Angus said quietly. Ruairi glared at him. It was apparent that somebody didn't trust him. He was happy he had brought along his gun. He wasn't always sure of how far his camaraderie went with the older generation, especially those that had left Ireland willingly.

"I would advise you not to look for a reason to," Ruairi said, temperamentally. "Neither of you has been charged with my keeping and I can assure you that neither of you would be able to keep me." The shadow had taken up residence, giving his eyes a stormy countenance.

"Your man's already alerted the British Home Office. Either take care of him or stay away from him," Richard suggested in an even tone.

"And what if I refuse?" Ruairi countered. "What if I like his daughter?"

"If you like her then I suggest you don't put her in any danger." Angus locked eyes with Ruairi.

"Do what is simple," Richard felt he needed to be more direct. "Kill him now before this becomes complicated."

"But be careful. Don't get yourself caught," Angus clarified.

Ruairi was furious and his agitation was evident. Every day before yesterday he would have gladly killed General Gainsborough; but yesterday had changed everything.

"Don't let a woman distract you, Ruairi." Richard tried to pacify him.

Ruairi snorted as he kicked his chair back. "Have a nice day boys," he said as he walked towards the stairs.

Angus thought better of calling him back. He was afraid of those tempestuous eyes.

Thomas, Aisling and Mairtin lounged around a sheltered courtyard with ice tea and finger sandwiches. They had left Charlottetown straight after Gracie's engagement party and sailed to Miquelon to pick up a shipment of French champagne. A few hours later they had pointed the boat south and made their way to the port town of Halifax.

Thomas was lost in his own world, reading Shakespeare's sonnets for the hundredth time. Aisling was watching her little brother with intense affection. He was interacting with the pages as though they were a living entity; agreeing and disagreeing, satisfied with the conversation at hand. He was so passionate about the written word and so consumed by love and art. He could move Aisling to tears with a look that she swore came directly from his soul.

"And what do you think?" she asked softly, "Was Edward de Vere the real Shakespeare?"

Thomas took a moment to disconnect from the book. He looked up at her with wide, shining eyes. "It's a very convincing argument," he began, referring to Thomas J. Looney's dissertation, "but the romantic in me cannot separate William Shakespeare from William Shakespeare. I would rather believe in the young illiterate actor becoming the greatest of all playwrights, even if the evidence is against me."

"There's no mistaking that you are an Irishman." Aisling looked on him with adoration.

Mairtin looked up and scoffed, "You give the praise of the greatest playwright to an Englishman and she calls you a true Irishman? I'm ashamed to be privy to this conversation!"

Thomas gave Mairtin a serious look. "I'm not ashamed to admit my admiration for an English writer. I may not agree with their politics in Ireland but I cannot fault them in other facets of life."

Mairtin drew himself upright and leaned forward in his seat, challenging Thomas with his eyes. "And if Shakespeare were alive today and he forcefully expressed the belief that we Irish should submit to a foreign crown, would you be able to open fire on him in the streets of Dublin or Belfast?"

"Yes, of course," Thomas replied, without hesitation.

"You would kill the greatest playwright that you believe ever lived for his political beliefs?" Mairtin wasn't sure of Thomas' convictions.

Thomas had his answer ready. "One of the greatest Irish poets was shot to death by a British firing squad for his political beliefs. I see no difference."

Aisling knew her brother's faith in Pádraig Pearse had never faltered; even after his death, Thomas was following his teacher's voice.

Mairtin surrendered, "It's a credit to you that you can see them as more than an enemy. I would never be able to pull the trigger if I did."

Thomas was surprised. "I didn't think killing bothered you."

Mairtin sat back and closed his eyes. "Making someone a ghost has always haunted me."

Ruairi stood in front of the door to the room and sighed. His frustration at the outcome of the meeting had to be put aside before he entered. He couldn't believe General Gainsborough had gone to the British in less than twenty four hours. He leaned with one hand against the door and one hand on his hip.

He had figured out who the man was that they had on him at the hotel. He was a weasel of a man, couldn't have been easier to pick. Ruairi had walked straight up to him when he came in the lobby and pushed him into the men's room. He had pulled the gun out of his waistband and held the barrel up under the man's chin.

"You tell those boys that I don't need a babysitter, all right?" He let the hammer knock softly against the chamber, "Got that?"

The man had nodded quickly, the sweat forming on his tweedy brow. Ruairi had let go of him and shoved the gun back into its place. "Now go use the toilet. I don't want you soiling those nice pants." He was pretty sure it had been too late.

Ruairi exhaled slowly, knocked softly, and then opened the door. Inside, Gracie sat on the bed, pouting. She wore a black dress with sequins and beads and her hair and make-up were done.

"What's wrong with you?" Ruairi asked, noticing the protruding lip immediately. He felt like doing the same thing.

"My foot hurts and I don't believe that I can wear my new shoes!" she sniffed.

Ruairi took one look at the t-bar heels that were sitting beside her on the bed and he grimaced. "Do you really want to have to wear those?" he asked. "Even without a sore foot they look painful!"

He sat down on the bed and picked up her foot. It was bruised but there was no evidence of infection. He reached into his vest pocket and pulled out some tablets that he had picked up for her. "I went by a chemist on my way to the meeting. I even let myself be late, just so that I could make sure you felt better. Take two with water and then freshen yourself up," he smiled at her.

"Freshen up?" she was incredulous. "Don't I look fine enough?"

"Oh, you were going to go out looking like that?" he pretended.

Her eyes were wide and she didn't seem to know what to say.

He laughed, "You look gorgeous Gracie! I'm just teasing you."

Her face lit up. "I thought you were serious. Do you know how much this dress cost?"

"There's obviously no change left then?" he cringed jokingly.

"Well, I'm sorry to say no but I hope you will think it was worth it." Gracie felt she had to explain, "It was designed by this French woman that everybody's been talking about. They say it will be *the* dress of the season. Isn't it just fabulous! And then, with the little money I did have left over, I went and got my hair and make-up done! I feel just wonderful! Aside from my foot," she added hastily.

"Well, then. Aren't you going to thank me?"

"Thank you?" she asked, mocking him, "I think you still owe me for that kiss!"

He laughed, "I think you'll have to kiss me again if you want it to be even! It was good, but not *that* good!"

She couldn't help but enjoy the attention that he was paying her. She blushed happily, "I don't think that your chances are very good at tricking me into kissing you a second time!"

"I don't recall that being exactly what happened, my dear, but I don't believe I'm in any position to argue with you." He knelt down and held her shoe out to her.

She slipped her foot in and watched while he buckled it up. "No, I don't believe you are."

Downtown, Gracie and Ruairi walked through the street, Gracie leaning heavily on Ruairi. He was pretty sure that the pills had numbed the pain but she seemed to like to be close to him.

The day had turned overcast and there was a cool breeze blowing in off the water so Gracie snuggled closer to Ruairi. She was starting to feel very comfortable with him as long as she didn't look him in the eye. When she did, her heart beat became irregular and she felt a warm sensation throughout her entire body. It almost made her feel sick.

One of the side streets they walked down had a tiny little café in it and Ruairi led her inside.

"Would you like a cuppa, Love?" he asked.

She was starting to like the way he called her 'Love'. She hoped he wouldn't stop using it. She nodded her head. In a few short minutes, she was sitting across from him, smelling the tea as it steamed up under her chin. He pulled out a notebook and wrote something down hastily.

"What are you writing?" she asked. "Is that a diary?"

He frowned. "Not really, it's my notebook. It keeps me organized."

"So there are no secret love letters in there?" she pried. She wanted to know more about Ruairi O'Neill.

He chuckled. "I leave the language of love to my brother Thomas. I wouldn't know how to write that sort of nonsense!"

"Nonsense?" she squealed. "Love letters aren't nonsense! If I were to ever receive a love letter, I would cherish it as my most prized possession."

"Are you telling me that you have never received a love letter?" He was shocked. She was an extremely beautiful girl. "I thought a girl like you would have inspired poetry from every lad you chanced to meet."

She couldn't hide that his words had flattered her. "Johnny is the only boy that's ever been allowed to court me and he doesn't have much time for writing."

"So, what are you going to do about the Bexley boy?" he asked her gently.

"Let's not talk about Johnny," she said stiffly.

He raised his eyebrows at her. "That sounds serious. Is it over between the two of you?"

"I doubt that my father will allow it to be over." She stared into her teacup.

"Surely your father wouldn't want you married to a cad like that?" Ruairi asked.

Gracie felt a tear slip down her cheek. "You know, don't you?"

Ruairi watched her face colour with embarrassment. "Aye, I know," he admitted, "Rosaleen told me the whole story."

"It's so humiliating," she muttered under her breath.

Ruairi leaned towards her, his eyes sparkling. "I'm sorry to say that I wasn't all that unhappy with the news. It made you a free woman at just the right moment."

Gracie knew he was just teasing her but her blue eyes began to water. She looked away quickly and tried to blink the tears back.

Ruairi didn't know how to react, "I'm sorry, Love. I didn't mean to upset you," he said softly, reaching for her hand.

She pulled back automatically and composed herself. "You are very forward," she chastised him.

He smiled apologetically. "I mean no harm, Miss Gainsborough. I wasn't raised with all your manners and like," he surrendered to her easily.

She sighed and shook her head.

"Now what?" he asked her.

"You think I am a snob."

Ruairi grinned at her. "No, I don't. I just think you need to laugh more. Did Johnny make you laugh?" he asked her, suddenly serious.

Gracie nervously picked at the teacup. "I'm sure he was lovely. I did like him once," she said, detaching herself from the subject of the conversation.

"Lovely, eh? Not really the kind of word I would want my girl using when she described me." He winked at her.

"And how would you want to be described? Violent? Criminal?" The words popped out before she could stop them. Her emotions were all over the place.

"You know, it amazes me how quickly you can go from sweet to sour," he mused. "No, I would want her to describe me as unpredictable, manly, charming, *sexy* . . ." he lowered his voice at the last word and said it in a way that made her throat dry and her lips wet. He saw her try to swallow and lick her lips at the same time and he smiled. She was nervous again and he liked it. He continued, "Do you want to know how I would describe you?"

"No, I've had about enough of you making fun of me for one day, thank you."

He pretended not to hear her. "I'd say you were spoiled, pretentious, judgemental and extremely . . ." he stopped.

"Yes?" she asked him sarcastically.

"Extremely seductive." He held her eye across the table. When the last word sunk in he watched her expression change.

"Really?" she asked softly.

"Really," he matched her softness.

"You shouldn't speak to a lady like that. It's vulgar," Gracie suddenly remembered herself.

Ruairi just sat back and watched her blush. He found himself enjoying his ability to set her off balance.

CHAPTER 7

William Gainsborough and Lucas Bexley sat in the parlour at the Club. They had just finished a round of golf.

"Have you made any decisions regarding Gracie and Johnny?" Lucas was still hoping to salvage his son's future.

"Well, obviously I feel that we need to discredit the Hamilton girl's claims so that my daughter doesn't look ridiculous when she takes him back. And of course he will have to make amends with Gracie in private." William was not as concerned with Johnny's infidelity as he was with the shame that it had brought on his daughter.

"And as for the Irishman that embarrassed my son?"

William's eyes grew cold. "I've made some enquiries," he hesitated, smoothing his hair and looking around furtively to ensure their privacy. "According to my contacts, it shouldn't be too hard to make it look like a rum deal gone south."

Lucas smiled. "That's what I wanted to hear."

Genevieve sat in the backseat of the black Ford staring across the street at the house that Rosaleen Jameson lived in and wondered how she could conduct this with so many prying eyes. She shifted in her seat. The dark blue jersey skirt she was wearing hugged her lower body perfectly making her look ten years younger. But the girl would always be youthful compared to her. Genevieve didn't know how she could keep pace with one so young and so unequivocally beautiful.

Genevieve watched her on the porch swing with two men and wondered if she was able to trust the girl. Everything about her made Genevieve nervous. Her black, glossy hair, her long, slender limbs;

every part of her body was foreign and yet, so familiar. She reminded her of the women of Montmartre, fiery seductresses like smouldering cigarettes in dark alleys.

Genevieve wasn't quite ready for this. She leaned forward and tapped the driver on the shoulder, indicating that it was time to move on.

As the car pulled away from the curb, Genevieve leaned her head back against the seat and sighed.

Ruairi looked over at the girl and found himself wishing she was someone else, anyone else. Not the daughter of the man that he was most likely going to have to kill.

"Well, where are you taking me tonight?" Gracie asked. They had left the little café and were sitting on a bench watching the ships passing in and out of the harbour. Gracie hadn't felt like walking too far down the pier so they had found a quiet place to just sit. She wanted to try to get to know him but he didn't say much about himself.

"First, we'll have dinner. I know a lad who owns a restaurant that looks out over the water." When she smiled at the thought of the romantic gesture, he corrupted his voice with a dodgy accent and continued, "I thought maybe I could tempt you with some seafood before taking you to an illegal establishment and plying you with liquor so that I don't have to sleep on my own tonight."

Her smile faded and her eyes widened. He started to laugh, "I'm just teasing you again, Love. How's your foot?"

She shook her head and smiled again. "A little sore but it's all right."

He held out a hand to her. "Do you still need to lean on me?" he asked.

She blushed again. "Maybe just a little bit," she said as she put her hand in his.

As they walked down to the restaurant on the water, Ruairi explained to her that they were meeting up with Mairtin and Thomas. She was a bit uncomfortable with the thought of the two extra men but she wanted desperately to make him happy with her.

The restaurant sat on the piers between fishing warehouses and once inside, Gracie noticed that there was a steep set of stairs that she would have to manoeuvre in her new heels.

"I think I'm still going to need your hand," she whispered to him.

He smiled down at her. She liked the way the skin at the corners of his eyes crinkled. He was a few years older than her, she was sure of it, but that only made him all the more attractive.

He leaned over to talk to the hostess that greeted them at the bottom of the stairs.

"Liam's expectin' me," he said to her.

"You must be Ruairi," she said, her voice as Irish as his.

"Aye."

"Your boys are waiting as well," she said, turning to lead them up the staircase.

"Grand," he replied.

Gracie took a deep breath and started the climb. When they got to the top, she looked around in awe. There were white linens on the tables and the whole room was dim, with only candles lighting the area. The reflection in the windows made it look like there were hundreds of little flickering flames going on into eternity. The sun was almost set and the sky was pink and orange with the faintest hint of darkness coming on.

"Your kind of restaurant?" Ruairi whispered into her ear.

His breath on her neck made her stomach flutter and all she could do was nod. He led her across the narrow room to where three men and one woman sat. One of the men stood up, offering his seat to Gracie. The other three stared at her, obviously surprised to see her.

"Good evening, Ruairi," the standing gentleman stuck out his hand. Ruairi shook it.

"Liam, this is Gracie. Gracie, Liam."

Gracie nodded to Liam. Liam nodded back.

"What the hell is she doing here?" Mairtin hissed, not even bothering to attempt to disguise the question with a cough.

Ruairi glared at him. "She's with me. Any more questions?"

Mairtin growled at him in response.

"Gracie, this lovely gentleman is Mairtin Fitzgerald," Ruairi continued to glare at him until he acknowledged her. When he finally nodded his head, it was with such a violent jerk that it looked like he had sneezed without the sound. "Are you all right, Mairty?" Ruairi laughed.

"I'm allergic to squirrels," he responded.

Ruairi just rolled his eyes. Gracie was confused but figured it must be some underworld code that she wasn't familiar with.

"This is Thomas, my little brother," Thomas stood and leaned in, kissing her on the cheek. "And this," Ruairi said, motioning to the young woman, "this is my sister Aisling. I'm not sure what she's doing here but I'm sure we'll find out."

At this, Aisling smirked at him and then stuck out her hand to Gracie. Gracie awkwardly shook it and then she let Ruairi lead her around to sit in the chair being offered by Liam.

"Ah, Ruairi, this came for you about an hour ago, compliments of Shorty." Liam produced a small envelope from his jacket pocket and handed it to Ruairi. Ruairi slipped it into his jacket pocket without even glancing at it.

"It's about bloody time," Ruairi said, half under his breath.

Gracie fidgeted in the seat. Liam hadn't pushed it in underneath her and the conversation made her uncomfortable enough.

"Well, if that will be all, I have some other guests to attend to. I'll send over the beverages." Liam slipped away.

The table stayed quiet. Gracie tried to pull her chair underneath her inconspicuously. She looked over at Ruairi to catch his attention but he was watching Aisling intently.

"So, what are you doing here?" he asked his sister.

"Well, I had a few days off from the hospital so I thought I'd just come over with the lads and have a little holiday." Aisling averted her eyes.

Ruairi turned his attention back to Gracie, "You see, Gracie, Aisling here works as a nurse at the hospital. When she isn't at work, she likes to play nurse with Mairtin over there but I'm not supposed to know any of this so everybody tries to come up with excuses as to why Aisling shows up everywhere Mairtin is."

"You sound like a very protective older brother," Gracie remarked.

A little dimple appeared in Aisling's cheek and she fought hard to keep it unnoticed. Mairtin cleared his throat and looked around as if he hadn't heard Ruairi. Thomas openly laughed. It was a generous laugh. Gracie liked him immediately.

"Protective doesn't begin to describe Ruairi when it comes to his family," Thomas revealed.

"I see," Gracie said softly, trying to hide a smile. She looked up and caught Aisling looking at her. Suddenly, Aisling's face broke into a smile and her cheeks flushed pink. Gracie's smile came out too and the girls shared a giggle.

Back in Charlottetown, Rosaleen sat out on the porch with Karl and Stavros.

"I overheard a bit of the details of last night outside my office," Karl picked at his fingernails while he prompted the conversation.

"She was a wild one," Stavros agreed. "What the hell did the cooks do to my lobster though?" he complained.

Karl flicked a piece of fingernail at him.

"Ew!" Rosaleen made a face at them both, "What did you overhear Karlie?"

Karl hated when she called him that. He felt it emasculated him. "I heard the O'Neill boys may have known the Gainsborough's from a previous life."

"How fascinating," Rosaleen said dryly.

"Are you really not going to tell me anything?" Karl was annoyed.

"Ask him yourself," Rosaleen lifted her legs and lengthened them out until they rested on Stavros' lap. Stavros suddenly couldn't concentrate. He just stared at the curve of her ankles.

"I don't have a death wish," Karl pouted.

"I think I've already died . . . and gone to heaven," Stavros moaned, as he slowly touched her kneecap with his index finger.

Rosaleen kicked him in the ribs and he coughed, half winded. "Sorry," she said sarcastically. "Reflex."

She turned her attention back to Karl, "All you need to know is that Ruairi is very good at everything he does and your connection with him will keep you from having to work on the fishing boats in the dreadful cold. Your association with him is purely business and any indication of friendship strictly involves poker and racing. There are no drunken confessions between the two of you and there never will be. Don't forget that."

Karl cursed at her under his breath.

Quicker than anything, her foot shot out from Stavros' lap and nailed Karl in the nether regions. He doubled over. Stavros winced in sympathy.

"Bloody reflexes!" she said, smiling to herself.

"So how was the meeting?" Thomas asked Ruairi in between bites of his halibut.

Ruairi looked over at Gracie and shook his head.

"Why can't I hear this?" Gracie asked.

"Because you're a Gainsborough and you'll go home and tell your Da," Mairtin said in a dull voice.

Aisling gave Mairtin a look across the table. He just shrugged his shoulders back at her.

Gracie tossed her cutlery onto her plate and looked around the table. "I want to know how everybody came to know my family. I'm sick of everybody knowing everything except me."

Ruairi closed his eyes and inhaled deeply. He had a feeling she was going to start asking the hard questions. He exhaled. "Just eat your food. No one here really knows anything or anybody."

"No," she had a stubborn look on her face.

Ruairi wiped his mouth with the white cloth napkin. "Gracie, please. This is not the place to have this conversation," his voice was low and had a tone in it that the rest of the table knew quite well.

They were all surprised when she continued to argue with him.

"Well, then, answer my questions and we'll be able to keep the conversation to ourselves. Don't make me raise my voice." Her steel blue gaze was locked on Ruairi.

Thomas had fully stopped chewing to see how his brother would react. Strangely, the girl seemed to have him at her mercy. Instead of losing his temper, he reached across the table, took her hand and squeezed it.

"Gracie, some things are better left unknown. We don't like your Da much. That's all you really need to know."

"You tried to kill him. I think there are a few more details you could tell me."

"Unfortunately, he *didn't* try to kill him," Mairtin snorted. Under the table, Ruairi booted Mairtin's kneecap. Mairtin's face contorted in pain and he glared at Ruairi. Aisling shrugged her shoulders at Mairtin and looked smug.

"What do you mean he didn't try to kill him?" she pleaded, but Ruairi had forced his silence.

Ruairi faked a smile at her. "Eat your dinner, Love."

Gracie sighed but finally picked up her fork and slowly ate her dinner. She pretended to be too involved in her meal for any further conversation but she listened intently to the others around her. It worked until Aisling asked about Johnny.

"So, Gracie, how long have you been with Johnny Bexley?"

Gracie automatically stopped chewing. She struggled to swallow her food. The table waited politely for her answer. "I was introduced to him by my brother when we first arrived in Charlottetown but I guess it became formal about a year ago."

"Did you think that you would end up marrying him?" Aisling asked.

Gracie nodded. "He was the only boy I'd ever kissed."

"I can't imagine only having kissed one man!" Aisling looked horrified.

Thomas swatted her playfully. "What kind of Catholic girl are you?"

Gracie's eyes flitted over to Ruairi. He grinned at her but never said a word.

"It was terrible that he never finished the speech last night. We're awfully sorry about that," Aisling added, noticing the odd exchange between Gracie and Ruairi.

"I'm not," Gracie said forcefully.

All eyes were suddenly on her, waiting for an explanation. Thomas, Aisling and Mairtin had left Charlottetown before the rumours had begun circulating.

"I'm surprised you never heard, really. I thought it would be common knowledge by now. He's cheating on me," Gracie sniffed and looked down at her plate. "He's been courting Lana Hamilton behind my back. I'm not sure how they managed to keep it a secret for this long, to tell you the truth. I must seem an extremely silly girl."

"Are you sure about this Gracie? I mean, it could just be a rumour," Thomas instinctively tried to protect the girl's feelings.

Gracie finally looked up, large tears streaking her perfectly applied make-up. "I'm sure. He didn't even try to deny it," she said steadily, her big eyes looking shamefully into Ruairi's.

Ruairi clenched his jaw as he watched her cry. He hadn't realized how much her pride had been hurt until then. "He doesn't deserve you, Love."

Aisling patted Gracie's hand across the table. "There, there, Gracie. Ruairi's right. He's not worth the tears." As she comforted the young English girl, she had to wonder whether Gracie's emotions were due to Johnny or somebody else. She knew her brother well and would have to watch him a bit more closely.

Billy jogged up the stairs to his bedroom to change for the evening. He had his shirt unbuttoned by the time he shut the door. When he spun around he found himself half naked in front of a reclining Rosaleen Jameson. She smiled at him from the bed and patted the spot next to her.

He chuckled, "Why am I not surprised that our first time alone in years involves you breaking into my house?"

She gave him a lazy smile. "I enjoy a dramatic entrance."

He walked over to the bed, took her hands in his, and gently dragged her up to standing, "What are you doing back in my life, Rosaleen?"

She leaned back from him and studied him closely. "Do you not want me here, then?"

Billy hesitated noticeably, "Of course I want you here but I'm wary of you this time." The implication hung in the air for a long while.

"You should always beware of a woman."

His eyes sparked. "Don't toy with me Rosaleen," he warned. His patience was very nearly gone. "Are you here for me?" he was aching to know.

"I am here for you," she said easily, "I promised you that one day I would come to you."

"I never believed you," he admitted.

"Well, here I am, God as my witness." She held her hand over his heart.

"And are you here forever?"

"That depends on you," she said slowly.

"Put me out of my misery, Rosaleen. What is this all about?"

"I have to tell you something," she looked at him intensely, "I'm sorry that I couldn't tell you back then."

Billy noticed a shift in her confidence. She was suddenly nervous, vulnerable. "You could have told me anything," he said.

She shook her head, "Not at the time. I didn't want to put you in danger," she revealed, her voice so soft he could barely hear her.

Billy thought back to the ambush, the shots fired, the gun in his back, "How could I have possibly been in any more danger than I already was?"

She faltered, "Billy, there are so many lies that could have killed you." She moved towards the window.

"All I want to know is the truth," Billy pleaded with her.

"The truth involves so many people."

"This is between you and me."

His words broke her. She felt all of the internal walls caving in and her body became weak. She reached out and he caught her, pulling him towards her and holding her to his chest. It felt so good to be in his arms again.

He gently pushed her upright and tilted her face to his, "Tell me."

"Promise me that you won't hate me for it."

"Nothing could be that bad, surely," he said, but Billy dreaded what was coming.

"I went to William with information about the ambush the day before it happened," she struggled to know where to start.

Billy blinked in confusion. "The day before?" He assumed he must have heard her incorrectly.

"Aye," she said very softly.

Billy covered his eyes with his hand. Flashes of memory from the nights he spent with her were split by the screams of his comrades as the shots ripped through the lorry. He lost track of his breathing and he felt disorientated. "Are you saying that my father could have prevented it?"

"Aye," she murmured regretfully. The truth was painful on both sides.

"Why are you telling me this?" he asked. He felt as though he were suffocating.

"Because you need to know how much I loved you . . . how much I love you before I . . ." she stopped talking and reached for him.

"I don't understand," he was choking now.

"I had to trade information on Ruairi for your father to believe me." Rosaleen still couldn't say the words without feeling repulsed at what she had done.

His face was white. "Why didn't he act to stop it?"

She began to second guess whether the truth was worth the hearts that she would break. She thought better of continuing. "I don't know," she lied.

Billy stood in shock as he thought about his comrades. He doubled over and dry heaved. He found his way to the floor and sat himself against the wall. He had his eyes closed to keep the world still. When he opened them, she was kneeling before him.

"You said that you love me." He reached forward and placed his hands along her jawbone.

"I do love you," she was nodding and kissing the inside of his wrists.

He leaned his head back against the wall. "I've waited so long to hear you say that." The seconds ticked by as he tried to sort through his emotions. They were layered and tightly interwoven. "Why did it take you so long to come to me?"

Rosaleen sank forward and melted into him. "I didn't want to risk your life again. I had convinced Ruairi to let you live. If he would have found out . . ." she knew that Billy didn't need to be reminded of how dangerous Ruairi was.

Billy was quiet for a moment as he tried to regulate his breathing. "Rosaleen, I need to understand why I'm still alive. Why didn't he leave me to bleed to death?"

"Because I ordered him not to," she began, her voice shaking.

"I don't understand why he listened to you, though." Billy failed to see how she had so much power over Ruairi.

It was a difficult concept to explain. "You took an oath swearing to defend the crown when you began your military service."

Billy nodded.

"Ruairi swore to defend me."

Billy stared down at the girl in his arms. "You are his Queen," he realized finally.

"To him, I am Ireland. I am Roísín Dubh," her voice caught. "He is in love with me."

"Rosaleen, if he finds out that I've touched you . . ." Billy could taste the bile again and couldn't continue.

He felt her grow cold with his thoughts.

"Ruairi won't kill you now. I can promise you that. He may never forgive me but he won't lay a finger on you."

"How can you make that promise after what you just told me?"

Rosaleen thought about the letter from Maggie that had laid out her destiny. She knew that Billy would never understand Maggie. "You'll just have to trust me."

Ruairi had changed the subject and the table was now spending a pleasant enough time chatting easily about Charlottetown and the differences between the old world and the new.

"I love that nobody knows me here," Aisling was saying, "nobody knows who my Grandda was or what the family business was."

Mairtin shrugged. "I sort of miss that, actually. People seem a bit colder here, less neighbourly."

"How could you say that?" Thomas asked, shocked. "Maria dropped off some baked goods just yesterday for us boys and Valerie has been taking good care of Mickey," he pointed out.

Mairtin laughed, "She has at that, but I don't believe it's been in the baked goods department."

Gracie looked up in surprise. "Are you speaking of Valerie Logan?" Gracie had heard many rumours regarding Ms. Logan but had never made her acquaintance. She was considered the most fashionable feminist in Canada. Even if her politics were barely tolerated by most of society, invitations to her social engagements were highly sought after.

Aisling smiled, "She's become a good friend since our arrival."

"I've been dying to meet her! My father won't allow us to attend any of her parties but I hear she is the most exciting of ladies," Gracie gushed.

Ruairi winked at her. "Maybe we will have to organize a chance meeting for you."

Gracie was thrilled with the idea. She found herself enjoying Ruairi's attentions more and more. She was surprised at how easy it was to talk with him, even laugh with him. If she didn't know better, she would have actually thought that she was attracted to him.

But that couldn't be. His abrupt manner and callous language was enough to assure her of that. She also disliked the company he kept. She felt so out of place with his friends. Although they tried to make her feel comfortable and his brother and sister had attempted to be charming, Mairtin had her on edge. They were much too different from her.

They finished their desserts and headed down the stairs and out into the cool breeze. Ruairi approached her with a cheeky look on his face. "Now Gracie, you have a choice. What we do tonight is completely up to you."

Gracie was intrigued.

"I know of a place that we can go, but the establishment might be a bit shocking for the likes of you. If you trust me though, I'd wager you would have a good time there."

"And what is the other choice?" Gracie asked, knowing that he was already hoping she would go for the first idea.

"Well, I could take you back to the hotel and we could just have a quiet evening and turn in early if you would prefer but I think that would be a rather boring end to your first rebellious weekend."

"I think you might be selling the girlie short if you think that a private night with her would be boring!" Mairtin laughed perversely.

Thomas shoved him hard towards the water. Mairtin stumbled but kept his footing. "I do apologize for him Gracie; he hasn't been properly socialized."

Gracie felt her cheeks redden. "Maybe it would be best if you take me back to the hotel. You don't have to stay with me, you can go out. I'll be fine on my own." She jutted out her chin and tried her best to look independent.

Ruairi smiled, his eyes never leaving hers. "No," he said, openly defying her for the first time. He knew he was risking a scene but he was almost sure he had figured out how to persuade her. "I want you to come with me."

"But you said it was my choice and I don't want to go out," Gracie said stubbornly.

Ruairi shrugged, his smile widening. "I lied."

A shadowy look passed Gracie's eyes but Ruairi diffused it quickly. "Ah, come on Gracie, I swear you'll have a good time!" he laughed, wrapping an arm around her waist and scooping her up. He twirled her around until she giggled helplessly. "I'll even dance with you," he whispered in her ear. Flirting and flattery could get him anywhere with this girl.

"Where would you have learned to dance?" she asked, doubting his abilities.

"Ah! It's a secret, Love!" He put her down, sliding his hand down her arm until he found her hand. He slipped his fingers through hers and then tucked her entire arm beneath his so that she was held firmly to his side.

She looked up into his eyes as a wave of giddiness washed over her. Maybe she could be attracted to him after all.

Aisling watched as her brother helped the Gainsborough girl up the street. She had apparently stepped on a fish hook earlier in the day. She was a nice enough girl and very beautiful but Aisling didn't like the way Ruairi was treating her. She hoped for his sake that he wasn't becoming attached to her. Mairtin made his feelings very clear. As a gorgeous woman and as a Gainsborough, she was a deadly combination and should be kept far away from Ruairi. He thought it was about time Gracie knew the truth. He wasn't going to let Ruairi dig himself his own grave on either side of the Atlantic.

Mairtin knew how Ruairi's meeting had gone. He had been called in an hour later for his own meeting. No matter what, he would be loyal to his friend but he understood where the concern came from. Ruairi could be very volatile and the boys were just trying to make sure he wasn't going to drag the army into something personal. They wanted to make sure they had one level head watching Ruairi's back. So, Mairtin was given his orders.

Gracie clung to Ruairi's hand. They stood in front of an alleyway door that had a tiny little window at the top with three bars in it. Thomas whispered something through the bars and the door swung open. Ruairi led her into a smoke filled room that was dimly lit and filled with all sorts of slippery creatures. In the middle of the far wall, there was a bar set up. A piano in the far corner was played by a man in top and tails and a dark woman with bright red lips swayed beside him. She opened her mouth and her voice was like caramel. A nearby woman recognized Thomas immediately and dragged him into the center of the room, wrapping her arms up around his neck.

"Poor lad didn't even get a drink first," Aisling laughed.

"That's what happens when you deal in love and poetry." Ruairi smiled at his sister.

"Good thing we don't know anything about love," Mairtin said loudly. Aisling swatted him and laughed. They moved off to a booth in the corner leaving Ruairi and Gracie standing just inside the door.

"Are you okay?" he asked her.

She nodded, taking it all in. She had never been to a speakeasy. She had heard fascinating stories about police raids and mob murders in America but of course, Billy and Johnny had never allowed her near an actual illegal establishment.

"So, do we dance?" she asked him, feigning disinterest.

"Not yet," he said, taking her hand and leading her towards the bar. "What do you want to drink?"

"A glass of champagne would be lovely," she said.

He laughed at her. "No champagne, Love. Not with me! Let me pick for you."

Gracie wrinkled her nose. He pulled out a stool for her. His fingers slid across her shoulder blades as he helped her up. She felt the goosebumps race across her skin. He leaned over her and spoke with the barman.

Two tumblers appeared in front of them and the barman poured an amber coloured liquid out of a big bottle. He filled the tumblers a quarter of the way full and then walked away.

Ruairi picked up his tumbler and held it up to her, "Come on, let's see how brave you are."

Gracie picked hers up and he clinked his glass with hers.

"Sláinte!" He smiled at her, then, he put the cup to his lips and drained the glass in one gulp. "Go ahead," he laughed when she took a sniff of it. "Just toss it back."

Gracie did as she was told. The liquid tasted all right but once she swallowed she could feel her chest and her throat burning. She coughed.

"What was that?" she choked out.

"Irish whiskey!" he was still laughing, "Did you like it?"

"I haven't decided yet," she coughed again. It made him laugh harder.

"Why did Mairtin say he was allergic to squirrels?" Gracie asked. She was dying to know what that meant. She was sure it was some kind of rum running code.

Ruairi shook his head, his smile was teasing. "Mairtin calls people he doesn't trust squirrels."

"Why?" Gracie didn't get it and the fact that it didn't have an exciting connotation disappointed her.

"Mairtin has a strange sense of humour. He doesn't like very many people."

"He doesn't even know me!" She was shocked.

Ruairi chuckled, "That doesn't matter much to him. You are rich so that immediately makes you suspect. He thinks that rich people are manipulative and sneaky."

Gracie furrowed her brow. "Well, I guess some rich people are like that," she conceded, "but I'm not."

"Really?" he asked, cocking his head to the side. "And how are you so different, Gracie?"

Gracie was caught off guard and she didn't know how to respond. "Well, I'm here . . . with you . . . in a speakeasy."

"Look around, doll," Ruairi said, gesturing to a few of the booths surrounding the dance floor. "Do you think all of these people are poor bastards like me?"

Gracie looked around. Everybody was dressed fancy. All of the women had their hair adorned with feathers and jewels and their makeup was painted on. The men wore their hair slicked and their shoes shiny. "Well, not all of them," she hesitated.

Ruairi laughed.

"Why is that funny?" she asked defensively.

"Most of these guys are making more money than your precious Da." Ruairi glanced around and then secretly pointed out a guy near the piano in a mustard coloured suit. "See that man? He's got more money in his clip than your Da does in stocks."

"Not a chance!" Gracie shook her head.

Ruairi looked on her with amusement, "You don't know much about the rum trade, do you?"

"Of course not! I'm a lady," Gracie was coolly defiant.

"Aye, that you are," Ruairi sighed.

Gracie was taken aback, "You make it sound like being a lady is boring."

Ruairi was slow to respond, "I like women more than ladies."

"And what, may I ask, is the difference?"

He shook his head. "We need to get you to Valerie sooner than I thought."

"What does this have to do with Valerie Logan?" Gracie was thrown by the sudden turn the conversation had taken.

"Valerie is a *woman* who will change your life." Gracie went to ask another question but he silenced her with a finger to her lips. "Ah! That's all I'm going to say. You are going to have to meet with Valerie for yourself to learn more."

"You're nothing but riddle after riddle, Ruairi O'Neill."

"And you're an open book, Gracie Gainsborough."

She only protested lightly and he knew she was enjoying the little game. He realized that he liked playing games with her.

The way he was looking at her, a crooked smile on his face, aroused her curiosity. "Why are you looking at me like that?"

The smile faded. "I'm having a good time with you," he said seriously.

She looked at him queerly. "Why do I take it that you're surprised by that?"

"I just would have never thought . . ." he started, abruptly stopping as another thought led him in a different direction. "You aren't as spoiled as you come across."

Gracie laughed, "Yes I am. I'm spoiled and pretentious and difficult and I don't think that's a bad thing."

"Neither do I," Ruairi said softly, reaching a hand out to touch her face. "You deserve to be spoiled."

They stared at each other intently. Ruairi wondered if he could just have her for a moment; a very short, very intense moment. That was all he needed.

"Dance with me."

It wasn't a question, Gracie noticed, it was a demand. She realized that she liked the way he spoke to her. She liked his confidence. She put her hand in his and let him lead her to a spot on the floor. The music was lazy and hypnotic, slow enough to dance close.

He put his hands on her and she felt herself give in to the strength of them. He led her through the motions easily enough but she found herself unable to connect her thoughts to her feet. She was too focussed on the heat of his breath on her neck, the warmth of his body pressed up against hers, and the beat of his heart. To know whether or not he was a good dancer was unneccessary. The only thing she knew for sure is that she had never danced like that before.

Ruairi let his hands travel gently up and down her back. She was so tiny and fragile in his arms. The more he tried to distance himself from her, the closer he pulled her. He could feel her opening up to him and he was fully receptive to it. He encouraged her gently with his eyes knowing that it was the wrong thing to do. But selfishly, he couldn't stop himself. He had her for tonight.

He bent down to her ear and whispered softly, "I'm still an Irish rebel." His eyelashes brushed against her cheekbone. He felt even the slightest touches as if they were a brand.

"I might be an English one," she answered back.

He laughed softly, his breath tickling the nape of her neck. She responded by nuzzling further into him.

"I think I like you," she said dreamily.

He kissed her forehead softly. "I think I want you to like me."

Thomas disentangled himself from a throng of women and made his way towards Ruairi, who seemed to be too at home in the arms of the Gainsborough girl. "I need to borrow some money for the buy in." He motioned to Ruairi to follow him.

Ruairi looked down at Gracie, uncertain of what to do with her. "Will you be okay for a couple of minutes by yourself?"

"Order me another Irish whiskey and I might feel courageous enough," she smiled weakly. He took her back to the barstool and ordered her another and then walked off with Thomas. They went through a door and disappeared. Gracie noticed a big man standing off to the side of the door. She shivered. She took a sip of her whiskey and made a face.

"Hello, Woman," Mairtin sat down beside her. He spoke slowly as if he thought she couldn't understand him.

She looked at him and sighed. "Don't tell me you're my babysitter?"

He smiled a sardonic smile. "I'm not cut out for such tasks. I just wanted to talk to you."

"About what?" Gracie was uneasy. She found Mairtin eerily magnetic. He was rough and hardened but there was something behind his eyes that intrigued her.

"How about we discuss your father?"

Gracie looked at him, surprised.

Mairtin didn't give her time to answer. "You obviously know that Ruairi kidnapped your brother and shot your father." He got right to the point. "Well, that's not really how it happened. Does the name Rosaleen Jameson mean anything to you?"

Gracie nodded her head. How could she forget the beautiful young woman who had rescued her? "I met her in the powder room at the party last night."

"Four years ago, your father met Rosaleen and used her to get information about the IRA and Ruairi."

Gracie felt a bit nauseous. She had a feeling she knew what he meant by the term 'used'. She swiftly finished off her second whiskey. It still burned.

It didn't take Mairtin long to fill in the details. He said it so easily, like he was telling her a vulgar bedtime story. "Rosaleen can be a very selfish girl. She was sick of the fighting and the long stretches without Ruairi and she thought that your father was an easy escape from a life that she didn't want to live. She ended up pregnant and when Ruairi found out, it drove him mad. Instead of keeping a safe distance and allowing us to kill William, Ruairi went after your Da himself. He was involved in the ambush that your brother was almost killed in, not that he had any idea that your brother was in that company. Everything went wrong that day and whether it was due to the fact that your Da had been informed that we were going to ambush the lorry or whether it was just bad luck, I don't know. It was supposed to be a simple arms retrieval but shots were fired and chaos broke out and somehow, Ruairi ended up with your bleeding brother as a hostage."

Gracie couldn't breathe. It was so much worse than she could have imagined; so bad that it was impossible to believe. She looked around for the barman and waved him over. "I need another one," she said, tears threatening to spill over. The barman poured the same amount but she waved at him to keep pouring. When her glass was almost full, she finally stopped him. Mairtin and the barman raised their eyebrows at each other. She looked at Mairtin. "Are you lying to me?"

"Why would I lie to you?" he asked.

"You are saying that my father knew that there was going to be an ambush but he did nothing to stop it. Why would he do that? Why would he risk my brother's life?" It was a damning accusation.

Mairtin shook his head. "We aren't clear on that part. Ruairi wasn't supposed to be in Dublin and we think that maybe your Da knew that too. He had the Black and Tans out looking for Ruairi near Balbriggan. Maybe he thought Billy wasn't in any danger. Our boys weren't supposed to open fire. It was just supposed to be an arms hold-up."

"How did my father save Billy from Ruairi?"

"He didn't." Mairtin took a swig of his drink, "Thomas and I took your Da hostage. Ruairi had no intention of killing your brother, just your Da," Mairtin paused, he was unsure of the rest of the story. Ruairi had never spoken of it since. "Ruairi wanted to make sure that Billy was transported back to his barracks safely. While we were out releasing your brother, something went very wrong. We came back, two of our boys were almost dead, there was blood everywhere, and both William and Rosaleen were gone. Ruairi looked for her for days and when he finally found her, she had been badly beaten. It's a wonder the baby survived."

"My father beat her?" Gracie was horrified.

Mairtin shrugged. "Rosaleen says he didn't. Her story is that he had somehow slipped the ropes he had been tied with, laid in wait and put a knife to her throat. She was forced to drive him to Dublin Castle and from there he let her go."

"So then, what happened to her?"

'She says she was attacked the next day in an alleyway. Four soldiers viciously beat her." Mairtin rolled his head, cracking his neck.

"Obviously none of us believe that story but it is what it is. We never got another chance to kill your father. Until now," he added.

"Is that why you are here?" She felt like she was fighting for air.

He looked very serious. "If you want your father to live then you need to stay away from Ruairi," he warned.

Gracie heard the threat clearly. "Well, I never planned on . . . I mean, I'm not . . . but . . ." she was stumbling over her words and couldn't seem to put a coherent sentence together.

Mairtin cut her off harshly, "Do you hear what I'm telling you?" He scowled at her, "He and your father cannot coexist. Do you know what that means? That means one of them will end up dead." He watched her reaction with blazing eyes. When he was sure that the words had taken effect he softened but only slightly, "It would be best for everyone involved if you just stayed away."

"The war is over," she said angrily, "and he told me that he wouldn't hurt me." Her chest was constricting and she struggled to breathe.

Mairtin's eyes hardened and he suddenly looked very determined. "The war isn't over for him. Do you really think he gives a damn about you? His family and Ireland are all that he cares about. Rosaleen is his family. We are his family. You mean nothing to him. He wants your father dead for what he did to Rosaleen, Gracie. He loves Rosaleen. Where does that leave you?"

Gracie knew there was only one answer to that question and the weight of it was crushing her. Her hands were shaking. She looked up and saw Ruairi coming towards her from the door on the other side of the room. Thomas was behind him, looking disgruntled. She suddenly realized she didn't know either of them at all.

Gracie slid off the stool and stumbled away from them, feeling her first real pangs of fear. She was in a dangerous situation with dangerous people. She needed to get to air.

Ruairi was only a few feet away from her when she bolted. He narrowed his eyes, unsure of what was wrong with her other than the obvious intoxication.

"Gracie!" he called out to her. She kept moving away so he reached out, grabbing her arm and pulling her around. "Gracie, where are you going?"

She yanked her arm out of his grasp and glared at him. "I can't let you do this, Ruairi. I'm leaving."

"Do what?" he asked, bewildered by her erratic behaviour. Then he noticed Mairtin sitting on the stool beside where he had left her. Ruairi shot him a nasty look. Mairtin just stared back, unapologetic.

"You cannot use me to kill my father!" She stumbled, mumbling something under her breath that sounded vaguely like 'Irish bastard' and tried to make it to the back of the room where the stairs were.

Ruairi looked over at Thomas who was trying desperately to hide his laughter. "This isn't funny. She's feckin' serious and very drunk! How the hell am I going to calm her down?"

Thomas shrugged, pulling a barstool towards him as a buffer between himself and his unpredictable brother. Aisling had gone to stand beside Mairtin and was scolding him quietly in his ear. Ruairi turned on Mairtin, enraged. "What the hell did you say to her?" he hissed.

Mairtin met his glare with an equally fiery look. "I told her the truth, Ruairi. She needs to know what you are going to do."

"I don't even know what I am going to do!" he snarled. He debated whether to chase her out or finish the fight at hand but he knew Gracie had to be the immediate priority. "This isn't finished," he threatened Mairtin.

Mairtin nodded, glowering at a furious Ruairi. Both boys were extremely stubborn. There was a heavy silence and then Ruairi followed Gracie out into the alley.

"Gracie. Stop running, Love," Ruairi called out as he caught up to her. She was off balance and completely disorientated.

She whirled around clumsily. "I don't want you to call me that anymore! Just let me go, Ruairi."

"Ah, Gracie!" he sighed. "Nothing's really changed. You knew I had shot your Da. We were at war. Just calm down."

"Did you really just tell me to calm down?" she snapped at him. "Do you really think it's normal to be calm with a man who plans to kill me and my family?"

His laugh had a bitter edge to it. "I'm not planning on killing you. Gracie, you came to me. Both times! You came down to the docks and jumped on the boat and told me you were coming with me. I didn't lure you onto the boat. You came to me and I've done nothing but make you comfortable."

Her look turned savage. "You're just trying to gain my trust and then, when I turn my back . . ." she gave him a disgusted look and turned away.

He took advantage of her position, grabbing her roughly from behind, clamping his hand over her mouth and whispering cruelly in her ear, "When you turn your back I'm going to kill you is that it, Gracie?" He spun her around and slammed her up against the stone wall imprisoning her in the tiny alleyway. Her bright blue eyes were full of fear and he could feel her body trembling as he pressed against her. His angry face changed into a sad smile and he dropped his hand from her mouth. "Why would I want to kill you, Gracie?" His breath was sweet and hot and her thumping heart was loud.

"Because you hate my father; because you're Irish and I'm English; because you're Catholic and poor and . . ."

"You don't know why, do you Gracie? You have no idea what this war is about. You've probably read a few newspaper articles about the 'Irish Problem' and because your Da fought over there you think you might know what happened."

"I know what happened. Mairtin just told me," she whispered, feeling like she might lose consciousness at any moment. "Ruairi, I'm so afraid."

He lowered his forehead onto hers, trying hard to fight the urge to shake her. He could feel his insides twisting and he grimaced. "I promised I would never hurt you. Please don't be afraid of me."

"Can you promise me again?" she asked him, barely able to breathe.

"I promise I will never hurt you." He felt her relax a little bit into him.

"Will you promise not to harm my family?" her voice shook as she asked it.

"I promise not to harm your mother or Billy," he said honestly.

Gracie tried to push him away but his body was massive compared to hers. "Promise me that you won't hurt my father!"

He gripped her shoulders and stared into her eyes. "I can't do that, Gracie. We have a history, and men like us don't change our opinions very easily."

"Then don't make any more promises to me," she said angrily. "Your words mean nothing."

He growled loudly, a deep throaty sound, "Gracie, I have no choice. You don't understand."

"You're right, Ruairi. I don't understand. Because you do have a choice and you are choosing to be a monster." She used every ounce of strength in her little body to shove him aside. She stalked towards the mouth of the alley, feeling the chill as soon as their bodies parted.

Ruairi cringed. The accusation hurt. He didn't feel as though he had much of a choice. "Gracie, look at me," he called to her, "I need to explain something to you."

She turned but left her eyes to trace the scars on the cobblestones.

"Gracie, there is a war going on and I'm in it. It's my job to fight . . ."

She cut in, "I get it, Ruairi. I'm the enemy."

"You aren't my enemy." Ruairi looked deep into her eyes. "Just because you're English, doesn't mean you're the enemy. But your Da is. Dammit, Gracie, he left Rosaleen pregnant and half dead. He ordered the killing of friends, family members . . . Can't you understand how much I hate him? Maybe I am a monster. Maybe I always have been. But tonight, I'd damn well protect you from anything." He stopped, hesitating only for a moment, "So maybe when I'm near you, I'm as close to human as I'm ever going to be."

"You're wasting your breath," her eyes were full of hatred. "You will never convince me that you are human."

"I understand," he said quietly. He couldn't force her to forgive him for his beliefs.

Gracie began crying and turned away again and ran to the main street, painfully aware that she was still vulnerable to him.

Ruairi followed a few paces behind her. He felt exactly like he had the morning before, when he had taken her out of the harbour, asleep on his boat. He had gotten himself into something that he couldn't control. He would have to break their association the moment she got off the boat in the morning. It was what was best for her. He shook his head sadly. It wasn't what was best for her. It was what was safest.

He followed her up to her hotel room. She went straight to her little pile of clothes that she had been wearing earlier and picked them up.

"What are you doing, Gracie?"

"Packing up my stuff," she said, sniffing.

"We can't leave until the morning. I promise though, as soon as there is light I'll wake you up."

She shook her head, "I just can't stay in this room. I want to go sleep on the boat so that we can leave earlier," she said. "I just want to get away from you."

"I have a separate room. I won't be anywhere near you," he said.

"I want to leave now," she maintained stubbornly.

"It's a long drive to the boat," he could no longer hide his frustration, "and it won't be very comfortable to sleep there." He watched her for any expression. She didn't seem to care. He sighed. He was completely at a loss for how to comfort her, to get her to even look at him again. "Ok, let's go to the boat. I'll just pay up downstairs."

"I'll go wait on the street."

"It isn't safe. I won't let you go anywhere alone."

Her laugh was almost manic. "It's not safe?" she echoed him hollowly. "You think I'm safe here in this little room with you?"

"You are safe with me," he said quietly, painfully.

She pushed away from him, almost knocking herself over in the process.

"The car isn't on the street," he said, putting his hand out to steady her. "I parked it a few streets away this afternoon for safety reasons. You should stay here while I go fetch it."

She brushed him off, "I'd rather walk down to it."

He looked at her. She was limping badly but wouldn't accept his arm.

"I need to sober up," she confessed angrily. After that she remained silent.

Rosaleen lay beside Billy and pulled the blanket up under her throat. She had promised him that she would warn him before she told Ruairi about her betrayal. It was too dangerous not to. Then they had made love. She was surprised by the depth of her feelings for Billy; feelings that she knew would shatter the pedestal that Ruairi had built for her.

She wrapped the blanket around herself as she tiptoed out onto the balcony. She stared out over the harbour and the black water and thought about drowning. She was in over her head anyway.

She was only twenty-two when she was introduced to General Gainsborough. She was dining at the Shelbourne Hotel and he had seen her across the room and sent over a drink. He was powerful and commanding and he lavished money and attention on her. She was so sick of the fighting, sick of her father and Ruairi being gone for weeks, sick of listening to her mother crying in the room beside her. He promised that the British Army were there to help. They were going to fix all of Ireland's problems. And a man like him, well, he could do anything.

The tears slipped down her cheeks and she wiped them away angrily. Ruairi had warned her over and over to stay away from him. He had pleaded with her. But what did he know? He was running around fighting for Ireland dirty, hungry and poor with a pistol that kicked to the left and a rusty knife.

She had tried to justify her disobedience to him by telling herself that she had been a fool in love. But she knew the truth. She was just a fool. The General had bought her confidence with fine clothes, jewellery and fancy dinners.

William had left her when he realized that she would never give him Ruari O'Neill. At first she had been devastated. At her lowest point, she had begged him for one more chance. He had promised to meet her in a room at the Shelbourne but he never came. His son had shown up instead. Then she had found out that she was pregnant. Ruairi vowed he would kill General Gainsborough twice if he ever had the chance.

As the months went by, Rosaleen was reminded more and more of Billy but she had never allowed herself to believe that he was thinking of her too. She swore to herself that she would take the truth of who had fathered her child to her grave.

An unfortunate day in the middle of September changed her mind. The IRA had orchestrated two strikes, one in Dublin and one in Balbriggan. Ruairi was to be in Balbriggan but the attack in Dublin had caught Rosaleen's attention. Billy Gainsborough was a member of the company that had been targeted for an arms raid. She knew that her only chance to ensure his safety would be to inform General Gainsborough and have the raid disrupted. It had never occurred to her that William would demand something in return. She listened in horror as he telephoned the barracks in Gormanstown. The Black and Tans were given their orders to pick Ruairi up in Balbriggan.

On the morning of September 20th, 1920, Rosaleen woke up in a cold sweat. Ruairi was asleep beside her, his arm rested protectively over her swollen belly. She clung to him, tears streaming down her face when he tried to leave her for Balbriggan. She knew what the Black and Tans were capable of. She begged Ruairi to stay in Dublin and he finally relented, sending one of the younger boys in his place and overseeing the ambush in Dublin from a safe spot on North King Street instead.

Rosaleen had thought she had averted the disaster until she saw Billy step out of the lorry in front of Monk's Bakery. William had gambled his son's life. She held her breath and prayed that he would just lay down his weapon. She screamed when the first shot was fired. When it was over, Billy's body lay face down on the street. One British soldier was dead and a few more were seriously injured.

She remembered pushing Ruairi out of the motorcar, forcing him to risk his life for the Gainsborough boy.

Rosaleen muffled her sobs with the blanket as she remembered Ruairi's face when he had heard the news. The injured soldiers had died and Kevin Barry had been arrested. Ruairi was furious with her. He had pulled a British soldier to safety and unknowingly left one of his own under the lorry; one that would now be on trial for his life.

Ruairi had no choice. He sent Thomas and Mairtin to capture the General and bring him in. He would destroy William's credibility with his son and with the British Army. Then he would kill him.

Rosaleen knew that Billy would remain alive as long as Ruairi had no knowledge of their affair. But William once again used his son's life as collateral.

In an effort to silence him and keep Ruairi free from the truth of her betrayal, she disappeared with William, trading her conscience for his version of tactical manoeuvring. He had promised her sanctuary but she awoke in the streets, brutalized and broken.

By the time Ruairi found her, she had already heard. It had been all over the wireless. Eighteen year old Kevin Barry had been sentenced to death for his part in the ambush. And Balbriggan had been burned to the ground.

A cold breeze snapped her back to the present. She squeezed her eyes shut to stop the tears that were falling but the memories began replaying themselves again. An explosion of colours appeared on her eyelids and she could see houses and shopfronts ablaze. The Black and Tans raided Balbriggan in reprisal for the shooting of RIC Head Constable Peter Burke that afternoon. They were seeking out one suspect in particular but no mercy was paid to the rest of the town. Families ran screaming from their houses as the town was set alight. Seamus Lawless and Sean Gibbons were captured and bayoneted to death. Ruairi O'Neill was never found and Rosaleen would never be able to bring herself to imagine what would have happened if she hadn't begged him to stay in Dublin.

The day after she arrived home with her baby girl, her father was shot by Black and Tan commanders. The day after that, her mother took her own life. Ruairi was on the run again, slipping in for midnight visits and leaving long before dawn. He would sleep next to her but he refused to hold her.

Rosaleen crouched down and rubbed her eyes. She needed the images gone. She needed to leave Ireland. She couldn't smile at the same people and love the same land that she had helped desecrate. Her guilty conscience followed her down every street and around every corner. She wanted a new life for Kathleen and she needed to let Ruairi move on. He had wasted four years of his life protecting her from the stares and gossiping, while also fighting the Civil War. He had made sure that Kathleen wouldn't be taken away from her by the Catholic Church and Rosaleen had never had to fear destitution.

As always, Ruairi had saved her.

She looked back at the black water.

"What are you thinking about?" Billy asked softly from behind her.

"Death," she answered him truthfully.

Billy looked across the water. The moon had drawn a pathway to the night. He wrapped his arms around her. She was freezing. It was easy to think of death on a night like that. "Come back to bed," he said as he led her away from the balcony.

Rosaleen fell asleep in Billy's arms. He held her tightly to his body and she felt safe for those precious few hours. But when she woke up the darkness brought back the fear. She carefully slid her body out of his grasp and tiptoed out into the hallway.

She saw the double doors at the end of the hall and couldn't help herself. She slipped silently into the room. He was there with his beautiful wife. Rosaleen studied her carefully. Everything about her was perfect, even in her sleep and Rosaleen envied her. Except for the man sleeping beside her, she had everything.

She looked at William and felt her insides tighten. She imagined him cold, lifeless, bloodied.

She turned to leave and noticed how badly her hand shook as she closed the door behind her.

CHAPTER 8

G racie limped her way along the cobbled streets, careful not to turn her ankle in her new heels. Ruairi had tried to take hold of her arm a couple of times but she continued to make it very clear that she didn't need or want his help. She desperately needed more of the pain tablets he had bought but she wasn't ready to break her silence.

In her head she kept going over what Mairtin had told her about her father's actions. She remembered the few times William had spoken about his time in Ireland. He had convinced her that the Irish were a horrible race; heathens running around murdering each other with pitchforks and shovels. She thought back to the breakfast where she and her mother had sat, horrified by his account of the Easter Rising in 1916. He had spoken of his devastation that allies would turn on the Crown in the middle of the greatest war the world had ever seen, splitting England's defences and leaving her vulnerable to German advances. He had detailed the act of treason; Pádraig Pearse leading his Irish Volunteers to a Republic, entirely separate from Great Britain, owing no allegiance to her King. He had shown her the pictures of the Dublin General Post Office as it smouldered under the weight of a week of British shelling. She remembered how proud she had been of her countrymen when they had executed the leaders; a wall of stone painted with the blood of traitors.

Tonight, she had no pride left. Not in her country, not in her family, and not in herself. She felt she was complicit in the death of a nation.

Suddenly, her stomach turned. She leaned over and vomited. She tried to turn away from Ruairi, embarrassed, but when she moved, she retched again. He was at her side immediately. As she stood, doubled over, he reached around and gathered her hair, pulling it away from her face. She vomited until there was nothing left in her. Then she began to cry again.

He was like a beautiful masterpiece, painted with colours that Gracie had never even known existed. But the moment that she had touched him, the picture was ruined and he was suddenly something ugly, scarred and imperfect. She heaved.

Ruairi picked her up and carried her down the last street to the motorcar. She had no energy left to resist him.

Ruairi could barely hear her breathing as they drove towards the boat. He forced himself to focus on the bright white path of the headlights while all around him the shades of grey faded to black. He set his jaw and forced himself to show no emotion. Inside, he beat himself up for letting this happen. He should have killed General Gainsborough that night so many years ago. It would have destroyed fewer lives. The Gainsborough family would have never known, to them William would have died a hero and Gracie would have had nothing but wonderful memories of her father. It was Ruairi's fault for not aiming at his head the moment that he had him in his sights.

He slowed down as he approached the boat. He looked around carefully and then parked near the dock.

"I'm just going to check the boat, make sure everything's okay," he said softly. He didn't trust taking her on board without knowing there was nobody else waiting for him. She didn't need any more scares that night.

After a thorough check of the boat he helped her from the motorcar and took her aboard. There was one tiny bunk in the cabin where he would put her and he would spend the night on the deck, guarding the door to the cabin.

She sat on the wooden floorboards, slowly unbuckling her shoes. He knelt down in front of her and checked her foot again. It was swollen and bruised.

"I have some water in a jug in the cabin. I'll give you some more of those tablets and you can rinse your mouth out. I'm sure you don't have the best taste in it right now. I'm sorry about the whiskey. I shouldn't have made you drink it," he was very quiet, his voice husky.

"It wasn't the whiskey," she finally responded. She wiped her eyes, exhausted. "Was what he said true? Did my father really use Rosaleen to get information to . . ." she couldn't bring herself to say kill, "to hurt all of those people?"

"Aye."

"Did he really send the Black and Tans out to hunt you and kill you?"

"Aye."

"I'm sorry," she said, leaning her head against the cabin.

Ruairi looked at the girl sadly. She didn't seem to understand war. "It's not your fault," he said softly.

"Can I ask you one more question?" she asked.

"Of course you can."

"Did he really know that you were going to ambush the lorry?"

Ruairi grimaced. He tried a diplomatic answer. "I don't believe he intended for your brother to get hurt."

"That wasn't my question."

Ruairi hesitated, "I can honestly tell you that what happened that day was out of your father's control. It was out of all of our control."

Gracie let out a heart-wrenching sob. "They didn't go looking for Billy until hours after though, right?"

Ruairi looked away. He knew where she was headed. He had asked the same questions, over and over.

She pressed on, "If he had tried to save Billy, they would have ambushed the ambush. Do you know what I mean?"

Ruairi knew what she meant. He couldn't look at her. He suddenly understood Billy's compulsion to protect her from the truth.

But she had uncovered the lie. "I need to know why you saved Billy."

"Rosaleen made a deal. Billy lives, William dies."

"I don't understand." Gracie reached up for help to stand.

Ruairi lifted her gently. "Neither do I," he sighed. "Or at least I tell myself that I don't."

Gracie looked up at him. "What do you mean by that?"

Ruairi reached down and brushed her hair back from her face and then kissed her forehead softly. "I mean nothing, Love; nothing that makes a difference anyway."

Ruairi produced a jug of water. She was standing near the front of the boat. She rinsed out her mouth, and leaned over the railing. He couldn't help but smile watching her, with all her class, spitting over the side of a boat.

She turned back to him to get the tablets and noticed him watching her. "I'm really attractive now, aren't I?" She shook her head.

"You're beautiful," Ruairi said seriously.

Gracie's eyes watered. The way he was looking at her made her tremble. He had taken the most horrible moment and made it wonderful.

Before he knew what he was doing, he had closed the distance between them.

He put his hands on her hips and pinned her against the railing. He slowly lowered his head and kissed her lips. She didn't pull away. Instead, she moved her body as close to him as she could. She opened her mouth and let him explore the heat inside her. He tightened his grip on her and lifted her until she was seated on the railing. She circled her legs around his body and nuzzled her head into his neck. He could feel her tongue and her lips and her hot breath.

He had to stop her. His body was screaming at him but he knew that he had to protect her from himself.

"Why?" she asked him, breathing heavy.

He swallowed, trying to relax his body, "We can't be together, ever. It's just wrong."

"Let me be with you, Ruairi, even if it's just tonight. I . . . I need this." She looked up at him with pleading eyes. She wanted him to hold her together. She would break if he let go now.

"Believe me you don't want to do this."

"I need to do this," she repeated, leaning in to kiss him again.

He kissed her back but pulled away early. "You want a man like Johnny."

"Johnny is an unfaithful dog." Her big blue eyes watered. She hesitated, and then admitted, "I knew what I was doing when I came down to the docks. I wanted to be with you then and I want to be with you now."

"I have nothing to offer you. I'm a monster, remember?"

Gracie looked down at his body. "I don't know what you are but I want to find out." She unbuttoned his vest.

He groaned, "I'm dangerous, I'm a bad . . ." He kissed her again, very close to losing control.

She pulled at his shirt to un-tuck it. A thump as the pistol hit the deck quickly brought Ruairi back to reality and he backed up.

"What was that?" she asked looking down at darkness.

Ruairi hesitated, "A gun."

Gracie's face froze. "You *were* going to shoot me."

Ruairi tried not to laugh at her outright. "The gun is for protection, Gracie, and I had no intention of shooting you. I promise." He hugged her to him and pulled her off the railing, setting her down on the deck. He picked up the gun and handed it to her. "You need to trust me, Gracie, you are safe with me. I think you'd shoot me before I ever shot you."

The gun was heavy in her hands. She gave it back to him quickly, not liking the feel of it. He slid it into the pocket of his trousers.

"Do you always carry a gun?" she asked, morbidly curious.

"No. Just when I think I might need it."

"Why did you need it today?"

"The meeting I went to was a bit tense."

"Was it with other rumrunners?" she asked, her eyes big.

He laughed again, "What do you know about rumrunners?"

"Nothing," she chirped, "but I heard that you are one."

He smiled. "The meeting was with some of the old boys from Ireland. They had some messages for me." He looked at her. He realized that the best way to leave her would be to tell her the short version of the truth. "They don't want me having anything to do with you or your family because of the unfinished . . ." he drifted off.

"The unfinished business with my father," she said quietly.

He sighed, turning away from her. "I'm sorry, Gracie, I shouldn't have touched you like that."

Gracie was silent for a moment. She felt a strange mix of feelings tumbling around inside of her. "What if, just for tonight, we put all of this aside?" she asked him.

He wrinkled his forehead. "Why would you want to do that?"

She walked towards him, stopping only when she was close enough to put her hands on his chest and feel his heart beat jump at her touch. "For you, stealing my virtue would be second only to killing me in terms of hurting my father. And for me, giving myself to you is a tiny bit of penance for what my father has done."

He smiled down at her slowly. "Being with me would be like doing penance?" he asked amused.

She shook her head, blushing softly. "No, not really but I have no other way of making it look like a sacrifice on my part."

"What changed your mind? It was barely an hour ago that you were screaming at me in an alleyway. You told me we could never be friends, now you want to be my lover." He watched her closely and saw her struggling with something deep down inside. "Or is this just about getting back at Johnny?"

"No!" Gracie was adamant, and then she softened, "I mean, maybe at first it was, I just wanted someone to give me attention, but now . . ." Gracie felt the nausea again as she thought about the words that she had said that had led them to this moment. "I don't want to hate you, Ruairi, I want to fall in love with you. There is something so beautiful about you but it's hard to make out," she paused. "So, just for tonight, I want to keep looking."

"Gracie, I can't afford to fall in love with anyone; especially you."

"Because of Rosaleen?" she asked.

Ruairi felt an angry stirring. "Rosaleen has nothing to do with this."

"Mairtin made it clear that you love her and only her."

"I did once." His words seemed far away.

"You don't love her anymore?"

Ruairi bit his lip. "I still love her. Just a bit differently than I used to."

"So there's room for someone like me, maybe?" She kept her eyes downcast, scared of another rejection.

Ruairi lifted her chin. "I think you managed to squeeze yourself in there, somehow," he smiled at her, "but nothing can come of it, no matter how much I feel for you, Love."

"I know that it could never be forever between us but maybe we could just have this moment." She leaned up towards him, letting his slow breathing sweep across her face.

"Maybe," he said, very softly, before kissing her again. "But Gracie, I'm not going to . . ."

She put a finger to his lips. "Please don't say no to me. Not tonight."

He chuckled. "Nobody says no to you, do they now?" It was going to be a long night for his screaming body. He held out his hand to her. "Dance with me, Gracie."

"There's no music," she said.

"Wait here," he said, stealing quickly into the cabin and then returning with a gramophone.

"I can't believe you have that on board," she giggled.

He looked down at it. "It's not mine. But I wouldn't have thought it of the guys who own it either. They must have some very long days fishing."

She put her hand in his and he pulled her to him. They danced under the stars until Gracie's foot hurt too much. Then, she took two more tablets and led him into the cabin.

"Can you undo my dress for me please?" She turned her back to him.

He smiled at her impeccable manners. Even in sordid situations she was nothing less than classy. He undid the clasps and helped her slip it over her head. She had on a black silk slip underneath and a black garter belt holding up her black stockings. She made sure he watched as she undid the straps on the garter belt and slowly rolled the stockings down. She stood up and started to unbutton his shirt. Her fingers trembled. He clamped his hands around her wrists to stop her but she just leaned in and kissed him. He groaned.

Soon, she had his shirt off and was working on his undervest.

"Are you sure this is what you want?" His brown eyes were very serious and very dark.

She nodded, her blue eyes glistening, "Please don't try to talk me out of this."

Afterwards, they spent the night clinging to each other on the little bunk. She prayed over and over that the morning wouldn't come but right on cue, the morning sun poked its way into the tiny cabin. Ruairi sat up and stretched. Gracie tried to pull him back down to her but he pulled away from her gently.

"I have to get you home," he said quietly. He stood up, pulled on his undervest and pants and put the pistol back in his waistband. He walked outside to find Mairtin having a cigarette on the dock.

"What the hell are you doing here?" Ruairi hissed, jumping down onto the dock.

Mairtin gave him a steady look. "We're all a bit worried, Ruairi."

Ruairi rubbed his face and growled. He reached for the cigarette and took a long drag. "It's all fine, Mairty. I'm taking her home and cutting all association. She already knows."

Mairtin shook his head. "Aye, you say that, Ruairi. But you seem to have a way of picking up strays. You try to take care of everybody and I'm just here to tell you that it's none of your concern what happens to that girl. You didn't mess up her family. It was messed up long before you were involved."

"You don't think I know that?"

"I think you know it, but I think you think you can fix it. Killing the General isn't going to fix it and not killing him is going to make it worse. You need to stay away from her." Mairtin took the smoke back and flicked the ashes.

Ruairi knew he was right of course but it was already too late. She was burned into every crevice of his consciousness and his body was now intimately attuned to hers.

"Don't you want him dead?" Mairtin looked at him, trying to pry into his thoughts.

Ruairi sighed. "Of course I want him dead. It's just more complicated than that."

Mairtin slapped him on the shoulder and butted out his cigarette. "It's only more complicated because of that girl. Let go of her now and then we'll figure out what to tell Rosaleen when we get back. Once we have that sorted, you'll see things clearer."

"You've been told to watch me, haven't you? They want somebody looking over my shoulder that I won't kill." Ruairi knew the way upper command worked.

"Well, you did a number on that poor kid yesterday and they figured I could keep an eye out for you without seeming suspicious."

"Did you tell them you have trouble moving without looking suspicious?" Ruairi teased.

Mairtin looked down. "You know I wouldn't . . . I'm just here to make sure you don't do anything rash."

Ruairi nodded. "Honestly Mairtin, which of the two of us has the better record for wise decisions?"

Mairtin's smile looked more evil than pleasant. "They don't know me very well, do they?"

"You'll tell me anything I may need to know?" Ruairi's question was more of a demand.

Mairtin nodded and then walked off down the pier.

"Say good morning to Aisling for me," Ruairi called after him.

Mairtin kept his back to him but stuck up his middle finger as he walked away.

Gracie lay in the tiny bunk, listening to the creaking of the boat as it rocked in the early morning breeze. While she waited for him to come back to her she thought about her reasons for being so impulsive. They seemed less clear now, not that she would have made a different decision this morning. She just needed him to reaffirm her feelings.

He appeared in the cabin again, seeming a bit off balance. He was rummaging through his canvas bag for something. "Are you going to get up?" he asked her.

Gracie sat up on her elbows. "I was hoping maybe we could talk."

"About what?" Ruairi asked lightly, not looking up. He didn't seem to be able to make eye contact.

"About last night," Gracie felt slightly awkward now, wondering if she hadn't been good company through the night.

Ruairi eyed her warily. "Why don't you get dressed and you can talk to me while I ready the boat?"

Gracie sat up further, pulling the blanket up around her chest as she moved. She was suddenly very self-conscious. "I want to talk now."

"I can't . . . I can't talk to you while you're . . ." He motioned to her state of undress.

"You seemed fine with me like this last night," she grumbled.

"Yes, but last night we were . . . and this morning we aren't, so . . ." It was Ruairi's turn to be self-conscious. He didn't trust his self-control. "If you don't put some clothes on, I'm going to end up back in bed with you and we'll never get on with this."

Gracie blushed when she realized his reason for averting his eyes. It made her feel strangely satisfied. "You know, we could just go back to bed for an hour or so."

Ruairi smiled and reached for the door. "We've got to be clear about this, Gracie. It's too easy to make a mess of it. It's going to be hard enough as it is to stay away from you now."

Gracie looked up, searching for his eyes. "It is going to be hard," she agreed. "I wouldn't have thought so."

"Really? I had no doubt in my mind." He smiled gently and left her alone to get dressed.

She put on the light blue jersey shift from the day before. It was more appropriate than the black dress. When she finally appeared on deck, the sun was already bright in the morning sky. She shielded her eyes with her hand as she watched him prepare the boat for the trip. He was more handsome than ever this morning and Gracie found herself fantasizing about running away with him. They could leave now, just sail away. She smiled.

"What are you smiling about?" he asked as he strode by.

"Nothing, really," she lied.

He smiled back at her. "I bet I could guess."

She raised her eyebrows and looked at him expectantly. He was quiet for a moment as he concentrated on manoeuvring the boat into open water. "You're thinking exactly the same thing I am. You're wondering what it would be like if we just took off together."

Gracie began to deny it but her cheeks gave her away. "You were thinking that too?" she finally conceded.

"I've been thinking it all night. It wouldn't work out though, even if we were very far away," he stated.

"Why not?" she asked, following him around the boat.

"I'd get sick of you," he said casually, leaning over the railing and looping a large white rope through a carabineer on the side.

"What?" she squeaked, instantly offended.

He rolled his eyes. "I'd definitely get sick of that!"

They both started to laugh. He grabbed her arm and spun her around so that she was caught between the railing and his body. They were quiet as their bodies reacted to the closeness. She felt him lifting her in his arms but she saw nothing but brightness. She wove her fingers through his hair, kissing him hungrily. He pulled back long enough to make sure they were far enough out of the harbour and then he lay her down on the deck and gave in.

"I have to check our course," he whispered softly to her. Her eyes were closed and he wasn't sure if she was awake.

She smiled gradually, "I hope we're lost."

He chuckled, "You are making my life very difficult, Gracie Gainsborough." A few minutes later he returned to her. "I'm sorry, Love, we're not lost."

"Hmm . . ." Gracie pretended to pout but it got lost in her smile as he lay down and nuzzled back into her chest. The sun was warm and delicious and Gracie didn't want to move.

"You wanted to talk before," Ruairi reminded her.

Gracie slowly opened her eyes. "I wanted to know how we were going to do this."

"Apparently not well," Ruairi laughed.

Gracie sighed. "Are you going to stay in Charlottetown?" she tried to keep her voice light.

"No. I'm only here for a few more weeks. Rosaleen needs to get settled and then . . ." he trailed off.

"Where will you go?"

"Home," he said quietly. His accent was thicker on the word.

Gracie suddenly felt the weight of his head on her chest. It felt like it was pushing all the air out of her lungs. She gasped for a breath.

"Are you okay?" he rolled over, bracing himself over top of her.

She felt hot tears streaming down her face and the harder she fought to stop them, the faster they came. "I'm sorry, I don't know what's come over me."

"Ah, Gracie," he sat up, pulling her to him and rocking her gently. "I'm sorry I dragged your little heart into all of this."

"Don't apologize, Ruairi, please don't apologize for making me feel wanted," she managed to say.

He pulled her to him tighter and cursed the General over and over in his head.

Billy knew the moment Rosaleen had left. The space beside him had suddenly gone cold. He had struggled with whether or not he should follow her but he had thought better of it. It was too dangerous with Ruairi in the dark.

He had lain awake for another hour, remembering every second of the first time. She had been wearing a black evening gown and an obscene amount of diamonds. She was sitting at the vanity when he entered the room and she had seen him in the mirror. She didn't turn around, just stared straight at his reflection.

"He isn't coming, is he?" she had asked softly.

He had shaken his head no but hadn't taken his eyes off of her reflection either. She was much more beautiful than he had ever imagined a woman to be; stunning, in fact.

She had dropped her head. He could clearly see the tears shining off her face. "He didn't believe I would give him Ruairi then." She had lifted her gaze back to the mirror, the full effect of her sorrowful eyes locked on Billy. "He was wrong."

Billy had felt the tragedy in her voice. "I'm sure he loved you."

She turned and smiled at him, a strange smile; the type of smile that makes the masters weep into their paintbrushes. Her tears dried up as quickly as they had sprung and she had him under her spell. "Well," she had said finally, "I don't think that much matters now, does it? Would you like a cigarette?" She held a jewelled case out to him.

He took one, even though he never smoked. It gave him something to do with his shaking hands. He lit hers for her and then stood back, watching her smoke hers while his just burned away to a stub.

"Well, then, I guess I should leave," she had said with a steady voice. She had picked up a few belongings while she had smoked the cigarette and now she was ready to quit the room. As she had walked by him he had caught a trace of her perfume and reacted without thinking.

Just a gentle arm on hers, turning her towards him. It was the way she looked up at him through her thick lashes. She looked so vulnerable that he had kissed her. And then he had made love to her.

They made small talk for most of the rest of the trip. Gracie asked about Mairtin and Thomas and what their role was in the Irish Republican Army. Ruairi couldn't tell her much about what they did but he didn't mind telling her about who they were. He wanted to make sure she knew that they were human.

"Thomas is just like any little brother," he said, smiling. "He's always up to something and always needing me to get him out of it!" He paused, "Mairtin's different. He's tough to understand if you don't know him. He's a bloody good lad though and the best man to have at your back."

"He seems a bit mad to me," Gracie said.

Ruairi laughed. "He is mad! And he's rough. He can take down the best of them. He stands among the best of them too," he continued quietly. "I trust him with my life."

"I guess as a soldier, that's pretty important," Gracie felt compelled to listen to Ruairi about these men that she had once regarded as nothing more than murderers.

"In the end, it's all we have," Ruairi agreed.

"I've never known anyone to value life so much and so little at the same time. You desperately want to live a life of freedom and yet you are willing to kill and be killed to get it. It all seems so hypocritical to me. And anyways, didn't Ireland become a Republic in 1921?"

Ruairi stared out across the water at the mass looming on the horizon. "You're speaking about the partition of the South from the North. There's no such thing as freedom in the North . . . for either side. I can't abandon the North. I grew up in Belfast and my Ma is still there. I was only in Dublin for the Rising. I haven't really had a home since."

"Can you explain this partition to me?" Gracie asked.

"I wish someone could explain it to me," Ruairi said wryly but he relented. "In essence, the British government thought they could appease both sides by keeping the six northern counties part of Britain, and allowing Home Rule to the rest." Ruairi sighed. "And thus began the Civil War. Not really the freedom that we all wanted."

"What is the freedom you all want, really?" Gracie wondered aloud. "I mean, in truth, none of us are ever really free. I don't think I'm free. I have to do what my father tells me to do until I marry, and then I'm at the mercy of my husband." She raised her eyebrows and continued, "The suffragists can stomp around all they like but where does it get us, really? So should I pick up a gun and start shooting all the men? I ask you."

Ruairi chuckled. "Gracie Gainsborough, I don't think I gave you enough credit! That is an interesting point."

"Well, defend yourself to me! Make me believe that your cause is just," Gracie implored him with shiny blue eyes.

Ruairi took her hands and wrapped his fingers through hers. "To the philosophers, freedom is nothing but a lofty ideal; the ability to do whatever one wants without social or moral constraint. But take it out into the streets, take it to the common man and you have a different definition of freedom. Gracie, I'm not fighting for an ideal, I'm fighting for my life. I don't care about my philosophical freedom; I care about my physical and my spiritual freedom."

"By spiritual do you mean being Catholic?" she found herself entranced by Ruairi's passions. She was amazed at how mesmerizing he could be. She was pretty sure that if he continued he would also be powerfully persuasive.

He shook his head. "Religion is only a very small part of the spiritual. I mean the core of who I am; my essence, my spirit, my soul. I'm fighting for the freedom to just live," he paused before adding, "without fear."

"And yet you are instilling fear into the lives of those you've chosen as your enemies. What of their freedoms?"

Ruairi leaned back against the railing and sighed. The wind rustled his hair and the morning sun dipped his features in gold. "I have to take care of myself and my family."

They were both silent for a moment. Then Ruairi cleared his throat, "Can I ask you a question then?"

Gracie looked up and nodded.

"I can't fall in love with you for many reasons, not least because you're William Gainsborough's daughter. But why can't you fall in love with me?" His eyes burned with curiosity and something else that Gracie couldn't read.

"Because you want to kill my father," she said simply. She knew that was her best answer.

"So, if that wasn't my destiny, would you want to be . . ." he hesitated, almost choking on the words, "my girl?"

Gracie squinted as she looked out at the water. The sun was throwing spears of brilliant light off of the water's surface and the effect was almost blinding. "No," she lied. It was easier to lie to him than to make herself any more vulnerable. "You aren't a suitable match for me," she said, somewhat detached.

"Is that your way of saying I don't have enough money to marry you?" he asked directly.

"Well, honestly Ruairi, do you think that you could make a woman like me happy?"

He read her much better than she read him. "Yes, I do."

She sighed, exasperated. "How would you entertain me?"

He chuckled. "I think I've got that figured out."

She couldn't help but smile. "I'm serious. I'd have to give up my whole life for you."

"And you would do it if I asked you to." His eyes watched hers for any hint of an argument but there was none. She just stared back at him, unblinking. Then she dropped her eyes and he thought he could see them watering.

"Ask me to," she whispered.

He kept his eyes on her. "I can't do that to you."

"Ask me to give it all up," she demanded softly.

"And what if I kill your Da?"

Gracie flinched and the tears spilled slightly. She quickly wiped them away with the back of her hand. "Part of me thinks he deserves it which is terrible I know, and I'm sure that will change," she began softly, "but most of me doesn't believe it could happen. I can't believe that you are a killer."

Ruairi closed his eyes and sighed. "I don't know how to make you understand but this war is my life."

"So even after all of this, after me, you still want to kill him?" she asked, not daring to look at him. "Mairtin said you and my father can't exist together. Is that true? Is that why you came to Charlottetown?"

He grimaced. "I'm here for Rosaleen but she lied to me, Gracie. She knew your father was here and I think she thought that if I came over, I would kill him as soon as I saw him and then it would be done. This has to end, one way or the other."

The tears that had threatened unleashed themselves. They were angry tears. "Why is it so hard to just let it go?"

He shook his head slowly. Her fierce reaction made him wonder whether her loyalties were now split. "It's my job, Gracie, and I should have done it years ago."

"Why didn't you?" she asked impulsively. Her hand flew over her mouth as she realized how much she wished he had.

He hesitated, "I should have."

She stared at him, incredulous. "I can't believe you just said that."

"What did you want me to say?" he asked calmly.

Gracie leaned back against the cabin door, unable to look him in the eye. "You should have lied to me."

"I'll never lie to you."

"It would be better if you did," she said squarely.

He shook his head. "You need to accept who I am."

Gracie sighed. "I've always fancied my father a hero. I used to tell everybody that my father was a war hero."

Ruairi looked at her crushed face. "He can still be the hero and I can still be the traitor. Nobody would disagree with you. You don't have to believe me."

"It's not about whom I believe, Ruairi. It's about who is telling the truth."

Ruairi reached over and touched her face very gently. "The truth changes every time the story is told, Love."

They were in Charlottetown harbour by mid-morning and neither Ruairi nor Gracie was eager to say goodbye. After the boat had been tied up and all of their stuff put on the dock, Ruairi turned to her.

"So, have we said everything that needs to be said then?" he asked softly.

She tilted her head and looked up at him. "It seems the only thing left to say is goodbye."

He gazed back at her, "If you need me . . ."

Gracie put a finger to his lips to stop him. "Don't promise me that you'll be there. I can't bear to hear that."

"Don't marry Johnny."

"I might have to. I'm sure my father has already worked out a suitable apology for him to give to me. I told you, I'm no freer than you are."

"There are a million men out there . . . some will even be rich enough to keep you entertained," Ruairi argued with a sad smile.

"They're all the same, Ruairi. I know lots of wives who have husbands who have mistresses. It's just the way of the world."

"I wouldn't do that to you."

"Yes, well, I can't have you now, can I?" she reminded him softly.

"Well, if you do marry the gobshite, can you at least promise me that you'll have your own sordid affair?" he asked, a cheeky twinkle in his eye.

Gracie winked at him. "I already have."

He laughed heartily. "That's a good girl."

"You aren't really going to kill him, are you?" Gracie asked one more time, hoping for some sort of promise.

He avoided the question. "This will probably be the last time we have a chance to speak to each other. You won't see much of me from here on out. I'll be headed back to Ireland soon."

She stepped forward and wrapped her arms around him. He let her kiss him one more time. "Please don't . . ." her tiny voice cracked.

He cringed slightly. "I'm sorry, Gracie," he whispered into her ear. Then he pushed her away from him. He picked up his bag and looked her in the eye. "Take care of yourself, Miss Gainsborough." He turned and walked off down the dock and disappeared.

Lana Hamilton had decided to take a stroll along the pier before stopping in at Audrey Gilmour's for the open house.

She hadn't gone more than a few hundred metres when she had seen them. Gracie Gainsborough was with the Irishman again and they were looking at each other with a strange familiarity. Then Gracie had leaned in and clutched him to her in an intimate embrace. Lana could feel the heat rising in her own blood as their lips met and she watched the rum runner's hands move slowly around her waist, gripping her softly at the ribcage. Then he had pushed her away but the intensity had remained, suffocating Lana as if all of the air had been allotted to the two lovers breathing heavily into each other's mouths.

Lana licked her lips and smiled. Now she had a scandal worth talking about.

Genevieve sat across the table from the other ladies lost in thought. She had played tennis in the morning and then all of the women had decided to have lunch at the Club. Every one of the ladies had expressed their condolences about the shameful way that the engagement party had been disrupted but Genevieve knew that they were all secretly enjoying the gossip. Eleanor's absence that morning had fuelled talk that there was a growing rift between the two women. Truth be known, Genevieve had never liked Eleanor Bexley, she had just tolerated her for the sake of the friendship between Lucas and William.

Genevieve had been anxious since yesterday when Billy had told her that Gracie had gone away with Norah. She hoped that Gracie wasn't too distraught over the way the night had ended. She was actually elated that her daughter had escaped marriage so narrowly. But she was sure that her daughter would be crushed by the circumstances.

She had also done a lot of thinking about her brush with Rosaleen Jameson. She didn't know whether she admired or hated the young woman. She blamed the affair entirely on William and she intended to make him pay for it for the rest of his life, however long that would be. But she was wary of the girl as well. Genevieve was not about to be a mere pawn in this dark queen's chess game. She had moves of her own to play.

She tried to bring herself back to the conversation at hand. It was something about the latest temperance meeting. One of the women was adamantly saying that laws would have to get stricter if they were going to keep Prince Edward Island dry. She was sure it was the same lady she had seen guzzling champagne at the party.

"How does this place operate so openly?" she was asking, "I mean, everybody knows that Mr. Johansen commiserates with bootleggers and that he has gallons of liquor in the basement."

The ladies all tried to look angered by this but Genevieve knew that each one was secretly hoping that the others wouldn't blow the whistle on the Club. Liquor was the only thing that kept these women relatively tame.

Genevieve's eyes perused the room and landed on two gentlemen outside on the patio, beyond the doors. She excused herself and made her way towards them. One of the gentlemen was the owner of the club, Karl Johansen. Genevieve was interested in the other one.

After Genevieve had left the table, Mrs. Chatham leaned over the table conspiratorially and whispered loudly, "Eleanor says there's trouble between Genevieve and William."

"I heard William had an affair and Genevieve hasn't allowed him to come to her bed since she found out," said Mrs. Lexington.

"Do you want to know the truth?" Juliette Hamilton sat near the center of the gathering and had a smug look on her face. "I've heard from very reliable sources that William moved his mistress and their daughter over to Canada just a few weeks ago. One day, just recently, Genevieve saw a little girl that looked remarkably like Gracie when she was young. The child was sitting in the bakery alone at a table, so Genevieve went in to have a closer look at her. Apparently, she had quite the conversation with the little girl until some young man appeared, claiming to be the little girl's father."

Mrs. Chatham's eyes were big. "Did Genevieve confront William?"

"Nobody's quite sure. In public Genevieve and William are still acting as if they have the perfect marriage and of course my source isn't able to be around for the private conversations."

"Who is your source?" Another lady asked hungry for gossip.

Juliette Hamilton smiled mischievously. "I've been sworn to secrecy, Ladies. You'll just have to be content to know that this is the truth," she paused dramatically, "but there is something curious about the whole thing. His mistress is an Irishwoman."

The salacious nature of that accusation was enough to keep the ladies occupied for the rest of the afternoon.

Genevieve stepped out into the sunshine and smiled at the men. "Lord Michael," she said graciously, extending her hand to him.

Mick grinned and took her hand in his. "Didn't I tell you to call me Mick?"

Karl gave him a funny look.

"Do you know Mr. Karl Johanson?" Mick asked, motioning to him.

"Of course," Genevieve said. "It's a pleasure to see you again, Karl."

Karl nodded at her but wondered if she saw. Her eyes were focussed on Mick. He decided to excuse himself and allow the lady her privacy. When he was gone, Mick cleared his throat.

"Genevieve, wasn't it?"

"*Lady* Genevieve," she corrected him, teasingly.

"Well, Lady Genevieve, what brings you out on this lovely day?" Mick knew he was a bit out of his element so he would have to rely on his wit to charm her.

She blushed as she responded, "Just morning tea after an early tennis lesson. Do you play tennis, Mick?"

He smiled at her, "No, I prefer the sport of kings."

"A punter then, I suppose?" she asked.

He laughed, "You surprise me, Genevieve. I think there is a bit of commoner in you."

She feigned a look of disdain. "How dare you?"

"Do you frequent the races?" he asked her.

"Occasionally when my husband feels we ought to be seen together," Genevieve said dryly.

"And how often is that?" he asked, looking her over.

"Why do you ask?" she pursed her lips.

"I was just wondering if you had to be seen with him next Sunday or if you might want to attend the races with me?" There was a mischievous twinkle in his eye.

"I'm a married woman, Michael, it wouldn't be very proper for me to be seen out with you."

"I don't think you care much about being proper," he said slowly, "but I was more thinking that it would be a wonderful chance for you to meet Valerie."

She raised her eyebrow and then laughed, "You must have read my mind. That is exactly why I've sought you out."

He leaned in close and whispered to her, "Unfortunately, that is why most ladies have been seeking me out lately. I fear Ms. Logan may be slightly more fetching than I am."

"I doubt that is the the truth," she laughed. Their eyes met. Genevieve smiled at him and looked back in at the ladies drinking their tea. "Is there any chance that I could meet with her before next Sunday?"

"Do you have plans right now?" he asked.

CHAPTER 9

Rosaleen sat by herself with a cup of tea in the small kitchen of the two story walk-up that she shared with the rest of the Irish crew. The house was a vibrant blue with white trim and a little white veranda out the front.

"Cuppa tea?" she asked Thomas as he stumbled into the kitchen. The lot of them had turned up not long after Rosaleen had woken up. She had walked aimlessly around Charlottetown thinking about her predicament before returning home and passing out on the porch swing.

He smiled. "I'd love one."

Rosaleen made the tea and let it steep for a few minutes. She kept her back to him, not wanting to make small talk. She had too much on her mind and Thomas was too much of a gentleman to speak honestly with her.

"Milk and sugar?" she asked, forgetting how he liked it.

"Just sugar, thank you, and lots of it."

She giggled. "Here you are," she said, handing a teacup to him.

He took a sip and made a face. "A wee bit strong. You're definitely your Ma's daughter. I can remember her tea. It used to make my stomach ache." He winced.

"Ma used to say I made it so that my spoon stood up in it."

Thomas smiled. "I think the spoon hopped out and ran away before it rusted!"

"Trying her tea?" Aisling's voice piped up from the doorway. "You must not have had the pleasure before! I obviously should have warned you about it."

Rosaleen gave her a dirty look then turned back to Thomas. "Ungrateful, she is."

Thomas laughed cheerfully as Ruairi walked in.

"I didn't realize you were back," Rosaleen said, staring at Ruairi. "You're a bit worse for wear, aren't you?"

Ruairi was fairly dishevelled. His trousers were wrinkled and a few of the buttons on his shirt were missing. "Long night and early morning," he said stiffly. "Where the bloody hell were you last night that you didn't make it to bed?" Ruairi had seen her curled up on the porch swing when he had come in.

Rosaleen glared at him. "None of your business." She didn't like what his tone implied.

"Were you with him?" he asked directly, a slight snarl in his voice.

"By him, I'm assuming you mean William?" Rosaleen's eyes hardened.

Ruairi ran his fingers through his hair and sniffed. He didn't answer her.

"No, I wasn't with him. Not that it is any of your concern."

"Then who were you with?" Ruairi pressed.

Rosaleen flicked her hair back from her face and squared her chin to him. "I was with Billy."

Ruairi groaned. "Ah, bloody hell Róisín!" He slammed his palm down on the bench top then reached out to pour himself a cup of tea.

"Calm down. I made you some breakfast." Rosaleen pushed a plate towards him. She thought that would be enough to appease him. It was loaded with food that none of the others had had the pleasure of. She was obviously trying to make up for something.

Ruairi looked at her. His jaw twitched. "I think you and I need to have a chat."

"How about we leave this unsavoury business till after breakfast, hmm?" Aisling nodded towards Kathleen, who had just pattered into the room. Ruairi understood. He went over to the little girl and picked her up, tossing her casually up over his head. "Good morning, my little faëry," he whispered as he kissed her on the cheek.

"Where were you last night?" Kathleen asked Ruairi in her best effort to sound disappointed even though she had a silly grin on her face. "I thought you were going to be home to tuck me in? Peggy doesn't tell me any stories."

"Didn't you know I was in Halifax?" he asked back, giving her a bear hug, and then placing her down on her chair at the table.

She shook her head and her black curls bounced around her face. He laughed and tugged on one playfully. "We'll have to get Auntie Maggie to come over. She tells the best stories," he said as he sat down next to her and devoured his meal.

When he had finished he pulled the little girl into his lap and cuddled her to him. "Would you like to go for a swim at Auntie Valerie's a bit later?" he asked her.

Her face lit up. "Yes!" she cried, "I'll go find my bathers!" She climbed down from his knee and ran as fast as her little legs would go up to the second floor.

Ruairi looked around at the rest of the table. "I think you all need to find yourselves something to do as well."

Each pair of eyes turned to look at Rosaleen who was still standing near the sink.

"Well, let's get on with it then," she said flippantly. "Obviously Ruairi has something he needs to say to me." Deep down a tiny ball of fear was knotting in her stomach.

The table cleared quickly and the room emptied. Rosaleen turned to face Ruairi.

"It's over," he said to her.

"Don't be so dramatic," she chastised him. "What is over?"

"Whatever game you are playing with the Gainsboroughs. I'm moving you out of here."

"You can't do that!"

"I can do whatever I damn well please!" Ruairi exploded. "I can't take this anymore, Rosaleen. I've got people watching me because everybody's wondering when I'm going to have had enough of your shite. And this time I have! You're going to get me killed or worse!"

"You're the one spending weekends with the girl! If you'd just do your fecking job we could get on with this," she yelled back at him.

"And what's my fecking job?" he asked angrily.

She hesitated, realizing she had made a dangerous turn. "You're supposed to be here for me!" she finally yelled.

There was a spark in his eyes. "Do you know how much I have done for you already?"

"Then go!" she screamed at him, "Go and leave me here!"

"You know that I can't do that! You know that I won't leave you unprotected!"

"Why? Because of some ridiculous geis that Maggie laid on you while she danced around the fire when we were children? Grow up, Ruairi! Stop believing in the faëries and the Fianna and for God's sake stop believing in Ireland!"

Ruairi went cold with anger. "I don't protect you because of a geis, I protect you because I love you," his voice was like steel. "And Ireland is the only thing I do believe in; Ireland and you."

Rosaleen slammed her teacup down, shattering it on the hard benchtop. "Well you need to stop believing in me too! I am not Ireland and I am not yours!"

"You don't know who you are Roísín! That's the tragedy! But God knows you aren't mine! I was never good enough for you, was I?" His eyes burned indignantly. "But you seem to forget that if it wasn't for me, you would be in a Magdalene laundry repenting for your sins!"

"I never asked you to take care of me! I didn't need you!"

"No, you didn't, did you? General Gainsborough was looking after you so well, wasn't he? You've got one bastard child to the father; do you think you need one to the son?" His words stung.

"I hate you!" she picked up the teapot and threw it at him. It smashed against the wall. Then she ran up the stairs, tears streaming down her face.

It wasn't until she was gone that Ruairi saw that Kathleen had come back into the room. She looked up at him with her big blue eyes full of tears.

"You aren't really going to leave us are you, Ruairi?" she asked in her soft voice.

Ruairi squatted down beside her and pulled her onto his lap. He sighed and stroked her hair as she settled into his chest. "I'm sorry, my little love, I didn't mean for you to hear all of that." He took a deep breath. "I'm not leaving you anytime soon."

Genevieve was intrigued by Michael Fitzgerald. He had a gentle way about him even though his voice was rough and his character unpolished. He was beautiful in the most bizarre sense of the word.

He had taken her down to the water and they sat against the wall of the cannery recently purchased by himself and his son. He had planned on meeting Valerie there within the hour. He had some saltine crackers and bits of cheese stored in a little lunchbox and he had pulled a bottle of wine off of a boat that they had gone by. Genevieve had argued that it was too early for wine but he had insisted and she had given in. They sat across from each other, both leaning against different piles of crates.

"What were you doing at the engagement party, Michael?" Genevieve asked.

"Mick," he corrected her.

"I prefer Michael," she countered. "Is that a problem?"

He gritted his teeth. He knew why she was refusing to call him Mick but he chose to ignore it. There were other ways of making her come around. "I was there with Ruairi O'Neill," Mick levelled with her.

"I figured as much. It seems a bit suspicious that two lots of Irishmen would arrive uninvited."

"I take it there weren't too many Irishmen on the guest list?" Mick asked, a bit tersely.

Genevieve tried to smile at him. "Don't judge me," she said quietly.

Mick softened. "I wouldn't dream of it."

"So, if you know Ruairi, I assume you know about his connection to the family?"

"Aye," Mick nodded. He took a bite of the cheese and then offered it to her. "I would have offered you the first bite," he said, "but I wanted to make sure it was still safe to eat!"

She laughed and took the hunk of cheese. She took a tiny bite and then handed it back. She stared at him expectantly.

"I'm not sure what you want me to say Genevieve," he gazed back at her steadily. "I'm a bit out of my depth here."

She shrugged her shoulders. "I don't know. Just say something."

Mick hesitated. "I'm sorry that your husband is such an arse," he said finally.

Genevieve laughed so hard that she thought she would cry. Mick just sat and watched her eyes dance.

Gracie made her way home quickly. She was feeling rather sore in places that she never knew she had muscles. All she wanted was a warm bath and fresh clothes. Halfway home she stopped suddenly and began to turn around and then she stopped again and shook her head. She didn't want him, she chided herself. She couldn't want him. He had nothing to offer her. She took a deep breath and swallowed hard. She had to let him go. She walked on.

Tears began to slip down her cheeks. She hadn't expected to feel anything afterwards. She wasn't supposed to care about the rugged rebel. He had been an easy indulgence, someone to ease the pain of her shattered confidence. And all he could become was a memory that she would hunger for during the lonely years to come.

She had to accept the life she was destined for.

She wiped away the tears, closing her eyes to concentrate on her breathing. Her composure returned, steeling itself against the influx of raw emotion. She passed the gate and crossed the lawns with long leggy strides and let herself in through the front door.

"Gracie!" Johnny's voice called out from the great room.

Gracie groaned inwardly. She took a deep breath and conjured up a smile that only passed for pleasantly bored. "Yes, Johnny?" she answered, appearing in the doorway.

He was standing beneath one of four massive chandeliers in the room. "Come here to me," he beckoned her.

"Say please," she answered back, her tone feisty.

Johnny pursed his lips. He figured she would be difficult. "Please."

She walked towards him, her neck elongated and her chin tipped up to the left. "What can I do for you?" she asked him politely.

"Let's not be so formal, Gracie. I'd like to speak frankly with you about what has happened and how we can try to fix it."

Her face was a chameleon. He could tell that she was furious inside but her tone was only passively aggressive and her features were as smooth as ever. "I don't really believe there is much to discuss."

Johnny said the words as he had rehearsed, "I want you to know that there is no truth to the rumours that you heard and I sincerely apologize . . ."

Gracie cut in, "Johnny, we both know that my father has coached you in what to say to me. I don't want to hear it. You are going to have to show me that you want to marry me. I want proof that I am not about to make the biggest mistake of my life."

Johnny tried to swallow but his throat was too dry. "How can I prove that I love you?" he asked nervously.

She gave him a patronizing look. "Oh really, Johnny, don't be so naïve! This is no longer about love. This has become a match of convenience. Prove to me that there is a strong enough reason for me to marry you without love."

Johnny wasn't sure how to react. "Is this how it is to be between us then?" he asked, his face hardening.

She put her hands on her hips. "Is it really so difficult to believe?"

He avoided the question. "I'm not sure how to win back your favour if you think so little of my affection."

"Just be on your best behaviour," she instructed him simply, "I may eventually feel something for you in time."

She watched as he struggled to contain his frustration with her. She wondered what had ever attracted her to him in the first place.

He stepped forward to embrace her. It was awkward and stiff. His arms slid around her mechanically and he pulled her in close, too close. He buried his face into her neck and inhaled her sweet scent. The smell was too thick, too sweet. There was something else there as well, or rather, someone else; someone strong and musky.

He pulled away from her and looked into her eyes. He felt the colour drain from his face and his nose wrinkle in distaste. Beneath the surface she was laughing at him.

"Will you let yourself out?" she asked, a perversely satisfied smile playing on her pink lips. "I'm in desperate need of a bath."

Rosaleen lay face down on her bed, hiccupping and sobbing, her eyes swollen and her nose running. He should have come up by now, full of apologies and gentle caresses. Instead, she heard the front door slam shut and his footsteps down the footpath followed by little skipping feet as her daughter chased after him.

Rosaleen punched her pillow viciously. She couldn't figure out how she had made such a mess of everything. She cursed brokenly as she struggled to breathe between the torrents of tears. She hated herself for what she was doing to Ruairi but it seemed like every time she tried to let him go, she somehow dug her claws deeper into his heart.

Thomas came into the room and wrapped her up in his big arms, rocking her until she went limp. He pulled the covers up over them and soothed her with her poem. "Little Rose, be not sad for all that hath behapped thee," he delivered the lines as he stroked her hair away from her face. They had all learned how to comfort each other. "A Roísín ná bíodh brón ort fé'r éirigh dhuit," he repeated the line in the Irish, hearing Pádraig Pearse's voice in his head. As he recited for her and for Ireland, Rosaleen drifted off to sleep.

That night, Rum Row glistened against the black horizon. Ruairi could see the red glow of the *Leda* from well out and he wove his way towards it magnetically. Three full-bosomed ladies of the night greeted him as he put his feet on the love-worn deck.

"Where's Mags?" he asked.

A buxom brunette put a finger to his lips. "Why don't you give me a go? They call me Charlotte."

Ruairi chuckled at the thought of the rhyme that he could make with that. "Well, Charlotte, as lovely as you are, I have a thing for redheads!"

"Don't they all?" a husky voice floated up behind him.

He turned around as a conflagration of hair, breasts and legs flew at him. He caught her as she pressed her hot lips against his chest and neck.

"What did I do to deserve this sort of hello?" Ruairi held her to him. He could smell Ireland on her; burnt peat and faëry dust.

"You were born, my Love, you were born!"

"I take it the men of the Atlantic aren't fulfilling all of your desires?" Ruairi tucked her wild hair behind her ears and held her face in his hands, more to stifle her kisses than anything else.

She rolled her peridot eyes. "My desires will never be met by a man who rolls over and asks me how much he owes me."

"Have I taught you nothing?" Ruairi chastised her, "The money should be on the table before the goods are produced."

"Always trying to take care of me!" Maggie clucked her approval. "Speaking of goods, I've got something for you to taste."

"That's what I'm here for, Love." Ruairi followed her down through private holds and to a hatch hidden beneath a thin cement floor.

A few barrels of whiskey were stacked haphazardly on top of crates full of bottled rum and gin.

"How is it coming along?" Ruairi watched as Maggie poured a tumbler full of amber liquor out of a jar placed on top of the furthest barrel.

"Well, for being in oak for only six months, I'd say I'm onto something. But don't be expecting as smooth as you're used to," Maggie wagged a finger at him. "And remember, I made this batch before we decided to go top shelf. The next batch will be a bit more refined."

Ruairi swilled the whiskey around in his mouth and then swallowed slowly, too slowly. Maggie laughed as the alcohol scorched his throat. "Bloody hell! They couldn't accuse us of watering it down!"

"I haven't tested the other two barrels." She motioned to the other samples she had packed.

"Hand me a tap," Ruairi instructed.

"You can't shut her out," Maggie warned suddenly.

Ruairi looked up at her. "Not you too," he groaned.

"She's made mistakes, sure, but not out of malice." Those green eyes singed Ruairi's conscience.

"What do you want from me, Maggie? I'm still here," Ruairi argued.

"No, you aren't. You've already gone back to Ireland to die. I can see it in your eyes."

"It's just a lack of sleep that you see," Ruairi grimaced. "And don't be accusing my eyes of anything. We all know what your eyes are capable of. Do you have a spoon?"

Maggie produced one from the folds of her skirt. Ruairi poured whiskey from the second barrel into the spoon and lit a match, holding it to the spirit. A blue flame arose from the spoon.

Maggie smiled. "Safe. Want to check the proof?" She held out a vial of gunpowder but Ruairi already had a mouthful of the sample.

His face twitched as he swallowed. "Proofed!" he laughed.

"Think it will sell?" she asked.

"Damn sure it will sell. It is better than anything they've got on the market over here, matured or not. Tastes like gold compared to the shite they're selling everywhere else." Ruairi tested the third barrel with the same result.

"Want to see something fearsome?" Maggie asked with a twinkle in her jaded eye.

Ruairi sat down and watched her uncover a flask in the corner. She poured the liquid onto the spoon and struck a match. This time, the flame was the colour of her hair. "Lead burns red and makes you dead," she whispered chillingly, watching the distillate disappear.

"Did you make that?" Ruairi was horrified.

Maggie gave him a look of utter disgust. "How dare you? Of course I didn't make it. My still is made of top quality materials, not second hand junk."

"Well, where'd you get it?"

"Some eejit who was obviously trying to kill me." Maggie was quite casual about the whole thing.

Ruairi wasn't. "Where the feck is this eejit?"

Maggie barely looked up. "At the bottom of the ocean where he belongs."

CHAPTER 10

T heir conversation was so easy. Genevieve hadn't been herself for so long and yet with him, she felt transparent in the most liberating way. She found herself telling him things that she would never tell anybody else. Things like how she had resented moving to England permanently for William, how she had never wanted children but how she didn't regret the ones she had, and how she wished sometimes that she could just run away and never come back.

"Why don't you?" Mick asked.

It was a simple question that required a simple answer but Genevieve found that no matter how she constructed the sentence, it never really captured what she felt inside.

Finally she just went with, "I can't."

"You won't," Mick countered.

"I can't."

He scratched his silver hair. "Do your legs work?"

She nodded.

"Then you can, you just won't."

She laughed, "Is everything this simple to you?"

He thought for a minute. "Aye," he said, "it is that simple for me. It's that simple for Valerie too. I think you need her in your life."

"I'm not so sure. I've heard that Valerie Logan is a very dangerous woman," Genevieve gave Mick a sideways glance.

"I've heard that too!" A brash female voice spoke up from somewhere behind them. "Shockingly dangerous is the rumour!"

A wide grin opened up Mick's toughened face. He stood up and greeted Valerie Logan with a passionate embrace. Genevieve was caught off guard and didn't know where to look.

"I didn't realize that you two were . . ." she gestured.

Valerie gave Mick a surprised look that didn't fade when she turned her eyes back to Genevieve. "That we were what, Darling?"

"Together," Genevieve finished.

Mick chuckled but said nothing.

Valerie gave a coy smile. "I'm not sure whether we've realized it yet either. Neither of us go much on talking," she paused. "Well, that's not quite the truth. He doesn't go much on talking," she clarified. "I'm quite the talker."

Genevieve laughed. She liked Valerie immediately. "It's a pleasure to finally meet you Ms. Logan."

"Unless I am to call you Lady Genevieve, which I highly doubt that you could persuade me to do, then I suggest you call me Valerie and not Ms. Logan," the fiery red-head instructed.

"Genevieve will do just fine," she was assured, "I'm not fond of my title."

"I'm not fond of it either," Valerie was blunt, "If I were you, I would have insisted on being the queen!"

Genevieve couldn't contain her laughter. She enjoyed a candid conversation.

Valerie looked Genevieve up and down. "Are you interested in fashion?" she asked suddenly.

Genevieve became very self-conscious. "Why do you ask?"

"I'm looking for a business partner," Valerie said seriously. "I think you need to come to my home this evening."

Gracie dressed and fixed her hair and make-up so that she was ready to accompany the family to the Gilmour's open house. She waited with a cup of black tea for her parents to arrive at home. When they did, she dutifully told them that she had spoken with Johnny. William was elated. Genevieve smiled tightly. There were no questions about where she had been or who she had been with. It was enough for William that things between her and Johnny might be smoothed over.

Billy met them at the open house. He was less than thrilled about her willingness to give a second chance to Johnny. He knew something must have happened while Gracie was with Ruairi but she refused to discuss it.

Johnny saw the hatred in Billy's eyes and kept his distance. He accepted the well wishes of the family friends but he knew that it was obvious to everyone that the relationship was strained.

Lana Hamilton and her Peacock Brigade flounced around like she had nothing to be ashamed of. They even had the audacity to approach Gracie and pretend that they were still great friends. Gracie refused to acknowledge the girls and spent the afternoon beside the pool with Norah. But Lana would not be ignored.

She waited for an opportunity to pounce. When Norah went in search of refreshments, Lana sat down beside Gracie. "So, I wasn't really sure if you and Johnny were still together after I saw you kissing that dockworker this morning," Lana's tone was upbeat, "but I guess true love can get over anything, right?"

"You saw . . . ?" Gracie's stomach turned.

Lana smiled and nodded. "Saw the kiss? Yes, it was quite a kiss! But don't worry; it will be our little secret," she giggled conspiratorially.

Gracie was furious to know that she had been caught out by Lana Hamilton. "He isn't a dockworker," she glared at Lana, quickly defending Ruairi.

Lana feigned innocence, "Oh, does he work at one of the factories? I'm sorry I don't know him at all. He doesn't associate with my family."

It took all of Gracie's willpower to control her temper. She knew exactly what Lana was up to and she was angry with herself for not being more discreet this time. She narrowed her eyes and smirked at the girl in front of her. "Well, that's too bad. You should spend more time down at the docks. You're the type of girl that the sailor's would appreciate. Then you might find yourself a husband and stop sleeping with everybody else's."

Lana glared at her. "Be careful, Gracie. I could ruin you with this."

Gracie challenged her, "Go ahead, I dare you."

The lawns were abuzz with talk of William's mistress. The ladies that had been at morning tea had spread the gossip to those that hadn't and now it was all anyone could talk about. Genevieve was mortified.

When she was finally able to excuse herself and make her way to the car, her hands were trembling noticeably. She tucked herself away in the back seat of the motorcar and clutched at her hands as they shook in her lap.

She had no idea how she was going to be able to disentangle herself from this mess. It was one thing to consider it, but quite another to actually go through with a divorce. She had sufficient grounds with adultery and was confident that if she went to the Supreme Court, the divorce would be granted. However, she had her children's reputation to consider. She could easily move back to Paris and maintain a fashionable reputation as a divorcée but if her children were to stay on Prince Edward Island their standing in society would suffer greatly. Islanders were extremely traditional and Genevieve didn't know if she could gamble her children's future just to ensure her own happiness.

Gracie looked down at the piece of paper in her hand. She had left the Gilmour's around the same time as her mother but had taken Billy's car and chauffeur. She sat staring at a massive house on Haviland Street, across from Connaught Square. It was Valerie Logan's house.

Gracie knew very little about the woman. She was an extremely wealthy and fiercely independent widow. Her first husband, Randall Logan, had been a dairy farmer. Valerie had known nothing of the land and less about love. The illegitimate child of a prostitute and a sailor, Valerie couldn't have had a worse beginning. She was abandoned at the door of St. Dunstan's Cathedral and to this day she refused to pass by without lighting a candle and saying a prayer.

Valerie had met Randall on the side of the road while she was out for a walk. She had gone up the island for a few days to visit a friend near Summerside. His horse had thrown a shoe. She had held the horse for him as he had tapped the shoe back on. He had fallen hopelessly in love with her and he married her within the week. Their romance had been full of emotional extravagance and caprice. Although he had no money, he had lavished on her more love than she could have wished for in a hundred lifetimes. And she had been happy.

But the romance ended as quickly as it had begun. A careless horse-riding accident claimed his life and Valerie was left shattered and alone.

She never re-married, instead choosing to invest the little money she had from selling the dairy cattle into a fox breeding venture near Tignish. It had been a wise decision. A silver vein of fur proved golden for Valerie Logan. With her new financial freedom, Valerie became a figure head for the feminist movement. She was not one for pickets and petitions however; she raised awareness by throwing opulent parties that were invite only and extremely provocative affairs.

Gracie wondered why Ruairi wanted her to meet Valerie. In Gracie's views, she seemed a very precarious woman to introduce a young lady to. She pushed open the car door, stood up and straightened her dress. She was determined to find out.

Ruairi sat at the bar staring into the bottom of his tumbler. He hadn't really been in the mood to go out but it was Thomas' birthday and everybody wanted to celebrate. The whole crew had gathered at a smokey establishment on Sydney Street. It was an unlikely speakeasy, an average home from the outside, a delightful little tavern on the inside. Its former walls had been knocked down to make one large room, split in the middle by a massive maple bar. The music was mellow and the conversation light.

Ruairi avoided the craic. He sat, moody to the point of petulance, examining the viscosity of his drink.

"You liked her didn't you?" Aisling pulled up a barstool and sat close to him. She was determined to drag him out of his mood.

"Mmm . . ." Ruairi's little smile gave him away.

Aisling smiled too, and Ruairi's smile gave way to a head shaking grin. "I don't think I've ever seen you smile like that over a girl."

Ruairi laughed. "She was a bit of fun."

"So why not have a bit more fun?" Aisling pried. She had heard that Ruairi was ready to pull up anchor and head south to New York.

Ruairi's mouth returned to a scowl and he remained silent. He tapped the bottom of the tumbler against the bar distractingly. Aisling continued to stare at him until he spoke. "It isn't right. She deserves better than that."

"Better than you? I never thought there was better than you," she tried flattery. When that didn't work, she switched tactics. "I know I wasn't the most supportive person when you brought her out in

Halifax but maybe you are on to something. We are in a new country now, and if she could make you stay . . . away from Ireland . . ." She was annoyingly persistent. Both she and Thomas were hoping to keep him from going back.

"Ireland is home," Ruairi growled.

"Home is where we all are . . . alive," Aisling stressed. "Don't you want to live Ruairi? Actually grow up? You can't play soldier boy all your life . . . and if you do, it will be a very short life."

"I have to finish the job and get out of here," Ruairi muttered. "I don't have time to play the lover."

"Finish what job?" she asked, putting her drink to her lips. "Setting up the crew or killing the General?" she was teasing him.

"Both if need be," Ruairi held her gaze to see the reaction. She choked on her drink. He smiled.

"Is that what Rosaleen wanted to begin with?" she asked him.

"She's doing a good job of pretending it wasn't," Ruairi's voice was accusing. Ruairi began to tap his tumbler again. "I think she wants him dead, one way or the other, she just doesn't want to be responsible for it," he said through gritted teeth.

She sighed, "That's why you pulled back from Gracie even though you are clearly smitten with her and that's why you had that screaming match with Rosaleen this morning."

"I'm not smitten and Rosaleen deserves more than a bloody screaming match." He was so angry with her. "I warned her about that bastard. Now look at the mess we're all in. If he gets in my way, and we all know he will, I'll have to kill him, I'll have to destroy another family, I'll have to destroy Gracie," he groaned. "She doesn't deserve that, Aisling. This should have been done a long time ago."

Aisling sighed, "I'm sorry, Ruairi. Sometimes I wish you didn't have a conscience. I wish you were a bit more like Gerry."

"Aye, and that's because Gerry's your favourite brother," he teased her gently.

"Ha! That's a laugh! Gerry as my favourite," she giggled. "No, I love all of you for very different reasons. But I've never had to worry about Gerry. I just always knew he'd turn up fine. You and Thomas are different. Thomas is too casual and you, well, you're just too good for this life."

Ruairi squeezed his sister into his chest, practically knocking her off the barstool. "You give me too much credit, baby girl."

"You know, Ruairi, you can let Mairtin do it if it needs to be done," she said slowly, "and then she couldn't blame you."

He shook his head. "She'd still hate me. Even if I don't pull the trigger, she'll believe it was me."

"Then she doesn't deserve you," Aisling stated firmly, patting her brother on the back.

"We just need to leave town, and the sooner, the better." Ruairi stared down into the tumbler. The bartender ambled over and refilled it finally.

"What about the whiskey and what about Maggie? This business isn't going to transport as easily. We have everything set up here."

"We can run this whiskey all down the East Coast. We just need to get away from General Gainsborough so that I don't have to kill him."

She sighed, "Why don't we take a trip to New York just for the weekend? We'll go see Gerry and I'm sure he'll be able to give you some clarity."

Gerry was the oldest of the O'Neill's. He had narrowly escaped with his life during the War of Independence and had turned up in New York where he had set up a lucrative bootlegging venture. He funnelled money back to the army to help with the increasingly tight finances. Gerry and Maggie had started distilling their own whiskey a few years back and the recipes were ageing nicely. Now that Ruairi had landed, it would be up to him to corner buyers and set up a distribution crew. He and Gerry often had late night cryptic telephone calls to sort out all of the details and the brothers had fallen back into the easy rhythms of relying on their bonds; even though they had yet to lay eyes on each other on this side of the ocean.

"We'll catch up with Gerry soon enough. We both know he'd just tell me to shoot the General now, before there is even a sniff of trouble." Ruairi put his head down on his arms and stared up at his pretty little sister.

"Aye, you're probably right. That boy was always too quick to pull the trigger," she paused. "Either way, you have to forgive Rosaleen. She needs you right now, you know."

Ruairi grunted, "I don't know if I can forgive her for dragging me back into this."

"You are a stubborn arse, you are. But you'll forgive her. You always do." She patted his shoulder and then leaned in and gave him another cuddle.

Thomas pattered across the room, a drink sloshing in one hand and a cigarette in the other. He gave his little sister a sloppy kiss on the cheek.

"Happy birthday little brother," Ruairi turned and held up his glass to Thomas. Thomas shoved his cigarette in Ruairi's mouth to free a hand, saluted the drink and then grabbed it and drank it down. Ruairi laughed.

"Never thought I'd be spending my birthday in Canada," Thomas sighed. "I miss Ireland. The booze is better."

"And it's legal," Ruairi added.

"Yeah, what's with this Prohibition shite, anyway?" Thomas was loud and unsteady on his feet already.

"Ah, comeon Thomas, you'd be out of a job if it wasn't for Prohibition!" Stavros yelled brightly.

Thomas held up the drink he had been carrying. "Then here's to Prohibition!" he yelled. "Drinks are on me!"

Rosaleen watched Ruairi from across the room. She knew she had to tell him the truth soon. She just didn't want to see that look of betrayal on his face when he figured out that once again she had chosen another man over him.

"What are you thinking about?" Stavros penetrated her thoughts, "Is it dirty?"

Rosaleen glared at him over her drink. "Remind me again why we invite you to come out with us?"

Stavros smiled in a manner that he thought was sexy and batted his very short eyelashes at her. "Because you think that one night you will get me drunk enough and I'll come home with you."

Rosaleen pushed back her chair and left the table. She would rather chance another horrible fight with Ruairi than be relegated to Stavros' idea of romantic overtures. She sat down beside Ruairi and smiled at the bartender.

"Another round, Joe," she said to the bartender behind the maple slab. He was about as unsteady on his feet as Thomas was.

Ruairi just stared down at his once again empty glass. They sat in silence for a few moments.

"Are you going to continue ignoring me?" she finally asked, nervously picking at her thumbnail.

"I'm not ignoring you."

"My mistake. Usually when I sit down beside you, you at least acknowledge my presence."

"I'll grunt next time."

"Thank-you."

Silence. Joe, the bartender, slammed the drinks down in front of them, inadvertently spilling them over the sides.

"You're ignoring me again."

"No, I'm not."

"He just put a drink in front of you and you said nothing."

"That's not ignoring you."

"Well you ignored the drink."

"I'm sorry. I didn't realize I was supposed to acknowledge the drink. Should I grunt at it?"

Rosaleen threw her hands up. "What do you want me to say Ruairi? I'm sorry for what I said to you this morning. I know that you have sacrificed so much for me but . . ."

"But what, Rosaleen? What else do you want?"

"Nothing, Ruairi, I swear!"

Ruairi downed the drink. "You're full of shite, Róisín. You brought me here to kill him."

Rosaleen knew she was in for it when Ruairi used her Irish name. "That's not exactly true."

"Nothing you have told me in the last few years is exactly true, is it Róisín?"

"Ruairi, please don't think that way," Rosaleen begged him. She could feel her chin quivering. He was the only person in the world that could make her cry.

He groaned angrily. "He would have been dead already if . . ." he stopped himself.

"If what?" Rosaleen had always wondered why Ruairi had shot him in the shoulder instead of the head.

But Ruairi wouldn't answer her question. "From the very beginning you've been lying to me, Róisín, and you're still lying to me. And I'm tired. I can't keep doing this. If you want me to kill William, I'll do it. It will be the last thing that I do for you. Then I'm going home."

Rosaleen bit her lip to keep the tears at bay. She knew she would have to tell him the whole truth. She just didn't know how. "Ruairi, I need to be honest with you . . ."

"Honest with me? Jesus, Mary and Joseph Róisín, honesty would have been a good place to start," he snarled, "but it's too late now. Now you just need to stay out of my way."

She caught her breath. "Have you told the girl what you plan to do?" she asked, referring to Gracie.

He glared at her. "I had to. She deserves the truth. When I care about someone I tell the truth, no matter how much it hurts."

His loyalty to the Gainsborough girl upset her. She crossed the line in a few careless words. "This all would have been easier if you hadn't gotten mixed up with her."

Ruairi's eyes blazed. "This would have all been easier if you hadn't whored yourself out to a British General."

Her mouth dropped open and she slapped him full across the face.

Ruairi stood up slowly, knowing the whole bar was waiting for his reaction. "Did that make you feel better, then?"

She sat frozen as he pushed passed her, swallowing back any feeling that was trying to escape its internal cell.

William watched as Genevieve sat at her dressing table, putting the finishing touches on her make-up. She was wearing a navy silk and organza gown. Her hair was pinned neatly at the back of her head and she wore a thin navy headband set with diamante studs. In her ears hung large chandelier diamond earrings and her wrists glittered with diamond cuffs.

"You look lovely this evening," he said, appraising her from a distance.

"Thank-you," she said simply. He noticed that the words didn't have their usual frosty tone to them.

He spoke again, to see if he could pull her into conversation, "Where are you going this evening? I wasn't aware that you had an event on."

"I don't really," she lied, "I'm just having a night out."

William narrowed his eyes. "A night out where?" he questioned her.

She licked her lips. "Actually, I'm meeting with Valerie Logan this evening."

"You will not!" he bellowed. William had been adamant that his family had nothing to do with Valerie Logan. Although the divide between old and new money had been stripped away by the war, William had made a point of rejecting any advance by the local feminist.

Genevieve squared her shoulders and faced her husband. "I will."

"This is not a negotiation." William took a step towards her.

Genevieve refused to take a step backwards. "You're right, it's not. I am going to Valerie's home tonight. Goodbye."

William stood open mouthed as his wife strode by him and left the house.

It was to be an evening of canapés, impromptu monologues and operatic solos in honour of the fox. Ms. Logan's ballroom had been transformed into a dazzling gallery draped with various interpretations of the human body dressed in fox stoles, coats and hats. Valerie was ready to take her love of premium furs to the next stage. She wanted to not only grow the furs, but to make them into something beautiful, something wearable. The designer that Valerie was mentoring was a young dandy from Montreal named Gustav. He had earned a reputation for enjoying certain pleasures that had kept him on the fringes of fashionable society. Ultimately it meant that he was never hired by those whose social position demanded a certain adherence to moral rigidity; those who cared to make a rich investment. Valerie meant to change that by taking his work to those who frequented many of her 'events', those with less traditional views of art and culture, but enough money to make the evening worthwhile. She also thought it would be fun to invite a few of those who would extremely disapprove of him. This would fuel an interesting debate and Valerie loved an argument.

Gracie waited impatiently in the library. The house was not furnished in the style she was used to, rather, it was quite modern, artsy almost, yet comfortable. Gracie stared up at the painting on the wall in front of her. It was geometrical shapes in vivid colours. As she was trying to decide if she liked it, her thoughts were interrupted by the clicking of heels on the black tiled floors.

She turned just as a petite woman with short red hair glided into the room. She was magnificently put together, everything polished and perfectly angled. She was younger than Gracie had imagined her, maybe forty.

"What can I do for you?" she asked breezily.

Gracie bit her bottom lip. She wasn't quite sure how to answer that. She took a deep breath. "My name is Gracie Gainsborough. I'm here to meet you on recommendation of a frie . . ." she stopped herself, "of an acquaintance of mine, Ruairi O'Neill."

The woman's face remained neutral. She continued to meet Gracie's eyes politely but did not offer any contribution to the conversation.

Gracie fidgeted uncomfortably. "I'm sorry; I'm not sure what else to tell you. He didn't say why we should meet."

The woman's face suddenly broke, and a feline smile spread across her face. "Well, then, if we are to meet, then meet we shall. It's lovely to meet you." Valerie came closer to Gracie and extended her hand. "You're a Gainsborough?" It was a rhetorical question. She assessed Gracie in a sweeping glance and smiled. "You're like your mother." The way she said it was obviously complimentary.

"You know my mother?"

"Not well, but I daresay I will soon. She'll be here tonight, actually." Valerie beckoned for Gracie to follow her. "Come, Darling, let's have this discussion while I dress. I'm already late."

Gracie walked behind the woman and caught sight of an enclosed courtyard where about twenty women lounged on pillowy settees and decadently overstuffed armchairs.

"I'm sorry," Gracie apologized, stopping immediately. "I didn't realize you had company. I'll come back some other time."

"Nonsense," Valerie waved dismissively, "I always have company. We'll have to get right to the point though as I really do have to get this evening underway." She led Gracie into a large bedchamber. "Now, tell me, Gracie Gainsborough, why have you really come to see me?"

Gracie looked confused. "Honestly, I came because Ruairi mentioned that I should meet you."

"Do you always do what you're told?" Valerie wondered more to herself than to Gracie.

Gracie watched as the woman floated around the room, piecing together an outfit that made her look like a couturier's muse.

"What type of occasion are you dressing for?" Gracie asked curiously. She was intrigued by the magnitude of the social event that would warrant such an extravagant display of wearable art.

"I have organized a fur exhibition for Gustav," Valerie paused, momentarily losing her train of thought as she ran her fingers over a silk sash. Her finger caught and she cursed shamelessly. "He has done an entire collection using furs from my Summerside foxes." Valerie stopped fussing with the fabric long enough to concentrate on the young girl in her room. "Would you like to come?"

It didn't take long for Gracie to make up her mind. "I would love to. I feel I've been missing out on something extremely important."

Valerie accepted the compliment graciously. She reached out and took Gracie's hand. "Let's find you something suitable to wear."

"I'll just slip home and dress. It won't be any trouble at all." Gracie didn't want to chance ruining one of the masterpieces in the wardrobe before her.

Valerie silenced her with a wave of her hand. "Tut, tut!" she admonished. "We don't have time for that!" She turned back to her wardrobe and pulled a gold dress from the rack that had fringed layers of beads and sequins dripping from it. She slipped into it and then grabbed another dress from the same rack. It was a similar style in a bright blue. "You'll wear this tonight," she said to Gracie brusquely. "I insist. You will be my guest of honour."

Genevieve had her back to the group of women but she overheard one of them comment on her attire. "She was supposedly considered fashionable overseas but I just can't see how! Look at how form fitting that dress is! Nobody wears corsets anymore!"

"She isn't wearing a corset, that's how thin she is. She barely eats!" a rotund lady quipped.

"And what did she do, buy out Harrod's before she left London?" another woman huffed.

Genevieve smiled to herself. The candour of wealthy women amused her greatly. She stopped listening to the gossip long enough to be greeted by a prominent member of the legislature that was just arriving. Valerie was obviously powerfully connected.

She had wandered through the open house, trying to find her hostess but the mysterious Valerie Logan was nowhere to be seen.

She stepped out into the cool westerly that blew across the back patio. She was surprised to see her daughter surrounded by a throng of unfamiliar faces, laughing gaily as though she knew the crowd well. She caught Gracie's eye and waited while she made her way over. Genevieve embraced her daughter warmly.

"You aren't angry with me for being here, are you?" Gracie asked timidly.

"How could I be when I'm here myself?" Genevieve brushed a wisp of her daughter's hair behind her ear tenderly.

"I didn't know that you knew Ms. Logan," Gracie was actually quite shocked that her mother was there. She was dying to know how Genevieve had convinced William to allow it.

But Genevieve avoided revealing much. "I just met her this afternoon. I came to have a look at the furs."

Before the conversation could progress, Valerie swept towards them. She leaned forward and kissed Genevieve on both cheeks. "I'm so delighted that you are here."

"So am I," Genevieve said politely, "I wouldn't have missed it."

Valerie laced her arm through Genevieve's. She turned back to Gracie briefly, "Go mingle, Darling, and let me have your mother all to myself."

Gracie dutifully nodded and stood back while Valerie led Genevieve back into the warm glow of the house.

Rosaleen caught local fishermen Jimmy and Charlie as they headed out on a midnight run to Rum Row. They were happy to take her with them and so she stood, her arms crossed firmly over her chest, looking out over the harbour as the boat pushed through the black waters, the breeze blowing her dark hair around her face. She watched the lighthouse flashing in the distance and thought about home.

Ruairi had always said that she was Ireland to him; she was Roísín Dubh. He had sworn to live and die for her alone. She had thought that if she could change who she was, she could change his fate. She shuddered as the wind shouted the truth in eerie voices. She folded her hands over her face and cried.

Old Charlie came over and rubbed her back. He barely knew the girl but he could tell she was a troubled soul the day he had met her. The Irish called her the Black Rose and he knew why; her beauty drew admiration but her thorns made her untouchable.

Genevieve stood beside the golden woman and thought about the opportunity that was being offered to her. Valerie had asked her to invest in the development of a distribution network for the furs. Genevieve's Parisian past had afforded her certain contacts that would be vital to opening up the European market.

Norah Bexley approached and gave Genevieve a knowing smile. "It seems as though Valerie had been monopolizing your attention. I hope she is at least giving you a decent discount."

Valerie laughed, "Oh, Norah, you sound like a jealous boyfriend I once had!"

Genevieve was amused. "I take it you two have already met?"

Norah kissed Valerie hello. "Met? Madame, Valerie is an addiction. Just having met her would never be enough!"

Genevieve raised her eyebrows. "Is it because of you then that my daughter secured an invite?"

Norah looked around and frowned. "I didn't even know Gracie was here."

"She's outside with the younger ones," Valerie directed. Norah nodded and moved off in that direction.

Genevieve looked at Valerie questioningly. "Do you know how my daughter ended up here?" she asked.

Valerie knew better than to betray the young girl's association with Ruairi. She played coy, "Maybe she was in the market for a beautiful fox fur coat!"

Norah found Gracie wandering past canvas displays of female sexuality. "What are you doing here?" she exclaimed.

"I am the guest of honour according to Valerie Logan," Gracie laughed, avoiding the question.

"I didn't know that you knew Valerie and I thought you hated politics!" Norah embraced her friend. "You won't even read a newspaper for fear of getting ink on your hands!"

"How could I hate something I know nothing about?" Gracie joked.

Norah grabbed Gracie's hand. "Come, there are so many people to introduce you to!"

She led Gracie to a large group of young people gathered around a feather light model wearing one of the stoles that Gustav had designed.

"It's brilliant isn't it?" the model was fingering the fur seductively.

"I've never seen fur of such quality," a slight young man offered. "I would love to meet the designer of the pieces."

"Valerie must have him hidden away in one of her boudoirs," a lanky young woman with a cigarillo in hand looked around furtively. "Apparently he's every bit her type of man."

"I believe he may be every bit my type of man as well," the young man's eyes twinkled merrily.

Gracie smiled at the comment. She supposed she should have been shocked by it but she wasn't. She listened to the swirling conversations, fascinated by these lives that seemed so exotic to her own. The feminine world was on show. The visible realm entertained her eyes with naked representations of primal power and carnal mastery. It was as though Valerie's home was enchanted; women were more fascinating, their words more glamorous, and their bodies more alluring.

As bewitched as she was, her mind wandered back to the masculine. She kept wondering where Ruairi O'Neill was now and whether or not he was thinking about her.

Ruairi leaned heavily on the veranda rail, a cigarette hanging casually from his mouth. He had calmed down slightly and was able to convince Thomas and Aisling that he would be alright on his own. But he wasn't alone. She was still lingering on his body and on his mind.

Rosaleen took off her heels to climb the rickety rope ladder that was slung haphazardly over the port side of the *Leda*. It was Moonshine Maggie's boat and she had set anchor on the other side of the Rum line; the other side of the law. The *Leda* was a floating brothel in the middle of Rum Row. A line-up of trawlers and cutters lay scattered three miles off the coast of Cape Breton, outside the reach of the ever vigilant Coast Guard, selling liquor, ladies and luck and Maggie's boat specialized in all three.

Rosaleen found her friend lying face up on the deck, her red hair spread around her head in a halo of fire. She was staring at a sky full of stars.

"I never get tired of it, you know," she whispered, her husky voice floating up to Rosaleen. "The sky is so much bigger here."

"It's the same sky," Rosaleen said, unhappily.

"It couldn't be," Maggie insisted.

Rosaleen sighed and lay down beside her.

"Did you tell him, then?" Maggie asked, hearing the sadness in Rosaleen's voice.

"No, but we had a fight. He said some awful things to me."

"Did you deserve them though?" Maggie asked.

Rosaleen felt the tears snaking out of the corners of her eyes, "Every word."

Maggie rolled over and put an arm around Rosaleen's body. "Did you come for advice or just a warm body?"

Rosaleen turned her head to look directly at Maggie. "Advice."

"Call Gerry."

CHAPTER 11

Sunday morning Gracie sat at the breakfast table on the right hand side of her father. Everything was different now, as if suddenly, she had woken up no longer in her body, but watching from above to find some hidden meaning in it all. She stared at her father between bites of her croissant and wondered whether he was ashamed of his double life or if he justified it as part of being a man; and if that justification was enough.

"What's on your mind, Gracie?" He noticed her watching him.

She tried to smile. "Nothing Papa, I'm just thinking."

"Well, pet, don't do too much of that. You'll end up with lines on that pretty little face of yours." He patted her hand and went back to his breakfast.

She looked down at the hand that rested on hers. She tried hard to convince herself it wasn't as bloody as Mairtin had said it was.

Later the family attended church and Gracie sat between her father and her mother. William reached out and put his arm around his daughter, his hand caressing her shoulder lovingly. Gracie felt herself cringe and her mother stiffen. His touch suddenly felt all wrong. Mairtin's words rang in her ears and she couldn't silence them. Questions formed in her mind. She questioned being rich and she questioned being poor. She questioned war and peace and every state in between. She thought of Ireland and England. What had gone so bloody wrong? She looked up at the cross hanging behind the pulpit and wondered why death seemed the only way to atonement.

After church, the family drove over to the Club for brunch. It had become the thing to do on a Sunday.

William and Genevieve sat at a table with Lucas and Eleanor and the Nicholsons, a family that had moved up from the Southern States. Eleanor and Genevieve were avoiding speaking directly to each other by pouncing on Milly Nicholson. Milly loved the attention and her soft southern voice had lulled everybody into a passive mood.

The younger sets sat off at a table of their own on the patio, surrounded by the other heirs and heiresses of Charlottetown society.

Johnny sat beside Gracie, his hand resting lightly on her arm. He had been very dutiful and affectionate to her, annoying Gracie to no end. She had developed an aversion to being touched by anyone.

Norah had excused herself and was off saying hello to a young man she had met the night before, and Billy was sitting across from Johnny, pointedly ignoring his former friend and discussing the many advantages of the technological advancements in trans-Atlantic communication with a young lawyer from Pennsylvania that had recently started working at the firm.

Gracie tried desperately to look interested in the conversation but she was finding the charade draining. Her thoughts kept slipping back to the dark cramped cabin that had become her personal heaven. She had to physically fight to stop the blood from rising in her cheeks as she relived the racier moments of that night. She couldn't help herself; she had slowly become obsessed with her memories.

Norah reappeared at the table giving Gracie an outlet for her restlessness.

"Did you see the dress that Marie Chalifoux is wearing? Apparently her dressmaker in Paris is still sending her all of the latest styles. According to Clarisse it's costing Henri more than half of his annual salary to keep her from divorcing him and running off with that barrister from Chicago," Norah whispered

"Barrister?" Billy snorted. "You mean mobster! Have you seen that chap? The only thing he knows about the law is how to break it!" he laughed. "Come on, boys, let's go play some tennis." The boys jumped up from the table eagerly, Johnny trailing behind the group.

Norah and Gracie barely acknowledged them as they left. They were too interested in Marie Chalifoux to care.

"Poor Henri! He sure has his hands full with Marie. That woman is an absolute dragon!" Gracie made a face as she looked over at Marie. "But I can't help but admire her, I mean, she does have fabulous taste!"

"She does, doesn't she?" Norah agreed. She dropped her voice again, "Gracie, have you noticed the looks you are getting from the Peacock Brigade?"

Gracie looked up to see that the full attention of Lana Hamilton's table was being paid to her. "I don't care. After last night, I've realized there are much more interesting people on Prince Edward Island. I think I'm done with Papa's crowd. They are dreadfully boring in comparison."

"Don't let your father hear you say that," Norah warned. "I do agree with you though. I'm tired of our regular routine. I'm going to Valerie's meeting on Tuesday night. Are you going to come?"

"Um . . . yes, yes of course I'm going to go." Gracie was distracted by the sudden disappearance of Lana Hamilton. She was becoming extremely uncomfortable under the stares of the rest of the Peacock Brigade. "Norah, something is going on over there."

Norah turned just as her brother came back from the courts, his face constricted into contained animosity. "Gracie, may I speak with you alone?" He stood, motioning for her to stand also.

Gracie pursed her lips and sighed. Lana was back with her group now and looking over at Gracie smugly. There was nothing Gracie could do except follow Johnny away from any straining ears.

Out on the other side of the patio, a warm breeze blew in off of the water. Gracie inhaled deeply, trying to keep herself calm.

"I'm not exactly sure how to begin this conversation," Johnny was cautious.

Gracie noted his attempt to hide his irritated tone. "Johnny, if this has to do with Ruairi O'Neill, you need to understand that it was all just a big misunderstanding," Gracie cut him off, doing her best to make her voice as smooth as honey.

"Did you kiss him on the docks yesterday morning?" Johnny asked pointedly.

Gracie folded her arms and jutted out her lower jaw. "Yes," she answered, looking off towards the water. That was the least of her transgressions.

"Then I didn't misunderstand anything," Johnny snarled. His face changed suddenly into a soft smile and he put an arm around her as two gentleman passed within earshot. As soon as they were gone, the smile faded and his hand on her back slid around to grip her arm fiercely. "I knew there had been someone else, someone to make you feel better about the whole thing with Lana. But I don't need these kinds of embarrassments, Gracie. You do not hang around docks and men of ill-repute and you do not flaunt your affairs in public. I will not overlook these types of things. Do you understand me?" he hissed.

Gracie's face contorted in anger. "Who do you think you are? Do you really believe you are in any position to threaten me?"

Johnny glared down at her. "I'd be very careful, Gracie. I would doubt that your father will side with you in this matter." He still had her by the arm.

She winced, partially because she knew he was right and partially because his fingers were digging into the skin of her upper arm. "Johnny, you're hurting me." She tried to pull her arm away but his grip tightened. His other hand cupped underneath her jaw. To an outsider, it would look as if they were about to kiss but to Gracie it felt like he was going to crush her skull in his fingers.

"If you ever embarrass me again Gracie, you will regret it. Your father has already expressed his desire to destroy that Irish bastard. One word about this and his desire will become a reality," he sneered. "Don't tempt me."

His face changed back into a composed and genteel look. "Now that we have that sorted," his grip relaxed, "let's go back inside and forget all of this ugliness, shall we?" He held out his arm to Gracie.

Gracie felt real fear at his last threat. If her father went after Ruairi, Ruairi had sworn to kill him. Shakily, she put her hand into the crook of Johnny's arm and allowed him to lead her back into the restaurant. She didn't know what else to do. She didn't notice Mairtin Fitzgerald standing off to the left of the doors but he noticed the faint purple marks that were beginning to appear on her arm.

Rosaleen stayed at home with Kathleen on Sunday. Ruairi had disappeared without speaking to her, leaving her beneath the weight of the words that were still unspoken.

She picked up the phone and asked the operator for a Gerard O'Neill in New York.

As the operator put through the call she watched her little girl playing with a doll that Ruairi had given her. She wondered if he would still love Kathleen when he knew the whole truth.

The line was busy.

Johnny stewed over the news of Gracie's tryst. He wasn't satisfied with the outcome of his conversation with Gracie and he was a man who believed in instant gratification. It wasn't long before he excused himself and went to speak privately with William Gainsborough. He had every intention of telling William the rumour, exactly how he had heard it but somehow, in the heat of the retelling, the truth was stretched by his angered imagination. His girl, his soon to be wife had been defiled by that *Irishman*. The word was foul enough in his head but it was somehow even worse on the tongue. He spit it out and watched the General's countenance change.

William's temper got the better of him. It was one of his more glaring personality faults but he had never tried hard to change it.

He was determined to confront her immediately. He would not let her spoil the family reputation or her own chances to marry because of a dalliance with Ruairi O'Neill. He would stop her nonsense and pull Genevieve into line as well. He was tired of his wife's petulant quarrels with him. He was the man of the house and she would do well to remember that. He would make sure of it.

"We'll sort this out, my boy. Don't you worry about a thing, we'll sort this out," he told Johnny, his jaw set in a hard line.

Johnny nodded quietly, his hand quivering just slightly in his lap.

William watched the ladies with their cups of tea on the far side of the dining room. He crossed the distance with long, athletic strides, his vitality returning with each step. His anger enlivened him. He put a strong hand on his wife's shoulder.

"I think it is time for us to leave," his tone was demanding.

Genevieve didn't move. "Let me finish my tea."

"No," William barked. He tried to soften his voice when he realized he was creating a scene. "No Dear, we must go home immediately. Fetch Gracie and take the motorcar. Johnny will drive me home."

Juliette Hamilton was on her feet. "I trust everything is alright, William?" she feigned concern.

William smiled at her. She was a clever woman and he respected that. "Yes, Juliette, everything is fine. I'm just exhausted and would like to spend the afternoon with my family."

"Then should I fetch Billy as well?" Genevieve was collecting her purse and glaring at William.

"No, don't disturb Billy," William's look sent shivers through Genevieve. "His presence won't be necessary."

Genevieve looked over at Johnny. He wouldn't meet her eyes. She looked back at William. "I'll see you at home then," she said. She was worried about what she had consented to. She quickly turned away from the table of women, knowing that for the rest of the afternoon, she and her husband would again be the topic of conversation.

Gracie and Genevieve had barely shut the front door when William and Johnny burst out from the study. They stood staring at each other in the hall, neither party knowing what to say to the other.

William spoke first. "Let's go to the parlour. We will be having a family discussion," he growled.

"If this is to be a family discussion then Billy should be here," Genevieve replied evenly.

"Do as you are told!" William yelled.

Both Genevieve and Gracie shrank back from him. They followed him into the parlour. Gracie sat nervously on one of the lounges. Johnny's eyes were shifty and unsettled. William paced with his hands behind his back.

"What is this about, William?" Genevieve asked.

William turned on his heel to glare at her. "You would already know if you were as dedicated to your daughter's upbringing as you claim to be!"

Genevieve flushed angrily at the accusation. "What does that mean, William?"

"Do you know where your daughter was yesterday morning?" he challenged her. "Gracie, why don't you tell us where you were and who you were with?" William turned his full, glowering attention on her.

Gracie sat in disbelief. She found herself angry at her father for assuming he had any right to question her in front of Johnny after his indiscretion. When she looked up, her eyes were hard. "Why doesn't Johnny tell you where I was, *Papa*?" she stressed the title with icy emotion. "He seems to know so much about my whereabouts. Or actually, is it Lana Hamilton who knows where I was? Her name seems to be coming up an awful lot lately, don't you agree?"

Johnny faltered, feigning confusion, "I'm not sure what she means . . ."

But Gracie, like her father, wanted a captive audience in her presence. "How *is* Lana Hamilton, Johnny?"

Johnny glared at Gracie. "This has nothing to do with Lana."

Gracie smiled viciously. "Oh, I think it does." She turned her eyes back to William. She felt strangely empowered by her tryst. She stood up and walked directly over to him. "I spent the morning with Ruairi O'Neill, but I gather you already knew that. What you probably don't know is that I spent the night with him too!"

His open hand hit her face with a resounding crack and her tiny body crumpled to the floor. "You little whore!" William shouted. "You will stay away from him or you will find yourself out on the street!"

Genevieve gasped, falling to her knees beside her daughter. Gracie clung to her mother in real fear. In all of his rages, he had never struck Gracie. William's hand stung and he realized he had hit her harder than he had intended to. But his adrenaline was like fire simmering just beneath his skin. He turned his attention to Genevieve. "I've had enough of this family acting in their own self-interests. Am I making myself clear?"

Genevieve looked down at the tiny trail of blood coming from Gracie's lip and tracing itself across her dress. "How dare you harm our child?"

"I will do whatever is necessary to keep this family from shame and ruin," he seethed.

"You are the one who has brought shame and ruin to this family! The whole island is talking about the illegitimate child, William." Genevieve was furious with him.

William's fist came down hard and fast to silence her. The blow sent her backwards and she clutched at her cheek as splinters of pain ripped through her skull. Gracie began to scream hysterically. Johnny sat stiffly at the window seat, not moving, not reacting.

"Hold your tongue! That child is not mine!" William shouted over Gracie's sobs.

Genevieve glared up at him steadily, the pounding in her head causing her to see double. She refused to cry but she couldn't stop her trembling.

William reached towards her. She pulled away but he was over top of her, trying to help her up. She stood absolutely straight as she watched him turn and pick Gracie off the floor. "Now, you will take Johnny back and I better not hear of any more foolishness concerning Ruairi O'Neill. I think the best thing to do is get this wedding planned and over with so that we can move on with our lives. Give me the ring, Johnny."

Gracie's legs were too shaky to stand on their own and William continued to embrace her as he jammed the ring back on her finger. It made her dizzy with revulsion. Every time she tried to focus on his face she saw a different man from the father she had known. He had become the monster that Ruairi had said he was.

Gracie found herself alone in her bedroom, lying on her bed. She clawed her way under the covers, pulling them tight around her shaking body. Everything seemed blurred together and Gracie found herself trying desperately to distinguish some sort of reality from the nightmare. She didn't know how long it was that she laid there before a violent sleep engulfed her.

Genevieve sat on the edge of the bed that she had shared for so many years with her husband. She could no longer pretend that their marriage wasn't over. She could live with the bruised skin and the hardened heart but she would not allow him to harm her children. She pulled a sheet of paper from her bedside table and wrote her brother's name at the top of it. She would post the letter first thing in the morning. It was time to seek refuge.

Billy hung around the Club for another couple of hours, having a few hits of tennis and a few snifters of brandy. He was trying to distract himself from the fact that he had not seen or heard from Rosaleen since she had fallen asleep in his arms.

He left the Club around seven o'clock and decided it was time to go to her.

He found the little blue house and stared at it for a moment. It was a charming little house, in good condition and well looked after. He liked it. It had character.

She opened the door looking startled to see him. "What are you doing here?" she asked, sliding through the half-opened door and shutting it quickly behind her.

"I came to see you," he said, wondering why she wouldn't invite him in. "Is Ruairi inside?" he asked nervously.

"No, but my daughter is home and I don't feel like explaining you to her."

"Oh," he replied, not sure how to take that, "Are you planning on introducing us soon?"

Rosaleen felt the colour drain from her face. "I'm not sure," she stammered. "I haven't decided yet."

"What is there to decide?" Billy asked. "If you came here to be with me then I am going to have to meet her."

"It's not that easy, Billy! Until I figure out how to handle Ruairi you need to stay away."

"So it's all on your terms then?" He was slightly annoyed with her.

"Unless you want to get yourself shot," she fired back at him.

Billy tried to diffuse the situation. He hadn't come to fight. "I'm sorry, Rosaleen. I just would like to be able to come and see you whenever I need you. I don't want to be always waiting for you."

"You have no right to demand anything of me," she spoke through gritted teeth, her nostrils flaring. "I'm not your private whore!"

"That is not what I meant," he stammered. She was twisting his words.

The door flew open behind her and Rosaleen turned in alarm. A tumble of red curls appeared and Billy was shocked by the depth of the green eyes that stared him down. "Keep your voices down," the woman's voice was warm and melodic.

Rosaleen cursed, "You scared the hell out me, Maggie."

"Kathleen's just in the kitchen having some milk before bed so just be a wee bit softer," Maggie warned.

"Can you just come out for a walk, Rosaleen? I've been thinking about how we can tell Ruairi . . ."

Rosaleen's reaction was fierce, "You will stay away from Ruairi!"

"Well, when are you going to talk to him? At least tell me that much," Billy pleaded with her.

Rosaleen turned away from him. She felt caged; the lies were closing in on her.

Billy took a step towards Rosaleen. He was desperate to hold her but Maggie put her hand up to stop him. Her green eyes flashed. "Go home King Billy," she said firmly. "Rosaleen will send for you when she's ready."

He stared at Rosaleen's back for a long moment, willing her to turn back around and come to him but she stood rigid and unmoving. Finally, he relented and made his way down the porch steps and out to the street.

Maggie watched him go, her eyes darkening as the Englishman was taken by the night.

Genevieve stood on the threshold of her new life. Valerie Logan reached out and touched the bruises with her fingertips.

"You are safe now," she promised her new friend firmly.

"I had to leave Billy and Gracie," Genevieve cried.

Valerie pulled her inside gently and wrapped protective arms around her. "We'll get them as soon as we can."

When he arrived back home, Billy knocked on Gracie's bedroom door. When she didn't answer, he let himself in. She lay on the bed, curled up beneath a mass of linens. Her tiny body was barely visible under all of the bedding. He sat down beside her and put his head in his hands, letting the rejection, the hurt and the anger settle somewhere deeper. When he felt calmer, he reached over and rubbed his sister's back.

It took her a few minutes to fully wake up. When she finally turned herself towards him he saw the red puffy eyes, the swollen lip and the broken demeanour.

Somewhere down the street, a young man narrowed his eyes and looked around to make sure no one had seen him walk up the steps of the house. He took a deep breath and adjusted his tie, and then he knocked on the door.

She opened it herself, a look of sheer adoration on her face. He liked that. Gracie hadn't looked at him that way in a long time. He smiled at her. She blushed.

"Hello Lana." He moved inside and slid a hand around her waist, pulling her to him gently. "Is anyone else home?" he murmured softly.

"No, Johnny," she breathed back. "We're all alone."

"Good," he said, as he shut the door behind him. He felt himself weaken. She was so much more exciting than Gracie was, especially with her clothes off. He grabbed a hold of the pearls and pulled her in to kiss her lips.

There was no fight in her. That was the way Johnny Bexley liked his women.

When the door closed, the lights from a black Ford switched on and the motor roared to life. Mairtin grimaced. He would keep an eye on Johnny Bexley. Even though the girl was a Gainsborough, Mairtin had seen the way Ruairi looked at her. She may as well have been Irish now.

Maggie led Kathleen up the stairs and away from Rosaleen who was intent on washing away her sins with whiskey. She was playing the mother now, her make-up gone and her wild hair pulled away from her face. As she brushed the little girl's hair and smoothed the bed linens, she wondered why Kathleen had never asked about her Da. It would have been natural for the little girl to start questioning the strange family arrangement that she was surrounded by but she never had. She was content to be taken care of by whoever was around when she was in need. She had never made strange or screamed endlessly for Rosaleen.

Maggie bent down and kissed the top of her head as she climbed into her bed. "Are you ready to dream, my Love?" she asked.

Kathleen tossed her curls from side to side. "I want a story!" she cried happily.

"What kind of story?" Maggie asked, her green eyes twinkling. She knew the response would be the same as it always was.

"A faëry story," Kathleen said through a mass of giggles.

"And why do you think that I'm only good for faëry stories?" Maggie tickled her playfully.

Kathleen sat up, looking straight into Maggie's bright eyes. "Ruairi always calls you a bean sidhe," she admitted to Maggie slowly, "but I think he's wrong."

"Do you? And why is that?"

Kathleen reached out and touched Maggie's pale fingers. "I've never heard you crying so you must not be a bean sidhe."

"Och, you're a clever one," she whispered to the little girl.

Kathleen leaned over and put her head on Maggie's chest. "Auntie Maggie, what is a geis?" she asked.

Maggie leaned her head back against the wall behind the bed. "A geis is sort of like a curse," she felt her voice changing over the words.

"Do you know anybody who has a geis on them?" Kathleen continued her questioning.

"Where are these questions coming from, Love?" Maggie could hear the question that the child really wanted to ask.

Kathleen picked at Maggie's long, red fingernails and remained quiet for a while. When she spoke, it was very softly. "Mammy said that Ruairi is only here because he believes in the geis that you put on him."

Maggie wondered what would have possessed Rosaleen to tell Kathleen that. "Oh Kathleen," she breathed out heavily, "that was all just games when we were young."

But Kathleen refused to forget about it so easily. "What was his geis?" she asked again.

Maggie closed her eyes. She remembered that night around the fire when she had stared through the flames at Ruairi. She had seen Roísín Dubh, the black rose and she had seen death. He had called Maggie his bean sidhe ever since.

"Ruairi loves your Mammy very much. I used to tease him that he'd do anything to protect her." Maggie struggled to put it into terms that she would understand.

"Even die?" Kathleen's age had not protected her from the natural conclusion.

"Even die." Maggie took the little girl's hand and held it to her heart.

Kathleen inhaled deeply, slowly. When she let the breath go, she snuggled back into her bed. "Tell me the story about Caer and Aengus Óg," her voice was sleepy.

Maggie's eyes flashed emerald. She let go of the present and let her mind drift back to the world of faëry. "The goddess of dreams," Maggie exhaled as she kissed Kathleen's temple and stroked her hair back from her face. "Caer Ibormeith was a daughter of the Danaan prince Ethal Anubal, and she lived one year as a maiden and one year as a swan," her voice slowly faded into the other realm as the little girl fell asleep.

CHAPTER 12

Billy didn't go for his run that morning. He had slept beside his sister, wanting to be there for her if she woke up in the night. He had found his mother's note. She was gone and he hoped for her sake that she wasn't coming back. He stewed on his options which were few and none very attractive, but anything would be better than living under William Gainsborough's roof any longer. He had his trust fund and the money that he had saved since moving to Canada. He couldn't move the whole family out immediately, that would take time. He would lose his job, certainly, but there were other offers on the table. He thought about Ruairi and the money that had been pressed into his palm.

There was a cough as William walked past Gracie's bedroom door. Billy looked over at his sister and decided it couldn't wait. He rolled off of the bed and crossed the room to the door. By the time he was through it, his father was already downstairs. Billy chased after him as quietly as he could. He caught up to him just as his father entered his office.

Billy shut the door purposefully behind them.

William turned slightly towards him as he rounded his desk but wouldn't look him in the eye. "Are you back already from your run?" he asked after clearing his throat.

"I didn't run this morning," Billy's tone was terse.

William raised an eyebrow. "That's not like you," he stated, not knowing what else to say. He was pretty sure he knew why his son was in his office and he was braced for a confrontation.

"Did you think that I'd let you get away with abusing my mother and my sister?" Billy growled.

William sat down at his desk and avoided the question. "You seem quite fond of Ruairi O'Neill suddenly."

Billy shook his head in disgust. "This has nothing to do with Ruairi O'Neill."

William stared at his son. "My treatment of your sister has everything to do with Ruairi O'Neill. Are you not aware of her affection for him?"

"Gracie doesn't even really know Ruairi," Billy began to argue.

William sat back. "Apparently she knows him quite well," he paused, "intimately, in fact, according to her."

Billy was silenced. He tried not to appear as shocked as he was.

"If you weren't so concerned with Rosaleen, you may have been able to save your precious sister from ruin. Luckily, Johnny is a gentleman and will honor his pledge to your sister regardless."

"Johnny Bexley is no gentleman," Billy found his voice.

"That is quite an accusation coming from your lips," William's tone was harsh.

"What is that supposed to mean?" Billy had a feeling that he may have walked into a trap.

"I had an interesting discussion with Rosaleen the other night."

"Do you care to elaborate?" Billy shifted his feet unconsciously. He was slightly unnerved about what she may have said to him. He could clearly remember his father's face after she had kissed him at the Club.

"At this point, I just feel you need a sound warning about fraternizing with members of the Irish Republican Army."

"It is due to members of the Irish Republican Army that I am still alive," Billy clenched his jaw. "I had my own discussion with Rosaleen recently."

William narrowed his eyes. "So she has told you then?"

Billy fought to control his rage. He wanted to strangle his father for what he had done. "She went to you with information that would have saved three soldiers lives never mind the young boy that was hanged for their murder! It should have been your neck in the noose!" Billy could feel the tears, hot and sticky. "You gambled my life, your own son! The truth is I'm only alive because Ruairi O'Neill found his heart for half a second."

William stood up and faced his son with clenched fists. "You are only alive because Rosaleen couldn't bear to have the blood of her child's father on her hands." William had waited for the right moment. He knew his son had been deceived.

Billy hesitated, his mind uncertain. The conversation had suddenly become very confusing.

"Did you not think I would find out about the Shelbourne?" William pressed on, "I do think it was in poor taste given the history between her and me."

Billy went from hot to cold. "What does that have to do with Ruairi leaving me alive?"

"The child is yours!" William sat back down and leaned into his chair with a wicked grin and a clap of his hands. "You didn't know? Isn't that interesting? She looks so much like Gracie as a child except for that black hair of her mother's," William mused.

Billy felt his stomach twist. "The child looks like Gracie because you are the father."

"No, no I'm not. I hadn't been with Rosaleen for a year when she had the baby."

"That's not what you said back then." Billy felt the shifting sands of his father's words.

William sighed. "I had a gun to my head. I would have admitted to anything at the time. But the truth is much more complicated." He put a hand to his head and rubbed at his temple. "I did everything I could to save you once the shooting started at the bakery." He ground his teeth. "But you didn't need saving, did you? Rosaleen wouldn't have let you die knowing what she knew."

"Was it jealousy?" Billy asked. He felt sick to his stomach. "Is that why you let them go through with it? Did you want me dead because I slept with her?"

William pursed his lips. "I didn't care about you and Rosaleen! I cared about capturing and killing Ruairi O'Neill. I would do it again if it meant nailing that bastard."

Billy didn't try to hide his disgust. "You sacrificed three soldiers and your son for your own glory."

"I was serving my country."

"You were serving yourself."

"And what were you doing when you were sleeping with that whore? Obviously she had turned you. How many other missions did you compromise to protect her and her murderous friends?" William tried to shift the focus.

"I don't have to listen to this. My conscience is clean." Billy had played William's games before.

"I wonder if Ruairi will see it that way," William said calmly.

"If I was the father, she would have told me. It was different with me. She . . . '

"What? She loved you? That girl doesn't love anybody. She was just using you to get out of Ireland." William had wrestled the power away.

The accusation hurt, not least of all because of the way she had treated him the night before. "You don't know her," Billy argued weakly. He had no energy to fight; there was too much information to process.

"Let me ask you something. Why do you think she told me who the father is but not you?"

Billy swallowed hard but couldn't answer. His mouth was dry.

William was nodding his head as if the answer should be obvious to both of them. "She's just here for money, Billy. She doesn't give a damn about you."

Billy was overcome with anger and a much more brutal emotion, fear. He shook as he spoke. "Whether she loves me is not the issue. If that child is mine, then I will freely give her everything she is entitled to; love and money."

"She will not get a penny. She is a bastard," William swore.

"You forget that I am a lawyer. I am the one who will interpret the law," Billy pointed out, "and I can assure you I will interpret it in her favour."

"Are you threatening me, Billy?" William asked, almost too casually. His tone incensed his son.

Billy became irrationally calm. "I don't need to use threats. You are about to lose everything. I'm done with you."

"Are you just? You'll have nothing if you walk away from me."

"I'm my own man in this country."

William laughed at his son's naïveté. "You will always walk in my shadow."

"Not if I'm following Ruairi O'Neill," Billy spat out, not even sure if he meant what he was saying.

William looked his son in the eye. "Ruairi O'Neill is a marked man. If you stand behind him, you will be in the direct line of my fire."

Billy set his jaw. "Always one to shoot them in the back, aren't you William?" He left William screaming obscenities in response and went back up to check on Gracie.

In the quiet of Gracie's bedroom, Billy thought about what his father had told him. If it was true, Rosaleen's daughter was his daughter. And now he was homeless and most probably jobless.

Gracie groaned softly. She rolled over and looked at her brother with dull eyes. Billy reached down and stroked her hair off of her face.

"Good morning," he whispered.

She tried to smile weakly. The cut on her lip was too painful and limited her attempt. She licked it to try to moisten the crack but the taste of blood turned her stomach. "Did you stay here all night?" she asked quietly.

He nodded. "Of course I did. I didn't want you to wake up alone."

Gracie reached for his hand.

Billy inhaled sharply. "Gracie, I'm going to move out."

Her eyes went wide and she sat up quickly. "You can't leave me here!" she cried.

Billy put a finger to her broken lips and hushed her. "I won't. Not for long anyway. I just have to get myself set up and then I'll get you out of here."

Gracie crawled up on her knees and grabbed Billy by the shoulders. "Take me with you now, Billy," she begged. "I can't stay in this house! Not anymore!"

Billy put his hands on his sister's cheeks and sighed. "It's not that easy. I have to find us a suitable place to live and I have to make sure that I can support you. Just give me a few days and I'll try to get you to Valerie's with Maman. Be the perfect daughter and stay away from Ruairi O'Neill. I promise, Gracie, I will take you out of this horrible house."

Gracie's shoulders began to shudder and she buried her head in her brother's chest. He wrapped his arms around her and whispered softly into her hair, "I will never let him hurt you again, I swear."

Hours passed but Gracie couldn't move from her bed. Billy and her mother were gone and the house was silent. Her mind kept slipping backwards through time, tracing the links to Ruairi and Rosaleen. It was a convoluted past, so much bound up by myth and mystery. She felt the inherent need to find her own truth.

She tiptoed down the stairs and looked around to make sure she was alone in the big house. She shut herself in William's study and looked around slowly. The room was dark. The curtains were still drawn. The wood panelling made the room seem small, almost claustrophobic.

She looked at the clock and wondered where she should begin. She had limited time. A cabinet stood in the corner closest to her. It was locked but she knew where William kept all of his keys. As a child she had played many a day away beneath her father's desk and she had found the little cut-out space in which his keys were anchored.

Her thin finger prodded around beneath the top slab until she found it again. They were there and the cabinet opened. She stared in at the masses of files before her, not knowing exactly what it was she was looking for, what word in cramped handwriting would implicate one man over the other.

The files were labelled according to many different things; some had dates, some had names of people while others had names of places. She sifted through the first few but they were mostly dockets and tax information. The second lot were more interesting, with letters from the British Foreign Minister's office and the minutes from meetings held with Winston Churchill; but there was nothing concerning Ireland.

She continued to search, emptying file after file. She looked back at the clock as another hour chimed into existence. It was one. Her father would be home by three o'clock. Every Monday afternoon since the weather had turned fine William had played golf with Lucas, Richard Kennedy and Benjamin Cole. They would then indulge in copious amounts of brandy before they retired to their homes for dinner with their respective families.

Gracie sighed. She sat atop mounds of paper, useless scraps of information documenting her father's every move. Except the ones she was interested in. She stood up and stretched. Her heart had calmed itself sometime during the shuffling and sorting and her mind had numbed itself completely. She left the room in search of a cup of coffee to help her keep her eyes open and alert.

She returned with the bone china cup and saucer steadied perfectly the way her mother had taught her. As she perused the piles on the floor, looking for a fresh place to start, her eyes fell upon a thick file that had landed near the base of the cabinet. She kicked the nearby files away from it revealing its label in bold black ink. "JAMESON".

Her hand trembled enough in her rush of excitement that she dropped the cup and saucer, the china shattering on impact with the cold marble tiles on the floor, the coffee splashing over everything within a three foot radius. Gracie scooped up the file without so much as a glance at the mess and hurried over to the desk.

She gasped as she opened up the file. The first insert was a newspaper clipping. The headline read "The Sack of Balbriggan" and the picture showed Black and Tans standing in front of a burning block of row housing while mayhem ensued behind them. Gracie skimmed the story with her hand clutched to her throat.

Gracie felt the hot tears turning icy, the further they slipped from her eyes. She sat back, not knowing if she should continue. Her mind tried to pacify her with excuses but her strangled heart fought hard to make her emotional response so strong that she couldn't deny it. She knew she would have to keep wading through the horror stories to convince herself of what she was beginning to believe was the truth.

What she found made her feel ill. There were detailed lists of what were known as 'Sinn Feiners' giving names, addresses and next of kin. The list had been updated on several occasions as evidenced by the date at the top of the page. Beside their names, in her father's handwritten script were words such as *warned, lifted,* and *dead.* Gracie scanned the names for any she may recognize. She found Mairtin and Michael Fitzgerald as well as Thomas and Ruairi O'Neill. Beside their names were written the words *active.* She shivered. There were other names that made her cry; two Jameson's, one O'Neill and one Fitzgerald, all dead. There was one O'Neill that had words beside it that made her feel a fluttering of hope that her father hadn't always been successful. Beside Gerard O'Neill the words read 'escaped Mountjoy-believed to be in America'.

The next few documents related to Rosaleen Jameson. There were personal documents that listed everything from her date of birth to what types of literature she fancied. Gracie felt as though she were suffocating when she realized that on this specific piece of paper, Rosaleen had been slowly dehumanized into a few categories of words. Then there were the medical records which included a copy of the birth certificate of Kathleen Jameson; William Gainsborough was listed as the father.

She continued on until the file was exhausted. It was clear that Ruairi and Mairtin had been telling her the truth about her father's career as a British General. He had been behind countless raids, tortures and executions. Until she had met Ruairi, she would have argued that no matter how brutal or manipulative or sadistic, he was just doing his duty to his country. He had signed up for a war and he was doing a bloody good job to try to win it. But now all of those Irish names had faces and one face in particular was forcing her to question everything she had ever been told.

She pushed back from the desk, at a loss for where the rest of the information might be hidden, if there was any. She slowly paced around the tiny room. She had made an absolute mess of it with papers strewn everywhere, the broken china and the coffee. She was lost inside her thoughts when the study door flew open.

William stood staring in disbelief at his daughter. She had ransacked the room and now stood on top of scattered piles of important documents. "What the bloody hell are you doing?"

Gracie moved behind the desk to put an obstacle between her and her father. He was blocking the door. "I was looking for something," she stammered.

"And did you find it?" William's voice was constricted.

Gracie looked down at the file that lay open on the desk. "Yes, I believe I did."

William took a step towards her. Without taking his eyes off of her, he closed the file on the desk and tucked it under his arm. "Then you best be on your way," William's words were short and steady.

Gracie nodded and made a move to leave but he caught her arm as she brushed by.

"There's more, if you are interested." He glared down at her.

Gracie could smell the brandy on his breath. "I don't know what you are talking about."

"I have files on him too. They're in the safe. Do you remember the code?"

Gracie pulled away from him and felt her back against the book case.

"It's your birth date, in case you've forgotten." His smile was insincere. "I just want you to get the full picture of what happened over there. I wouldn't want your opinion of me tainted."

Gracie was too afraid to speak. She just wanted to get away from him.

"Maybe another time then," his tone was cold. He held her in his gaze a few moments longer and then moved away from the door.

She bolted, running all the way back to her room and locking the door behind her.

Gracie didn't surface from her room again that day or the next. She desperately wanted to go back to her father's files and read what was written about Ruairi but something down deep told her that she had read the words before, too many times. Ruairi had spoken for himself and she had believed him. She didn't doubt that he had done things unimaginable. He had never denied that. But he had his reasons and who was she to judge them.

She didn't know how to confront the feelings that were keeping her awake at night; the voices that were telling her to do things that were wild and unheard of in her world. The courage to act on her night-time revelations eluded her and so she clung to the daytime in which everything became clear; it had to be left alone.

She couldn't risk putting Ruairi in danger. Gracie now knew what Mairtin had meant when he had told her that nothing good could come of their brief affair but a wound had opened up that refused to clot. All that she was made up of was seeping out of her, bleeding her of her own self.

In an attempt to blot out any idleness that may allow thoughts of Ruairi to unsteady her resolve, she spent the days following the confrontation plotting her escape; not just from her father's house, but from her life as a dependant woman. But every night, her body would mislead her mind and she would dream of his hands all over her, his lips moving softly in the space between her neck and shoulder and his eyes, burning intensity into the furthest reaches of her soul.

For Ruairi, the last few days had been difficult at best. He was a disciplined man, never giving in to foolish whims or flights of fancy. Even when he seemed at ease, his mind was carefully calculating the possible consequences of every word and action. Spontaneity was a state of mind for him. He could easily live in the moment as long as that moment had been given due consideration in the moments before.

But she had gotten to him. She had a way of blurring reality and making the past seem like an intangible thing. There were moments when he actually forgot what he was supposed to be doing in Charlottetown. And in those brief moments, he knew he was in danger of losing himself to her; and of getting himself killed.

There was an easy solution; get himself and the others out of Charlottetown as quickly as possible. And that is what he intended on doing.

CHAPTER 13

O n Thursday morning Ruairi sat on the porch smoking a cigarette. His feet pushed against the veranda rail and rocked him back and forth on the porch swing. He watched the clouds building over the harbour and wondered whether there would be an afternoon storm or if it would blow off. He wasn't good with weather patterns. Mick was though. He had grown up on the land in Galway and he seemed to know what the weather was going to do before the sky knew. He would ask Mick. There was no point in going out for the shipment from Miquelon if he was going to get himself killed in gale force winds. He was taking one of the bigger boats this time and was going to meet Stavros and Thomas offshore. They were supposed to have taken *The Phoenix* out after breakfast and would be on the north side of the island at about eight that night. It would be a long day for them but hopefully lucrative. They would unload Ruairi and make the runs to shore. *The Phoenix* was much faster than the Coast Guard ships and they would have the liquor distributed all over Prince Edward Island by the the middle of the night if all went well.

Mairtin kicked open the screen door and came out to sit across from him. Ruairi stopped swinging and stretched his legs out over the side of the bench, lying face up.

Mairtin opened a flask and took a long drink.

"How do you drink that stuff this early in the morning?" Ruairi asked, half disgusted with Mairtin's drinking habits.

"Early? I've been up since four," Mairtin defended himself. "Half the day's already gone."

"Where did you go this morning?"

"In to get the messages," Mairtin replied.

"Anything interesting?"

"We aren't going out today, plan was called off. Same plan is a go for Monday except Stavros isn't available so I'll take his place."

"What happened?" Ruairi hated it when they couldn't make a transfer. He actually enjoyed the work. He felt lazy just sitting around, playing poker and drinking. He'd never been in a job where he wasn't living hand to mouth.

"The transfer to Miquelon got picked up. We'll have to wait for a new supply to come across."

"McCoy will be extremely happy to know he has our supply of Irish whiskey to keep him going then," Ruairi smiled.

Mairtin agreed, "It's too bad we haven't figured out how to make Champagne. We wouldn't have to go up to Miquelon at all."

"Someone will have to alert Stavros and Thomas or they'll be wondering what the hell happened to us," Ruairi chewed his thumbnail as he spoke.

"I'll fetch them," Mairtin replied.

Ruairi sank back in the swing and closed his eyes. "Anything else?"

Mairtin was slow to answer, "There's a message for you from HQ." He handed him the sheet of paper that the note was written on.

"And what do the big boys have to say?" Ruairi raised his eyebrows waiting for Mairtin to fill him in. "I take it you've already read it?"

Mairtin nodded, lighting his own cigarette and taking a long drag. "I think you should read it for yourself."

This particular message had come through the day before. He had been slow to pass it on, rereading it over a dozen times. They'd been ordered to stay put possibly for the full year. The Royal Ulster Constabulary had begun a campaign in the North and Ruairi's presence back home would only complicate matters. They would call him home when his safe landing could be assured.

Ruairi re-read it a few times. "And what are your thoughts?" Ruairi asked.

"You wouldn't listen to me anyway."

"Would you listen to you if you were me?"

Mairtin looked confused as he tried to decipher all of the 'yous' in the question. When he finally figured out what he was being asked he sighed, "You should stay." His words were simple.

"Should I stay with her?"

"A woman's not worth that kind of trouble."

"That's a bit of a worry when you're courting my sister," Ruairi's tone had a hint of caution in it.

Mairtin smiled, "I'll rephrase that. *That* woman's not worth that kind of trouble."

"I'd wager she is. Greater men have gone down for less."

Mairtin shrugged. "And what if you're wrong and it gets you killed? Or worse, it gets somebody innocent killed?"

"Is there really anybody innocent left?"

Mairtin just puffed on his cigarette. "I'm pretty sure we were all born damned," he finally said, a stream of smoke punctuating his prognosis.

"Speaking of the damned," Ruairi looked up at Mairtin, "did you hear about young Billy leaving the big house?"

"Me Da was going on about something to that effect this morning. The old dame left as well." He snuffed the cigarette out against the railing of the veranda. "Apparently Valerie opened up the whole west wing of the house for her."

"Do you get the feeling that we are just puppets in this play?"

Mairtin exhaled loudly. "I do get that feeling," he said, patting Ruairi on the shoulder as he walked stiffly passed him and back into the house.

Ruairi took advantage of his day off by taking Kathleen down to the bakery. He had to do something useful or he would go mad. He walked the couple of blocks with the little girl, happy to have a moment in the sun with somebody whose concerns revolved around missing doll clothes and catching butterflies.

Kathleen pranced beside him, her little fingers entwined with his. He looked down at her and laughed. She had been in such a hurry to get ready that she had put her shoes on the wrong feet. He tugged on her hand to get her attention. She looked up, her big blue eyes radiating joy.

"You have your shoes on the wrong feet, Love!" he laughed.

She looked down, flexing her right foot in front of her and examining the shoe. She looked back up at him with a silly grin. "Oops!" she giggled.

Ruairi knelt down and unbuckled the first shoe and then the second. She hung onto his shoulder as she lifted each foot for him to slip the shoes off.

She leaned her face in close to his ear. "Who is that lady, Ruairi?" she asked in a whisper.

Ruairi looked up quickly and saw Genevieve Gainsborough watching them from the doorway of a shop across the street. He turned back to Kathleen, switching the shoes with a bit of haste now. "No one special," he quietly answered her. He did up the buckles and patted her on the head. "There. Perfect."

As he stood up and took her hand again, he saw the Lady step up onto the curb a few feet from them.

"You look like a father," she smiled at them.

Ruairi swallowed. "I'm not her father," he answered quickly, almost defensively.

"He's not my Da!" Kathleen laughed like it was a joke.

She met his eyes. "I know," she paused, looking at the girl hesitatingly. She leaned down close to her. "I'm Genevieve."

"I'm Kathleen," said her two and a half foot counterpart.

"How would you like to get a sweet from the lolly shop?" Genevieve asked brightly.

Ruairi was anxious to get on his way. "I don't think that's such a good idea. We're headed to the bakery."

Genevieve looked up at Ruairi furtively. The hat she was wearing was pulled down low and cast dark shadows over her face. "I would really like to speak with you."

"I can only spare a few minutes," Ruairi said tersely.

She straightened up and he saw the bruising around her eyes. "It will only take a moment, I promise."

"Oh, please Ruairi! I'd really like a lolly!" Kathleen chimed in.

Ruairi sighed and relented, "Alright, but we must be quick."

He followed Genevieve and Kathleen down the street a few shops. Once she had satisfied Kathleen with a treat and sat her down at a table, Genevieve beckoned Ruairi to step aside with her.

He spoke first, "Is that why you left him, then?"

Genevieve tugged the hat down self-consciously. "I didn't come here to discuss that."

Ruairi stood in front of her, his arms crossed. "What can I do for you then, Lady Gainsborough?"

"Three things, actually. First, please call me Genevieve," she began.

Ruairi shook his head. "I don't think it would be appropriate given our situation, and I won't have much occasion to. You and I will not be speaking to each other very often, if at all, in the future."

"I know that you hate my husband, Ruairi. It's actually something that we have in common."

Ruairi raised his eyebrows. "That doesn't make us friends though."

Genevieve smiled sadly. "No, I suppose not."

"What is it that you have to say to me, Lady Gainsborough?" Ruairi's patience was wearing thin.

Genevieve's eyes darted to the child. She was completely lost in her own little world. "Does she know who her father is?"

Ruairi looked at her like she was crazy. "Of course not!"

"Who does she think her father is?" Genevieve pressed.

"It's never been an issue before." Ruairi felt his temperature rising. "Is it an issue now?"

Ruairi clenched his jaw. "What are you asking me?"

"Is Rosaleen here to find a father for her daughter?"

"No . . . no . . ." Ruairi faltered. He hadn't figured out exactly why Rosaleen was in Charlottetown but he didn't want to admit that to Genevieve Gainsborough. "She hates William now. She isn't here for him."

Genevieve narrowed her eyes. "I know she isn't here for William. I'm worried about Billy. He doesn't know, William never told him."

Ruairi's heart began to crash. "Told him what?"

Genevieve looked at Ruairi's panicked face and she blanched. "You don't know either," she realized.

"Told him what?" Ruairi's tone was suddenly hard and fierce.

"The little girl is Billy's child, not William's," Genevieve's voice was barely audible. "I thought it was obvious. William had quit her long before she fell pregnant."

Ruairi stared at Kathleen. She looked up at him, a rainbow of colours smeared across her chin from the lolly. He tried to even out his breathing. He held out his hand. "We have to go, Kathleen. Hop up."

"Ruairi, please wait," Genevieve begged. "I have more to say."

Ruairi's eyes had turned cold. "I can't hear anymore. Not from you." With that, he was out the door, the little girl turning slightly to wave goodbye to the pretty lady in the hat.

Billy lay on the double bed in the room he had rented at the City Hotel on Great George Street. He considered his situation. Lucas had fired him within hours of Billy leaving the Gainsborough house. He approached the other law firms as soon as he had checked into the hotel but William had already sent very direct messages to them. There wasn't a single businessman on the island that wasn't associated with William Gainsborough in one way or another. There was only one man who might employ him now. Billy bit his lip. With his skills, Bill McCoy had said that he could be very useful to Ruairi O'Neill.

A knock on the door distracted him from his thoughts. He was surprised to see Rosaleen on the other side. They stared at each other for a long moment.

"Come in," Billy finally said, holding the door for her.

She walked through and stood in the centre of the room, frozen for a moment. She couldn't look at him while she spoke. "I never told you everything I needed to say the other night."

He sighed. "Well, go on then." He watched her fidget nervously.

It took her three attempts to finally say the words. "Kathleen is your daughter, Billy."

Rosaleen stood silently as she waited for Billy's reaction. They stood a metre apart in the tiny hotel room.

"I know," he confessed softly. He wanted to know why she had suddenly decided to tell the truth. He watched her face closely.

Rosaleen was stunned. "You know?"

"William told me." He looked away from her. She had obviously made the decision to come to him on her own.

Rosaleen walked to the window and stared out across the street, unsure of where to go from there. "I suppose I shouldn't be shocked. I'm sure he has given you every reason that you shouldn't allow me back in your life. Has he said enough to discredit me in your eyes?" She turned back to him, her arms folded delicately across her chest.

"I think you've done a fine job of that yourself." Billy didn't allow any emotion to pass by his features. "Is it money you are after?"

"Is that what you think?"

"I don't know what to think," he replied truthfully. "I feel like such a fool."

"Billy, I swear to you, I am not here for your money! I came here for you. I want to be a family."

"Rosaleen, having me means having money. Do you think that point is lost on me?"

Rosaleen could see that he didn't trust her anymore. She had waited too long to tell the truth. She began to tremble. She hadn't eaten in days and she was barely sleeping. Her heart was beating too fast and her head began to throb. She reached for the table.

Billy watched as she turned pale. "Rosaleen, look at me!"

She could hear Billy's voice but it seemed miles away.

"Rosaleen!"

CHAPTER 14

As the evening descended, Ruairi found himself sitting in the kitchen of Stavros' house with a cup of tea in one hand and a sugar biscuit in the other.

He hadn't told anybody yet. He didn't know who to tell.

"Anyone hear any gossip around town today?" Stavros asked lightly.

"You're worse than a woman," Karl grunted.

"I've got some gossip." Thomas smiled mischievously.

"Well, out with it then," Stavros demanded.

"Young Billy Gainsborough might be a bit more like his father than we knew," he paused to wiggle his eyebrows, "There is a rumour around town that he has an illegitimate child! Apparently, it might be the reason that he's moved into the City Hotel."

Ruairi tensed. "Where did you hear that?" he growled.

"Genevieve Gainsborough was overheard talking to some stranger on the street."

Ruairi leaned forward and put his head in his hands, resting his elbows on his knees. He tried to picture every face that had been in the lolly shop.

"That dog!" Stavros crowed. "I would have never given him so much credit."

Even Karl was impressed. He whistled low. "That will give the ladies something to get wild over at morning tea."

Mairtin watched Ruairi with guarded eyes. "I need a cigarette," he said suddenly.

Stavros pointed to the veranda. "You better go outside, Maria hates when I smoke inside."

"I'm already on my way out." Mairtin motioned for Ruairi to follow him.

Ruairi looked over at Thomas. "You sure that's what you heard?"

Thomas nodded enthusiastically. "Damn sure. He's the talk of the town at the moment!"

Ruairi sighed. It was only then that Thomas realized his brother wasn't too pleased with what he had heard.

When Rosaleen opened her eyes, she was lying on the bed in Billy's hotel room. He was sitting at the little table, reading a newspaper.

"What happened?" she asked, struggling to sit up.

"You fainted." Billy slowly stood up and made his way closer to the bed.

She put her hand over her face, embarrassed. "I'm sorry," she mumbled, "I haven't eaten much lately."

"I thought that may have been the case." He held out a glass of water to her. "You need to take better care of yourself."

Rosaleen sipped at the water. "Will you please sit down beside me?"

Billy shook his head. "No, I don't think straight when I'm near you."

Rosaleen began to cry. She couldn't help herself. "So that's it then? You won't forgive me?"

"I don't know yet, Rosaleen!" Billy turned away in frustration. "You need to give me some time."

She put the water down and pushed her hair back shakily. It took her a few moments but she finally made it to her feet.

"Don't get up, Rosaleen. You can stay here and rest. I'll have some food brought up and . . ."

She was already at the door. "I'll be fine, Billy. I always am."

Billy watched her leave. He didn't make a move to stop her.

Ruairi leaned over the porch rail and lit his cigarette, passing the match over to Mairtin who stood beside him, facing in the opposite direction with his back against the railings.

"You're very quiet tonight," Mairtin pointed out. "I would have expected a little more of a reaction to that sort of rumour."

Ruairi was slow to respond, "I've had all afternoon to think about it. I was the stranger that Genevieve Gainsborough was overheard talking too."

Mairtin sucked heavily on the smoke in his mouth. "I have a feeling I'm not going to like the end of this story."

Ruairi put his head down and bent over the rail. "William isn't Kathleen's father."

The cigarette fell from Mairtin's mouth. He caught it, burning his fingers in the process. "Are you telling me Billy Gainsborough is Kathleen's father?"

"That's the rumour."

"Do you think it's true?" Mairtin was wild-eyed.

"Aye, I do," Ruairi's voice was full of sadness. "It makes the last few days a lot less confusing."

"You should go to Maggie. She'll know for sure."

"If Maggie knows, she's kept it from me for a reason. I need to go to Rosaleen. I want to hear it from her. I want to hear every damn word of it out of her mouth. And then maybe I'll finally be able to stop loving her," he said forcefully, trying to convince himself.

Mairtin flicked his cigarette butt off the veranda and quickly shoved another in his mouth.

"Are you all right? You have to breathe *some* oxygen to sustain yourself," Ruairi chuckled.

"No, I'm not all right," Mairtin spat out, irritated with himself for not having seen through her lies. "Rosaleen's messed up your life one too many times."

"This will be the last time. This is goodbye. I'm going back home and she's staying here."

"Why do you want to go home so badly? Is it because you want to fight for our country or are you just trying to get yourself killed so that it doesn't hurt so much anymore?"

Ruairi turned away from Mairtin. He would have never thought that Mairtin would be so perceptive.

Mairtin wouldn't let up. "Or are you scared you might actually love another woman more than Ireland?"

"I don't love anything more than Ireland." Ruairi's voice was hard.

"You are lying to yourself. The soil means nothing to you. It used to be all for Rosaleen but now every single one of us is Ireland to you, including Gracie Gainsborough." Mairtin growled, more at himself than at Ruairi. He wasn't the sentimental type. "If you go home, you won't be any closer to Ireland and you won't be any closer to her."

Ruairi leaned forward a bit further and took a deep breath. When he straightened up his face was hard and his eyes were dark. "And what am I supposed to do about that?" he hissed. "I can't change her name."

"Yes, you can. You can marry her. Make her an O'Neill."

Ruairi gave him a queer look. "What?" he asked in disbelief. "Wasn't it you who told me I couldn't fix everything for her? Didn't you say her life was screwed up and I should just stay out of it?"

"Well, we damn well can't stay out of it and you know it. We're already involved."

Ruairi stared at him, shaking his head. "You know, Mairty, you've never made much sense to anyone but this is absolutely absurd, even for you."

"She could have a life with you. You can get away from all of this, just run! Take her to New York and never go back to God forsaken Ireland. It's not going to change for a long time back home. You have to get out now. Let me clean up the mess."

"She's better off without me," he argued.

Mairtin took a long drag of the cigarette. "She's got bruises on her arm from that damn Johnny Bexley when he found out she was with you," he exhaled. "I'm pretty sure she may have had an altercation with William just after that as well. I was curious to know why they left the Club so suddenly so I followed Genevieve and Gracie home. There was a lot of noise coming from inside."

Ruairi kicked the railing hard and cursed in a foul manner. He buried his head in his hands and thought about the bruises on Genevieve's face. "I'm not meant to live a long life," he groaned.

"Me Da always said, you live what you're given," Mairtin said simply.

With that, the boys went back into the kitchen.

CHAPTER 15

On the fourth morning, Gracie appeared for breakfast. She was pale and dishevelled but she attempted a smile as she came into the parlour. William closed his paper and watched her sit down. Her lip was still damaged but it had begun to scab over. William felt a stab of regret as he watched her hesitate to look up at him.

"Good morning," she said softly.

"Good morning," William replied, trying to sound casual. "How are you today?"

"Well, thank-you," she forced a civil reply.

There was silence for a minute longer and then Gracie spoke again. "I'm going to call around to the Bexley's to see Norah. I've missed her."

"That's a good plan. Maybe you will see Johnny as well," William said pointedly.

"Yes, we have much to discuss. It would be good to see him," Gracie said quickly.

William relaxed. Maybe he had done the right thing after all. She didn't seem too broken and she was at least talking sensibly now. He leaned back in his chair and put a hand over, patting her on the arm. "I love you, Gracie."

"I love you too, Papa," she answered automatically.

Gracie walked the short distance to the Bexley's estate. The door was opened by a butler with a sour demeanour who showed her into the large Victorian sitting room. In less than two minutes, Johnny appeared.

"It's nice to see you, Gracie," he said casually.

She glanced up at him, indifferently. "I'm not here to see you," she replied.

He crossed his arms and glared at her. "At some point we have to settle this matter. For the sake of appearances, anyways."

"And how do we settle it for the sake of appearances, Johnny?" she asked coolly.

"I think you should go sailing with me this afternoon. I've just bought a new boat and it would be good for us to be seen out together. I've invited a few others so it won't just be the two of us."

Gracie cringed. She couldn't think of anything she wanted to do less but she knew if she refused him, he would go straight to her father again. She could also hear her brother's words, telling her to be good for just a little while longer. "Fine, if only for the sake of appearances," she added.

"Fine. Meet me at the docks at two," he snarled back.

"Fine."

Norah finally appeared, giving Gracie a reprieve from Johnny for a few short hours. The girls took a turn around the nearby park.

"So, have you seen Billy since he left?" Norah asked Gracie, still in shock from all of the details of the past few days. Rumours were being whispered all over the Club but hearing them confirmed by Gracie disturbed Norah. She hadn't expected any of them to be true.

Gracie shook her head. "He told me to wait for him and to try to be good until he comes for me. I never left the house until this morning. And I only left my room once." Gracie thought about the office and the files and her father.

Norah put her arm through her friend's. "This is all such a nightmare."

Gracie stopped walking and turned to face Norah. "I wouldn't care about any of this if I could convince Ruairi to run away with me."

"Is that what you really want, Gracie?"

"Yes, it is. I love him," she stated.

Norah nodded. "Then I'm happy for you."

"You don't hate me for what I'm going to do to your brother?"

Norah thought about Johnny and laughed. "I only wish I could be there when you jilt him!" She leaned in and hugged her friend. "After what he's done to you, he deserves everything he gets."

Norah left Gracie at the docks just before Johnny arrived. There were six others. Everybody was happy and smiling except their host who scowled fiercely at Gracie every time she so much as looked in a different direction. He hauled her around the boat by the hand as if the moment he let go of her, she would disappear with the Irishman again.

And he was right. They weren't even out of the harbour when a tiny craft caught everyone's attention. It was manned by Ruairi O'Neill.

Gracie waved at him excitedly. He smiled up at her.

"What the hell is that?" Johnny narrowed his eyes as he looked over the tiny craft that his rival sat on.

Ruairi looked around, as if confused by the question. "A sailboat?"

"That is a pathetic excuse for a sailboat," Johnny said arrogantly.

"I made it myself," Ruairi answered back casually.

"Did you really?" Gracie asked, leaning over to gaze down at him.

"I've always had an interest in sailing but never the time or money to have learned properly." He gazed back up at her, a playfully crooked smile turning up the left corner of his mouth.

"You'll never learn properly in that thing," Johnny spat out. "I'd sooner swim back than be seen sailing in that."

"What a rude thing to say, Johnny! Apologize immediately," Gracie demanded.

"I certainly shall not." Johnny glared at her. "If you'll excuse us, Mr. O'Neill, I believe our boat can withstand a bit more of the sea than that unfortunate vessel of yours and we'd best be getting on with it."

Ruairi nodded to him pleasantly. "Enjoy the day." As Johnny turned his back, Ruairi made a face at him prompting Gracie to giggle.

Johnny wheeled abruptly and grabbed Gracie by the arm, yanking her away from the rail swiftly.

"Ow, Johnny! You're hurting me!" Gracie yelped.

Ruairi clenched his fists. He was too far away to do much more.

"You were flirting with that snake!" Johnny continued more quietly, "You are my fiancée and you had better start acting like it."

He whispered ferociously in her ear, "Don't you dare make a fool of me in front of our friends again."

Gracie's features became dark and shadowy. "Yes, that would be tragic, wouldn't it?" Gracie's voice was loaded with sarcasm. She looked back over her shoulder at the widening gap between her and Ruairi. He was staring back at her, a cigarette in his mouth and trouble in his eyes. Her own eyes glimmered with a cheeky countenance.

She couldn't pretend any longer. She faced Johnny and handed him the ring. "I don't think I want to be your fiancée anymore. You are an ass." With that, she climbed onto the railing and jumped into the water.

"What? Gracie! Get back here!" Johnny yelled. But Gracie was already swimming. Johnny swung around wildly to enlist his party's help but they were all laughing hysterically.

When Ruairi pulled her up onto the tiny boat he was shaking his head in disbelief. "You're a bit of mischief, aren't you Gracie girl?"

"I'll be whatever you want me to be for the day," Gracie panted. Then she rolled over onto her back and began to laugh. "Is he still sputtering over there?"

Ruairi looked over at Johnny's sailboat and chuckled. He raised his voice and called out to him, "She's alright, mate. We'll see you on shore as long as this unfortunate little vessel makes it back in one piece!"

Johnny reddened as the laughter of everyone else swelled around him like the moving sea.

"I think you've just gotten yourself into some trouble, Missy," Ruairi reprimanded her lightly.

"I'd say I have," she paused and her face went serious. "What are we going to do about it?"

"We?" Ruairi raised an eyebrow.

Gracie pulled herself to her knees and reached for Ruairi, pulling herself into his arms and tipping her head to kiss him passionately. "We," she whispered when their lips parted.

Ruairi groaned, "Apparently *we* are going to have to get you out of your father's house."

"Will you have me?" her wet skin responded to every little breeze that blew across her.

Ruairi kissed droplets of water off of her shoulder and collarbone. "Living with me would ruin any chances we have of marrying you off to decent society."

"Fabulous. I've been looking for a way to attract those with less than reputable reputations."

Ruairi fought the urge to laugh. "I'm serious, Gracie. It would ruin you."

"I've already been ruined. At least let me get some enjoyment out of it."

Ruairi shook his head. "You are impossible."

"Impossible to say no to?" she asked hopefully.

He kissed her nose, then her mouth. "No, just impossible," he laughed good-naturedly. He stared at her lips and suddenly his face became very serious. "What happened to your mouth?"

Gracie pulled her lip in, trying to hide it. She didn't answer.

Ruairi took a deep breath and looked away. "I saw your mother's cheek yesterday."

Gracie remained silent.

"I can't let him hurt you, Gracie. You can't ask me to stand back and let him hurt you." Ruairi put a finger to her lips and traced their outline.

"I'm not asking you to do anything," she said. Her blue eyes begged him to let it go.

He gave in and kissed her again. "You amaze me."

She shook her head, a blush rising to her cheeks. "I don't know why."

"You're fearless."

Gracie looked at him in disbelief. "Me?" she argued. "I'm scared of everything. You're the one who's fearless."

"How so?" Ruairi was genuinely interested.

"Everything you do is so unconventional. You fight against entire armies. All I did was jump in the harbour and swim to safety."

Ruairi began to laugh. "I can't believe that you think I'm safe now!"

"What's that supposed to mean?" Gracie asked.

"Last time I fished you out of the water, you thought I was a crazy kidnapper. Now I'm your safety!" he continued to laugh.

Gracie laughed with him. "I still think you're crazy!" Her face sobered very quickly. "But you are my safety."

Ruairi's face darkened. "I'm also your danger. Your father won't be too pleased when Johnny tells him about this."

Gracie sniffed, "I don't care. I love you." She looked back over her shoulder at the three masted sailboat as it glided towards the mouth of the harbour. She knew Johnny was watching her. She crawled over to Ruairi and reached up to grab him by the hair. She pulled his face towards her and kissed his lips forcefully.

"Gentle," he teased her, pressing her wrist so that she released his hair.

"I thought you were tough," she teased back.

"No, not with you. I'm soft and weak and fragile." He leaned in and kissed her slowly. As she pulled away he bit her lip playfully, forgetting momentarily about the cut.

"Ow!" she giggled. "You hurt me!"

His face was serious again. "I will never hurt you," he promised her, stroking her cheek with his thumb.

"Yes, I'm afraid you will. You will leave me and go back to Ireland and that will hurt me more than anything else ever could."

Ruairi dropped his hand from her face and stared out at the water. "I'm sorry."

"Aren't you afraid to go back? Aren't you afraid of dying?" she asked softly.

He shook his head. "No, not really. I'm actually afraid to keep living."

"I don't understand," she said, pulling his hand up to her chest and cradling it near her heart.

He wrapped his fingers around hers. "Gracie, I have been fighting in different wars for almost a decade. I thought that one day it would end but we just seem to find new enemies. I'm exhausted. I have very little fight left in me."

"But I thought it was all over now?"

"Does it seem like it's all over to you?" His eyes were pained. "It's not over. It won't be over until we have our country back and I'll be dead long before then."

"Is Ireland really worth it?" she asked, her innocence touched a part of him that he had never revealed to anyone else.

He answered honestly, "I have to believe that it is."

She was quiet for a moment. "So, what are we to do about my living arrangements? Billy mentioned that I might be able to move in to Valerie Logan's house."

Ruairi agreed with that idea. "It's the perfect place for you. Your mother is there and I have easy access to you."

"So I still look virtuous, but really I'm one of *those girls.*"

"Did you hit your head when you jumped in the water?"

"Yes, right here," she smiled pointing to her lips. "Please kiss it better."

Ruairi relented and kissed her over and over while Johnny Bexley made his way out to sea.

William sat across from two thick-necked men. Both had square heads and mealy complexions. Neither wore a tie.

William handed the larger one a bulging envelope. "You'll get the rest when I see the casket," he said bluntly.

"Any preference to how it's done?"

William shook his head curtly. "Dead is dead."

Genevieve was relieved to see her daughter had received her invitation to afternoon tea. Billy had arranged to meet them as well. It had been days since she had seen her children and she had been missing them. William had denied her any access to the house and to Gracie and she was worried about how her daughter was faring.

Genevieve was wearing a beautiful fur jacket that Valerie had given to her as a gift. It was the first thing that Gracie noticed.

"That is gorgeous! You look so glamourous!" Gracie ran the fur through her fingers.

"Oh my Darling! How are you?" Genevieve put her arms around her daughter and held her tight. When she let go, she examined Gracie's lip and tears sprang to her eyes. "I am so sorry that I couldn't protect you from him."

"I should have never told him about Ruairi and me," Gracie would never allow her mother to take responsibility for her father's brutality.

"Is there still a 'Ruairi and you'?" Genevieve didn't want to pry but she was very concerned about her daughter's relationship with the Irishman. She would bide her time but she would have to discuss it with Gracie eventually.

"I think so," she smiled.

Billy came up behind her and kissed her cheek. She squealed and turned. He wrapped her up in his arms.

"I've missed you," she whispered in his ear.

"You have no idea," he whispered back.

They sat and Genevieve poured the tea. "What's the matter, Darling?" she asked, looking at Billy.

"I'm not sure I'm going to be able to support the both of you for a few months," Billy said quietly. "I'm having a bit of trouble securing a job."

Genevieve put her hands to her son's face and kissed him. "You don't need to be worried about that. I promise you, I'm going to be just fine on my own. I have had some money sent over from home and I think I may have found a way to make more."

Gracie took her chance. "Do you think that Valerie would mind if I came to stay there as well, just for a little while?"

"Not at all," Genevieve smiled. "It's why I asked you here today. Billy and I have spoken about it and we are both terrified of you being in that house by yourself. I ran it by Valerie and she is more than happy with you moving in."

Gracie was relieved. "Ruairi doesn't want me alone with Papa either. He thought that Valerie's house would be the perfect place for me."

"Ruairi?" Billy looked distressed at the mention of his name.

"I was with him this afternoon. I know you asked me to be good but it's just too hard to stay away from him."

"Gracie, we need to talk about this," Billy sighed heavily.

Genevieve reached over and stopped her son from continuing. "This can wait, Billy. Let's just focus on getting Gracie out of William's house."

Billy watched his sister as she left. She looked lighter and happier than she had in weeks. He looked back at his mother who was watching him carefully. "Did she really..?"

Genevieve sighed and nodded her head. "I don't know what to make of it," she confessed. "He must have been a gentleman about it. She doesn't seem at all injured."

Billy stared at the table. "I need your advice, Maman. I believe I may have injured a young woman."

Genevieve waited for her son to continue. She could tell he was hurting greatly.

"I just found out that I fathered a child in Ireland," he confessed. He was ashamed of the tears that began to fall but he was too tired to fight them. "I met Rosaleen Jameson at the Shelbourne Hotel in Dublin. She is Ruairi O'Neill's closest friend and somehow she had become involved with . . ." he began to cry openly. He was afraid of what the truth would do to his mother.

She leaned across the table to comfort him. "I know all about it, Billy. I knew about your father's affair and I knew about your affair."

"Did he tell you?" Billy was incredulous

"Eventually," she admitted, "but a wife knows. And so does a mother."

"I don't know how everything became so complicated!" he cried.

"What does she want?" Genevieve asked mildly.

"She says she wants to be with me but I'm not sure that I believe her." He looked up into his mother's eyes. He needed her to tell him what to do.

"What do you want, Billy?" she asked instead.

"I want to talk to Ruairi," he replied truthfully.

"Do you think that is wise?" Genevieve asked him. There was fear in her voice.

"No," Billy sighed, "but what choice do I have?"

"Is he really as dangerous as he's made out to be?"

Billy looked at his mother calmly. "Yes, he is," he assured her, "and when it comes to Rosaleen, he's the most dangerous man I know."

Rosaleen curled up on a settee in Valerie's courtyard, waiting to be given some undivided attention. She had come to rely on Valerie's advice. Valerie's views were unbiased. She had no reason to judge Rosaleen. She stared vacantly across the scattered potted plants and various collected objects from Valerie's travels. She was listless; tired of the emotional drain of keeping all of her secrets.

A curtain fluttered to her right and the shadow behind it was delicate and willowy. Rosaleen let her gaze slide to the shadow, willing it to move again. The form moved away from the window and she could hear footsteps on marble moving towards her from behind.

"I was wondering how long it would take for you to come to me." Rosaleen adjusted herself so that she could look directly at Genevieve Gainsborough.

Genevieve's smile was thin. "I'm actually surprised you haven't come to me."

"I'm not sure how you feel about me." Rosaleen shifted uncomfortably.

"How I feel about you isn't important." Genevieve sat across from her, smoothing her dress with her hands and then folding left hand over right as though she were speaking to a proper lady. "You should be worried about how my son feels about you."

"I am desperately worried about how Billy feels about me." Rosaleen made eye contact hesitantly.

"When I learned you were here, I was thrilled at first. I thought it would be wonderful for Billy to know his daughter, to have his own family. He seemed so distant since the war," Genevieve paused, breaking eye contact. When she looked back at Rosaleen, she saw the first crack in the young woman. She wanted to make her break for the pain she was causing her son. "I just came from him. He's an absolute wreck. I've never seen him so shattered."

"I love him but he won't believe a word I say." Rosaleen drew her legs into her chest and rocked herself.

"You deceived him!" Genevieve couldn't understand how the girl could be so naïve. "You've deceived everybody! Why should anybody trust you?"

Rosaleen angrily wiped a tear away from the corner of her eye. "Do you understand the position I was in back then? Both your husband and your son are alive because of my deception. You should be thanking me!"

Genevieve's eyes were cold. "Why should I thank you for having an affair with my husband? Why should I thank you for being involved in an army that would have thought nothing of killing my son? Your lies may have saved them in the end but they were only in danger because of your existence. It is taking all of my self-control not to wish you dead for all of the sorrow that you have caused."

Rosaleen could no longer hold back the tears. "And is that how Billy feels? Does Billy wish me dead?"

"No," Genevieve said flatly. "No, Billy's not like that. He just wishes you would have told him the truth when you knew that you were carrying his child."

"What can I do to convince him that I was only trying to protect him?" Rosaleen begged for advice.

"I don't think that you can. I think that Ruairi is the only person who will be able to convince Billy of anything now," Genevieve said quietly, "as long as he doesn't kill my son first."

Rosaleen put her head in her hands. "Ruairi won't kill Billy," she said, closing her eyes to hear Maggie's voice more clearly. "He may kill himself though," she whispered.

They had decided to meet that night. Ruairi had given him a dockside address and told him to be there by midnight. When Billy walked in, he saw Ruairi slouched down in a booth in the corner. He was writing in a leather bound notebook, his hat pulled down low and a cigarette hanging out of the crook of his lips. Billy sat down across from him. They eyed each other warily, neither wanting to appear overly tense.

"I hear that you're a free man." Ruairi flipped the notebook shut and shoved it inside his jacket pocket.

Billy threw up a hand carelessly. "That's the rumour. I thought freedom was supposed to be a good thing, though."

"This isn't a good thing?" Ruairi asked.

"It's too early to tell." Billy rubbed his eyes with the back of his hands. He was tired. He hadn't slept well lately. It may have been the bed at the hotel. Or it may have been the stress of unemployment. Or it may have been . . .

Ruairi cut into his thoughts, "The thought of freedom makes people do crazy things."

"I'm ready for a little bit of crazy in my life."

Ruairi half-smiled. "Are you then?"

Billy swallowed nervously. "So how do we do this?"

Ruairi openly laughed. "*We* don't do anything. You and I won't be doing any business directly. This is all above board. I don't want you compromising your golden boy image. There will be a girl, tomorrow night at the Dominion Day celebrations. She'll be your contact. Everything will be through her. That's all you need to know. Are we clear?"

Billy nodded.

"Good."

Both boys continued to stare at each other.

Billy looked away first. "You shouldn't have touched my sister."

Ruairi sat back and sighed. "I think what happened between your sister and I should remain private."

Billy couldn't bring himself to look at Ruairi. "I asked you to stay away from her."

"I did stay away from her. She came to me."

"You took advantage of her!" Billy accused him.

Ruairi clenched his jaw. "I only did what she asked of me."

"So you think that makes it alright, do you? My sister needs to be protected, not exploited."

"I'm not the one that she needs to be protected from. I've seen what your Da did to her." The flame of the candle on the table danced wildly as Ruairi spoke.

Billy's eyes pierced Ruairi's. "I don't need her left broken hearted when you decide to piss off home."

Ruairi's face became stony. "Billy, I'd be very careful if I were you. If it wasn't for my relationship with your sister, I'd have very little reason to leave you alive."

Billy groaned, raking his fingers through his hair. "I swear, Ruairi, I didn't know that the child was mine until a few days ago. I would have never left her if I would have known."

"I know." Ruairi looked off across the room. When he finally turned back to Billy the tension had left his face. "Don't blame her for what she's done."

Billy was silent for a long time. "Do you think she loves me?" he finally asked.

Ruairi leaned back, running a hand over his throat. "I hope so. It's the only thing that will make the sacrifice worthwhile."

"What sacrifice?" The lines between Billy's eyes wrinkled.

"My life."

"That's a tad dramatic don't you think?"

"You really don't get the Irish do you?" Ruairi narrowed his eyes. "Have you not read many Irish stories or poems then? She's Róisín Dubh and I've made a gospel of her, or so the song goes."

"The song?" Billy raised his eyebrows in disbelief. "Are you telling me you are going to let a song dictate your fate?"

"History repeats itself, over and over. I'm just one lad in a long line of tragedies."

"And Rosaleen is just one lass in a long line of Kathleen Ni Houlihan's?"

"Leading the men of Ireland to their death," Ruairi finished. He leaned towards Billy as he quoted the song that he had based his life on, "Thou hast slain me, O my bride, and may it serve thee no whit, For the soul within me loveth thee, not since yesterday nor today, Thou has left me weak and broken in mien and in shape, Betray me not who love thee, my Little Dark Rose!"

Ruairi drove across to Georgetown on the eastern tip of the island. He had business to attend to on a rocky outcropping where six men sat around a lazy bonfire. Ruairi turned off the headlights as he nosed into park. "It's unusually cold in Limavady," he called out after he slammed the car door. He hated speaking in code but he didn't feel like getting shot at tonight.

"Aye, that it is," came the reply.

Ruairi picked his way carefully through the rocks and then stumbled down the grass and sand embankment. He waved away the offer of a drink and pulled out a thick envelope from his coat pocket.

A stout man with a skiff of red hair reached for the packet, smelling it and laughing loudly. "I can always count on you to get a payment. What was the cut we agreed upon?"

"Ten percent," Ruairi held out his hand.

"A bit stiff isn't it?" The man squared his shoulders and looked around at the men gathered. They were all nodding in agreement.

Ruairi smiled easily. "You'll be a bit stiff if you don't hand it over."

"Easy now. No need to get cranky. I just think we might be able to work out a better deal; one that benefits both of us."

"I don't do deals," Ruairi warned, his patience wearing thin. "Give me what's owed and then I'll be off."

"We have to stick together over here, us Irishmen, or else we'll end up the same way we did back home." The stout man fingered the stack of money, slowly counting out a share for Ruairi.

"We only ended up that way because we did too many deals." Ruairi pursed his lips and glared.

"You're not doing yourself any favours, lad." A large man, dressed in plaid sat opposite Ruairi, his enormous features casting shadows in the firelight.

"Well, it's a good thing I've got the luck of the Irish with me then." Ruairi revealed a pistol strapped to his ribcage.

The stout man threw up his hands. "Whoa, backdown boyo. We were just making sure we weren't getting fleeced by you."

"Next time you would do well to remember it's not a question that needs to be asked," Ruairi stated clearly as he took the wad of cash being held out to him.

The men nodded and Ruairi backed away from the fire. As he scrambled back up to the car he could hear the taunts and curses that followed him.

Ruairi tied *The Phoenix* fast and clambered up the rope ladder. He looked around the deck of the *Leda*. It was a busy night. He caught sight of her hair just as she rounded the bow of the boat.

Maggie!" He called out to her.

She turned and her blood red lipstick broke into a lazy grin. She started to move towards him but the man at her elbow tried to pull her back. "Wait your turn!" the man spit at Ruairi. "She's my whore for the hour."

Ruairi's fist hit him in the temple.

Maggie sighed as she watched the man crumple to the deck. "Sure and there goes twenty-five dollars."

"Prices have gone up a bit," Ruairi noticed.

"Inflation," Maggie laughed, patting her breasts.

"I need you right now," he said.

"So do these lads," Maggie pointed out. She didn't like to be disturbed when she was working.

Ruairi met her eyes dangerously. She understood.

"Your boat will be the most private," she said.

He nodded and led her back down to *The Phoenix*.

"So she's told you then," Maggie assumed when they were settled across from each other.

"Hasn't said a word to me," Ruairi licked his lips. "What am I missing, Maggie? I thought at first I should go to her but," he stalled.

"But you think you might kill her with your bare hands if your suspicions are correct." Maggie's soft voice betrayed her hard body.

"Kevin Barry's dead," he began.

"Kevin Barry is dead because the British hung him." Maggie wanted him to think clearly, reason clearly. It was too easy to ask those questions.

"They would have hung me too."

Maggie felt the corset biting into her flesh. "She never went through with it. She loved you too much."

"She didn't love me enough," Ruairi swallowed.

"No, she didn't." Maggie understood his pain. She moved over beside him and put her arms around him. "You need to go to her and listen to what she has to say. And then you need to make your choice."

"It won't matter either way, will it?" Ruairi was asking her to see things again.

She closed her eyes to stop his questions. "Mick's onboard," she said. "You should go and have a drink with him."

Gracie stood at the front door, feeling strangely at odds with herself. She was excited by the prospects of living within the same walls as Valerie Logan but she was also dreading it. She felt inadequate next to such a woman; hopelessly inadequate.

The door was opened by a tall blonde Norwegian woman with muscular legs. Gracie followed her inside and found Valerie engaged in a shouting match with three top hatted men.

The men's faces were mottled red and purple and their voices were strained and high pitched. Valerie was obnoxiously loud for a lady and yet her appearance was rather refined. Gracie watched in shocked amazement.

"You cannot possibly allow this ceremony to take place," trilled a man with a Lincolnesque beard.

"I most certainly can. This is my home and I will do whatever I like in it," Valerie roared.

"The Church has strictly forbidden this union and as a member of our congregation we cannot allow you to take part in it." This time the yelling was done by a tall gangly man with a swan like neck.

"We will have you excommunicated!" threatened the third man with a podgy belly.

"Well, good luck buying the Cavendish property without my generous donation," Valerie threatened back, before catching sight of Gracie. "Tell me, child," she addressed her, "is there anything more romantic than a nun and priest wanting to marry each other at the age of eighty-seven? I mean, they've given entire lifetimes to God, surely we can grant them a couple of years of deviance."

Gracie didn't know how to respond. She giggled nervously, which was obviously the wrong thing to do as the shouting match recommenced at an even louder volume. It was a whole twenty minutes before the gentlemen finally stormed out, the whole thing left unresolved.

Valerie took a few deep breaths and then turned to the young girl. "I'm sorry for all of that ugliness. Now, what can I do for you?"

Gracie looked at her luggage awkwardly. "Um, did Maman not speak to you about . . ."

Valerie saw the trunks and hatboxes that amassed all of Gracie's spring and summer collection. Her hand flew to her mouth. "Oh!" she cried, "You are moving in! I forgot all about it! I don't have a room ready."

Gracie went white. "Will I have to go back to my father's?"

"No, no of course not. You can stay here as long as you like. Today has just been an awful mess for me." She squeezed Gracie's hand. "Come on now. Let's get you settled."

William sat in the men's lounge of the Club with a cigar and a brandy.

Johnny sat across from him, his hair slicked and his trousers pressed. "What am I supposed to say if I'm asked about what happened between Gracie and me?" He was irritated and humiliated.

"Nobody will ask you anything. That's not the way society works, Johnny. They'll just talk behind your back," Lucas reminded his son.

William puffed his cigar slowly. "My daughter has made a very unfortunate choice," he said calmly. "I assure you, I am going to make her regret it."

CHAPTER 16

Gracie awoke to the dull ache caused by another night without him and groaned in annoyance. She rolled over, burying her face in her pillows, trying desperately to shake the image of him that had painted itself on the insides of her eyelids.

Today was Dominion Day. It had been Gracie's favourite day of the year last year. The docks would be lined with buskers and food stands and the whole harbour would be filled with a carnival like atmosphere. The ladies would all be showing off new summer frocks and hats and the gentlemen would for one day, leave business at the office and give themselves up to the decadent sights, sounds and smells of their Canadian home. It was a day of revelry for all and Gracie usually basked in that kind of shameless exhibition.

But today was different. Today she felt like burrowing underground and hiding from the world. She bathed slowly in the steamy tub while thoughts of slipping under and never surfacing made her breathing erratic and excruciating. She had to spend the day dodging her father. Ruairi would be there but he didn't want to associate with her openly and although the thought of a secret romance was thrilling, the logistics of it dampened the excitement. She began to contemplate pretending she was sick and staying home when a figure appeared at the door.

"Good morning, Gracie."

Gracie gasped, "What are you doing here?" She was afraid to move as the bubbles formed only a thin cover over her body.

Ruairi shut and locked the bathroom door behind him. He began to undress.

"What are you doing?" Gracie squealed again.

"Having a bath," Ruairi said, as if it was a foregone conclusion.

Gracie blushed madly. "We can't do that . . . here," she said, looking everywhere but at Ruairi's very naked body.

"Why not?" Ruairi whispered loudly.

"There are people around!" Gracie was gesturing wildly.

Ruairi looked around. "Not in here, Love, it's just me and you." He smiled at her nervousness. "Scooch forward." He put a toe in behind her.

When she leaned back, she felt him all around her.

"I missed you last night," he whispered in her ear.

"I thought you were coming," she whined.

"I got held up," he said kissing her shoulder and her neck.

"Where?"

"At a brothel," Ruairi chuckled.

"I don't believe you!" she giggled.

Ruairi just smiled and slid further down in the water.

"Let's not go today. Let's just stay here."

"In the bathtub?" Ruairi teased.

"Sure," she laughed.

"You'll look like a prune in less than an hour and that's not very attractive. And I promised my other girlfriend I'd get her some candy floss."

"Your other girlfriend?" Gracie raised an eyebrow.

"Yes, Kathleen. She's gorgeous, and very sweet . . . . and she's three years old."

Gracie giggled again, "Rosaleen's daughter?"

"Aye. I can't let her down."

Gracie sighed. "Okay. I understand." She paused. "Ruairi?"

"Mmhmm?" His eyes were closed.

"Will you ever love me as much as you love Rosaleen?"

In a much smaller tub, Rosaleen slowly sponged the soapy water up and down her arms. The soap smelled of jasmine and citrus, fresh and lively. Rosaleen felt the power in this ritual. She was baptized in bathwater, clean for the shortest of moments before life would drown the purity within.

She sank back and let the water swallow her. He hadn't spoken to her yet. He had kept himself at a distance, barely looking at her. He was punishing her and although he hadn't left, she already felt abandoned.

When she came up for air, pushing her hair back off her face and wiping away the droplets of water, Aisling was at the basin with her back to the tub, gazing steadily at herself in the mirror.

Rosaleen swallowed her self-deprecation. "Good morning, Aisling," she said as she flicked water at her, spraying the mirror and missing Aisling.

Aisling turned, disrobed and grinned. "Room for me?" she asked.

Rosaleen laughed. "I haven't bathed with you since we were little girls! We'll never fit both of us in here."

"Well, we'll just have to make do. This is the only room in the house that doesn't have ears." She smiled, dipping a tentative toe in the closest end.

Rosaleen squished her legs up in front of her and Aisling sat down, the water sloshing madly over the tub. "Careful! You'll lose all the water!" she giggled as they tried to shift themselves into comfortable positions. "We're like a packet of sardines!"

"I've never seen a packet of sardines look so good." Karl's voice floated in, dry and humourless.

Rosaleen and Aisling looked at each other wide-eyed. "What are you doing in here, Karl?" Aisling shrieked, trying to cover herself.

Karl shrugged in the mirror while he began to floss his teeth. "Don't mind me. I won't be long, I'm just flossing."

"Well, floss somewhere else! This is a closed tub!" Rosaleen growled at him.

Karl glared at her. "I wouldn't be able to fit in there anyways!" he snorted as he took his string of silk to the door. He shut it with a bang and the girls dissolved into giggles.

"I will never understand that man!" Rosaleen said between fits.

"Two girls in a bathtub and he was intent on flossing his teeth! I think he's beyond understanding!" Aisling laughed, barely catching her breath.

When they finally settled down Rosaleen stood up, turned around and then sat back down with her back to Aisling. "While you're telling me why you had to share my tub, you might as well wash my back."

Aisling picked up the sponge and squeezed it over Rosaleen's shoulders. The water trickled down her boney blades. Aisling was shocked at how thin Rosaleen was becoming. "I wanted to ask you something," she began slowly.

"Mmhmm . . ." Rosaleen breathed. She knew what the question would be.

"Did you know the child was Billy's at the time of the ambush?" It was a broad question but her inflection made it very direct.

Rosaleen turned to look at Aisling over her shoulder. More water dove over the edge of the tub. "Aye, I did."

"Please tell me that you weren't the informer." Aisling's eyes implored Rosaleen.

Rosaleen dropped her eyes to the bathwater in response. "I was trying to protect Billy."

"What about Balbriggan?" Aisling feared the answer. The Black and Tans had arrived so quickly.

"How much of it do you want me to confess to?"

The water suddenly seemed cold to Aisling. Small drops of heat trickled down her cheeks as she thought of her brother running for his life. The face that stalked him was no longer that of the foreign enemy. It was his best friend. "How could you?"

Rosaleen didn't know how to answer her. She just shook her head as the tears slipped past her cheeks.

Aisling thought about that one single day; Kevin Barry's neck in the noose and the pillaging of Balbriggan.

"Please say something." Rosaleen reached towards her friend slowly.

The water shifted suddenly as Aisling pulled back. "Did you have anything to do with General Gainsborough escaping?"

Rosaleen couldn't answer through her tears.

"Oh God!" Aisling exclaimed.

"Ruairi was supposed to shoot him in the head. He was supposed to be dead." Rosaleen choked out between sobs. "But then Ruairi didn't kill him and he threatened to tell Ruairi that I had betrayed him! I didn't know what else to do!"

Aisling leaned over the edge of the tub. She thought that she was going to vomit. "You should have killed him yourself," she said quietly. "Did he order your beating?" Aisling needed to piece that whole night back together.

Rosaleen shook her head. "I can't talk about that."

Aisling was sick of the secrets. She stood up shakily and grabbed for a towel.

"Please Aisling, don't make me tell you," Rosaleen begged.

But Aisling wouldn't listen. She dried herself off and left the room with the towel wrapped around her. She was halfway down the hall when she heard Rosaleen's final confession.

"It wasn't William," she cried.

Aisling stormed back into the bathroom. "Who was it then? Was it Billy?"

Rosaleen looked up in alarm. "No, no of course not!"

"Then who was it?" A male voice was behind Aisling.

Rosaleen drew her legs to her chest to cover herself. Mairtin and Thomas were both glaring at her from the doorway.

"It was our own," she finally admitted. "It was retribution. I was seen leaving the Castle. Somebody obviously had their suspicions about me."

Thomas and Aisling began immediate denials. Rosaleen had been severely beaten. She had almost died. They couldn't believe their own comrades could have been responsible.

Mairtin stayed silent, locking eyes with Rosaleen. She gave the tiniest of shrugs.

"Do you know who it was then?" he asked.

He could tell by the look she gave him that she did. "And should we be counting ourselves lucky that they didn't kill you?"

Rosaleen swallowed hard. "I was told that it was only out of respect for Ruairi that I was left alive."

Mairtin nodded.

Aisling looked back and forth between her lover and her best friend. "You believe her?" she asked Mairtin, incredulous that he could conceive of the Army Council ordering this.

Mairtin closed his eyes briefly. "It happens all of the time. I've been ordered to keep our own in line before. I've been ordered to keep Ruairi in line if I have to."

Thomas turned cold eyes on Mairtin. "I'll split your skull if you even think of trying to keep Ruairi in line."

Mairtin glared back at Thomas. "Ruairi already knows about the order. I told him about it. Where the feck do you think my loyalties lie? All I'm saying is that retribution orders are common."

Aisling fought her insides. The revelations were making her physically sick. "You can't tell him any of this."

"I have to," Rosaleen said quietly, her face resting on the edge of the tub.

Thomas leaned back against the doorjam. "I think Aisling might be right, Rosaleen. Sometimes the truth isn't worth telling."

"The only person I would be protecting is myself." Rosaleen stood up and wrapped herself in a towel. "I'm going to tell him tonight."

CHAPTER 17

B illy picked Gracie up and walked with her towards the festivities. When they arrived at the waterfront, the docks were crowded with people wearing every colour imaginable and a band was playing somewhere down the pier. Gracie felt herself relax slightly as she breathed in the fresh Canadian air that she loved so much. Today it was laced with the smell of doughnuts and hot dogs and candy floss. Gracie couldn't hide her smile.

"Let's get some salt water taffy and candy floss!" She grabbed Billy's hand and dragged him towards the booth. "Your treat!"

Billy laughed and pulled out his wallet. "It's going to be an expensive day, isn't it?"

The Irish contingent walked the couple of blocks to the harbour. The group was unusually quiet. The rift between Rosaleen and Ruairi had taken its toll on all of them.

Ruairi walked near the front of the pack with Kathleen. He held the little girl's hand tightly. She skipped along beside him without a care in the world. Ruairi had promised her candy floss and now she couldn't wait to get to the carnival.

"How much farther?" she asked, for the third time that block.

Ruairi swung her up into his arms and shook her playfully. "You are driving me crazy, you are!" he exclaimed. "If you ask that question one more time I'm going to let Uncle Stavros sell you to the highest bidder at Rum Row!"

Kathleen giggled uncontrollably. "No!" she squealed.

Ruairi put her down and told her to count her steps until she got to the festival and then she'd know how much further for next year. Then he called back to Mick.

When Mick caught up to him he spoke in low tones. "I need you to take Kathleen for a little while."

Mick nodded, glancing sideways to gauge Ruairi's countenance.

"I'll be calm," Ruairi assured him.

"Go easy on her," Mick advised. "She's still the same girl you grew up with."

Ruairi sighed. "I know."

By now they were approaching the first of the vendors. There were people milling about everywhere and the air was laden with the smells of grease and sugar. The group paused, looking around at each other, not quite sure what to do first.

Kathleen grabbed Ruairi's hand again and tugged at it excitedly. "Let's go get faëry floss!"

"You go on ahead with Uncle Mick. I need to speak with your mammy." Ruairi handed her off to Mick, winking at her as she went. "Make sure he buys you both colours and save a bit of the pink for me!"

"You don't want pink!" she giggled, "Pink is for girls!"

"Well, I like girls!" Ruairi said cheekily. The little girl laughed along with everybody else without understanding the joke. Then she skipped off beside Mick, holding the old man's calloused hand between her baby soft ones.

Rosaleen looked over at Mairtin. He nodded at her.

"Can you keep an eye out for Maggie?" Rosaleen asked Aisling softly. "She said she'd come in for the fireworks."

Aisling was trying hard to pretend everything was normal. "Of course."

Gracie let a wisp of candy floss dissolve in her mouth. The sugar crystals tickled her tongue and she felt young and giddy.

"You aren't really going to eat all of that are you?" Billy asked.

"I'm going to make a serious attempt at it."

Billy plucked a tuft off the stick and took a few steps backwards as he shoved it in his mouth. He made a face as he swallowed and then licked his fingers. "You don't mind if I leave you alone for an hour, do you?"

Gracie's eyes widened. "No, Billy, no!" she begged. "You can't leave me by myself."

"I have to, just for a little while. You'll be fine," he assured her, "and then when we meet up I'll buy you a shaved ice."

"Am I three now?" she pouted.

"You're acting like it."

Gracie scowled, "Fine. Go. But I swear, if I end up married off to Johnny Bexley because Papa sees me unprotected, I'm holding you personally responsible."

Billy chuckled and pointed to something behind her. "I don't think you have to worry about that anymore."

Gracie turned and saw Lana Hamilton, her arm laced through Johnny Bexley's, smiling and laughing as if she had just carried off a grand coup.

"That doesn't bother you, does it?" Billy looked at his sister, concerned.

"Not at all," Gracie said haughtily, "they deserve each other." She turned her eyes back to her brother. "Well, go on then. I'll be fine by myself for a little while, but hurry back. I doubt I will be civil if either of them speak to me."

Billy leaned down and kissed his sister on the cheek and snatched another piece of candy floss before dashing off.

Genevieve and Valerie strolled down the promenade, stopping every few feet to say hello. For Genevieve, the charade was draining. She hadn't felt like coming out but Valerie had practically dragged her. Already three couples had remarked on how quiet she seemed and had asked if she was well.

Valerie took her over to a park bench and sat her down. "Is there anything I can do to gain your confidence?" she asked.

"I'm worried about my son. What Rosaleen has done has hurt him fiercely."

Valerie wasn't overly sympathetic. "Not intentionally, believe me. She was completely wrong in how she went about the matter but she really does love him. And she's hurting too, you know."

"It's not a competition," Genevieve replied frostily.

"I'm not here to fight about Rosaleen," Valerie sighed, taking Genevieve's hand.

"I apologize. I'm just being overly protective."

"There's no such thing when it comes to being a mother," Valerie assured her.

"Gracie is the one who really needs me at the moment. I'm not sure what to make of her involvement with Ruairi O'Neill." Genevieve was worried that her daughter hadn't quite thought through all of the implications of what she was doing.

"Gracie is a young woman now and I don't believe that what you think will be of much concern to her at the moment. Her heart is involved which means not much else is." Valerie put a comforting arm around Genevieve. "What else is troubling you?"

"I've been planning my escape," she said softly.

"Your escape?"

"I intend to invest in your business, Valerie, quite heavily, in fact. On the condition that I be allowed to stay in Paris as long as I like. I am sick to death of the stares and the gossiping. I want to be away from Charlottetown as much as possible."

"I'm absolutely fine with that, if you are sure that it is what you want. I can't think of a better representative in all of Europe, really. With you as the face of the company, I would say our overseas sales will be grand indeed." Valerie looked at Genevieve questioningly. "Have you discussed this with your children though?"

Genevieve shook her head. "You're the first to know."

"They may object, you know."

Genevieve sighed. "They can object all they like. I need to get out of here, away from William, away from all of this . . ." she motioned to the society set. "Paris is home to me. This place will never be anything more than a nightmare."

"Give it time, Darling," Valerie paused. "If it makes any difference, I want you to be in Charlottetown as much as possible. I enjoy your company. And maybe if we found you a new man here," she giggled.

Genevieve shook her head vehemently. "I don't ever want another man!"

Valerie laughed outright, "Careful, with words like that, people might mistake you for a feminist!"

"I can think of worse things," Genevieve said as she caught sight of Juliette Hamilton.

"What about divorcée?" Valerie raised her eyebrows suggestively.

Genevieve's tone was derisive, "I'm seriously considering it. I'm just waiting for legal advice on how much money he will take from me."

Valerie narrowed her eyes. "Money isn't everything."

"Says the woman with bucket loads of it in her *own* possession," Genevieve pointed out with contempt. "You forget that my fortune is now my husband's. Your brand of feminism, as you like to call it, is fine for your situation but it does not suit the rest of us women who are not lucky enough to lose our husbands before they disappoint us."

Valerie bore the remark graciously. "You may think it's easy for me to go around espousing feminist ideals but in truth, Genevieve, it's all I have to be passionate about. The love of my life is dead and believe me, politics is no worthy replacement. I long to know what it is like to have a man by my side; to have that internal struggle of how to keep the balance of my husband's life and mine in perfect harmony while maintaining a unity that goes beyond a shared house. But I have no family of my own to worry about and so I need not be cautious about the reputation I leave behind. I am free to think solely about how we as women can attain the life of equality and freedom that we so deserve."

"You live that life everyday. You do as you please, just like any man."

"And I cry at night when I am lonely, just like every woman."

"What about Michael?" Genevieve asked.

"Mick has had his one love as well. We could never be that to each other," she hesitated, trying to smile again. "He does wonders to scare the shadows away at night though."

Genevieve lifted her eyes to the woman beside her. "I'm sorry. I've been vicious to you even though it is me that I am angry with."

Valerie smiled sadly. "You needn't apologize. I can't begin to understand the amount of stress you are under right now."

"I really believe Paris will be the answer for me. I've been dreaming about returning since the war ended. "

"Are there no troubles in Paris?" Valerie asked.

"There's no William in Paris, not even a single memory of him."

"You shouldn't have to run away from him."

"I won't be running, Valerie, I'll be sailing."

Both women began to giggle like young girls. "Let's go home," Valerie suggested. "We'll have our own carnival."

Ruairi and Rosaleen made their way through the crowds towards the industrial wharfs. Ruairi sat at the end of one of the docks, his feet dangling above the lapping water. Rosaleen sat beside him quietly, listening to the wood creak beneath them as the old logs did their best to withstand the constant pressure of the ocean.

Ruairi looked over his shoulder to make sure they were alone, and then his eyes settled on her. "How long have you known?" he asked her.

"Known what?" she asked, confused.

"That Billy was the father," his voice constricted on the word.

Rosaleen dropped her eyes away. "The whole time," she said quietly. "How long have you known?"

"A few days," he answered.

Rosaleen put a hand over her mouth. "Why did you wait so long to talk to me?"

"I'll ask the questions," Ruairi snarled. He stared out across the water. "Was your whole purpose in coming here to tell him?"

Rosaleen took a deep breath. "It was to find out if we still had a chance to be together. I'm in love with him, Ruairi."

Ruairi barely kept his head above the wave of hurt that washed over him. "And why did you need me then? Wouldn't it have been easier without me in the way?"

"You are never in the way, Ruairi," Rosaleen feared that her words would fail her.

"No more lies, Rosaleen. You were my rose and I was the fecking thorn in your side." Ruairi gripped the wooden planks of the dock hard. "Why am I here?"

Rosaleen felt sick. She knew that she was ripping his heart out. "I wasn't sure how William would react to me being here. He had threatened to kill me if I ever tried to contact Billy. I knew that you would protect me."

"How long was it between William and Billy?" Ruairi wasn't sure he really wanted to know.

"I hadn't been with William in months."

Ruairi narrowed his eyes and pinned her with an angry glare. "Then how did you end up with Billy?"

Rosaleen began to cry silently. They were tears of fear and guilt and shame all mixed together. "I was supposed to be reuniting with William the night that I met Billy. William didn't show up."

"Why not?"

"William had left me before because I hadn't given him any useful information and so . . ." Rosaleen covered her face with her hands and sobbed. She was terrified to continue.

Ruairi clenched his jaw but made no other movements.

There was a long drawn out silence.

Rosaleen finally uncovered her face. She looked over at him and saw the pain in his eyes.

"So you decided to give me up," Ruairi finished for her. He knew her well enough. It was an easy conclusion.

"He never came. He didn't trust me."

"And if he would have showed up? What then?"

"It wouldn't have mattered. You were always one step ahead."

Finally he turned those eyes back to her. "It does matter. You were willing to have me executed so that you could be with him."

Rosaleen trembled beneath his eyes. She didn't know what to say. "You would have gone to jail. There were no . . . execution plans," she stammered.

"I had deserted the British Army and then joined the fight against it! I would have been shot!" he exploded.

"He told me he would have the charges changed," Rosaleen defended herself weakly.

"Did you really believe him?" Ruairi asked.

"At the time, I did," she faltered. "I know differently now."

Ruairi bit his lip to keep from lashing out at her. He was trying, desperately trying to stay calm. "I would never have chosen anyone or anything over your safety and happiness, never."

"I know that, Ruairi. I made a mistake."

"That's a bit of an understatement." Ruairi put a cigarette in his mouth.

Rosaleen reached into her little bag and pulled out a box of matches. She struck the match and reached up to light Ruairi's cigarette. Ruairi waved her hand away as he struck his own match.

Rosaleen let her match drop into the water. "With Billy, it was just one weekend, a very long time ago."

Ruairi felt his muscles tighten. "And you fell in love with him that quickly?"

She nodded slowly.

"Jesus, Mary and Joseph he must have been good. I've spent my whole life trying to get you to fall in love with me."

"Ruairi, please don't . . ."

He cut her off. "So it was you that informed the British about the ambush," Ruairi surmised. He had been suspicious of her all along but he had never allowed himself to truly believe it.

She inhaled violently. "I tried to protect Billy by going to William and stopping the ambush. I had to give him something so I told him that you would be in Balbriggan."

"You really didn't care whether I made it out alive, did you?" Her betrayal was so complete.

"Why do you think that I begged you to stay in Dublin that morning?" she cried.

Ruairi turned away from her in disgust. "Is that supposed to make it all alright then?"

Rosaleen wiped away the tears that kept falling. "I don't expect you to forgive me," she said.

"I don't know that I ever will." Ruairi couldn't look at her. "Did you help him escape?" he asked, referring to William.

She nodded helplessly. "He threatened to expose me as an informer and a liar."

"That's what you were," he whispered.

"I thought that if you knew the truth, you would kill Billy."

Ruairi shook his head. "Why couldn't you love me? I was the one fighting for you!" He broke down.

Rosaleen had never seen him cry and it terrified her. "I did love you. I just wanted more." Her words came out all wrong.

"What else did you want? I gave you everything I had."

Rosaleen was devastated by the look on Ruairi's face. She reached out to touch him but he pulled away. "I wanted a man who was going to live. You were trying to get yourself killed just to prove that you loved me enough."

Ruairi stood up and stared out over the black water. "I didn't want to live my life without you. I still don't. I would have fought a thousand men and died a thousand deaths for you." He swallowed and wiped his eyes. "Now one British bullet will be enough."

Rosaleen grabbed at his trousers as he tried to walk away. "Please don't leave me like this," she begged him.

"It's time for me to grow up, Rosaleen. I need to stop believing in Ireland and I need to stop believing in you." He took a step backwards, pulling Rosaleen down face first on the dock in the process.

"Ruairi!" she screamed prostrate, "Ruairi, please!"

But he was gone.

Billy wandered the festival by himself. He was in no mood to celebrate and did not feel like company. He was angry with himself for expecting anything from Rosaleen Jameson. She hadn't wanted him then, why would she want him now? He stood near a fiddle group and listened to their wailing melodies, his thoughts drowning in the rhythms of the Maritimes.

He looked up as William approached. He was with a gentleman of similar age and a young woman. She was blonde with pale eyes and an enigmatic smile. She wasn't looking at Billy, affording him the perfect opportunity to take her all in. She was long-legged and thin and her hair was cut daringly short.

She turned back and caught him staring at her and a blush rose to her cheeks. Billy could appreciate her modesty. Her lips quivered slightly as she smiled.

William gave a cool greeting to his son. "I trust you are well?"

"Very well," Billy answered, his eyes not meeting his father's.

"I've been asked to introduce you to Mr. Hanlon Harcourt and his daughter, Georgiana." William didn't look at all pleased to have to introduce his son. "Apparently Georgiana is in desperate need of some entertainment while she is in town and Hanlon knew that I had a son of her age."

Hanlon shook Billy's hand and clapped him on the shoulder. "A fine young chap such as yourself would know of all of the local amusements."

"I'm sure that we'll be able to find something to occupy her time," Billy smiled warmly at her. He put out his hand to her.

She slipped her smooth fingers into his palm.

"I'll leave her in your capable hands then, shall I?" William was abrupt. A hard look passed between father and son before William steered Hanlon off in a different direction.

"It's a pleasure to meet you, Georgiana. Where are you from?" As Billy asked his question, the fiddles rose in volume and Georgiana only saw his mouth moving. He took her elbow and guided her away from the music. "Lovely music but I'd much prefer your conversation."

Georgiana blushed again. "I'm sorry, I didn't hear your question," she said to him.

"I asked where you were from." Billy repeated.

"Ottawa, at the moment," she replied. "My father works for the government so we move around a bit."

"Well, Ottawa is the place to be when you work for the government." Billy wanted to keep the conversation going but he was finding himself at a loss for words.

Luckily, she seemed to want to continue their chat as well. "And you are from London, your father told me. What do you do here in Charlottetown?"

"I'm a solicitor." Billy found himself hoping she would be impressed.

She was. "That's wonderful. Have you always been interested in law?"

He shook his head. "No, I just sort of fell into it after the war."

"Well, aren't I a lucky girl? My first day on the East coast and I've met one of our handsome war heroes." She smiled up at him, her face dazzling.

It was his turn to blush. "I'm no war hero, I can assure you," he paused, not exactly sure of where to go from there. "Georgiana, can I offer to buy you a lemonade?"

"That would be lovely," she said.

Billy offered her his arm and he felt a sudden thrill as she put her hand around his bicep. She smelled like rose petals.

"Are you enjoying your time here in Charlottetown?" he asked, gazing at her while they walked.

"I am now!" she laughed, shyly.

"Good," Billy laughed too. "So am I."

They smiled at each other and melted into the crowd as one.

Rosaleen wandered, lost in a daze between the vendors and buskers and revellers. She felt nothing, smelled nothing, saw nothing. Her senses were paralyzed beneath the weight of her broken heart.

She tried to focus her eyes on something, anything to give her a frame of reference for her next movement. When the images in front of her finally sharpened, it was with disastrous results. Billy Gainsborough stood only a few feet from her with a beautiful blonde woman, her arm threaded through his. They were smiling at each other as if they were the only two people on the street.

He turned his eyes on her but there was no familiarity. She could have been anybody. He took a step in her direction, saw her and then stopped himself. His smile had faded and his face seemed frozen.

Rosaleen waited, praying that he would come to her and hold her while she fought the death inside. He was her last hope.

But he turned away, leaving her stranded in the grave she had dug for herself.

Billy looked back once. She was still standing in the middle of the street, looking shocked and disorientated. Pieces of him wanted to turn and go back for her, tell her she was forgiven and that they would try again. Other pieces hurt too badly. The most important piece felt completely shattered.

"Are you okay?" Georgiana asked Billy.

Billy exhaled and turned to the pretty girl. "Of course, I apologize, my mind wandered for a moment. You were saying?"

The girl giggled. "I was saying, that when Ruairi asked me to meet you, I thought you would be one of his rough and tumble friends. It's a nice surprise to meet a charming, educated, and handsome young man. I didn't know Ruairi knew any of those."

Billy looked up at the sky and inhaled slowly. "Ruairi, eh?" He shook his head and laughed. He hadn't even considered the possibility that this was the girl. "You're the girl that Ruairi was sending."

Georgiana gave him a strange look. "Who did you think I was?"

Billy pursed his lips and then smiled. "I just thought you were a beautiful somebody that fate had put in my way."

"Well technically, I am. Ruairi just happens to be fate in this circumstance!" She winked at Billy.

He laughed. "How is it that Ruairi manages to surround himself with such gorgeous women?"

Georgiana smiled. "Ruairi is well connected, let me assure you."

"I have no doubts about that," Billy breathed. "So how long do I get to spend with you before you disappear?"

Georgiana shrugged. "I'm not really going to disappear. You'll see me often enough."

"How's that?"

"You'll be working for my father. We're a close family."

"Your father? I thought he was with the government?" Billy was confused.

"He is," she confirmed.

"So..?"

"Ruairi called in a favour. He asked Daddy to give you a job. He said he would vouch for you personally so Daddy said yes. He adores Ruairi."

"But what does your father have to do with rumrunners?" Billy asked in a whisper.

"Nothing," she whispered back playfully. She watched him struggle to understand what she was telling him. When it was clear he wouldn't figure it out she gave him a clue. "He has a bit to do with policy making."

A slow smile spread across Billy's face. "Would that extend into Prohibition policy?"

Georgiana sighed satisfactorily. "Impressive! Ruairi really does have a smart friend!"

Billy laughed heartily and slung an arm around the beautiful girl as he led her off in search of a lemonade stand. "Tell me, my father isn't at all involved in this, is he?"

Georgiana shook her head. "Not in the slightest."

"How did you get him to introduce the two of us then?"

"Ruairi thought it would be a bit of sport, having your father introduce us. Just a subtle knife twist really," she said smugly.

"Very clever," Billy smiled. He might enjoy working for Ruairi O'Neill more than he originally thought.

Up and down the dockside the festivities continued. Day fell seamlessly to night and the streetlamps burned intensely, casting intimate shadows across the harbour.

Ruairi rarely felt out of control but his emotions made him vulnerable to the elements. His nerves were raw and he was struggling to maintain his balance. He narrowed his eyes. William Gainsborough was a mere twenty feet from him. His muscles strained and his blood surged. He flexed his fingers. He could break the General's neck in one movement. His pace quickened, he was closing the distance. There was no longer a reason to leave him alive.

The next step was like hitting a brick wall. He stepped backwards, stunned by the force of whatever had gotten in his way. Thomas' eyes burned into his and Mairtin's grip seized his forearm, dragging him off to the side.

"Not here, brother," Thomas whispered hoarsely. "Not now."

The rush of blood receded and Ruairi felt a cool clamminess wash over him. His rigid body turned to jelly as he slumped into Mairtin's shoulder. Mairtin steadied him and cast a weary glance over at Thomas. They had been lucky to catch him when they did.

Gracie saw him sitting on a bench. He had his head in his hands and Mairtin and Thomas were fussing over him as if he were about to be sick. She made her way over to him, despite Mairtin and Thomas warning her away with fierce glares. She knelt down in front of him and took his hands in hers.

"Are you alright?" she asked.

He raised his head to look at her. She was shocked to see his face so pale and his eyes rimmed red. A muscle twitched at the corner of his mouth but aside from that he remained perfectly still.

"Ruairi?" she felt a strange sense of panic. She put a soft hand up to his cheek. "Ruairi, speak to me," she implored him.

He exhaled. Then suddenly he was on his feet, dragging her with him. "You shouldn't be seen with me," he said, pushing her away. He could see Billy Gainsborough and Georgiana Harcourt standing a few paces behind her.

"Ruairi, please!" she was shaking her head, her forehead wrinkled with concern. "I'm worried about you."

His nostrils flared and Mairtin groaned, knowing all too well that Ruairi's temper was about to explode again. "Take your sister home, Billy," Ruairi demanded. "And keep her away from me. You were right, I can't be trusted."

Gracie turned and saw her brother behind her. She looked back at Ruairi and met his bloodshot eyes with her own temperamental ones. "I will not leave you, Ruairi. I love you," she stated firmly.

"Don't waste your love on me," he said.

Gracie stood in shock as she watched him disappear into the crowds. Billy put his arms around her and turned her face away.

"Mammy!" Kathleen cried gleefully. "Mammy, look at what Uncle Mick bought me!" The little girl raced towards her mother with a stick of candy floss in each hand, one pink and one blue. "Where's Uncle Ruairi? I want to give him some of the pink one!"

Rosaleen stared down at her daughter for a moment before she began to cry again.

"Mammy! Mammy, what's wrong?" Kathleen's eyes went wide as she watched her mother weep.

Rosaleen sank to her knees and Kathleen screamed, dropping her candy floss and falling on top of her mother. Mick grabbed them both up and called to Aisling to come quick.

"Take Kathleen home. I'll follow with Rosaleen," he directed.

Aisling nodded, scooping up the little girl and moving away from the scene as swiftly as possible. In her arms, the terrified little girl screamed for her mammy.

CHAPTER 18

The sea sparkled in the moonlight as if millions of sequins had been hand-stitched to the water. Gracie watched the fabric ripple in the midnight breeze. Billy had taken her back to the hotel but neither of them could sleep so they had wandered back down to the dockside.

"Do you think he's out there tonight?" Gracie asked sadly.

Billy gave her a sidelong glance. "Who? Ruairi?"

Gracie caught her breath. Ruairi's words had hurt deeply but she wouldn't allow herself to believe them. "It would be a lovely night to be out."

"It would," Billy began slowly. "Gracie, we need to talk about what happened between you and Ruairi in Halifax."

Gracie grimaced. "No we don't," she said firmly.

Billy took Gracie by the wrist and turned her towards him. "Gracie, I know that right now you think you are in love with him but Ruairi is not going to stay in Charlottetown. He is going to leave and you are going to end up heartbroken. You are already heartbroken. Look at what he did to you tonight!"

"Stop, stop, stop!" Gracie stamped her foot. "Don't you see? I'm grown up now. I'm making my own decisions and if I make a mistake, if Ruairi's a mistake, at least it's *my* mistake! I want to make my own mistakes!"

"Gracie . . ."

"No! I don't want to talk about this! You cannot tell me who to love!"

Billy groaned. "Gracie, I know that! But Ruairi is not just a mistake. He is dangerous; physically, emotionally, socially."

"No, he's not! You don't understand him!" Gracie defended him.

"You're right! I don't understand him!" Billy shouted back at her, "One minute he's planning ambushes and the next, he's dragging me from the rubble. One minute he's got a gun to my head and the next he's shaking my hand."

"He put a gun to your head?" Gracie's eyes were wide.

"Yes, Gracie, he put a gun to my head. And I wouldn't put it past him to pull the trigger next time."

Gracie was startled by the last comment. "Why would Ruairi ever have a reason to want you dead again?"

Billy fought against his urge to lie to her. She could no longer be protected from the truth. "Rosaleen saved my life back in Dublin but she had to give William information on Ruairi in return. If Ruairi would have been caught, he would have been court martialled and executed."

Gracie thought back to Ruairi's unstable eyes earlier in the evening. "Why would Rosaleen want to save your life over Ruairi's?" she asked.

Billy let go of his sister's arm. "That little girl of Rosaleen's is mine."

"Yours?" Gracie didn't understand. "How could she be yours?" She had heard the rumours around town but had discounted them as false. In her mind, William had fathered Kathleen.

Billy paused, not quite sure how to answer that. "I slept with Rosaleen."

Gracie was shocked. She thought about the birth certificate that she had found in her father's files. William Gainsborough was listed as the father. Her brother was also William Gainsborough. She began to stammer, "Do you love her?"

Billy sighed. "I did."

"You don't anymore?"

"I don't know how I feel anymore," he said honestly.

"You have a daughter," Gracie said slowly.

Billy looked out at the harbour and felt small. "I have a daughter."

Ruairi convinced Thomas and Mairtin that he was calm. He sent them home so that he could have time to think. He watched as they walked away, both looking back at him over their shoulders and then looking at each other as if they didn't know for sure if they could trust him.

He didn't go far. He walked over to the little park that overlooked the harbour and sat on a bench as the last of the merry makers straggled towards their homes. When he was finally alone, he found himself suffocating in a kind of emotion that he had never experienced before. It was a kind of pain that made breathing all but impossible.

And then, one by one, the tears fell. Crying was foreign to him. Crying was feeling and feeling was against his rules. It revealed all the grey that lay between the black and white. In one night his world had become monochrome. There was no opposition; no differentiation, just shades.

He had loved Rosaleen so hard and so long. In his heart there was no life without her and yet, she had left him long ago. He had died without ever really noticing.

Sometime, long into the night, Maggie appeared. She wore a white silk gown that fluttered around her legs. Her skin glowed translucent in the moonlight giving her an eerily evanescent quality.

She made her way towards him slowly, as if in a dream. She knelt down in front of him, taking his head in her hands and kissing his tears.

"Come with me," she murmured into his hair.

'Where?" he asked, not looking directly at her.

"To my faëry ring," she breathed.

He gave a tiny laugh, "I'm merely a mortal."

"Well, I want to make you merely immortal," she whispered.

He made the mistake of looking into her emerald eyes and never regained consciousness until the morning.

Ruairi spent the next morning brooding in silence. He had woken up in his own bed with a blinding headache and fresh ink on his chest. He had to look in the mirror to see what Maggie had tattooed on him; overtop of his heart she had drawn a black rose. She had failed to wipe it clean so it was still smeared with his own blood. He found that rather prophetic as he crawled back under the covers.

Thomas finally roused him from his angst and loaded him in the car with a few rods and drove up towards Cavendish. There was a good spot for fishing off the shore and fishing always soothed the brothers.

"Are the brakes still sticking?" Ruairi asked.

"Aye, it's worse now. There's a bit of a grind in them as well."

"I'll have to get underneath it tomorrow morning." Ruairi loved to tinker with cars. He might have been a mechanic if he wasn't so good with a gun.

"You'll miss Mass," Thomas chided playfully.

"Sorry Ma, I'll come next Sunday."

Thomas laughed. Mrs. O'Neill had dragged them to Mass every Sunday morning of their lives until they were sixteen. Then they were allowed to choose; but if they didn't choose Mass, she would guilt them into promising they would come the very next week.

"Got bait?" Ruairi asked.

"Aye, I picked up some cans off Joe yesterday."

Ruairi nodded and stared off at the horizon. "You ever miss Gerry?" he asked suddenly.

"Of course I do."

"You think he misses us?"

Thomas gave his brother a funny look. "I'm sure he does sometimes. Why?"

Ruairi shrugged. "I just wonder what it would be like if we went to New York."

"What about Ma?"

"She would come, if all of us were here. She would love it after she got off the boat, I think."

"So, you're considering it?" Thomas asked, trying not to sound too bright.

"No, not really."

"It sounded like you were." He kept his lips in a thin line to stop them from flipping into a frown.

"Just thinking out loud," Ruairi went quiet.

Thomas threaded the car along the narrow island roads. He was worried about Ruairi. Gerry was the only one who could talk Ruairi around when his moods overtook him. Thomas couldn't help but feel anxious when Ruairi was sullen and silent. It usually meant that trouble wasn't far off and after intercepting him last night on his way towards General Gainsborough, Thomas knew there was a good chance that this kind of trouble would be fatal.

When they arrived in Cavendish, Thomas followed a new road out to the water's edge. The waves were bothered on this side of the island and the sky was growing dark with clouds.

"Perfect for fishing," Thomas mused lightly.

Ruairi nodded absentmindedly and picked his rod out of the car and walked down to the rushes with his tacklebox in hand. He squatted down and sorted through his tackle until he found his favourite hook and then began rigging his rod for the session. All of this was done in silence.

"Ruairi!" Thomas groaned. "Just let it go, lad! I'm trying to get you to enjoy the day."

Ruairi threw down his rod and whirled around to face his brother. "What am I missing? Tell me what I'm missing and I'll enjoy the fecking day!"

Thomas stared at him. "What do you mean?"

"Why can't I just leave her here? Why do I feel so responsible for her?"

Thomas was worried by his brother's outburst. "Who are we talking about?" he asked, faking calm, "Gracie or Rosaleen?"

Ruairi glared at him. "Rosaleen," he snarled.

Thomas thought about it for a moment, trying to slow the conversation down. Ruairi was looking for a fight, to let off steam, so Thomas had to be extremely careful with his words or he would end up with a broken nose or a black eye.

"You love her," Thomas said seriously. "She's your best friend, she's your soulmate."

Ruairi clenched his jaw. "And what would you say if I had said I was talking about Gracie?"

Thomas smiled. "I'd say the same thing. You love her. She's your soulmate."

"Who are you, the fecking lovelorn poet now?" Ruairi snapped at his little brother. "I need a man's advice, not a poet's."

Thomas grinned. "The women always like the poets."

"Sure, and what would you recommend I do about this situation, Mr. Yeats?" Ruairi mocked him harshly. William Butler Yeats was one of Thomas' favourite poets and had become a mentor to him in the last few years. He was modern and he wrote about Ireland and the cause.

Thomas took a deep breath. "Well, you could stay; for both of them." He flinched.

But Ruairi didn't hit him. He just looked sad. "If I stay, someone will die."

Thomas fixed his brother with eyes that had seen into a future tainted by the past. "We all have to die eventually, Ruairi."

Rosaleen sat on the porch swing, staring off into the distance. Karl sat down on the railing and watched her for a long moment. She had always been guarded but today she had been more withdrawn than ever.

Aisling had told him to leave her alone but as much as he usually liked to avoid the uncomfortable intimacy that came with sharing a friend's grief, he felt that the girl needed somebody to talk to.

"Is there anything I can do?" he asked cautiously.

Rosaleen slowly raised her eyes to his face. He realized she hadn't even noticed him sitting there. "No," she responded flatly.

Karl nodded and looked away quickly. He contemplated sneaking back inside when she suddenly began to sob. He watched as her tiny framed seemed to shrink into itself as whatever it was that was hurting so badly consumed her.

Not knowing what else to do, he sat beside her and put an awkward arm around her shoulders. She sank into him more out of a need for stability than comfort. He let her cry, and didn't mind that she never told him what was wrong.

Then suddenly, she was on her feet. She barely looked at him as she threw out a quick explanation. "I have to call Gerry," she said and was gone.

Karl just shook his head and lay back on the porch swing, covering his face with his fedora.

Genevieve was led through the stately home by a podgy maid with black hair that had one large white streak through it, like a skunk. Valerie had summoned her to the patio. She wasn't surprised to find that she wasn't the only guest that Valerie was entertaining but who it was made her slightly uneasy.

Valerie gestured to the child. "Kathleen, this is Lady Genevieve Gainsborough," Valerie introduced the little girl.

The child looked up at Genevieve and smiled a bright, toothy smile. "I know you. You bought me a lolly."

Genevieve smiled back at the beautiful little girl. "Yes, I did." She reached down and stroked the girl's hair lovingly. "It was the least I could do," she said with a sigh.

"You're pretty," Kathleen announced with all of the candour that comes with innocence.

Genevieve laughed openly, "Thank-you, my Darling. That is very sweet of you to say. You're very pretty yourself." Genevieve knelt down so that she was face to face with the little girl. "You remind me of my daughter when she was young."

"Is she pretty too?" Kathleen asked.

"Yes, she's very pretty," Genevieve replied honestly.

Kathleen held up a doll. "Do you think she's pretty?"

"Oh yes! She's lovely! Where did you get her?"

"Uncle Mairtin bought her for me. Do you want to see my other dolls?" she asked, pointing over to an entire tea party of dolls.

Valerie watched Genevieve with admiration. When Kathleen was finally satisfied that Genevieve thought all of her dolls were pretty she moved out of earshot and went back to amusing herself as children often do.

Valerie smiled. "You were very kind to her."

"You forget, Valerie, she is my granddaughter."

"I'm amazed, Genevieve. I have to say, I thought you would be hesitant to consider her family. I mean, she is technically a bastard child," Valerie pressed on.

Genevieve was indignant. "I may be a touch conservative on some things, but you can't think me so provincial as to deny my own flesh and blood just because she was born outside of marriage."

"Well, I won't make that mistake again." She was quiet for a moment as she watched the girl. Then she asked, "Have you reconsidered Paris?"

"Not in the slightest." Genevieve pursed her lips.

"Have you told Gracie and Billy?"

"Yes, I had breakfast with them both this morning."

"And how did they take it?" Valerie took a sip of her tea.

Genevieve dabbed at her mouth with her handkerchief. "They took it rather well considering."

Valerie leaned back in the rattan chair. "I wanted to discuss the possibility of Mick accompanying you on your first trip, just to get you set up."

"I really don't think that's necessary," Genevieve lifted her chin with stubborn independence. "I'm sure I would be just fine on my own."

"I'm sure you would too," Valerie agreed, "but I would feel better knowing that you had someone there to take care of you those first couple of days. He wouldn't stay long. He would just see you settled."

Genevieve felt her eyes moisten and she dabbed at them with the handkerchief. Valerie had become a true friend. "How will I ever manage to be away from you for months at a time?"

Valerie leaned over and squeezed Genevieve's hand. "I doubt you'll have time to miss me. I'll probably have to sail over myself to drag you back here!"

Genevieve held up a lace gloved hand, "Can you imagine Mick in Paris?"

Valerie smiled slowly, imagining her lover in a designer suit, flashy cufflinks and wingtip brogues, standing in Trocadero with a macaron in his hand. "Yes, actually I can," she giggled.

CHAPTER 19

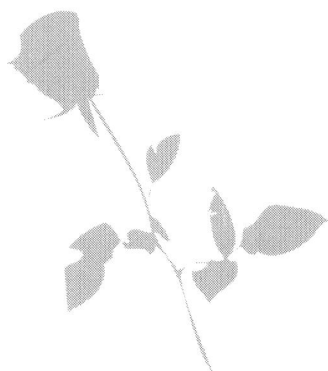

Gerry hung up the phone and leaned back heavily against the wall. Rosaleen's voice had trembled so much that the fear of God that Ma O'Neill had so strongly instilled in her boys crept into his soul.

He had known his brother was in trouble. He had felt it in his bones.

But he also knew there was no stopping Ruairi.

He packed his bags anyway. A loaded pistol nestled between his shirts and socks.

Rosaleen had volunteered earlier in the week to do a run with Ruairi but after the fallout from the night before, she had asked Aisling if she would take her place. Everyone was gathered in the parlour with a cup of tea when Ruairi came in ready to leave.

He looked at Rosaleen, in her jersey dress and bare feet and snorted. "Is that how you're coming in the boat?"

Rosaleen looked up at him with heavy eyes. "I'm not coming," she mumbled. "Aisling will give you a hand this evening."

Aisling stood up, tipping the last of her tea into her mouth and smiling at her brother. "We'll have a grand time!" she exclaimed, a bit too brightly.

Ruairi's glare made the room seem cold. "No. Rosaleen will help me." He turned frozen eyes on her. "Get dressed. I don't have time to wait."

Nobody could argue with those eyes.

Ruairi stood at the bow of the *Armada*, a tiny speedboat owned by a very wealthy Spaniard who thought it was delightfully amusing to be involved in the rum trade.

It would be a long night. He was dropping off two shipments and picking up one. The boats would arrive in two hour increments. He was trying to concentrate on finding some stars in the sky to keep his mind from wandering to the English girl and her English brother. Rosaleen sat a few feet from him, very still.

The weather had turned progressively worse as the day had worn on. By the time Thomas and Ruairi had returned from fishing, the clouds had mounted their furious attack on the sky and the whole island suffocated beneath grey rains.

Mick had warned Ruairi against taking the boat out. The seas were disturbed and not to be trifled with for a few cartons of rum, but Ruairi needed an outlet for his anger and challenging the seas seemed like an appropriately impossible feat.

There was very little conversation to keep either of them from noticing how precariously the boat was rocking. The waves grew stronger, tossing the little boat from side to side.

"I don't think they are coming!" Rosaleen finally screamed over the howling wind, holding onto the railing for support.

Ruairi knew she was right. He had known the moment they had left the harbour that nobody would be meeting them and as he watched the walls of water rising up out of the darkness, he knew they were in danger. He clenched his fists and looked at her. There was fear in her eyes and he had caused it. He had meant to cause it.

She saw the darkness dancing across his face. "We're in trouble, aren't we?"

"We'll be fine. We just need to wait it out. We won't get back into the harbour in these conditions." But his eyes refused to lie.

She drew a shaky breath and crawled towards him on her hands and knees. "I know you don't want to be near me right now but I'm freezing. Will you hold me?" she asked. Her face was stinging from the pelting rain.

His face was stony but his arms were warm. He held her to his chest while the boat was pitched violently around in the waves as if Manannan Mac Lir, the god of the sea himself, was angry with them.

Rosaleen pressed her head into Ruairi's chest and began to cry. His heartbeat was strong and steady. She clung to him, gripping his body with every ounce of strength. He was still alive and still with her. She still had him.

He instinctively tightened his hold on her. His arms flexed and he buried his face in her hair. He put a hand across her face, shielding her from the wind and rain.

She felt his lips pressing into her skull.

Suddenly Ruairi caught a glimpse of something solid through the pouring rain. "Oh shite!" he yelled, springing to action and fighting desperately with the motor.

"What's wrong?" Rosaleen screamed, trying in vain to be heard over the elements.

Ruairi pointed through the grey at a mass that was taking shape not far off the port side. "Rocks!" he yelled. "If we hit those . . ."

Rosaleen didn't need to hear the rest of the sentence. She knew what would happen if they hit those rocks.

Ruairi was scanning the shoreline as it loomed out of the darkness. He looked back at Rosaleen and shook his head. He dropped down, crawled towards her and gritted his teeth. "The water is our best option. The motor is gone. If we don't try to swim towards that clump of trees, we'll be in those rocks with the boat."

Rosaleen swallowed. "But if we don't make it to those trees, we'll drown."

Ruairi held her eyes. "I won't let you drown." He held out his hand to her.

Rosaleen never broke her gaze from his. She put her hand in his and realized there was no doubt in her mind that he would get her to shore.

The water was icy. Rosaleen was immediately disorientated but Ruairi still had her hand held tightly in his. He was pulling her upwards and her head broke the surface. As she gasped for breath a wave knocked her back under and her lungs filled with water. She felt Ruairi's body beneath her, pushing her back up. She began to panic; not for her life, but for his. He would drown himself to save her.

As the waves knocked her under over and over, she lost track of where she was in relation to him. Except for his hand, she had not felt him near her in what seemed like an eternity. She fought desperately to stay conscious but the lack of air and the churning water was winning the battle.

She wished she had had one more chance to tell him that she was sorry. Instead, all she could do was squeeze his hand and pull away. She wouldn't drag him down anymore.

Gracie paced Valerie's dining hall as they waited for dessert to be served.

"Gracie, sit down please, you are being very rude." Genevieve chided her.

"I just thought that I would have heard from Ruairi today." Gracie was beginning to panic. She had expected him to come running to her that morning, full of apologies for his words and behaviour.

Valerie reached over and squeezed Gracie's fingers. "I'm sure you'll hear from him after . . ." Valerie stopped talking quickly.

"After what?" Gracie asked.

"Just after, Darling," Valerie smiled thinly and then called to the nearest server to bring coffee.

Billy glanced over at Valerie and saw the concern in her eyes. A mighty storm had blown up across the Atlantic. "Is Ruairi on the boat tonight?" he asked suddenly.

Valerie nodded tightly. "And he's not alone."

Aisling sat rigidly in the parlour. Mick was beside her, rubbing her back occasionally but she refused to be comforted.

"I should be out there with him. It should be me out there. Not the mother of a little girl. It should be me."

"Nobody should be out there right now," Mick said, shaking his head.

There was a loud banging at the door. Thomas was the first one to get to it. Outside on the porch stood Billy and Gracie Gainsborough drenched and shivering from the rain.

"Is he here?" Gracie asked, her teeth chattering.

Thomas swallowed and then shook his head slowly.

"Tell me he's not out on a boat in this?" Billy moved through the doorway and caught sight of the bodies huddled together in the dark parlour.

Nobody answered him. He scanned the room.

"Where's Rosaleen?" he asked, his voice tense.

Again, nobody answered.

"Good God," Billy breathed. "How big is the boat?"

Mairtin finally looked him in the eye. "Not big enough."

The hours ticked by. Kathleen was curled up in Thomas' lap. Aisling paced by the window. Her figure was lit up periodically by lightning, outlining a shaken little sister. Gracie fell asleep on Billy's shoulder. Nobody spoke. Two wet figures materialized out of the darkness. Karl and Stavros slipped in. They didn't need to ask any questions, the tension in the room made all answers obvious.

Mick reached over and gripped Billy's shoulder. His wrinkled face seemed strangely taut. "If she comes home, you are going to make this right."

Billy felt the vibrations of fear in the old man's voice. "When she comes home," he corrected him.

Gracie woke herself up whimpering. She had a nightmare. Ruairi was standing high above her, leaning over the railing of a large ship. He was dripping wet and crying tears of blood as he waved goodbye to her.

Rosaleen opened her eyes. Ruairi was above her, wiping her face tenderly with his thumbs. He was caked in blood and dirt. He said something to her but it was muffled and she couldn't understand. She began to shake her head but the movement hurt too much. She squeezed her eyes shut and then opened them again. He was still there, his face worried and pale.

She tried to tell him she was okay but her voice was gone. She groaned. He smiled. She smiled back weakly.

He kissed her forehead and then her cheek. She felt warm droplets sliding down her jawbone. She turned her lips until she found his. He didn't pull away from her. His warm breath saved her soul and she tumbled back into incoherence knowing she was safe again.

Time dragged by in the little blue house. The storm broke and the blackness faded to grey which paled into dawn.

Kathleen opened her eyes and looked around. "Where's Mammy?" she asked sleepily.

Thomas rocked her gently. "She's not back yet, Love."

She struggled against his arms and climbed down off his knee. She padded over to the window and stared out at the morning fog. Her little face crumpled and a few tears slipped down her cheek.

Billy was the closest to her. He reached down and picked her up. She sobbed into his shoulder. Billy held her as close as he could while he hushed her softly. "I'm here now," he whispered, "I'm here."

Rosaleen finally awoke fully to see Ruairi sitting with his back to her. He turned around when he heard her sit up but he didn't say a thing. His eyes swept over her to make sure she was moving all of her limbs.

"We're alive," Rosaleen voice was ragged from the salt water in her throat.

"Mmhmm," he grunted. "How are you?"

She knew his concern was genuine but the hurt was back in his eyes. "I'm fine, I think. Everything aches but its all there." She reached up to look at a gash across his forehead but he ducked away from her touch.

"Are you still angry with me?" she asked quietly. She wondered if his kiss had been real or if she had imagined it while she was unconscious.

"Of course I'm still angry with you," he said in a flat voice. "Did you think one little storm would make me forget what you've done?"

"You have to forgive me one day," she said, speaking to his back.

"No, I don't. I can be angry forever. I'm good at angry," his voice was still toneless.

She fought the urge to cry. It hurt too much. "Fine, be angry with me forever, if you must, but I still love you." She was defiant. "Even after all that I've done, I swear that I love you."

"I know you do," he whispered.

Rosaleen looked up, not sure if she had heard him correctly.

He coughed. "Maggie came to see me after I spoke with you last. I don't remember much except . . ." he trailed off.

She waited.

"She told me some faëry tale about four cowardly men and a beautiful black rose."

Rosaleen inhaled sharply. "Interesting premise," she said slowly. "Was it a good tale?"

Ruairi shrugged. "It was if you like twists and turns and complex characters. I'm a simple lad. I like easy to follow stories."

Rosaleen rubbed her temple. Her head was pounding. "The only really important thing is the end. Did it end well?"

"Well, of course it did. It was a faëry tale," Ruairi paused. "I probably would have written a more gruesome ending for the four cowards but apparently they got what they deserved."

Rosaleen wrinkled her brow painfully. "How so?"

"A crazy red haired bean sidhe cast a spell on them; turned them all into eunuchs . . . or so the tale goes."

"That's a pretty good story." She tried to smile but that hurt too much too.

"Definitely helped me sleep last night," he waited until she looked at him before continuing. "I wish you would have told me that story."

"I couldn't risk what you would have done," she argued.

"How do you know what I would have done?"

"You're a creature of habit. Somebody hurt me. Your reaction would have been to kill them."

"And they would have deserved it."

"You were already in enough shit."

"So you were trying to protect me."

"I had good intentions."

He leaned back against a tree and stared her down. "I won't be angry with you forever; just a little while longer." A crack of a smile played on his lips.

"That's understandable." Rosaleen reached towards him and took his hand in hers.

Although his face had softened, the horrible pain was still in his eyes. "I'm so sorry that I took you out in that storm. I just felt so helpless without you, so lost . . ."

Rosaleen put a finger out to quiet him. "I don't deserve this. I don't deserve you."

Ruairi felt his own tears attack him viciously. "Why can't I hate you?"

"I don't know. I hate myself if that makes you feel any better."

He moved closer to her, still holding her hands. "No, it doesn't make me feel any better. I wish neither of us had any idea what hatred was."

She smiled bitterly. "Yes, that is the dream isn't it?"

"It's not supposed to be like this, Róisín, it's not. We were supposed to be lovers."

"We are lovers, Ruairi. That's why it hurts so much." There was a long silence. "Will you stay if I promise to love only you?" She was staring at his neck, memorizing the way his Adam's apple moved when he swallowed, when he spoke.

"No," he answered.

She wiped a tear away helplessly.

He sighed as he pulled her over to him and sat her on his lap, wrapping his strong arms around her and cradling her as if she were a child. "No, I won't stay. But I won't leave just yet. There's a man who has been left alive far too long and another who has been left alone far too long." Ruairi kissed her forehead roughly. "I'm going to take care of both of them."

Rosaleen put her head against his chest and listened to that strong steady heartbeat. "And what about the girl?" she whispered.

"I swore I'd protect my family the day my Da died. You're my family," he whispered back.

"And she's not?"

Ruairi sighed. "She won't want to be when I'm through."

It was a little after eight in the morning when the doorknob turned and two battered figures made their way into a fury of embraces and scolding. Aisling held her brother's face in her hands.

"Don't you do that to me again!" She beat her fists on his chest for emphasis.

He ruffled her hair and then squeezed her hard, avoiding making any promises that he knew he couldn't keep.

Thomas shook Ruairi's hand and cuffed him on the shoulder a few times, happy to feel the solidity of flesh and bone beneath his fingers.

Mairtin just pushed passed him, a cigarette already lit as he made his way through the door and out onto the veranda. He wasn't one for sentimentalities.

Ruairi noticed Gracie and Billy huddled together on the lounge. Gracie was pale and her eyes were big and round. "You look exhausted," he said to her, walking over and picking her up in one easy movement. She melted into him, burying her face in the crook of his neck. "I'm sorry." His words were soft and perfect. It was the only thing Gracie had wanted to hear. Without another word, he carried her out of the room and up the stairs.

Rosaleen watched them go, too afraid to look over at Billy. She felt the pats and hugs as one by one, the crew left her alone with him. When she finally turned back, he was in the same position he had been when she had walked into the house; sitting forward on the lounge, his elbows resting on his knees and his chin resting on clenched fists. His expression was unreadable but his eyes were full of emotion.

"What are you thinking about?" Rosaleen asked him. She just wanted to hear his voice.

"I'm thinking that I've never met anybody who can make me feel so angry, so afraid and so helpless all at once and then also make me so happy, so relieved and so in love."

"I wish I could only make you feel the last three," she said honestly.

"Do you know what I wish? I wish you would have told me three years ago about all of this. I wish you would have asked me what I wanted," he said.

"You have to understand Billy, I didn't think about what you would want, or what Ruairi would want. I didn't even think about what the child inside me would want. I was scared and all I can do is say that I'm sorry." She swallowed hard. "I'm so sorry. I truly believed I was doing the right thing at the time."

Billy stood up and walked towards the window. He stared out at the mists and fog and tried to sort through his muddled emotions. He could forgive and forget or he could just walk out of the house and forget.

"I don't know what else I can say to you," she whispered. She stood in the doorway, frozen by his indecision.

"Tell me why I can't live without you," he said.

Rosaleen moved into the room slowly. He felt a soft hand on his waist and her forehead pressed against his shoulder blade. He could feel her breath through the fibres of his shirt and it made him shudder.

Billy turned around, catching her chin in his hand and forcing her to look into his eyes. "Do you really love me?" he asked.

She put her lips to his to answer his question.

Gracie woke up, her hair, her arms, and her legs tangled around Ruairi. He was snoring lightly, his chest rising and falling softly. The sun was tumbling through the window, baking her exposed skin and making her feel sick. Her mouth was filmy and the smell of stale smoke permeated the house and invaded her pores. She untangled herself from her lover and glanced around the room for something to slip over her naked body. She saw a tweed vest slung over a chair in the corner as she pulled a pair of Ruairi's underwear on. She giggled to herself as she went passed the mirror and out the door.

Her feet padded quietly down the carpeted staircase, trying not to wake anybody in the crowded house. She wound her way into the kitchen and opened the door of the walk-in cool room. She was in desperate need of water.

Curled up in the far corner reading a newspaper was Karl, wearing nothing but undershorts, a tie and a black fedora. He looked up casually, as if his presence there was to be expected.

"I'm sorry," Gracie fumbled for words, "I was looking for the water jug." She scanned the shelves frantically, trying to look everywhere but at the man on the floor.

"Middle shelf, far right," Karl directed.

"Thanks." Gracie was relieved as she grabbed the pitcher and fled the strange scene.

Just before she shut the door, Karl called out to her. She stuck her head back in and looked at him straight on without thinking. "I beg your pardon?" she asked.

"Nice outfit," Karl enunciated slowly.

"Maybe I could borrow your tie next time!" Gracie giggled as she backed out and slammed the door.

William sipped his coffee slowly as Lucas devoured a plate full of scrambled eggs and bacon rashers. They were sitting in the large dining room that William now had all to himself.

"It will all be over tomorrow, William. I don't know why you're so tense," Lucas said between bites.

William grimaced. "Ruairi will be dead tomorrow but it won't all be over. I still have the matter of my wayward family to deal with."

Lucas stopped chewing and stared at William. "You've cut them off financially, right? So it won't be long until they realize how much they need you."

"Hanlon Harcourt asked me to introduce him and his daughter to Billy at the Dominion Day festivities. Don't you find that a bit strange? Why would he want to make the acquaintance of a junior lawyer?"

"Most likely he was trying to marry his daughter off. Billy is very eligible for that sort of match."

"It was more than that, though," William continued, "he kept asking me questions about Billy, even after they'd been introduced. He seemed especially concerned with Billy's job prospects."

Lucas used his tongue to suck bacon rind out of the space between his two front teeth. "That *is* interesting," he noted.

"A little bit too interesting for my tastes," William said dryly. "You don't think he would try to hire him, do you?"

Lucas picked up his fork and stabbed a roasted tomato. "Don't read too much into it, William. Billy doesn't have a hope in hell of getting a job that prestigious."

CHAPTER 20

Ruairi rolled over and pulled Gracie into his arms. "What are you doing with my vest on?" he asked.

"I had to go downstairs for some water," she replied lightly. A few seconds later she asked, "Does Karl seem odd to you?"

Ruairi thought about it for a moment and then shook his head. "No, why?"

"He was curled up in the cool room, half naked, reading the paper," she said slowly.

Ruairi chuckled. "What's odd about that?"

"What are your plans for today?" Gracie asked, noticing for the first time the new tattoo on Ruairi's chest. It was another reminder of his love for Rosaleen. She didn't like it.

"I've got a meeting at lunch and then I was planning on heading out to the horse races. Why? Do you want to come?" He kissed her on the lips, preventing her from answering for a few minutes.

When she finally caught her breath she nodded. "I have to have lunch with my mother but I'm sure I could be persuaded to dress up and be your date at the races."

Ruairi smiled and rolled onto his back, pulling her on top of him. "Well, you better scrub up good because there is a certain little girl that looks very cute in pink ruffles and hair ribbons."

"Kathleen will be there?" Gracie was surprised by that.

Ruairi nodded. "She likes beating the bookies."

Gracie's brow crinkled in concern. "She bets on the horses?"

"Don't look so shocked. She's made more money for me off the bookies than I do off of the rum!"

"You are teasing me." Gracie sighed.

Ruairi laughed. "I guess you'll just have to see it for yourself."

During lunch at the Club with her mother, Valerie, and a few members of Valerie's Women's League, she saw him. Gracie stared at the Irishman across the room. He sat side-on to her, his hardened features illuminated by the glare of the sun coming in through the enormous windows behind him. The large cut across his forehead made him look especially tough. He was smiling at the gentleman in front of him, that cheeky smile of his. Gracie felt her heart begin to ache. Every aspect of her being was longing for him; urging him to turn that smile towards her. Suddenly, every minute out of his reach was an eternity in hell.

He seemed to be lost in easy conversation, his hands floating carelessly in and out of whatever story he was telling. She liked the way he talked with his hands, usually when he got a little bit excited. She watched them, remembering the feel of them on her skin. They were big, strong hands that seemed so capable, so sure.

"Gracie? Gracie, Darling?" Genevieve's voice seeped into Gracie's consciousness. Gracie turned her head slowly, not registering yet that she was being spoken to. Genevieve held her daughter's gaze until she was sure Gracie was focussed again. "Gracie, we were just discussing tomorrow's fox show. Valerie has organized a high tea benefit beforehand in the garden for Agnes Macphail."

Gracie tried to look more interested than she was. "Is that the woman in parliament?"

"Not just *the* woman in parliament, Gracie," her mother chided her, "the *only* woman in parliament. Honestly, you would think you were raised under a rock."

Valerie had seen Ruairi when she had arrived. She knew exactly why Gracie was distracted. "Go easy on her, Genevieve. I don't think feminism and politics are on her mind at the moment!" She smiled knowingly.

Genevieve frowned. "I'm beginning to think I should have locked this young lady up in a very high tower."

Gracie smiled demurely. "Oh, Maman, you worry too much! High tea would be lovely but I would have to raid my wardrobes at once. I can't think of anything suitable to wear to meet the venerable Agnes Macphail!"

"You are cheeky, Madamoiselle," her mother couldn't help but smile at her quick recovery, "anything for a new dress!"

The ladies at the table all laughed politely.

"There is a wonderful fellow from Montréal in town at the moment, Gracie. He does exquisite work. You would do well to commission him for some frocks if you feel your selection is lacking." Carolina Spencer, the treasurer of the Women's League, addressed Gracie. "His craftsmanship is unmatched and the season really demands an assortment of looks."

"You simply must tell me his name then! I'll book him immediately on your recommendation." Gracie tried to sneak a look back at Ruairi but he had vanished. Her disappointment was evident.

"There's no need. He's staying in my home," Valerie corrected herself, "your home. He'll be doing a consultation for Carolina tomorrow at noon."

Carolina smiled warmly at Gracie. "I wouldn't mind at all if I had to share him with you," she said graciously.

"Is this the same man who designs the furs?" Gracie hadn't realized there had been a man in Valerie's home since the fur exhibition.

"Yes, Gustav, he's a dear friend and comes to stay often," Valerie licked her lips salaciously. "He's been slipping out of the house a bit lately, though. There seems to be many other diversions in Charlottetown."

Carolina shared a look with Valerie across the table. Their eyes were dancing.

"He sounds like a rare find." Gracie looked up at her mother. "Maybe you need to meet this Gustav as well, Maman!" she teased.

Genevieve feigned shock. "I don't believe I'm that Parisian!" She laughed.

Ruairi left the Club as quickly as he could. He had seen her out of the corner of his eye, sitting with all of the society ladies having lunch and gossiping. It had taken all of his self-control to leave without allowing himself the luxury of catching her eye, even for a few moments. He had no time to be distracted by her until the races.

He walked down towards the water and then veered off sharply down an alleyway no more than three feet wide. About twenty paces in he climbed a fire escape that led to the upper chambers of a local council building and then jimmied open a window on the third floor. They had been given a special allowance to use the building under the strict condition that they never entered through the front door. It wouldn't do to have the prohibition agents sniffing around a council owned building.

He took a quick look around and then crawled through the window. Inside Stavros and Karl were in the middle of another verbal sparring match while Thomas, Mick and Mairtin sat in various states of relaxation, ignoring the other two.

They all looked up expectantly when Ruairi shimmied through the window.

"Well?" Stavros turned away from Karl and put his hands on his hips.

Ruairi looked over at Mairtin and Thomas. "It doesn't seem to matter that the drop didn't happen last night because I just got handed a hundred and seventy thousand in cash."

Mairtin threw his head back and whooped. Thomas started to laugh. Stavros was so excited he wrapped his short arms around Karl's middle and squeezed him in an impromptu hug.

Karl looked distressed and pushed the little man off of him. "You're worse than a Jack Russell Terrier. Don't ever do that again!"

"So McCoy's men liked our hooch?" Mairtin was impressed.

"He told me it was the best whiskey his clients had tasted outside of Ireland," Ruairi bragged.

"Well seeing as we used the recipe from the best whiskey inside of Ireland, it makes sense!" Thomas laughed.

"He's given me another order; triple what he took last time."

Mick grinned at Ruairi, his leathery face folding into happy wrinkles. "Well done, lad. What does this mean for us?"

Ruairi knew what Mick was asking. "It means us boys have done our job here and can head back to New York at our leisure to plan our trip home. We'll do a few more runs with you and train the new crew but then we can go home."

"What about Rosaleen?" Mick's concern was evident.

"I'll make sure she's taken care of before I leave."

Mick wasn't satisfied. "I thought you'd been ordered to stay for a while longer?"

Ruairi shrugged. "It was more of a suggestion than an order."

Mick's smile faded. He nodded and swallowed and then opened his mouth to say something but thought better of it and just nodded again.

Ruairi levelled the old man with his eyes. "This was always the plan, Mickey. You don't have to stay. You can come home too."

Mick's face hardened. "I'm done with Ireland, Son. I wish you could be too."

Thomas waited until Ruairi was alone in his room later, dressing for the races, before talking to him about what he had overheard.

"Are you not even going to consider the possibility of staying?" he asked from the doorway. "I thought there was a chance that you might spend some time in New York?"

Ruairi was checking the stitching in the crotch of his suit pants. He had snagged it on his way through the window. He didn't turn to look at his brother. "No."

"Why not?"

"Because." Ruairi didn't feel like being diplomatic this afternoon. It was too warm for diplomacy.

"I thought this whole thing with Rosaleen was sorted?"

"It is." Ruairi's jaw twitched. "If Billy Gainsborough doesn't marry her, then Gerry will. She's always had a soft spot for Gerry."

"She's always had a soft spot for you," Thomas shot back.

"She doesn't want me. I'm going home."

"The Gainsborough girl wants you," Thomas argued.

"No, she doesn't. Not really. I'll never be able to give that girl what she wants."

"You have a hundred and seventy thousand dollars in your money clip. You could give her everything she wants, and yourself, every night." Thomas was not going to give up easily.

Ruairi finally faced him. "You are bloody daft for a poet, boy. I can't love her enough. I gave everything I had to Rosaleen. She tore the bloody heart right out of me!" His eyes blazed. "Gracie deserves more than what's left."

Thomas was frustrated. "Well, were you even going to talk to us about going back home? I mean, it's a pretty big risk to go back when we've been ordered to stay here and the whole damn British Army and Royal Ulster Constabulary is after your neck."

"You can stay if you like," Ruairi responded.

Thomas narrowed his eyes. His brother was becoming more and more difficult to deal with.

Race day on Prince Edward Island was not regarded much differently than any other day by most people. But for the few avid race-goers and those in the fashionable set, it was an extremely exciting day that brought with it the promise of scandal, gossip and the occasional win.

Gracie had always loved the races as a child in London, not only for the horses and betting, but for the fabulous frocks and finery on display as well. Gracie was sure that the ensemble that she had put together would keep her on the best dressed lists in the society papers. It was a simple shift of black silk with a dropped waist but the extravagant beadwork that adorned the fabric made the dress absolutely stunning. There were hundreds of pearl droplets cascading down the dress and although it made the weight of the dress almost unbearable in the heat, the effect was worth the lack of comfort. Her milliner had sculpted a divine fascinator of exotic feathers that dripped pearls. She felt beautiful.

She had asked Norah to accompany her and the two girls were smiling and laughing as they made their way trackside. As they wound their way through the hordes of people, Gracie found herself enamoured with the pageantry of the lower classes. Although the dresses and hats were less expensive than those in the marquee, she noticed a raw talent for natural fashion among her counterparts. Many of the dresses presented a rare allure that had Gracie following the lines of their wearer's bodies with her eyes.

She was surprised to see Rosaleen Jameson. Even in a crowd of beautiful people, she stood out as if she were brightly coloured and the world around her was in black and white. She was standing in the middle of a group of men, brazenly applying her red lipstick without the aid of a pocket mirror. Gracie watched in fascination. When she was done with the lipstick she pressed her lips together, rolling the bottom lip over the top in an overtly sexual way.

She suddenly flicked her eyes towards Gracie, impaling her with the force of recognition.

Gracie found her heart racing as the beauty made her way over to her, ignoring the pleas of the men that she was leaving behind. "Gracie Gainsborough, as I live and breathe." Her lips smiled but there was something dark behind her eyes.

Gracie and Rosaleen kissed formally on both cheeks.

"Rosaleen, I'd like to introduce you to Norah Bexley."

"I believe we've met at a few of Valerie's events." Norah smiled politely.

Rosaleen nodded and fanned herself with a delicate oriental fan that Thomas had given her last Christmas. "If you are looking for Ruairi, he and Billy went to place some bets."

Gracie smiled. "Do you think they have finally been able to put what happened in Ireland behind them?"

Rosaleen gave her a slightly patronizing look. "It's a bit more complicated than that." She was silent for a moment. "And Ruairi will never leave Ireland behind him."

"Or you it seems," Gracie said without thinking.

Rosaleen narrowed her eyes. "Have I done something to upset you?"

"No," Gracie sighed, "No, I just feel like I'm competing with you for his affection."

"He loves you," Rosaleen assured her through gritted teeth. It was difficult for her to admit.

"Not as much as he loves you." Gracie knew the truth. It was written all over Ruairi's body.

"I'm surprised a girl like you isn't trying to persuade Ruairi into marrying. Don't you want him to stay?" Rosaleen changed the subject.

"I can't ask that of Ruairi." Gracie's face was bitten by emotion.

Norah reached over and put a comforting hand on Gracie's shoulder.

"I used to think like that," Rosaleen confessed, a rare moment of feeling fluttering through her veins. "I was wrong. I could have asked him for anything. Now, I think you might be able to as well."

"He's made it very clear that he wants to go back to Ireland." Gracie was getting upset.

"You need to change his mind," Rosaleen replied. "And you don't have much time."

Mick sat on a lounge chair beside Valerie. He had wanted to go to the races with the boys but Valerie had needed to discuss the plans for Paris. He wasn't overly keen on heading to France but he understood the importance of having Genevieve accompanied and settled properly. It also provided him with an opportunity to meet with some of the champagne suppliers they had been doing so much business with.

He sighed and lit a cigarette. He was worried about Ruairi. Mick did not want him to return to Ireland. He would have preferred to have Finnigan Murphy board a ship with Mrs. O'Neill in tow and move the whole family over. Ruairi's return to Ireland would eventually lead to one thing and Mick would do anything he could to prevent that.

But he knew that Ruairi couldn't remain in Charlottetown either, with William Gainsborough alive and wielding so much influence. Mick was almost hoping that he would have his own chance to deal with the General. But he knew that there would be nowhere to hide. One wrong step and they would all end up in gaol.

"You seem preoccupied, Darling," Valerie broke into his thoughts.

"I just keep thinking about Ruairi. I don't know what I can do to convince him that he will do more good for Ireland from New York. My lads could run the whole East coast if they wanted to." Mick was referring to Mairtin, Gerry, Ruairi and Thomas. In his mind, they were all his.

Valerie patted his sun aged hand. "You have a lot of confidence in those boys," she said dreamily. She was reclining on her lounge, wearing a bathing costume and sunglasses.

Mick looked over at her and wondered how she always remained so placid. "They've never been a disappointment," he assured her.

"They must get that from you," she teased him flirtatiously. She reached over and fed him a piece of salt water taffy that she had bought at the festival. It was his favourite sweet and she had hidden it away until they had some time alone.

He sat back and chuckled. "I'm too old for you . . . for this," he gestured to all of the fine things that surrounded them. Mick had led a very simple life back in Ireland. He was a farmboy and wasn't very comfortable without mud and shit at his feet.

"I disagree," she began.

"Don't you always?" he asked with a cheeky grin.

She giggled. "I think that you are finally at an age where you can appreciate it all, don't you? It's all coming together for us Mick, don't you see? You and I deserve this."

Mick watched her carefully. They had agreed when they had first met that anything between them would be casual but lately Mick found himself spending an awful amount of time at her side. "Us?" he asked, surprised by her language.

She turned her face towards him slowly but remained silent. After a moment, she pulled herself up to standing and moved over to his lounger. She sat on the edge, staring down at him. Valerie slowly reached out and ran her fingers through Mick's greying hair. "I may not need another husband," she smiled, "but I do have a thing for silver foxes."

Rosaleen had a few rare moments alone after Norah and Gracie had wandered off. She looked over and saw Billy leaning casually against the lower railing of the members marquee. Her lips narrowed into a tight line as she watched him lean in and whisper something charming to the blonde girl from the Dominion Day festivities. The girl giggled flirtatiously and Rosaleen felt her stomach sink as she saw the genuine pleasure he took from her laughter.

Mairtin walked towards Rosaleen with Kathleen bouncing beside him in a pink frilly taffeta confection.

"Did you get a good look at all of the horses?" Rosaleen turned her attention to her little girl to numb the feeling that was slicing through her chest. Billy had not made her any promises yet and she had no right to demand them.

Kathleen nodded. "Uncle Mairtin wrote down all of my picks so that Uncle Ruairi can place my bets."

"Well, I hope you picked a few winners because Uncle Ruairi works mighty hard for his money."

"Oh, he won't be disappointed," Kathleen said confidently, as though she were a seasoned punter.

"Where is Ruairi?" Mairtin asked, looking around.

Rosaleen was busy fussing with Kathleen's hair. "I'm not sure. He said he had to go speak with Billy but Billy is now in the members marquee with some blonde girl that I saw him with on Dominion Day." Rosaleen bristled.

"Who's Billy?" Kathleen asked.

"Nobody, Darling," she said, her tone hinting at sadness.

"There's Uncle Ruairi!" Kathleen shouted, pointing upwards.

Mairtin and Rosaleen looked up just in time to see Ruairi approaching Billy. He was wearing a tailored cream coloured leisure suit which set off his tanned skin and dark eyes perfectly. Rosaleen had felt a familiar thrill when she had watched him getting dressed.

"What's Billy Gainsborough doing with Georgiana Harcourt?" Mairtin asked.

Rosaleen looked at him, surprised. "That's Georgiana Harcourt?"

Mairtin nodded.

Rosaleen smiled, relieved. "Well, it all makes sense then," she breathed.

"What does?" Mairtin growled.

"Billy's the new baptist."

"The new what?"

"The guy who pushes the hardline prohibition laws across Hanlon Harcourt's desk." Mairtin still wasn't catching on. "The guy who keeps liquor illegal in this country so that we continue to have a lucrative career; the moment Prohibition ends, we are out of a job, Mairty. Billy's job is to sit on staff with Hanlon and make it look like Hanlon is doing everything the temperance groups want him to do, thus keeping him popular with the electorate. We give a small cut to Hanlon and and we get a few federal favours," she explained.

"So, Billy's a Baptist, then." Mairtin rolled his eyes. "Delightful, another Gainsborough connection."

Rosaleen ignored his jibe and smiled. She felt herself relax.

"Do you have everything I need then?" Billy asked Ruairi as he approached.

Ruairi nodded to Billy and then leaned in to kiss Georgiana's cheek. "Miss Harcourt."

Georgiana blushed. "It's been a while, Mr. O'Neill," she said, breathily.

Ruairi shrugged. "I'm a busy man."

"I know," Georgiana laughed, "and you are keeping my father a very busy man."

Ruairi smiled. "Well, idle hands and all," he joked.

"Straight from the devil's lips!" She smiled. They stared at each other intently for a while. "So what are you two gentlemen up to? You both seem very nervous."

The boys grinned at each other. "It's possible that we might be up to something," Ruairi laughed.

"Should I leave before the law enforcement shows up?" she teased playfully.

"I don't think you have to run out just yet," Billy assured her, "but we should probably get ourselves back down to the turf."

Ruairi agreed with him. It was time. He gave Georgiana another gorgeous grin. "Tell your Da I'll be in contact soon. Take care of yourself, Miss Harcourt."

"It was lovely to see you, Mr. O'Neill." She put a gloved hand to his cheek.

He winked at her. "Always a pleasure."

She turned to Billy. "I'll be seeing you again very soon," she smiled. "It will be my turn to show you around Ottawa."

Billy nodded. "I look forward to it." When she left, his face sobered. "My father seems to be in attendance today." Billy threw a brief look in William's direction. He was with Lucas and Johnny.

"I've noticed him watching us." Ruairi looked directly at William with deadly calm eyes. He leaned his back against the marquee railing, a glint of metal at his waistband flashing in the sun.

Billy shook his head. "You cannot threaten him in public."

Ruairi furrowed his brow. "I'm not. I'm warning him."

"Do you have the other package?" Billy asked, shaking his head at Ruairi.

Ruairi hesitated. He looked down at Rosaleen, who was kneeling in front of Kathleen near the track, fixing something on the hem of the little girl's dress. She looked up and met his eyes. It was time to let her go. "I do," he said.

William stood off near the sandwich table, a cup of tea in his hand. He watched his son walk off with Ruairi O'Neill. He had seen the flash of steel and the glint in the Irishman's eye. He felt the space around him constricting. His heart was thudding in his throat and he felt sweaty and cold. He didn't trust his son and he knew that he was on borrowed time with Ruairi. The gun made him nervous.

He reached for Lucas. "I'm feeling ill," he gasped. He didn't feel safe, even with a hundred people around him.

Lucas turned towards him and saw the grey pallor of his skin. He grabbed William's elbow and motioned for Johnny to attend to William's other side. "We need to get him out of here before he faints."

The two men walked William outside the gates. Johnny had requested the car and Lucas escorted him home.

Billy followed Ruairi down through the crowds to where Rosaleen stood with Kathleen.

"Where's Aisling?" Ruairi asked her.

"Over there with Mairtin." Rosaleen pointed to a bench where Mairtin sat hunched over a pen and paper with a bookie beside him. Aisling stood, checking her make-up and hair in a little pocket mirror.

Ruairi grabbed Kathleen's hand and dragged her over to his sister. "Keep your eye on her for a minute," he ordered.

Kathleen looked up at Aisling as Ruairi strode away. "I don't know what it is they think I don't know," she said, shaking her head as if all grown-ups were a puzzle.

"What do you mean?" Aisling tousled her hair.

"Uncle Ruairi found my Da but nobody wants to tell me," Kathleen said bluntly. "I think his name is Billy."

Mairtin had stopped placing his bets to listen to the little girl. He looked up at Aisling with wide eyes. Neither of them knew how to answer Kathleen as she stared transfixed by her mother, her father, and Ruairi O'Neill.

Billy stood facing Rosaleen. She was looking between him and Ruairi, who was still a few feet away, worried that another fight was brewing between them.

"What is this all about?" she asked tentatively, trying to calm her nerves.

"We have a proposal for you," Ruairi said. His face was set with a charming smile.

Rosaleen was sceptical. "What kind of proposal?" she asked.

"The only kind women are ever interested in." Ruairi laughed.

Rosaleen looked confused. "Both of you are going to propose to me?"

"Sort of," Billy said slowly, taking her hand.

Ruairi took a deep breath. "Rosaleen," he began, "I have loved you since we were just kids. I always thought that one day I would marry you, one day we'd end up together, happily." He gave her little grimace. "So I bought you this," he said finally, producing a beautiful ring set with a square black onyx surrounded by tiny glittering diamonds.

Rosaleen gasped.

"We came so close to getting it right so many times," he paused, swallowing back the tears, "but I could have never gotten it as right as Billy did," he said, motioning towards Kathleen.

Rosaleen began to cry.

Ruairi handed the ring to Billy. It took him a moment to compose himself. "Take care of her. I love her more than anything."

Rosaleen threw her arms around Ruairi's neck. He pulled her to him and held her fast. "I love you, Roísín Dubh," he whispered.

"I love you, too." Rosaleen clung to him.

Ruairi finally turned her towards Billy.

A tear slipped down her cheek as he knelt down on one knee.

"Rosaleen Jameson, will you marry me?"

"Aye," she whispered, "I will."

Billy stood up and embraced her. Ruairi wiped his eyes as he watched Aisling hugging Kathleen. Mairtin just shook his head and went back to picking his horses.

Gracie stood beside Norah as the next race began. She still hadn't found Ruairi and she was becoming irritated. The day was almost over. The weight of the dress and the heat of the day were draining her.

Norah tugged on Gracie's arm. "Let's go place a bet on the next race," she suggested.

"I don't really know how." Gracie was hesitant.

Norah laughed. "I do! Come and I'll show you," she said excitedly.

They stood in the queue for the book maker and tried to keep their whispers low as they gossiped over whom they had seen and who was conspicuously absent. Both turned as they felt a strong arm slide across their shoulders and a warm body press between them. Ruairi kissed Gracie on the forehead.

"Where have you been?" she cried, cuddling into him.

"Taking care of something, my Love." He kissed her again, this time on the lips. Then he turned to Norah and nodded. "You must be Norah. We never officially met but I remember you from the docks."

Norah blushed. She couldn't help herself. "It seems like a very long time ago, Ruairi," she said, holding out her hand.

He shook it gently. "It does, doesn't it?" He turned back to Gracie. "I came to turn you girls away from your horse bets and propose something more illicit. How would you both like to go out to Rum Row?"

Gracie looked over at Norah who was shaking her head and pouting dramatically. "I'm so sad, I won't be able to come. I have a dinner date with the boy I met at Valerie's fur exhibition."

"Do you?" Gracie was delighted for her friend. Norah hadn't seen anyone since Henry had died. "That's wonderful news!"

"I do wish I could have come and I appreciate the invitation Ruairi," Norah apologized. "I've heard it's fabulously naughty out there!"

Ruairi laughed, "Some other time, then."

"You go, Gracie," Norah urged. "I must head home to get ready anyhow but you have to promise to tell me all about it!"

Gracie was grateful that Norah was such a good friend. She kissed her on the cheek and wished her luck. Then she tucked her arm in Ruairi's and let him lead her out the gates.

CHAPTER 21

On the other side of the world, Finnigan Murphy sat in a tiny cell in the Crumlin Road Gaol in Belfast.

He was trying to scratch out some meaningful phrase that would enshrine him in history; a poetic pearl that would carve his name into eternity. He had nothing.

He had sat for hours; time meant absolutely nothing in this place. There was always another second, always another minute that would go by.

He wrote one word . . . *Freedom* . . .

The whiskey had always helped him write. But there was no whiskey in here.

And there was no Thomas O'Neill. No Ruairi O'Neill. No Gerry O'Neill. They were the only brothers he had known. When his Ma died of consumption when he was thirteen, Mrs. O'Neill had put a spare pillow and blanket in the parlour for him. Whenever his Da would come home drunk and beat him for looking like his dead wife, Finn had a place where he could go and heal. Finally, Mrs. O'Neill had just made him a permanent bed.

He had stayed behind to look after Mrs. O'Neill. With the situation the way it was in the North, he had felt she shouldn't be left on her own. She had protected him and now it was time for him to protect her. Thomas and Ruairi were only supposed to be gone for a few months.

With Finn in gaol, Mrs. O'Neill was on her own. Word had come to him that the boys might not be back until the following year. He was angry with them and he was scared. Without brothers and whiskey, what did he have?

Freedom dies . . .

They had left him with a head full of ideals.

Freedom dies when . . .

They had left him with a head full of martyrs.

Freedom dies when love . . .

They had left him.

Freedom dies when love is born.

Gracie watched as they drew closer to the lights and noises of the offshore party. Everything else faded as her eyes took in the grand spectacle before her.

It seemed like there were hundreds of boats; all displaying banners advertising their onboard specialities. Rum, whiskey, gin, and wine were on offer; not to mention poker, cigars, and prostitutes.

Thomas weaved the boat in and out of the narrow alleyways made by the floating merchandisers. He called helloes to different revellers who leaned over the rails of their chosen stomping grounds as he passed by, flashing his trademark grin and waving like a wild man.

"Friends of yours?" Mairtin asked.

"Everybody's a friend of mine!" Thomas laughed.

"Especially when they're offering liquor and prostitutes." Stavros drummed his fingers on the side of the boat in anticipation.

Ruairi slipped his hand into Gracie's as he came up behind her. "I don't want you caught out by yourself, you hear me? You stick with me, Billy, Mairtin, or Thomas understand?"

Gracie nodded, burrowing into him. He rubbed her back and buried his nose in her hair. He would have preferred to stay home with her that night. He had no desire for her to be introduced to this aspect of his life but a celebration was in order.

They pulled up beside a rather dilapidated old cargo ship with a rickety rope ladder hanging down from about twenty feet up in the air. A red glow illuminated the boat against the black skyline.

"Do I have to climb that?" Gracie couldn't hide her fear.

Ruairi squeezed her. "Don't worry, I'll be right beneath you, helping you up."

"Goodness gracious," she squealed, as the rope wobbled and she slipped off of it on her first attempt. Ruairi caught her and muffled his laughter in her shoulder.

"Right, then," Mairtin shrugged his shoulders, "you can stay with the boat. It'll be a grand night without you to look after."

Ruairi cuffed him up the back of the head. "Steady up or you'll be staying down here with the boat."

Mairtin's eyes challenged Ruairi. "And who'll be making me?"

Aisling darted in between the two, turning to face Mairtin. "I will be, so get your arse up the ladder and never you mind about bothering Gracie tonight."

"She's got enough to worry about as it is," Rosaleen laughed.

Ruairi shot her a look. Before he could explain a wild face greeted them from up above. It was framed by unruly red curls and enough cleavage to drown a ship full of sailors. "There's me boys!" the woman shouted down. "I've been missing you lads! It's been weeks since you came 'round, Thomas O'Neill. Get up here and give me some cheap thrills and maybe I'll forgive you."

Thomas winked at Gracie. "Moonshine Maggie," he said. "Watch her around Ruairi. She likes him the most."

"Who's Moonshine Maggie?" Gracie asked, her eyes wide to take in the whole sight of the mad looking woman.

"A dear friend," Ruairi responded. His eyes shone as he looked up at the heavily made up harlot. With that he lifted her hands and placed them back on the rope. "Up you go," he prodded.

She had a choice of hands to help her over the railing at the top. Mairtin's calloused and rigid fingers reached towards her as did ten unfamiliar red-lacquered claws. She grabbed for Mairtin without hesitation and tumbled off the railing into his arms. She found herself hoping that he wouldn't immediately push her away. She was too terrified to turn around and face the madam behind her.

He didn't push her away. In fact, he actually pulled her closer, in an almost protective way. When she was finally released she found Ruairi in the clutches of those scarlet daggers. The colourful creation that was Moonshine Maggie was wrapped intimately around Ruairi's body. Her hands were twined around his neck and her lips were smudging their red fullness over his face repeatedly.

He had his arms around her voluptuous body and was rocking her back and forth as she kissed him. Gracie couldn't hide her shock and discomfort.

Aisling noticed. She put a comforting hand on Gracie's back. "We are all just pieces of each other, Love. Do you understand?"

"He'll never be just mine," she spoke softly as her heart dropped.

Aisling shook her head. "Ruairi belongs to all of Ireland."

Moonshine Maggie made her way through the crew, giving each and every one of them a passionate embrace. Billy was subjected to even more kissing and groping than Ruairi but he came through the ordeal unscathed aside from the smears of red lipstick all over his face.

When she finally locked her eyes on Gracie, the young English girl was trembling noticeably.

She became very still as she stood in front of the pale stranger. "Hello, beautiful girl," Maggie's voice was deep and steady.

Gracie shrank into herself. Ruairi was surprised by her sudden withdrawal from him. Instead of clinging to him, she seemed like she was trying to flee, trying to extricate herself from his grasp. He tightened his grip on her and watched Maggie's eyes closely.

Maggie pried her loose. She circled Gracie, appraising her as though she were making an expensive purchase. "So you've brought me an English girl to sacrifice. Interesting idea." She glanced over at Rosaleen and the two women shared a look.

Ruairi's stomach twisted as he watched her squirm under Maggie's scrutiny, isolated by who she was and what she represented to all of them. He stepped in front of Maggie and pulled Gracie back to him, pledging his allegiance to her and demanding it of the rest of them. He levelled both Maggie and Rosaleen in one burning gaze.

Maggie threw up her arms and relented immediately. She was never surprised or offended by Ruairi's expectations. Her hands and fingers and nails circled and wove around themselves. "He plays the martyr so well," she commented to the atmosphere. She dipped into a low curtsy, dropping her head in reverence to Gracie. "Welcome to the family."

Gracie's lips quivered as she tried to smile. Rosaleen turned on her heel and disappeared around the bow of the boat, dragging Billy behind her.

"Have you ever played poker?" Ruairi asked Gracie, who seemed increasingly interested in biting her nails.

"Yes," Gracie nodded, removing her thumb from her mouth. "Once or twice."

"Grand!" Ruairi laughed, not believing her at all. "Follow me!"

He took her hand and led her down into the first hold where eight round tables were set up and five men sat around each table. The enclosed space was filled with cigar smoke and profanity. Each table seemed to have at least two foul phrases that were tossed out in regular intervals.

A ninth and tenth table were hurriedly set up and a woman in a low cut dress held her hand out to Ruairi.

He passed her a wad of bills. "This is for the both of us," he said, indicating to himself and Gracie.

The girl nodded and shoved the bills down the front of her dress. She disappeared into the cloud of smoke but returned almost instantly with fists full of chips for them.

"We're betting real money?" Gracie gasped.

Ruairi gave her a queer look. "What did you think we were going to bet?"

"I've only ever played for matches," she said.

Mairtin groaned behind her. "Well, there goes that thousand."

Gracie's jaw dropped. "You just gave her a thousand dollars?"

"Two thousand," Ruairi corrected her. "The buy in was a thousand each."

The tables were ready and Ruairi sat Gracie down with Thomas and three men she had never seen before.

"I'll be at the next table with Mairtin," he said.

"You aren't going to sit with me?" her voice came out much higher than its usual pitch.

"You'll be fine, Love. If I sit beside you, I'll end up too distracted to play."

Thomas patted her hand. "I'll take care of you, don't you worry."

Gracie looked around at each of the three strangers and swallowed. They all looked extremely serious and not one of them had uttered a word.

The dealer began to shuffle. The cards were dealt. Gracie picked up her hand. Two aces and two tens with a six of hearts.

She asked for one and waited. Even the dealer chuckled.

"You may want to exchange more than one card," Thomas advised. "Do you know what hands you are looking for?"

Gracie kept to her game plan. "I want one card," she said evenly.

The dealer looked at Thomas, who shrugged. One card was placed in front of her.

Play continued around the table. The ante was upped. Gracie matched.

"I call," said the moustached lothario to her right.

Gracie laid her cards down. "Ace high full house."

It was Thomas' turn to drop his jaw while Gracie raked the chips towards herself.

Rosaleen led Billy into a tarted up bedroom.

"I wouldn't sit on the bed if I were you," she warned.

Billy cringed, looking at the purple velvet chaise in the corner. "I don't think I want to sit on that either."

Rosaleen laughed. "I'd say the floor is the safest bet."

Billy sat and stretched out his legs. "So, you brought me to a prostitute's boudoir to talk. What exactly are we talking about?"

Rosaleen giggled again. "I just wanted to talk about this . . . us."

"When it comes to us, there's never been much talking," Billy coughed.

"No, there hasn't," Rosaleen agreed. She bit her lip. "So . . . married . . ."

Billy laughed. "You make it sound dirty."

"I just don't want to be a Gainsborough," she said suddenly. "I mean, I want to keep my name."

Billy sighed. "That's understandable, I guess, given the circumstances."

Rosaleen was surprised. "Really? I thought you'd be angry with me."

Billy shook his head and reached out to pull her closer to him. "There's a lot of history with my last name that wouldn't be very appealing to you."

"I just hate William so much now. I know that I made a lot of mistakes but . . ."

"But he took advantage of you. I know that."

"Do you think that Ruairi knows that?" Rosaleen asked.

"I think Ruairi and I may be the only ones that understand just what my father is capable of." Billy hugged her to him.

She looked up at him. "I need to be honest with you about something."

Billy took a deep breath. "Your honesty is a fearful thing to behold of late."

"This isn't over. Ruairi still wants to kill William."

"Do you think we can stop him?" he asked slowly.

"No, I don't." She tried to find her courage. "So, I decided to telephone Gerry."

"Gerry who?" Billy's eyes were wide. He was pretty sure he knew who Rosaleen was referring to.

"Gerry O'Neill. Ruairi's older brother." Rosaleen watched Billy's face for a reaction. He looked worried.

"Why would you do that?" he asked.

"I thought that if Gerry came, maybe Ruairi would let him finish everything and then he and Gracie could maybe . . ." she trailed off.

"You're just full of surprises, aren't you?" Billy was shaking his head and looking grim.

"You're mad at me." Rosaleen noticed his withdrawal from her.

"I'm not mad. I'm just . . . just unsure of why anybody needs to take care of anything. Can't this just all end now?" Billy asked. "You do realize that although I understand why everybody hates him, he is still my father."

"I know. But Ruairi is Ruairi. I can't stop him this time. I just thought that it would be better if Gerry did it, and then you and Gracie wouldn't hate Ruairi."

Billy was overwhelmed by the enormity of the consequences that were involved. "Will you let me try to talk him out of it?" he asked.

Rosaleen nodded. "Of course I will. Just please don't mention anything about Gerry just yet. Ruairi doesn't know that he's coming."

Billy agreed. "I won't say a thing until you tell me to."

The cards continued in Gracie's favour. The foul language was now being thrown out all around her, mostly because of her.

"Are you kidding me?" the older gentleman seated directly across from her complained. He looked like he hadn't bathed in days. "How is it that she has won four hands in a row? Do you have something going on with her?" he asked the dealer.

"Did you just call me a cheat?" Gracie gave the old man a withering look.

"A filthy fucking cheat." He leaned across the table at her.

Thomas turned to his left and glared at the man. "Watch your mouth in front of the lady or you will be dealing with me." He leaned back and Gracie noticed for the first time a knife in a pouch on his belt.

The old man slid down in his chair and shut his mouth.

She smiled at Thomas. "Are you protecting me?"

"Well, somebody's got to. You're sitting up there like the National Bank of Gracie, all high and mighty like."

Gracie giggled and looked at her stack of chips. She was doing rather well for herself.

"What's going on over there?" Ruairi called out from his table.

"Gracie's robbing us blind!" Thomas called back.

Ruairi jumped up from his table and swaggered over. "Och, she is! Look at you, Gracie girl! I thought you'd said you only played once or twice?"

A sly smile spread across her face. "It may have been a few more times than that."

Ruairi leaned down and kissed her roughly on the cheek. "Now I understand what attracted me to you. I knew there was a bad girl in there somewhere!" He laughed as he went back to his game.

A few hands later, Billy and Rosaleen appeared.

"Gracie, come for a walk with me," Billy called to her from the door.

"I can't!" she called back, "I'm busy making money."

"Rosaleen will sit in for you. I'm sure she'll be able to win a few hands for you," he insisted.

"Take her away, will you?" Thomas teased. "I've already lost eight hundred dollars to her."

Rosaleen leaned over Thomas' shoulder and bit him playfully on the ear. "With a hand like that I can see why."

Thomas tried to shrug her off. "Get out of it!" he swatted at her, "Billy! Get a handle on your woman!" he laughed.

The third man, a quiet, burly Nordic fellow called.

Gracie smiled as she laid down a queen high straight.

"Wins again." The dealer pointed to Gracie.

The old man opened his mouth but Thomas shot him a look and he thought better of saying whatever it was that was on his mind.

"Cheerio chaps. I suppose I'll have to leave you with Rosaleen." Gracie pushed her chair back and stood up. "Not a single worthy poker face among them," she whispered loudly to Rosaleen.

Billy took Gracie back up to the deck. They stood at the stern, staring out over the churning water.

"How are you holding up?" Billy asked her.

"Wonderful! Did you see all the money that I just won? I bet I could buy my own house in a few more nights like this!" she crowed.

"Oh, good! Now Ruairi's turned you into a gambler!" Billy laughed.

"Blame Norah. She's the one who taught me how to play."

"That's not hard to believe! She's always been a bit of a wild one. You'd never believe she was a Bexley."

"She'd love it out here. I should bring her sometime."

Billy looked at his sister in disbelief. "You'd like to come back to Rum Row?"

"Why not?" Gracie was indignant.

"Gracie, you don't belong out here!"

"And where do I belong? The Club?" Gracie was annoyed with her brother.

"Yes! You belong at the Club. You're a nice girl, Gracie," Billy tried to remind her.

"Well, maybe I'm tired of being a nice girl. Maybe I like the things that not nice girls have."

"Like Ruairi?" Billy asked gently.

Gracie jutted out her bottom lip. "Yes, like Ruairi."

"You know, Ruairi likes *you* . . . the way you are."

"I'm ridiculous," Gracie pouted.

"What?" Billy was shocked.

"Even your beautiful Rosaleen thinks so."

"Gracie, that's not true. She envies you. You have the life she has always wanted."

"Well, now she has it with you."

"Yes, she does." Billy smiled.

"But what do I have?" Gracie looked down at the black waters. "I have nobody."

"You have Ruairi for right now," Billy tried to comfort his sister.

"I don't have Ruairi. He would never stay for a girl like me." Gracie turned to look at him full on. "Look at these girls! They've known him forever! And he adores them! He tattoos them all over his body. He does whatever they ask of him." She began to cry.

"He won't stay for them, either." Billy stepped forward and embraced her. "I know this is tough to hear, but Ruairi couldn't stay no matter how much he loved you."

Gracie struggled out of his arms. "Why not?"

"Because you are William's daughter," Billy took a deep breath but before he could continue, Mairtin's voice cut him off.

"Come here, Woman!" His voice was rough.

Billy looked up and Gracie turned around.

"Are you talking to me?" Gracie asked.

"Of course I'm talking to you. Come here to me!" He had another cigarette dangling from his mouth and a drink in one hand. The other hand was extended to her.

She slowly reached up and took it. His skin was as tough as he looked.

"Don't worry about her, Mairtin will take care of her," Rosaleen whispered in Billy's ear, coming up behind him.

"Did you win the game?" Billy slid his arms around her waist and kissed her.

She smiled. "It wasn't too hard. Your sister had a pretty good run going."

"You'll be nice to her, won't you?" He leaned back and looked at her meaningfully.

She sighed. "Yes, I'll be nice to her. She's your sister."

"She'll be your sister too," Billy pointed out.

Rosaleen made a face.

"Why don't you like her?" Billy was exasperated. "I adore Gracie."

Rosaleen scuffed her toe against the deck. "So does Ruairi."

"So you're jealous?" Billy guessed.

"Insanely," Maggie piped up as she slid in beside the couple. "So am I. Rosaleen was his one and only for the last forever. I thought that I would have been the next in line. Now there's a new girl in the bed."

"In the bed?" Billy raised his eyebrows.

"Figuratively speaking," Rosaleen added quickly.

Maggie did a little jig. "Figuratively, metaphorically, literally . . . every way possible." She stopped dead and turned her green eyes heavenward, "He's not stupid, Róisín, he knows what Ruairi was to you."

Rosaleen gave Billy a look of reassurance. "It won't be like that now, of course."

Billy nodded. "I know. I have nothing to be upset with him for. He took care of you when I couldn't. I'm nothing but grateful to him."

Maggie grinned scarily. "Grand! Now come to my bedroom!" she demanded.

Billy glanced at Rosaleen. "I don't have to sleep with her to be invited into the family, do I?"

Rosaleen laughed and shrugged her shoulders. "You never know what Moonshine Maggie's going to decide is tradition!"

Maggie turned and started her jig again. "'Tis just a toast that I'd like to give but if you're lucky, Moonshine Maggie might just fall in love with you some other time." She winked and danced off down the deck with Billy and Rosaleen smiling behind.

Maggie's bedroom was exotically dressed; the rugs were animal skins and the curtains had tassels. The bed was in the centre of the room and every other piece of furniture surrounding it was alight with candles.

A toast was being prepared when Gracie and Mairtin arrived. Maggie led Rosaleen and Billy in behind them. Most of the crew were crammed into the room. They were all handed tumblers with a finger of whiskey at the bottom.

"To the angel's share!" Maggie yelled.

"Sláinte!" the crew replied.

"What's the angel's share?" Billy asked.

Moonshine Maggie smiled provocatively. "It's the distiller's penance," she whispered, "the price we pay for our salvation."

Rosaleen wrapped her arms around his neck. "As wine or spirits age in their barrels, some of the alcohol mysteriously disappears. The rumour is that the angels drink it."

"That's quite a romantic notion," Gracie whispered.

Ruairi put an arm around her. "So maybe not everything I'm involved in is awful and criminal?"

"I don't think anything you do is criminal anymore," Gracie said.

Every Irish eye in the room turned to Ruairi.

Ruairi didn't give anything away. "Grand," he said. He looked over at Billy and saw a shadow pass over the young Englishman's face. Ruairi kept his eyes on Billy as he lifted his glass a second time. "To Billy and Rosaleen and most of all, to little Kathleen," he toasted.

"Sláinte," the voices rang out.

Thomas held up a newly refilled glass and cleared his throat. "I think we need to toast Bill McCoy for giving our whiskey top billing."

"Aye! To the Real McCoy," they unanimously responded.

"We may have gotten top billing but we still need to shoot for top shelf. There's a bit more tinkering with that recipe that needs to be done," Ruairi said.

"I don't know, Ruairi. I think that stuff is the best juice I've ever drank." Stavros defended their first batch.

Mairtin looked at Stavros and chuckled. "Aye, but we've all tried that shite that you make."

"I'll have you know that my bathtub gin will get you twice as drunk as the piss that you can get out here."

"It will also send you blind!" Thomas hooted.

Moonshine Maggie dragged a long fingernail across Ruairi's cheek. "You do realize that just because I was intimate with your man the distiller doesn't mean I am a whiskey baron?"

Ruairi nodded, a silky smile slipping across his face. "I don't want a whiskey baron. I want a whiskey baroness. I want to taste some sass in my spirit. That's why I came to Moonshine Maggie."

"Is that it then?" she played coy with him. "And all this time I thought you were just here to see my pretty face." Her make-up mask twisted into a grotesque pout.

"And you want it all triple distilled?" Rosaleen licked her lips and pinned him with a decidedly more seductive glare.

Ruairi nodded to both women. "I want it smooth. If we do this properly, we could corner the North American whiskey market."

"What about rye?" Thomas asked, rolling a cigarette.

Ruairi shot him a dirty look. "Do you consider rye whiskey? I don't know any self-respecting Irishmen who consider rye whiskey. Hell, I don't know any self-respecting Irishmen that consider scotch whiskey."

Mairtin grinned cheekily. "I don't know any self-respecting Irishmen."

They all laughed at that. Gracie watched as Ruairi's eyes lit up.

"Speaking of Irishmen," Maggie began, her feet starting to itch again, "Sing me a song . . ." she whined, "sing me my song!"

Ruairi threw his head back, "In Dublin's fair city, where girls are so pretty . . ."

Thomas joined in, "I first laid my eyes on sweet Maggie Monroe."

Their rendition of 'Molly Malone' was inherently different as not only did they sing about Maggie Monroe, but they changed her whole profession from fishmonger to streetwalker.

Moonshine Maggie danced with every male and female in the room and when the song ended, she curtsied and bowed as though she had just danced a beautiful ballet.

As the clapping subsided, Maggie and Ruairi shared a glance that made Gracie reach for him jealously. He brought her hand to his lips but kept his eyes on Maggie. "I think it's about time you gave up your night job, Madam Monroe."

Maggie gave Ruairi a mock stern look. "A woman needs honest work and this is about as honest as it gets."

"We need to talk, Woman." Mairtin grabbed Gracie's elbow as they filed out of Maggie's room. He dragged her up to the bar and bought her a drink. It was whiskey again but this time it was mixed with lemonade.

"You'll like it better," he said, handing it to her.

"I like whiskey just fine," she argued.

"Sure, and that's why you make such an ugly face every time you swallow," he said.

She reddened. She took a sip of the new drink. "That's delicious," she said, surprised.

He nodded. "I told you that you would like it."

"So what do we need to talk about?" she asked politely.

"Rosaleen and I need you to convince Ruairi to stay," he said bluntly.

Gracie groaned and took another sip of her drink. "Not this again."

"I don't have much time to say this so you need to listen to me," Mairtin instructed.

Gracie felt her throat closing up and the tears threatening again. "He's made it very clear that he won't stay. There's nothing I can do to . . ."

Mairtin grabbed her hand. "There has to be."

She tried to pull her hand away but he held it fast. "Like what?"

"Marry him."

"He doesn't seem interested in marriage," Gracie said softly.

"Then get pregnant. He won't leave you with a baby."

Gracie was shocked. "You cannot be serious!" she finally managed to tear her hand away.

"I'm deadly serious." Mairtin clenched his jaw. "If you don't do something, both he and your father are as good as dead."

Gracie turned away from him and sipped her drink. Her mind reeled. She couldn't do that to him, she wouldn't. When she finished the whiskey and lemonade she turned back to Mairtin to tell him to go to hell but he was already walking away from her. She looked around and couldn't see any of the other people she had come with. She tried to stand up and follow him but she was unsteady on her feet. She reached out to grab hold of the nearest thing and found herself holding onto the arm of a strange man. He leered at her and put his hands on her hips. She tried to move away but he tightened his grip.

"Well, hello sweetheart!" His breath reeked of cigars. He came close to her and leaned his body against hers. She tried to push him away.

"Don't get nasty, doll. You just let ol' Paul keep you upright." He put his lips near hers.

"Let me go!" she screamed at him. She was frantic. She started to cry but the stranger just laughed and held her tighter. She looked all around but saw nothing but blurred faces.

"Let me go!" Everything was fuzzy and the music was too loud and smoke kept being blown in her face. She felt claustrophobic or drunk. She couldn't tell the difference.

"Let her go!" Ruairi's voice was loud and threatening behind her.

Paul gave him a dirty look. "Mind your own business, you stupid tyke!"

The men around him laughed.

Suddenly, Gracie found herself in Thomas' arms. He had her safely tucked out of harm's way. She watched as Ruairi grabbed Paul by the throat and slammed him up against the port side railing. Two other men stood up to challenge Ruairi in Paul's defence. Without hesitation Ruairi smashed Paul's head into the top bar, knocking him out. The whole time he maintained eye contact with the other men. He turned to face one of them as Paul's limp body slid to the deck. The one in front of Ruairi took a swing, narrowly missing his jaw. There was a word from Ruairi in a language that Gracie hadn't heard before and Mairtin reappeared, squaring himself in front of the other defender. Ruairi threw his punch and his fist connected with the man's nose, spurting blood in a wide arc. The man doubled over. The blood made it impossible for him to see. Everybody on the deck cheered. Mairtin was next, punching his man so hard that he tumbled over a table and into the wall of the cabin.

"Not bad for a stupid tyke, eh boys?" Ruairi turned his back and walked over to where Thomas held a shaken Gracie. "I thought I told you not to go off by yourself," he reprimanded her. His breathing was a bit heavy but that was the only sign of exertion.

Gracie flung herself at him. It had all become too much for her to handle. "Marry me!" she cried.

Mairtin smiled as Gracie fell apart.

Ruairi gathered the hysterical, drunk English girl in his arms. "I'm going to take her home," Ruairi called to Thomas. "I'll send Karl back with *The Phoenix* to pick you lads up."

Thomas nodded. "If I don't see you before we head out in the morning, you make sure you're safe. I hate that you'll be out there alone."

Ruairi smiled at his little brother. "I'll be fine, Captain. Give Mags a kiss goodnight for me."

Thomas laughed. "What if she charges me for it?"

"Pay up! You know I'm good for it!" Ruairi winked and was gone.

Ruairi was quiet most of the way back to land. Gracie sat with her head in her hands. The rocking of the boat made her queasy and the phrase that she had inadvertently blurted out taunted her insides viciously.

Why had she let Mairtin get inside her head? Now she had ruined everything.

Ruairi docked the boat.

She crawled to the side and hauled herself onto the wharf where she lay face down debating whether the earth would spin slower if she flipped to her back. She heard Ruairi's soft chuckle somewhere behind her.

"Are you laughing at me?" she moaned.

"Yes." He couldn't help himself. He hopped off the boat and knelt down beside her. "Do you think you can stand up if I give you a hand?"

"No," she answered.

"Okay then." He lay down beside her.

"What are you doing?" she asked, turning her head slowly to look at him.

His face was inches from hers. "Lying beside you so you aren't alone."

The word pricked her conscience. She reached for his hand. "I'm terrified of being alone," she admitted.

Ruairi squeezed her hand but was quiet for a long while. Finally he asked, "Why does being alone scare you so badly?"

"When I'm alone, I have trouble believing you really exist. I have trouble believing I really exist," she paused. "Am I making any sense?"

"You're making perfect sense," he whispered. Ruairi let go of her hand and curled his legs back underneath him.

"I don't want you to kill my father," she moaned. "I don't want you to go back to Ireland and die. I want you to stay. Everybody wants you to stay."

Ruairi was quiet again for a long time. Gracie closed her eyes and listened to the lapping waves. It calmed her. So did the sound of Ruairi's breathing.

"Sit up, Gracie girl," he said finally.

She dragged herself up to face him. He looked so serious.

"I love you," he said suddenly. "The only way that I can marry you is if we move far away from William. I would have to pack up everyone and move us all down the coast to Atlantic City or New York."

Gracie rubbed her eyes. She thought she must have fallen asleep. She stared at him and blinked heavily a few times but he seemed to still be there.

"What are you doing?" he asked.

"I'm sorry." She stared at him harder. "I'm confused. Why am I moving to Atlantic City?"

"If I'm going to stay we need to . . ."

"You're going to stay?" Gracie was ten steps behind. "Why would you stay?"

"Because you asked me to marry you." He smiled at her. "And I'm saying yes."

"You're saying yes?"

"Aye, I'm saying yes."

CHAPTER 22

They went over the boat with their usual thoroughness. Mick was handy at pretty much everything which had made him a vital part of the Irish crew.

"So you think these clouds will blow off?" Ruairi asked one more time.

"She'll be fine, nothing to worry about, son." Mick's eyes had scanned the skies but found nothing of consequence.

"You've been quiet lately, Mickey. Anything bothering you?" Ruairi asked casually.

Mick shook his head. "I'm just trying to figure out a woman."

Ruairi raised his brows. He wondered if Mick was referring to Valerie Logan. He had never heard Mick ever mention any of his women before. He knew there had been a few but there had never been talk of them. "I think women are more of a mystery than us Irishmen."

Mick nodded. "I think you might be right."

Out of respect he didn't push for details. "You're a man of few words, Mickey. I like that about you."

Gerry O'Neill watched as the Atlantic Ocean slipped by. The Statue of Liberty was behind him, waving goodbye as he sailed back into the trap that was Ireland's ideals. He had sworn never to go back. He had seen all he needed to of martyrdom in the church and on the battlefield. He was now a Sunday Catholic and a Sunday soldier. He dropped his quarter in the offering plate and said his three Hail Mary's. He ran a few cartons of rum and whiskey and sent the cheque back to the army council. He had bought his way into Heaven and out of Hell.

And then he'd heard her voice on the line. That crimson angel, that black rose begging for the boy who'd sold his soul.

Ruairi met the shipment in Miquelon before it was even unloaded. He paid the money and went smoothly onto the next phase of the plan.

He would meet Thomas and Mairtin at the Rum Line and unload the champagne that went along with Bill McCoy's whiskey order. Thomas and Mairtin already had the whiskey onboard *The Phoenix* and they would make the drop for McCoy as well buy a shipment of rum to take back to Prince Edward Island. While they completed their run, Ruairi would set his course towards Belle Isle to meet the Québécois runners who would deliver the supply that would go over land to the locked Prairie Provinces.

It would be a long night but it would be lucrative.

Karl felt uneasy about the request but knew he couldn't say no to the Lady. When Mick answered the telephone he sounded tired.

"Mick? It's Karl. You busy?" Karl was all business.

"Not really, just tinkering with the brakes on that car of the boys." Mick hated the phone and held it as far away from himself as possible so that it sounded as though he was down a well to the person on the other end of the line.

"What was that you said?" Karl barked into the mouthpiece.

"I'm not busy!" Mick shouted back.

Karl pulled away from the earpiece. "You don't have to yell at me, Mickey, just speak up."

Mick cussed him.

"See? I heard that just fine," Karl said wryly.

"What do you want?" Mick was getting surly.

"I want you to come down to the Club and have a drink with me."

"I'm busy," Mick said.

"You just told me you weren't," Karl reminded him.

"Fine, but I won't be there for an hour," Mick relented. He could use a drink.

"Swell, that gives me time to finish up some paperwork."

Gracie wandered the streets with Norah, window shopping arm in arm. They had analyzed every word that Ruairi and Gracie had spoken the night before, reliving the moments over and over again.

"I can't believe you are engaged to Ruairi O'Neill!" Norah squealed.

Gracie giggled blissfully. "I can't believe I proposed!"

"I know! That's so daring; so feminist!"

"Valerie would be proud of me!" Gracie declared.

"When is he going to give you a ring?" Norah asked.

"He wants to take me shopping in New York. He wants me to meet his older brother before we get married."

They both squealed at the same time.

"Tell me again what the note said this morning."

"It said, 'Good morning, my Love, I'll be out on the boat most of the night but not a minute will go by that you won't be on my mind. Meet me on the docks at five o'clock tomorrow morning and don't be late. Love, Ruairi'."

"That is so romantic!" Norah fanned herself with her hand.

"I'm getting married!" Gracie grabbed Norah by the hand. This was how it was supposed to feel. "I'm getting married!"

Genevieve sat at the long wooden bar, her feet dangling off the floor because of the height of the stool. She felt far too visible. She pulled her cloche down over her eyes as far as she could and stared at her drink. Karl had said that he would direct Mick over to her the moment he came in.

She fidgeted with her skirt suit and her jewellery and sipped on her cocktail as though it were water. Suddenly he was behind her. She knew because she could smell his aftershave.

"I'm betting I'm not going to see Karl for the rest of the afternoon," he spoke softly, almost nervously.

She turned but wouldn't make eye contact. "And you are a betting man."

He nodded stiffly. "Aye, that I am."

Genevieve took a deep breath. "I've taken the liberty of booking our trips to Paris. I know that we hadn't officially agreed on a date but I'm anxious to leave Charlottetown as soon as possible."

"Paris, France?" he clarified.

She nodded but still refused to look at him. "We leave next week."

"That's impossible." He shook his head slowly and reached into his pocket to pay for the beer that was put in front of him. "I can't be ready to sail that quickly."

"Oh." Genevieve stared down at her hands which rested firmly in her lap.

"Why are you in such a hurry?" Mick was curious.

Genevieve faltered. "I ran into William this morning."

Mick sighed. "I can understand how difficult this must be for you." He tried to sympathize but it wasn't a strength of his.

Genevieve tried to calm her trembling fingers. "He threatened us," she whispered.

Mick couldn't make out what she had said. "I'm sorry, I didn't hear you. What did you say?" He reached out and tipped her face up so that he could see it. The sunlight hit her cheekbones and her carefully applied make-up showed translucent. Mick dropped his hand as he saw the outlines of the fresh bruises.

"He threatened us," she tried to repeat but she broke down in the process and fled to the Ladie's room.

Gracie arrived back at Valerie's house at half past noon. She wanted to give Carolina Spencer enough time to accomplish her business with the designer before she arrived. Carolina was in the ballroom with the Québécois coutourier. He had her standing on the grand piano while he made adjustments to the incredibly intricate dress that he was working on.

Carolina smiled at her broadly as she approached. "Isn't he extravagantly romantic?" she asked, her laughter bubbling up before she even finished the question. "He is no ordinary designer!"

Gracie didn't know how to answer but she didn't have to. A voice from the far side of the room made her turn. "He is no ordinary man!" Valerie Logan materialized smoking a cigarette near the doors that led out to the veranda.

"Gracie, this is Gustav. Gustav, this is the vivacious Gracie Gainsborough."

The young designer stopped to appreciate the attention that was being lavished upon him. He looked up at Gracie and smiled seductively. He reminded her of a raven, slick, polished and dangerously edgy. "They told me you were beautiful but they scarcely did you justice," he said, his English enriched by his lilting accent. He took her hand and pressed it to his lips. "I cannot wait to get you undressed."

Gracie blushed madly.

"He's perfectly indecent, is he not?" Carolina smiled naughtily as she winked at Gracie. "Please refrain from telling your mother anything that you hear this afternoon!"

"Is Maman not here?" Gracie was surprised.

Valerie shook her cigarillo instead of her head. "I can never keep up with your mother. She was gone long before I managed to get out of bed this morning."

Gracie watched curiously as Gustav's fingers worked meticulously along the hem of the gown. There was intricate embroidery at the bottom of the fabric that Carolina had designed on paper for Gustav to copy onto the dress. Carolina was incredibly talented artistically but she claimed arthritic fingers had put a stop to her imagination.

"Have you considered going with Genevieve to Paris?" Carolina asked Gracie from her perch.

Gracie fingered the keys of the piano. "I thought about it, I mean, I love Paris but . . . I just don't think I'm ready to move again."

Carolina sensed that Gracie was evading the question. "That's fair. But what will you do here?"

Gracie sat down at the piano bench and played a few chords. "I'm sure I can find something to occupy my time," she said, a sly smile spreading across her lips.

Valerie finished smoking and came to stand beside Gracie. "I've been hearing some interesting rumours." Valerie examined Gracie's left hand as it rested on the keys but noticed it empty.

Gracie was coy, "Is that so?"

Valerie frowned at her playfully. "It's not polite to keep secrets," she whined.

Gracie laughed in response.

Valerie wondered if a little inducement would help to confirm the gossip. She snapped her fingers. "I think we need champagne! I'll be back in a moment, ladies. Do not fear!" With that she swept out of the room.

Gracie watched Gustav's stitches closely. She was fascinated by the work.

He looked up and smiled at her. "Do you play?" he asked.

She looked down at the keys and smiled. "Yes, yes of course I play."

"Then play for us. I love music while I work."

"Oh, I couldn't!" Gracie tried to manoeuvre out of the task. She really just wanted to watch him finish Carolina's dress and start on designs for hers. She was saved by Valerie swirling back into the room with a flourish of champagne glasses all around.

"Drink up, we have much to discuss and discussions are better when fuelled by alcohol!"

Gracie couldn't help but giggle. She tried to pace herself but it wasn't long before the bubbles had their desired effect on her.

Gustav motioned for her to come to him. "What type of dress do you desire, my lady?" he asked, twirling her in front of him as though they were dance partners.

"I need an evening gown and two cocktail dresses." She smiled sweetly. "And if you do your job right, you may be making a wedding gown in the near future."

Valerie and Carolina both stopped mid-sip to stare at the young woman.

Gracie curtsied before her captive audience. "You heard right. I'm about to become Mrs. Ruairi O'Neill."

William arrived at the Club with Lucas to spend an afternoon in the men's lounge. His recent ill health was preventing him from playing golf. He could see his wife through the patio windows. She was publicly humiliating him, openly defying him by living with Valerie Logan and consorting with Michael Fitzgerald.

"I can't believe that your Genevieve has become a feminist." Lucas was in no mood for charity, practically spitting out the 'f' word.

"She's not my Genevieve anymore," William breathed heavily. "She's become an absolute disgrace. I told her so this morning. She wanted to meet to discuss our separation."

"And?" Lucas prodded.

"It didn't end well. She's become so difficult of late that there only seems one way to reason with her and it involves no speaking at all. I'm actually rather surprised to see her out."

"Who is that gentleman that she is with?" Lucas didn't want to aggravate William but his curiosity got the better of him. "I've seen him around town quite a bit recently."

"Michael Fitzgerald," William said with obvious distaste.

"I take it that you have made his acquaintance?" Lucas noted the hint of colour in William's voice.

William tugged at his collar. "He's connected to Rosaleen and Ruairi," he offered. The British Army would have had a field day with all of the Irish rebels in Charlottetown. William had been corresponding with the London Home Office to try to find out as much as he could about why the Irish contingency was in Charlottetown. The more he found out, the more he got worried. So far it seemed that Ruairi O'Neill was acting of his own accord and hadn't been sent to Canada for any specific purpose. William hadn't decided which scenario was worse. "He's a bloody criminal."

Lucas decided to change the subject. "That reminds me," he sniffed the air, "we will have to watch the time if we want to be well clear of here before the raid." Lucas nudged William with his elbow.

William nodded sullenly.

"After tonight it will all be over," Lucas continued, trying to brighten his friend's mood.

William shook his head. His authority was waning and he knew it. He had become a permanent fixture in the everyday gossip of the island. "Even if I had them all killed, I will have still lost, Lucas." William tried to loosen his bowtie. He felt rather hot. He drank some water and looked around but the room began to spin. He tried to stand up but he lost his balance and toppled forward, into the coffee table.

Lucas looked down at William's convulsing body and yelled for a doctor.

It wasn't long before the rendezvous boat showed up on the horizon line and Thomas and Mairtin got busy organizing the crates for a quick offload.

"I've never seen those boys before." Thomas said, eyeing McCoy's crew through binoculars.

Mairtin shrugged his shoulders. "I'm sure McCoy has quite a few guys to rotate."

"What a bunch of rubes! Wait till you see what they're wearing!" Thomas laughed.

"I'll do business while you pass up the liquor." Mairtin worked out the order so that they could get out off the line quickly. Even though the sun had set, it wasn't quite dark and they would have to be extremely vigilant to avoid being caught by the Coast Guard.

Mairtin got a hand up from a burly man in grey trousers with a white singlet under an open, tucked in light blue button up shirt. His suspenders were a fancy addition for the job he was doing. He walked over to the cabin and reached inside. Mairtin was watching the progress of the liquor when he felt a sharp tap on the back of his skull.

Thomas bent down to reach for another crate. As he hoisted it up over his chest he found himself staring up at four pistols. He didn't even have time to yell Mairtin's name before they opened fire on him. The bullets embedded themselves in his chest and he felt each one as the blood exploded outwards. Then he felt nothing.

Genevieve turned back to Mick and Valerie. "I should probably follow them to the hospital."

"I hate to admit it, but you probably should, if only to learn how serious his attack was," Mick agreed. Valerie had come as quickly as she could when Mick had called her. She had lied to Gracie, not wanting to upset her without knowing for sure what the problem was. When she had arrived at the Club she had fixed Genevieve's make-up and then forced her to drink gin and tonics to calm her spirits. She was in agreement with Genevieve that it would probably be best to send her to Paris immediately and give William a chance to settle down. Mick didn't seem to have much choice.

"We'll be here if you need us," Valerie said kindly. "It's been ages since Mick and I had dinner together."

"Who said anything about dinner?" Mick grumbled. "I came down for a drink."

"Well, then order another round because I'm parched." Valerie held up an empty glass.

Genevieve was grateful for their friendship. She turned back and watched the two of them from the front of the Club. They were staring lovingly into each other's eyes.

She hadn't been gone more than five minutes when the police charged through the front doors of the Club yelling 'RAID' over the shrieks and screams of scattering patrons.

Mick scanned the crowd for Karl and saw him being handcuffed near the south exit. As he turned back around to direct Valerie, a blow to the temple left him crumpled on the patio tiles.

Ruairi slowly made his way back from Belle Isle towards Prince Edward Island. The drop off had been effortless and the money was already neatly rolled in a wad in his pocket. He scanned the water for unwelcome traffic but saw nothing. Although his boat was empty of evidence, he didn't want to deal with the Coast Guard tonight.

As he navigated his way through the Gulf of St. Lawrence, he saw lights suddenly flashing a distress signal off his port side. He swung around and headed for it. *The Phoenix* bobbed lazily in the black waters. Ruairi could only see one figure in the boat. His stomach twisted.

He pulled alongside and then walked over to the rail. He almost vomited. There, amongst the shattered glass and broken crates, Thomas' blood mingled with the spilled whiskey. His body lay, crumpled over the only crate that remained intact. In the bow, Mairtin stared back at him, black and blue and swollen from the temples down.

Ruairi turned his back and tried to suck in a breath. He doubled over and tried again to breathe. Just when he thought he would surely suffocate he heard Mairtin's raspy voice call his name.

He leaned over the rail again and tried not to look at Thomas' body. Mairtin was looking up at him. "I'm sorry, Ruairi."

Ruairi willed himself to breathe. He shut out everything else. "Can you stand up?" he asked Mairtin.

Mairtin nodded and stood slowly, painfully. The boat rocked gently and out of the corner of his eye, Ruairi saw Thomas' hand slide down the crate and into a puddle of blood laced alcohol. "I tried to bring her home," he motioned to the boat stiffly, "but I must be leaking fuel from somewhere."

Ruairi nodded and closed his eyes as he lowered a rope down to Mairtin. Then he tied the other end to the railing. He would have to tow *The Phoenix* into the Charlottetown harbour.

He helped Mairtin up onto the deck. They couldn't look at each other. It was an entire hour of silence before they finally entered the harbour.

"They think they got you," Mairtin said finally.

"Who thinks they got me?"

"Whoever the bloody Brits hired." Mairtin tried to remember their words as they had thrown his body back onto *The Phoenix*. "One of the shooters said something about thinking Ruairi O'Neill would have been a giant because of they way William had described you."

"Did you tell them any different?"

"No. They think they got me too." He lifted his shirt and pointed to a bloody graze on the left side of his abdomen. When his body had hit the deck, one of the men had fired a shot at him. He had been extremely lucky that it had been carelessly aimed.

Ruairi clenched his fists. "Good," he said evenly, "then they won't be expecting you when we catch up to them and blow their brains out."

The hospital room was very quiet. William lay sleeping. He had been heavily medicated. Genevieve sat beside the bed watching his chest rising and falling while her mind contemplated the fragility of life.

A nurse came in. She had a beautiful auburn bob and startling eyes. She smiled at Genevieve and Genevieve thought she looked familiar.

The nurse set about wiping down William's forehead and checking all of the gauges and pumps. She wrote a few things in the chart and then turned on her heel and walked towards the door.

"How is he?" Genevieve called to her, not wanting to be left alone with him again.

The girl turned back. "He'll be just fine. He just needs his rest."

Genevieve rose and walked towards her. She read her name tag quickly. "What does the doctor say, Aisling? Are his infections worsening?"

The girl looked slightly uncomfortable. She shifted her weight and looked down. "The infections have spread and the doctor is trying to minimize the damage that the infections are doing to the vital organs. Time will tell but I'm sure the doctor will be able to tell you more."

Genevieve exhaled slowly and closed her eyes. She was tired. Actually, she was exhausted. "Aisling, do you think it would be all right if I went home for some sleep or should I be staying here tonight?"

"I would suggest you go home," The girl, Aisling, clipped the word. With that she gave a tight smile and walked towards the nurses' station.

Ruairi had gone through all of the motions. *The Phoenix* and *The Siren* were moored and all evidence of alcohol was disposed of. There was just the body left to deal with; his baby brother's body.

"How are we going to . . . ?" Mairtin couldn't bring himself to finish the sentence.

"We'll have to carry him to Maggie's distillery and then come back with the car." Ruairi felt his chest tighten as he thought about lifting Thomas' limp body.

Mairtin tried to swallow but his mouth was dry. Blood had congealed on the corners of his dry lips and he could taste it every time he opened his mouth. "Maybe we should go and get some help."

Ruairi shook his head. "I just want to move him now, before anyone sees him."

Mairtin nodded.

Ruairi stepped down onto *The Phoenix* and bent down to grab Thomas' arm. It was still warm.

He lost his mind in that one touch. He crumpled to his knees and scooped Thomas' body up, cradling him and crying.

Mairtin turned his back, unable to watch Ruairi fall apart. His own wracking sobs drowned out the words that Ruairi whispered into his dead brother's ear.

"The sea shall roll in red waves, and blood be poured out, every mountain glen in Ireland, and the bogs shall quake, some day ere shall perish my Little Dark Rose," he swore his oath on Roísín Dubh. "I'll be with you soon, little brother." He kissed Thomas' pale forehead roughly. "I will be with you soon."

Gracie walked towards the docks in the dark early morning. The sun had yet to rise but the moon had lost all strength.

She saw Ruairi jump down from the rails of the fishing trawler. He had a small bag slung over one shoulder and his trousers were dirty. He wore a trilby pulled down low over his eyes. When he turned his body towards her she saw a smear of blood on his white cotton shirt.

She shivered. She wanted to turn around and pretend she hadn't seen him; go away and come back when he had cleaned himself up so that she wouldn't have to ask any questions; but she couldn't move. There was something bigger than her holding her in her place.

That's when he turned and saw her standing there.

He stared at her. He couldn't bring himself to call out to her. She would have to come to him.

Mairtin came up behind him. He too was covered in blood. They had just finished cleaning out the boat. He noticed the English girl standing there and he clenched his jaw. It could only end badly between the two of them now. Mairtin covered his battered head with his hands. Losing control now would do Ruairi no favours. "Do you need me to give you some time?" he finally asked.

"Aye," Ruairi was having trouble speaking. "I need you to go let the others know."

Gracie watched Martin walk away and she waited until they were alone. She was only fifty feet from him but it felt like miles as she walked towards him. She stopped when she was about five feet away.

"I'm not late, am I?" she asked softly.

He shook his head slowly. Then he took off his hat and pulled his shirt over his head. He looked at the blood stain and then tossed it onto the boat behind him.

"What happened?" she asked. She was terrified to hear the answer. She had known all along that Ruairi might kill William but it hadn't prepared her for this image of him, cold and soaked in blood.

Ruairi was very still for a moment. Then he took a shaky breath and said, "This isn't William's blood."

She moved towards him slowly, carefully. She didn't want to know any more than that.

With the strength he had left, he pulled her to him. "Tell me you could have loved me," he whispered.

She looked up into his eyes. "I do love you," she whispered back. She stood up on her tip toes so that she could reach his mouth. Slowly, their mouths met and she felt his rigid body relax against her. "I will always love you," she said.

"You could love a monster?"

"No," she said, "but I could love you. You are not a monster."

He helped her up onto the deck of *The Siren*, and led her into the same little cabin that they had spent their first night together in. They never spoke a word as they turned to face each other in the cramped, musty little room.

Ruairi clenched his teeth and swallowed. He wasn't sure why he was complicating the situation but he knew that he needed her now. He needed her to humanize him. He tried desperately to calm the emotions that rolled like waves through his chest. He didn't want to scare her, didn't want to hurt her. He needed to be tender, gentle, soft, but his muscles were tensed and his movements full of force. He hoped she could soothe him with her touch.

"Are you sure you want to do this now?" she asked him quietly, her voice barely a whisper. She could see he was struggling and she was a tiny bit afraid of him.

He reached for her. "I need you now." There was urgency in his voice and it sent a surge through her body. She felt herself pull him on top of her and then everything slowed down.

Where their skin met she could feel ice and fire at the same time. Every sound seemed intensified; his breath in her ear was like a windstorm, his heartbeat like cracks of thunder. And she could taste him and he was sweet, so absolutely delicious. Her mind was ablaze with the overload of sensations and then for the briefest moment, there was nothing. And then everything. And then, drifting into the memory of it, she sighed.

He listened as her heartbeat returned to normal. He gently kissed along her collarbone and could feel the little flutters that each touch of his lips produced.

He lifted himself onto his elbows to be able to look down on her face. She gave him a shy smile and shut her eyes in self-consciousness. Her cheeks were flushed and her skin glistened with moisture.

"You don't know how beautiful you are," he whispered.

She opened her eyes slowly and stared up at him. The intensity had not left his eyes but there was suddenly something else there as well.

He kissed her lips and she felt the icy fire again.

"Gracie?" he breathed, his lips brushing hers as he spoke.

"Mmm?"

"Gracie, I need you to promise to do something for me." He stopped kissing her and waited until she looked into his eyes again.

"Anything."

"I need you to go back to Valerie's house and stay there until I come for you."

The fear in her voice betrayed her, "I don't want to leave you."

"Why not?" he asked gently.

She began to tremble and tears sprang to her eyes. "I'm scared you'll disappear." Her words rushed out.

He shook his head and held a finger to her lips. "I won't leave. I promise. I'll come to you later, in the middle of the night. Leave your balcony door open."

"Okay," she whispered. She would agree to anything tonight.

He nodded. "Good," he grew silent for a moment. "Gracie, I need you to promise me something else."

She groaned softly. "What?"

He ran his finger along the base of her throat lightly and then kissed the tip of her chin. The sensation sent chills through her. "Promise me you'll forgive me for everything I'm about to do."

Gracie's eyes widened as she understood the implications of his request. She stared into his eyes and saw misery deep inside. She circled her arms around his neck and wound her fingers through his hair. "I will love you no matter what," she said slowly.

"No you won't," Ruairi said, his muscles tightening again and his jaw clenching. "But it means the world to me that at this very moment, you believe you could."

He left her at the gate to Valerie's house. They had walked in silence. Gracie was too scared to ask him any questions. He had held her hand the entire way, squeezing it gently as if he were afraid she would try to pull it away.

At the gate he had held her tenderly, breathing her in and memorizing her face with his hands. He had pulled her arms up around his neck, leaning into the gate, softly crushing her between the iron bars and his body.

"I'll come back to you tonight," he had whispered, kissing her hungrily. "I'll need you again tonight."

She only remembered to breathe when he had disappeared into the morning mists.

When Genevieve awoke there were two friendly faces waiting for her at the bottom of the staircase. Mick sat, with Marie Antoinette wriggling around him. Marie Antoinette bounded towards her and nuzzled into her legs. Genevieve reached down, picking the dog up and cuddling it to her chest.

"Was she bothering you?" Genevieve asked tiredly.

"No, no," Mick waved it away.

"They're such beautiful creatures, aren't they?"

Mick looked sceptical. "I used to be a farmer, Genevieve, sheep and cattle. So, unless a dog can work, it's nothing but a pan-licker!" he said.

"Well, then, you'll have to give Marie Antoinette the benefit of the doubt. Since there are no sheep around, I guess we'll never know!"

Mick looked at the well-groomed, hairy little beast snuggled up against her breast and shook his head. "I think we know, but we might have to make an exception if we are to get anywhere here."

Genevieve smiled. "I think you're right." She caught his eye and held it for a moment. "He hasn't woken up yet." She looked at him more closely. She saw a blue shiny bruise on his right cheekbone.

"What happened, Michael?" she asked concerned.

Mick sighed. "There was a raid at the Club just after you left. Your man was waiting for me when I turned around."

"Who? William was at the hospital."

Mick shook his head. "Someone he hired."

Genevieve didn't understand. "What do you mean? Someone from his office?"

"A friend of the British Army."

"William's retired from the Army."

Mick caught her hand and held it. "Genevieve, he'll never retire from this. He wants to see us swing."

Genevieve looked away. She was ashamed of the reflection of herself that she could see in Mick's eyes. She was married to a horrible man; she had been an accomplice to horrible things.

He read her mind. "I don't blame you for any of this, Love. I just want you to know that it will have to be dealt with. I'm sure I wasn't the only one to receive a visit."

"If this is what I've caused, then I'll leave tonight. I cannot allow him to harm you in an attempt to get at me."

"This isn't about you, you just happened to end up in the middle of it," Mick sighed. "He's after us, Genevieve. He's trying to kill Ruairi."

"The war is over, Mick. He may not like you but he's not going to kill you."

Mick shook his head sadly. "The war isn't over, Genevieve, look at my face."

CHAPTER 23

Ruairi found Rosaleen waiting for him on the porch swing. She was pale and motionless as he approached. He could see the gun in her hand as he climbed the steps of the porch.

"Where is he?" she asked.

He took the gun away from her swiftly.

"Where is he?" she cried louder.

Ruairi pulled Rosaleen to him and held her tightly. "You need to go back inside now."

"Where is William?" she screamed. "I want him dead!"

"He will be, Love. Now go inside."

Genevieve was surprised to find Billy and Gracie sitting in the front parlour with a cup of tea. She smiled thinly and joined them. She reached for Gracie's steaming cup and took a sip out of it.

"Is everything okay?" she asked them softly.

Billy nodded and motioned for her to sit down. Genevieve looked at her daughter and noticed the peculiar way she was sitting, tense and alert.

She sighed. "I have some news. Your father has had a turn and is in the hospital. Most likely he will be fine but . . ." she took a deep breath, "I think it's best if you both go and see him this morning."

Billy rubbed his face. He was tired and had very little energy left for his father. "Is it absolutely necessary?"

Genevieve laced her fingers together in her lap. "He's still your father, Billy. If he dies, you may wish . . ."

"I won't have any regrets," Billy said firmly.

Gracie just sat there and absorbed the conversation.

Genevieve turned her attention to her daughter. "Gracie, what's wrong? You're so quiet."

Gracie's tears were spent. She was hollow and unsettled.

"Gracie, are you sure you're alright?" Genevieve repeated.

Gracie nodded her head vacantly. "Of course, I'll be fine."

Both Billy and Genevieve noticed Gracie unconsciously twisting and pulling at her necklace.

"Is that the necklace from Ruairi?" Genevieve asked her.

Gracie began to cry at the mention of his name. Genevieve looked at Billy. "She won't tell me," he mouthed to her.

"I'm going upstairs," Gracie said shakily. With that, she stood up and left the room.

Billy and Genevieve were silent for a few moments.

"I'm worried about her. She seems so overwhelmed."

"Well, her entire world has shifted in the last few weeks. She's had no time to process everything." Billy was worried too. "Did she tell you about her engagement to Ruairi?"

Genevieve shook her head. "I found out through Valerie. I never saw Gracie yesterday. I never thought I'd see the day when both my children married Irish rebels."

Billy shook his head. "They are both a lot more than that, Maman." He knew he would have to explain. "I have these lucid memories of her from the night I was held hostage. There was this moment when I was barely conscious. I thought I was going to die and then I heard this voice. When I finally got my eyes open, she was overtop of me, sponging the blood off of my forehead. I remember thinking that if I could just touch her back, as gently as she was touching me . . ." he hesitated, a bit embarrassed. "Well, she didn't seem real at the time but now she's so real it's frightening."

And Billy knew that he had a reason to be afraid. "She is my absolute heaven and my absolute hell," he groaned, almost feverishly. "I have these moments where it's like I'm back there, and I have these flashes of people and voices. But, I haven't been able to put it all together yet. All I know is that the only time I've slept through an entire night without nightmares is when I spend the night with her."

Genevieve had tears in her eyes as she listened to her son's memories. The war had stolen so much from the young men that fought in it. If their bodies weren't dead, their souls were. "I wish I knew more about what happened to you over there." She put her arms around him and remembered all the times he had run to her when he was a little boy. She had been there to kiss all of his hurts away. Then he had gone off to war and the scars he came back with were beyond her reach.

He hugged her back. "One day, I promise I'll tell you."

"You'll be careful, won't you? These relationships seem so risky to me."

He gave her a half smile. "Falling in love is always a risk, Maman."

Billy had gone up to see Gracie one more time before he went out. She was sitting absolutely still on the edge of her bed, lost in some memory.

"Are you sure you don't want to come back to Ruairi's?" he asked. "I'm headed over to see Rosaleen."

Gracie wondered if she should tell her brother about the bloody shirt but then decided against it. He would ask all of the questions that she hadn't had the courage to.

She shook her head. "I think it's best if I stay here."

"Are you sure you don't want to talk about something?"

Gracie looked up at him with a blank face. "I'm positive. Everything is fine."

Billy sighed but left her room. He didn't know what to make of it so he felt he should leave before he upset her any more.

Rosaleen was at the door before he knocked and when she opened it, Billy saw the tear stains and the red-rimmed eyes. His heart began to race.

"What's wrong?" he asked, reaching for her.

She pushed away his hands and kept her distance. "I think you should stay away from me right now."

"Why? What have I done?" he asked bewildered.

Her lower lip began to tremble and she lost control of herself. "They killed Thomas last night," she cried out.

"What?" The words floated over Billy and stayed just outside his grasp.

The door opened wider as Ruairi pulled Rosaleen backwards and stepped in front of her. "My brother Thomas . . . they killed my brother," Ruairi growled at him.

Billy felt sick. "Who killed your brother?" he asked, already knowing the answer.

Ruairi's eyes searched for something far away in the distance. "Go away Billy boy. You shouldn't be seen here today."

A chill ran through Billy as the door closed on him. The war had followed them.

Mairtin was waiting for Aisling at the front doors of the hospital. She couldn't wait to tell him who her patient had been. Such a strange world they were living in.

As she bounded out the door, he turned to face her. She gasped when she saw the cuts and bruises.

"What happened, Love?" she asked him, gently putting her hand to his face and inspecting the damage.

He grimaced under her touch but couldn't speak.

She clenched her jaw. "Mairtin, tell me what happened," she demanded. She tried not to let her mind imagine the worst. She had to hear it from him.

He made a strangled noise and wouldn't look into her eyes. "Thomas is dead," he choked out.

"Thomas?" Aisling was shaking her head. "You mean Ruairi. He was after Ruairi," she stated it like a fact. Mairtin had to have his facts wrong.

Mairtin didn't say anything more. His silence rattled her.

"Thomas? Why Thomas?" She was in disbelief. "Why Thomas?" she screamed at him.

Mairtin let her yell. She turned and ran back towards the hospital. Mairtin had to lunge at her to stop her.

"Let me go!" she screamed. "I'm going to kill him!" She kicked and scratched, trying to get away.

Despite his aching body, Mairtin held her tight. "Just wait, Aisling," his voice caught. "Just wait and let Ruairi kill him good and proper like."

She finally tired herself out and let him carry her home in silence.

They gathered in the parlour where his body was laid out.

"We'll have to take him to the church. Have a proper funeral," Mick said quietly.

"Tomorrow," Ruairi said firmly. He wanted Thomas to have one last night in a familiar place. After all, his eternal resting place would be on foreign soil.

"Are you sure that you can identify the men?" Mick asked, looking at Mairtin.

Mairtin nodded. "We can take Shorty's cutter. I telephoned Liam and he sent some fellas out to the Halifax Row with a description of the men we are looking for. If they are there, they'll be held up for us."

"And what if they've already headed south or run ashore and headed inland?" Mick wanted to be prepared.

"I'll fecking find them," Ruairi swore. "They can't be too clever. They killed the wrong bloke and left a witness alive. They are practically begging to get shot."

Rosaleen stood off to the side, refusing to allow anyone to comfort her. Her body trembled constantly and every few moments she would double over in agony. She had Thomas' hand in hers, she couldn't let go. Aisling was near his head, trying to burn every detail of her brother's face into her mind.

Ruairi looked to Mick, who was staring intently at him. "Are you ready?" he asked.

Mick pulled out the guns from the china cabinet and distributed them to Mairtin and Ruairi. They all checked, loaded, and rechecked their weapons.

Ruairi looked down at Thomas and his resolve hardened.

Maggie stood by the rail of the *Leda* staring out into the watery shadows. Her green eyes were so dark that they were almost black tonight and her red hair blazed with fury. She stood, outlined by moonlight, framed only by the dark horizon. She drew in a deep breath and tipped her head up to the heavens and screamed until the taste of blood ran down into her soul.

Ruairi walked down the rocky stretch that reached around like the curve between his index finger and thumb. Valerie's house was dark. He needed to replace the images that were flashing through his mind with her body. She would be his atonement.

He climbed easily to her second storey balcony and pushed open the door that she had dutifully left unlocked for him. She sat up in bed as he made his way into the room, her eyes travelling the length of his body and then back up to his face, assuring herself that he was in one piece.

He met her eyes. "I thought you would be asleep," he whispered hoarsely.

She shook her head. "I was worried about you."

The corners of his mouth turned upwards into something that wasn't quite a smile. "You needn't worry about me, Love." He sat down on the edge of her bed and she settled back into her pillows. He touched her cheekbone with the back of his hand and sighed.

She put her hand in his. "I don't know what to say when you are like this," she murmered. There was such a tortured look in his eyes that she had to look away. She caressed the back of his hand with her thumb and stared transfixed by the lines in his skin. She turned his hand over and ran her smooth fingers along the creases. His hands were a bit dirty and she rubbed harder to remove whatever it was that was . . . she stopped rubbing. It was more blood.

He grimaced, painfully aware of what she could see. He noticed the struggle in her eyes.

"Get undressed and come to bed," she said softly, turning his hand back over as she kissed it. She would not allow herself to think about where he had been or what he had done.

He pulled his shirt over his head first, revealing something black and heavy in the waistband of his trousers. She shivered as she watched him pull the gun out and put it on the night table beside her. He looked at her, his expression unreadable as if he didn't know whether to apologize for it or ignore it. She took his hands again and then kissed them both. "I still love you," she whispered into them, looking up meaningfully into his eyes.

She saw him struggle to breathe and his body went rigid as if he were fighting himself internally. He pulled her up towards him with such force that she gasped.

"You still can tonight," he said, his voice strangled with emotion. He kissed her hard and came down heavy on top of her. He was stronger this time, more sure of himself with her. He let go and gave in to the wild demands that coursed through his veins.

Gracie had woken early but he was already gone. She dressed quickly and left the house, searching for him in the misty morning. She walked down the empty streets and shivered from the chill that hung in the air.

She stopped in front of Province House and stared at the imposing façade. She hadn't slept well at all after the warmth had disappeared; her dreams were interrupted by images of beauty smeared with blood.

Not far from her, Ruairi sat on the steps of St. Dunstan's Cathedral, smoking his second cigarette of the day. He had thought that facing God would give him some clarity but instead it had made him more confused. Was he to fight and kill for his country, for his family? Was that forgivable? Or should he turn the other cheek? He thought about Mick and Mairtin's black and blue faces. There were no more cheeks left to turn.

Thomas' death had brought back all of the reasons he had enlisted in the IRA. He had lived on adrenaline for so many years, hiding out on the run, eating and sleeping in cellars, barns, and attics; dodging bullets and nooses every step of the way.

But now there was her. She stayed right on the periphery of a humanity he would have to black out. He had tried to drink her away at dawn but she only got blurrier, never disappearing. He inhaled and felt the burn as the smoke went down into his lungs.

He exhaled. There should have been choices. There should have been alternatives. But it was just kill or be killed. There had been so many before him; Emmett, Pearse, Collins. Each had chosen different paths. Each had ended up dead. They would all end up dead. He was sure of it.

It didn't seem to matter. He wondered how the next generation and the generation after would see it. Would it ever change? Would there ever be a choice?

Last night there had been no choice. He had listened to the decision as it was dictated to him by the voices of the past. He dropped the cigarette butt and ground it under his foot. The bodies would just be washing up in the Halifax harbour.

William had been awake for a few hours when Lucas came in with the news.

"How are you feeling, old chap?" Lucas asked, faking cheer.

"Fine, fine. Just tired is all."

"Are you sure? I have news that may upset you."

William narrowed his eyes. "Go on."

"A few mercenaries interrupted a rum transfer and shot dead Ruairi O'Neill."

William smiled. "And you thought that would upset me?"

Lucas continued gravely, "Only it wasn't Ruairi O'Neill. It was his brother Thomas."

William's face went white and the smile disappeared. "Does Ruairi know yet?"

Lucas didn't dare meet William's eyes. "He's already retaliated. All four of the mercenaries are dead; single bullets to the back of the head. They were found on the rocks near the Halifax harbour mouth this morning."

William felt the panic wash over him. At any moment, Ruairi would kill him for this. He had only had one chance to catch Ruairi off guard and he had failed.

Ruairi felt himself enter a darker space. The next bullet would end his relationship with Gracie. He couldn't expect her to forgive him for killing her father. But he would pull the trigger. He knew he would and the logic that had made him feel pure and righteous for so long now seemed distorted and gratuitous. He would continue the cycle. He would destroy another family; take another father away from his children.

She was suddenly in front of him. He blinked but she was still there, materializing out of the dew. She smiled up at him, her childlike innocence piercing his conscience. She had no idea the things he was capable of. He would have to tell her. She would have to make a choice.

He took a deep breath. "Your father tried to have me killed, Gracie." He took another moment to compose himself. "Thomas is dead. He was shot to death by four hired mercenaries who thought that he was me."

Gracie looked up at him in shock. Her first instinct was to deny it. It didn't happen if she didn't believe it. She started to shake her head. "My father's in the hospital, Ruairi, he couldn't have hired men to shoot Thomas. He was in the hospital," her voice got stronger at the end.

But Ruairi's eyes stayed strangely calm, strangely detached. "Gracie, my brother is dead. I can show you his body." Ruairi had wanted to say such different words to her. He had wanted to beg for a lifetime with her. Now he just wanted her to know, before anyone else was killed. She was the only one he didn't want to be brutal to.

Her lower lip began to quiver and she took a step backwards. "You're a rebel and a rum-runner, Ruairi; you must have lots of enemies. How could you assume that it was my father that . . . ?" she stopped. She had been staring at him the whole time but it wasn't until right then that she saw the tears. "You're crying."

He swallowed and looked away from her. He wasn't ashamed of the tears. He was devastated that he would never have the chance to touch her under normal circumstances again. He was devastated that he had lost his brother. He was devastated that it wasn't him dead, an end to his tormented life.

She caught her breath. Denial gave way to searing pain. His brother was dead. Thomas . . . was dead. She closed the distance between them and put her hands up to his cheeks. He put his hands over top of hers and she watched helplessly as he broke down an arms length away from her.

"I'm sorry, Ruairi. I'm so sorry." She was overwhelmed by his grief.

He suddenly pushed her away from him, forcing her back down two steps. "Gracie, you need to know where I was last night."

Gracie tried to climb back up the steps towards him. "You were with me last night, Ruairi."

He held her back. "Gracie, don't make this hard." He was adamant that she hear him out.

"I'm trying to make this easy."

He could hear in her tone that she didn't want to know the truth. "I killed four men last night, the men that killed Thomas."

Gracie felt her airways constrict. "Four men," she whispered, her voice floating away. "Did you kill my father?"

"No. I didn't kill your father." He pressed his lips together and then clenched his teeth. "Walk away now, Gracie. We can't be together anymore. It's gone too far."

"Don't you want me?" she asked, her face dissolving.

"Of course I want you, Gracie. But I can't put you through this."

"Can't it be over now?" she asked naïvely.

"No." His eyes hardened. He loved her but there was a line plainly drawn. She would have to cross to his side or he would have to walk away.

"I told you that I'd love you no matter what."

"You won't love me after this."

"Let me try."

"No."

"We were going to get married," she cried. "We were going to run away from all of this."

"I'm sorry, Gracie." He had nothing else to offer her.

She hesitated but only slightly. Then she slammed her little body into his. He steadied her against him, holding her tightly. He ran his hands up to her face, tilting it towards his. Their lips met and Gracie wrapped her arms up around his head, gripping his hair with her fingers. But he easily loosened her hands and backed away again.

"That was goodbye, Gracie. I'm sorry."

He retreated into the dark cavernous mouth of the Cathedral and left her standing alone on the cold, hard steps.

CHAPTER 24

Gracie stood, alone on the steps of the Cathedral. She wrapped her arms around herself and hugged tightly, afraid that she would disappear without him. Ruairi was gone. Thomas was dead. Her father was a murderer. Ruairi was going to kill her father. She began to tremble. Her legs gave way and she hit the steps hard, sliding down a few more before her body came to a rest, crumpled and heaving.

The next feeling was soft. There was someone behind her, someone who smelled of spicy earth, lifting her gently.

"There now," the voice was hushed but heavily accented. "The hard stone is no place for such a beautiful head."

Gracie could feel long spindly fingers brushing her hair away from her face and smoothing the skin of her cheeks. She opened her eyes and saw Moonshine Maggie, only it wasn't the same Maggie. No longer dressed as the hardened prostitute from the *Leda*, Maggie's face was clean of make-up and her hair was pulled back. She looked young and innocent. Her nails were short.

Gracie was drawn to her eyes. They were bright, like two limes. As she focussed on them, she heard a voice, quiet but persistent. "Codladh sámh, a ghrá mo chroí," it sang. The words were foreign but she clung to them as though she understood them.

Maggie closed and opened her eyes slowly, like an extended blink, and the voice disappeared.

Gracie felt her body grow heavy and then the sky went black.

When she opened her eyes, the surroundings were familiar, too familiar. She was back in William's house, back in her old bedroom. She sat upright looking around in fright.

She ran down the stairs and found Billy in the kitchen. He was reading a newspaper, with a cup of tea turning cold in front of him. He looked up at her when she burst in, his face pale and drawn.

"What are we doing here?" Gracie asked, panicked.

"I brought you here. You fell outside the cathedral and knocked yourself unconscious. Maggie brought you to the hotel and I brought you here with me."

"But why . . . why are we *here*?" Gracie's eyes were darting around as if she thought William was going to come around the corner and fly into a rage.

But Billy was lost in his own obsessive paradigm. He kept running his finger down the page that he had turned to and then shaking his head and staring off into the distance for a few seconds. "If I were dead, if Ruairi had shot me, this wouldn't be happening," he said suddenly.

Gracie stared at him. "What?" she asked, bewildered. Her head was throbbing.

"Ruairi was going to kill me and William. But he didn't. And now, William has killed Thomas. If William and I were dead, Thomas would still be alive."

Gracie was disturbed by Billy's line of reasoning. "Don't say things like that." She walked over to him and sat down in the chair beside him. "I can't bear to think of you . . ." she couldn't finish the sentence. "I can't bear to think about Thomas," she admitted.

Billy released a long, sorrowful sigh. "It's not just Thomas now." He handed the paper over to her and pointed at the front page story.

Gracie read the headline 'Four Bodies Found in Halifax Harbour'. She felt herself beginning to shake and she tried to read the story without actually seeing the words.

"Did you know any of them?" she tried to keep the fear out of her voice.

Billy shook his head. "No, but I know who killed them."

Gracie narrowed her eyes. "Who?" she asked softly, dredging up the memory of Ruairi in bloody clothes. She heard his voice telling her he had killed four men.

Billy's eyes watered again. "Ruairi killed them. They were hired to kill Ruairi but they shot Thomas by mistake. If you don't believe me, there are telegrams all over William's office and I guarantee you, somehow this will all get covered up by tomorrow. Ruairi retaliated. It is how this war goes."

Gracie sat very still in her chair. "I believe you."

"Is he going to kill William?"

Gracie nodded.

"Unless Ruairi is killed first," Billy's voice broke.

Gracie wouldn't allow that thought to penetrate. "He can't die. He's not meant to die."

"According to Maggie, he is," Billy despaired.

"She's wrong," Gracie said through clenched teeth but as she said it, she heard the voice again and those strange words. She shivered.

Billy closed his eyes and clenched his jaw. "Gracie, there's something about Ruairi that makes me question everything I know about right and wrong. It used to be so clear to me, but now," he hesitated. "In the end it's my fault that Thomas is dead. His blood is all over me." He opened his mouth to say something more but before he could he was interrupted by the slamming of a car door outside. He jumped out of his chair and walked with long purposeful strides towards the door.

Gracie stood up slowly and followed him, holding onto the walls for support. Every time she blinked she was confronted by the bloody shirt and the dark eyes and words that spoke to something deep down inside of her. She wondered who's blood would be on her.

William had forced his early release from the hospital. He felt he needed to be somewhere that he could stay in constant contact with the British Army. He needed advice. Lucas had called Johnny to help bring him home and they had just pulled up to the Gainsborough house when Billy threw open the door and charged towards them.

"What's wrong with you?" William asked from the last step of the granite porch. His son's face was a sickly shade of white and his eyes were bloodshot.

Without warning, Billy grabbed William by the neck and threw him up against the house. His thumb and forefinger pinned William's adam's apple and threatened to crush it.

"What the hell are you doing?!" Lucas yelled, rushing up the steps.

Billy slowly turned his head towards Lucas. "Back off or I'll kill you all," he vowed in a low voice. "I've spent years killing men. Three more on my conscience is nothing."

Gracie appeared at the doorway, her face filled with fear. Her eyes darted between the men.

"You had him killed didn't you?" When William didn't answer Billy pulled his father's head forward and then smashed it back into the white siding. "Didn't you?" he screamed.

William gasped. "Billy, no, of course not. I had nothing to do with it. I was sick, in the hospital."

"Don't lie to me." Billy's face was inches from his father's. "Who did you send to kill him?"

Gracie's heart began to race and she felt her legs trembling. She watched the frail man that was her father squirming at the hands of her brother.

"Did you know they are all dead? And he's going to kill you too!"

William began to choke under the increased pressure from Billy's hand. "Let me go and I'll talk to you," he gagged. "I can't talk like this."

Billy released him. "I didn't have anything to do with it, I swear, Billy." He knew he had to talk quickly. "When a few of the boys back home found out Ruairi was in Charlottetown they decided to kill him now rather than take the chance of him coming back to Ireland and causing more of a disturbance. I tried to tell them to let it go, that Ruairi was no longer a threat but they wouldn't listen. I only found out this morning when they shot the wrong O'Neill that they had already put a plan in motion."

"His name was Thomas," Gracie's voice was so soft that they didn't hear her. She was trembling violently.

Billy was shaking his head. "It's all lies, William! The Army had nothing to do with this. They told you to leave it alone! I found the copies of the telegrams. You bastard!" He was furious. Enough people had died in Ireland. They didn't need to continue the killing in Canada. "You do realize he will kill you for this?"

William's eyes went cold and he glared at his son. "We will get him, I promise you, we will get him. He is an enemy of the Crown and we will get him. Just like we got that paddy brother of his, we will get him."

"His name was Thomas!" Gracie screamed.

Billy turned and looked at her. "Gracie, are you . . ."

"His name was Thomas! He was gentle and funny and good. He was a poet . . ." Gracie began to hyperventilate. She bent over and felt her airways close. The ground started moving and then it blurred altogether. She felt Billy holding her steady but all she could see was Thomas laughing, Thomas reading, Thomas dancing. He had been so alive just a few short hours ago.

"Come on, Gracie, breathe for me now," Billy commanded her. William tried to get close to console her but Billy shoved him away with one hand. "She doesn't need you anymore," he snarled at William.

"I'm her father. She'll always need me."

She began to cough.

"That's a good girl," Billy tried to soothe her. "Just take some deep breaths."

Gracie gave herself an extra moment before she straightened herself up. She turned to face Billy, steadying herself on his arms. "I can't be near him anymore."

Billy nodded and cupped her cheeks in his hands. "Let's get you out of here. I've said what I needed to say."

William grabbed at his daughter as she began to walk away. Billy turned and hit him square on the jaw, dropping him to his knees. "You better stay there and pray," Billy snarled.

Gracie leaned on Billy heavily as he drove towards Valerie's house. As Billy parked she took in her surroundings. She hadn't noticed the ivy creeping up the façade before. Today it was the first thing that caught her eye. It made the house look safe; hidden and protected.

Billy reached out to open the door. He was surprised when it opened by itself, until Valerie appeared, stepping outside and partially closing the door behind her. Her eyes were red and swollen and she was dressed down in black tailored pants and a light knit sweater.

"I think its best right now if you both go back to Billy's room at the Hotel. I'll have some clothes sent over for Gracie."

Gracie dissolved into tears. "Do you all hate us now? We can't help who our father is!"

Valerie took the girl in her arms and calmed her. "I don't hate you. It's just with everything that's about to happen . . ."

The door swung open behind them and Rosaleen appeared, tear-stained and dishevelled. She flung herself at Billy. He caught her and held her tightly.

"This doesn't change anything between us," he said, holding her eyes. "This isn't your fault."

"I got him killed by coming to you!" she sobbed.

"Hush. Nobody's to blame but my father," he tried to reassure her but he knew her feelings of guilt ran deep. He turned back to look at his sister. Valerie was holding her as she fell apart. "He's ruined so many lives."

"War has a tendency to do that," Valerie sighed, rubbing Gracie's back gently. The girl was shaking so badly she could barely stand. "I think we need to lay this girl down. Come, Darling, I'll take you to the sitting room where you can settle yourself."

After Gracie was fussed over enough, Valerie turned back to Billy. "I'm sorry to have been so inhospitable at first," she tried to smile. "I'm not sure who I'm supposed to be protecting."

Rosaleen shuddered. "There's not going to be anyone left to protect soon."

"That's enough talk of death, Rosaleen," Valerie scolded her lightly.

Billy looked over at Rosaleen. After her initial tears, she had pulled herself back from him and composed herself stoically. She was sitting beside him, her dark long legs tucked up underneath her. She wasn't quite leaning into him and he realized she was using the tiny physical separation as a representation of the barrier between them emotionally. "Is there anything I can do?" he asked her, trying to engage her again.

She shook her head, pressing her lips together. "Ruairi's at the church. The boys are trying to organize the funeral."

Billy motioned to Valerie, "Can I speak with you in the kitchen, maybe?"

Valerie looked at Rosaleen. She shrugged half-heartedly. Valerie nodded and Billy stood up to follow her. Before he left, he reached down and patted his sister's hand. "Just stay here. I'll be back in a moment."

The room was silent for an interminable length. Rosaleen stared at the beautiful blonde creature that was stretched out on the sofa across from her.

Rosaleen raked her fingers through her raven hair and swung her long legs out in front of her to stand up. She reached over to a gold and crystal drink cart and poured two tumblers full of liquor. Then she knelt down in front of Gracie, holding one of the drinks out in front of her.

Gracie looked uncertain but took the drink.

"Drink it. It will make you feel stronger."

"Then just give me the whole bottle."

Rosaleen gave a little laugh. "You sound a bit like me."

"I wish I were more like you. You seem to be able to handle anything."

Rosaleen shook her head. "I don't handle things well at all. I've made a mess of everything."

"Please don't hate me," Gracie said, putting the tumbler to her lips.

Rosaleen would have normally found her naïveté annoying but instead, she found it refreshing that a girl only a few years younger than her could still be so innocent. "My daughter looks a lot like you," she said, a rare smile played out on her lips.

Gracie teared up. "I'm sorry that my father was such a monster to you."

Rosaleen tilted her head, her hair tumbling over her shoulder. Her eyes suddenly seemed distant. "He wasn't always a monster to me," she said softly, the lilt in her voice was like a lullaby. "And if it wasn't for him, I would have never met your brother and had my daughter . . ." she looked down at the floor, stopping herself. "I think you should go see Ruairi. He needs you."

Gracie rolled onto her stomach, tucking into herself. "He told me goodbye. He told me that I won't love him anymore after he . . ." she trailed off. She couldn't say the words.

Rosaleen looked her straight in the eye. "He's just afraid. He's lost so much already. But no matter what he has said, he needs you."

"He's going to kill my father."

Rosaleen reached over and took the tumbler from Gracie, setting it on the floor.

"Can you blame him?" she asked.

"No." Gracie couldn't.

"Can you forgive him?"

Gracie closed her eyes and shook her head. "I don't know."

Rosaleen nodded sadly.

"Am I awful?" Gracie cried.

"No. No, you're human." Rosaleen reached over and wiped a tear from Gracie's eye. "You have very little time left. Stay with him until he crosses that line."

CHAPTER 25

William sat alone in his study thinking over his options. It had only taken one phone call from a well placed friend before the police search was called off. The newspaper would run a story in the morning labelling the killings as 'mob related'. But that still left the problem of Ruairi O'Neill.

And Ruairi O'Neill didn't have a reputation to protect.

When Billy and Valerie came back into the sitting room, Gracie was gone.

"She went to find Ruairi," Rosaleen stated, as if that were an answer that shouldn't terrify Billy.

"Why? Why would she go near him at a time like this?" Billy began pacing back and forth.

"He won't hurt her." Rosaleen watched him from the sofa.

"How do you know?"

"I know Ruairi," she said simply.

"My father just had his brother killed. It wouldn't be too hard to imagine . . ."

"Ruairi is not crazy," Rosaleen said sharply.

Billy threw his head back and groaned. "Do you know how hard that is for me to believe?"

"I know that when Ruairi had reason to kill both you and your father that night in Dublin, you both lived to see the next morning. That's all the belief you should need."

Billy looked down at her. His expression softened. "If you asked him not to kill William . . ."

But Rosaleen was already shaking her head. "I won't ask that of him. Not anymore."

"Not even for me?" he asked.

"Not even for you. Ruairi needs me to choose him this time and I will."

Gracie looked back up at the massive doors of the Catholic Church. She had never been inside one before. She had been to church every Sunday growing up; Anglican church. Today, she felt like a Godless heathen. She was trembling badly, afraid that she was damned forever in the eyes of a God she didn't really know all because of the man she was born to love. She stepped inside tentatively. The air was strangely still and there was no sound at all. The light in the church was ethereal yet desolate. Shadows bounced off heavy beams and thick columns. The size of everything in the church seemed exaggerated and Gracie felt her insignificance acutely. She looked down the long center aisle and saw him. He looked small too. He was kneeling in the first pew with his head down. A coffin stretched open in front of him, beckoning.

Another figure came out from behind a massive pillar. As he made his way towards Ruairi, Gracie recognized Mairtin, his face badly bruised. She watched him as he waited. Ruairi raised his head and slowly stood up. He took a small card from Mairtin, read it and then handed it back. The two men just looked at each other. Mairtin nodded suddenly and turned to walk up the aisle.

"What are you doing here?" he barked when he saw her. The question echoed continuously and then suddenly, the sound was swallowed.

Ruairi spun around. She couldn't see his eyes. She needed to see his eyes. Mairtin continued towards her. "What the hell are you doing here?" he roared again. "If you don't stay away you'll be the next one in a coffin." His threat was loud and penetrated every corner.

"I'm sorry," she cried, the words bursting from her half in fear, half in grief. "I'm so sorry," she sobbed.

Mairtin stood in front of her as she slumped to her knees hard. Ruairi growled, a low angry sound, like a caged animal. Mairtin looked back, warning him not to move towards her, to stay in the shadows.

He looked down at Gracie. Her shoulders shuttered as they rose with her breathing. "I told you in the beginning how this would end." He stepped around her and walked out of the church with a single minded purpose.

Gracie stared up at Ruairi. Her knees ached and a chill was creeping into her bones. She slowly stood up and took a step towards him.

He shook his head at her.

She took another.

"Don't do this, Gracie," his voice was tired.

She kept coming.

He began to retreat. His back was against the coffin. He closed his eyes, willing her away.

"Just give me one more night," she begged him.

He opened his eyes. She was in line with the first pew. If he reached out, he could touch her.

"One night," he whispered sadly.

Mairtin sat with Aisling, Maggie and Mick in the parlour. None of them could accept that Thomas was dead. None of them could imagine burying Thomas anywhere but home.

"What is Ruairi's plan?" Mick asked Mairtin. He felt helpless. He had sworn he would protect the boys when their father had died and he cursed himself for not being there with Thomas. He could barely look at Mairtin, with his cuts and bruises, without realizing he could have lost him as well. But he wasn't a man for emotions. Instead, he had loaded his pistol and gone with Ruairi to find Thomas' killers. Now he was ready to do whatever was necessary to take the General down and keep Ruairi alive.

Mairtin looked up at his father's leathery face. "Not really sure, Da, he's pretty quiet about it all. But if he doesn't act soon then I'm going to do it myself," Mairtin threatened.

Ruairi walked in just then and glared at Mairtin. "You'll let me deal with it," he growled.

Mairtin glared back at him but stayed silent. Ruairi was dealing with enough and Mairtin knew it.

"Did you pay him a visit?" Mick asked Ruairi.

Ruairi shook his head. "I want to get Thomas buried first."

"I'd rest easier if we had him dead before Thomas was in the ground," Mick said gently. He knew this wasn't the best time to push Ruairi into action.

"It'll be in my time."

"How are you going to kill him?" Aisling asked.

Ruairi ignored the question. "Where's Rosaleen?" he asked. Nobody seemed to know.

Rosaleen stood on the pier, shielding her eyes with one hand as she looked out towards the harbour mouth. She was impatient. She dropped her hand and looked around. A few young dock workers stood off to one side, huddled together. Occasionally, one would look back at her and smile. She glared at him.

Her heart ached from all the bruises and scars. She had been careless with her trust, reckless with her love. She needed to grow a thick callous across the soft tissue. She needed to be the woman that everybody thought that she was.

On the horizon, a large ocean-liner rolled into view. The closer it slid, the more intense her conviction was. It wasn't long before she could make out the individual bodies and then, the individual faces. He stood, arms slung over the high railings, one leg propped up on a low rail. It had been a few years but he was still unmistakeable.

Emotion overtook her. Her throat was tight and the tears appeared unbidden. He didn't know yet. His baby brother was dead and he didn't know.

People streamed off the boat and hugged and chattered away noisily but neither he nor she moved for a long while. They just stared at each other. Her face was like stone. Something had changed, he knew by her eyes.

When he finally came down the gangplank, he wrapped her up in a crushing hug.

"What's happened, Love?" he whispered low into her ear.

Rosaleen sobbed into his shoulder. He rocked her back and forth. She caught her breath. "It's Thomas," she managed to say.

Gerry was very quiet. "How bad?" he finally asked.

When she didn't answer him, he knew.

"Tell me what happened."

"He was shot to death," her voice shook, "during a whiskey transfer."

Gerry tried to ask the right questions, whatever they were. "Did he suffer at all?"

Rosaleen swallowed hard trying to dislodge the emotion. "No, he died pretty quickly. Mairtin was there with him."

"Do we know who..?"

Rosaleen stared at her hands. "Ruairi killed all four late last night. He's planning on killing William in the next couple of days, I assume."

Gerry felt his body slowly numbing. "You are going to need to tell me everything, Rosaleen. I don't want to be half-informed."

Rosaleen looked up at him, her face drenched with tears. "I don't know what you mean."

He stopped and looked her dead in the eye. "You have a way with half-truths. I need to know exactly why the General isn't dead already. If my brother is wrestling with some kind of tortured conscience, I need to be ready for it." Gerry wouldn't let her look away.

"Has Ruairi told you anything?" she asked, ashamed.

"I've got the gist of it. You slept with the son, Kathleen belongs to him and you almost got Ruairi killed in the meantime."

Rosaleen looked away. "He's forgiven me." She couldn't bear Gerry judging her now.

"He always does."

Rosaleen nodded sadly. "Yes, he does."

"What's happened with the daughter?"

"He was ready to run away and marry her two nights ago."

"And now?"

"He won't listen to reason. Mairtin is itching to pull the trigger but Ruairi won't let him. He's convinced he has to do it himself."

"So why hasn't he?" Gerry was confused.

"William was in the hospital, he had some sort of turn. Ruairi didn't want any witnesses. I don't think he's planning to just walk in and shoot him."

"Does he know I'm coming yet?"

Rosaleen shook her head.

"Why not?" he narrowed his eyes. He looked exactly like Ruairi, suspicious of her every move.

"I want you to do it." She stared at him, unblinking.

He grimaced, "Ruairi will be furious."

"But he might stay. And if he stays, he lives."

Gerry shook his head. "He won't stay."

"Will you do it?" She was stubborn.

He put a muscular arm around her and led her across the street. "Of course I'll do it." He took a deep breath to calm himself as he thought of Thomas. "I'd be happy to do it."

They were standing just outside a little café and she stared through the window at all of the people inside, having their tea, eating lunch, living normal lives. "Do you want a cuppa tea?" she asked warily.

Gerry looked at her. She looked exhausted. He nodded and opened the door for her. He put his arm around her again and gave her a gentle squeeze. "I know you're worried about him, Love, but you can't change him."

She nodded but couldn't look at him, afraid if she made eye-contact that her emotions would spill out. They didn't speak again until they were seated with a pot of tea in front of them.

"What am I supposed to say when he asks me why I stepped in?" Gerry wasn't fond of lying to Ruairi.

"He won't ask," she said shortly.

"Why not?"

"He won't know you are here."

Gerry shook his head wildly. "No bloody way! I'm not going to do this without him and I'm not going to miss Thomas' funeral."

Rosaleen argued back. "You have to. If Ruairi even suspects that you're here he'll rush this and end up hating himself. He knows how quick you are to pull the trigger."

Gerry furrowed his brow. He wasn't convinced by her logic. "If he wants to finish this, then I think you should let him."

Rosaleen grabbed Gerry's hands and forced him to listen to her. "If he kills the General, it will be over for him and the daughter. He will go back to Ireland and he will die."

Gerry grimaced. "And you really believe that he'll stay here if he doesn't have to kill the General?"

"He won't have a reason to leave."

"There is still a war on back home."

"He can do his part from over here. Nobody else will have to die," Rosaleen pleaded with him. "Ruari's seen too much death." There were tears in her eyes again.

"We've all seen too much death."

"Ruairi thinks he's going to hell because of it."

"He doesn't really believe that," Gerry said.

"He told me he did," she said sadly. "He thinks we're all damned now."

"He's not going to hell. Ruairi needs to realize that even the angels have messes to clean up." He smiled at her. How could any of them be damned for a war that had been raging since before they were born?

"Rosaleen, I'll do whatever you ask but I'm going to see my family and I'm going to my brother's funeral. I'll deal with the fallout from Ruairi when I kill the General." Gerry wasn't going to give in on that point.

Rosaleen finally agreed. "Fine," she said. She heard Maggie's voice whisper that none of it would matter in the end.

Ruairi had to look again at the face that had appeared in his bedroom doorway. It had been years since he had seen that face.

"What the hell are you doing here?" he almost fell off his bed.

Gerry reached out to Ruairi. "I came to see how my little brother was holding up." His face was serious. "How are you holding up?"

Ruairi stood up and shook hands. "I can't believe you're here," he answered.

"Well, I figured it was as good a time as any."

The boys eyed each other with smiles that said a million things. When Ruairi's faded, Gerry knew what was coming.

"When did she call you?" he asked suspiciously.

Gerry sighed, "About a week ago."

"When did you find out about Thomas?"

"This afternoon."

Ruairi nodded and stared at the floor. Gerry stepped forward and hugged him. Ruairi put his arms around his brother and felt the bond that they had always shared.

"She wants you to kill him, doesn't she?" Ruairi pursed his lips.

Gerry's voice quivered with emotion, "It makes sense, Ruairi. Nobody else needs to know."

"I'd know." Ruairi's jaw was clenched.

Gerry could be just as stubborn though. "So what?

"So, I need to finish this."

"Thomas' death isn't your fault."

"Yes, it is. I could have killed William years ago but I didn't."

Gerry sat on the bed. "I'm still vague as to why you didn't."

Ruairi punched the wall. "I had every intention of it."

"Then why did you shoot him in the shoulder?"

Ruairi shook his head. In hindsight, it seemed ridiculous. "I thought that if I let them both live, that she would realize that I was the better man," he admitted. "I thought she would finally see how much I loved her."

Gerry narrowed his eyes and folded his arms across his broad chest and waited.

"My plan was to completely discredit the bastard, put him under suspicion from his own. I thought in the end, they would probably do the dirty work for me."

"And you would get the girl," Gerry finished for him.

"Instead, our brother is dead," Ruairi put his head in his hands.

"Three years later!" Gerry exploded. "Nobody could have seen this coming!"

"Maybe not, but I still need to kill him myself."

"And what about his daughter?" Gerry asked.

Ruairi stared at the wall. "She knows what has to happen. She knew from the start."

Gerry pulled a telegram out of his pocket and handed it to Ruairi. "If you are sure about going home then you need to see this."

Ruairi read the piece of paper and his face went white. "Dammit," he whispered.

Finnigan Murphy, Thomas' best friend and practically a brother to the other boys had been arrested and was being held in the Crumlin Road Gaol in Belfast on suspicion of the brutal assault of three Royal Ulster Constabulary officers. Ruairi felt defeated. Finn was one of the gentlest lads he knew. There was no way he had assaulted anyone. He was only being held for one reason.

Gerry watched Ruairi closely. "I'm going to go back for him."

Ruairi nodded. "There's not even a question."

Ruairi met Gracie down at Mick's cannery. It was a cool evening and Gracie was wearing a sweater set. A strand of pearls sat delicately on her collarbone. Ruairi reached out and ran his fingers across the pearls. He let his fingertips trail beneath the pearls. Gracie closed her eyes and concentrated on the feel of his hands on her.

"Follow me," he said, kissing her lightly and then taking her hand.

He led her through the warehouse to the back wall. He moved a few panels, revealing a door.

Gracie stepped inside to see a massive room behind the cannery's walls. It was filled with oak barrels and copper wires and large vats. "What is this?"

"This is where Maggie makes the whiskey," his voice was almost reverent.

Gracie was astounded by the scale of the production. She had pictured the bathtub stills that the temperance groups were always railing against. "This is incredible, Ruairi."

He nodded. "My brother Gerry helped her set it all up," he paused. "My brother's here now, Gracie."

Gracie turned to look at him. "Here in Charlottetown?"

"Aye."

"Did he come for the funeral?"

Ruairi hoisted himself up onto one of the barrels. "Rosaleen asked him to come last week. He didn't know Thomas had died until this afternoon."

Gracie's eyes watered. "How awful for him to arrive to such sad news."

Ruairi swallowed. "Gracie, he came to kill your father. Rosaleen thought that if he did it, then you and I could stay together and I wouldn't go back to Ireland."

Gracie stood absolutely still as she absorbed what Ruairi was saying.

"Are you going to let him?" she asked finally.

"No," Ruairi told her the truth.

Gracie bit her lip. She turned away from him so that he couldn't see her face and ran her hands over the oak. "So, this is where the angels steal from?" Her voice was soft and steady.

It took Ruairi a minute to figure out what she was talking about. "Rumour has it," he nodded. "Maggie says that every so often, she can feel them around her."

"I wish I could feel them. I always feel so alone."

Ruairi pushed himself off the barrel and stood behind her, drinking her in. "You're not alone, Gracie."

"I will be soon."

For the first time, Ruairi's conviction wavered. "I was so sure of myself until you turned up. I always want to live when I'm around you."

Gracie shuddered as her heart heaved. She leaned forward onto one of the whiskey barrels and tried to steady herself. She couldn't imagine a life without Ruairi. "I want so desperately to be able to forgive you."

"I don't deserve your forgiveness, Gracie."

"Yes you do." Her tears fell over the barrel. "But I don't think I'm strong enough to give it to you."

Ruairi turned away from her and began to cry. He had known this moment was coming but the pain of it had not been numbed.

Gracie felt her skin prickle. There were spirits all around her. "Tell me that it's just the whiskey that the angels are hanging around for," she cried.

Valerie lay beside Mick in the large canopy bed. "Are you asleep?" she asked him quietly.

He rolled over to look at her. The bruise on his face was dark and ominous.

"I'm scared Mick." She buried her nose in his neck.

"Scared of what?" he asked.

"I'm scared that you were right. That William won't stop until you are all dead."

Mick turned onto his back and stared up at the ceiling. After a moment's silence he spoke. "I don't think any of us will have to worry about William for too much longer."

CHAPTER 26

Gracie watched the sun rise with Ruairi's arms wrapped tightly around her.

"It's time to let go," she said.

Ruairi pulled her closer. "I don't know that I can."

She met his lips with hers and kissed him over and over again. Her hands travelled all over him, memorizing the map of his skin. "This is how I want to remember you," she said softly, "remember us."

His kisses travelled down her body; every touch meant to be the last but followed by one more.

She stepped back from him. He forced himself to release her. She took another step back, fighting every natural instinct. "I love you," she said.

"I love you too," he choked out.

He watched helplessly as she walked out the door.

William had to read the telegram twice. The second reading confirmed his fear. The British Government had withdrawn their support. They wanted nothing more to do with the unsavoury business that had already accumulated a body count of five. If Ruairi O'Neill came back to Ireland, he would be dealt with. Until then, William was on his own.

Gerry, Maggie, Mick and Rosaleen sat in Valerie's courtyard drinking and discussing Gerry's next move.

"I'm going tonight at ten o'clock," Gerry confirmed.

"Do you think Ruairi has any idea?" Rosaleen asked.

Gerry shook his head. "He's already made his plans to kill him at midnight. He wants to bury Thomas on the same day that he takes his revenge."

Mick looked worried. "How long do you think he will have before the police come for him?"

Both Rosaleen and Gerry looked at Maggie for an answer.

Maggie smiled. "The police won't even question him," she declared.

Gerry was sceptical. "Ruairi will be the first and probably only suspect, Maggie."

But Maggie was insistent. "They won't question him."

"Well, if they do, I'll confess to it," Mick offered. "I'm not going to let him go to gaol for this."

Gerry patted the old man's shoulder. "I would pity any officer who tried to arrest you. Not a single one of us would let you be taken in."

"I would go to hell for any one of you boys. Gaol would be easy."

Maggie narrowed her pale green eyes and focussed them on Mick. "Ruairi will not be questioned," she repeated a third time.

Rosaleen knew better then to question Maggie's talents but she couldn't quite grasp Maggie's conviction. "You weren't testing the whiskey before reading the star charts this morning, were you?" she asked.

Maggie began to laugh, an eerie cackling laugh that made Gerry's skin crawl. She stood up and began to move about the courtyard. Her laughter floated away and an even creepier silence filled the space.

Gerry watched Maggie closely. She was acting stranger than normal, moving about the space rhythmically in a circle. Her head was thrown back, her eyelids were fluttering and her lips were moving. She was speaking to someone who wasn't quite there.

Rosaleen completely ignored the performance. She sipped her whiskey and stayed oblivious to whatever rain dance or prayer was going on behind her.

Gracie hugged the pillow to her chest and cried. She was alone now. She had let go. Only, he was still there, in that ache, in that wound. In that shadow that sent a shiver down her spine as it passed over her. He was gone. And she was alone.

It was time.

Ruairi's Catholic conscience had been arrested years ago by the hell of the Great War. He had perfected many strategies to silence his moral compass when duty called but the Holy Ghost haunted him when his defences were down and his heart was stronger than his mind.

He believed that his soul had been compromised and although more than one priest had determined to convince him otherwise, he never allowed himself the forgiveness that confession promised to deliver. Regardless, he had knelt time and time again, revealing his darkness to the weary ears that were trained to hear more than words could say.

He entered the cavernous cathedral and genuflected beside the first pew. He knelt down and bowed his head, allowing himself to open up inside. He was heavily burdened and meditated deeply on his transgressions.

After a few moments of silence, he had the strange sensation that someone was beside him. He looked up quickly but to his surprise, he was still alone. He grabbed the pew in front of him and struggled to his feet but a veil fell in front of his eyes and the church went black.

William retired to his room with the help of his two nursemaids. They set about fluffing his pillows and turning down the bedcovers as he slowly disrobed. He looked at his ageing figure in the mirror and thoughtfully patted his soft stomach. He sucked in and tried to tighten up. He winced as a pain shot through his abdomen. He inhaled deeply and squeezed his eyes shut as he waited for it to pass. When he opened his eyes he noticed his belly had snuck back to its previous unfit state.

The nursemaids waited patiently for him to take his medication and lie down. They pulled the covers up over him and said goodnight. One lingered a bit longer by the bedside while the other made a quick exit, turning out the light as she went. William caught the young girl's wrist and she leaned down with a smile on her face. He kissed her roughly and she giggled.

"Goodnight, General Gainsborough," she said in a high breathy voice. There was a hint of something in it and William allowed the arousal to wash over him. Even that brought him pain now but it was still an enjoyable pain. He adjusted himself and groaned. He was alone.

William saw the organza curtain move out of the corner of his eye and he fumbled to sit up. It rustled again and he assured himself it was just the night breeze. He settled back into his pillows but he still felt uneasy. He tried to see the outlines of his furniture but the moon provided very little light. Everything was very dark shades of grey. He squinted, trying to force his eyes to see something. What he saw made every muscle in his body tighten instinctively.

On the other side of the room, a match was struck and the outlines of Ruairi's face materialized in the dancing flame. A cigarette was lit. With a flick, the match went out and a cold terror knotted itself in William's chest.

He struggled up onto his elbows and pulled the cord on the electric lamp. A soft glow illuminated the room. There was nobody there. His heart thudded. The thought of Ruairi was making him crazy. He couldn't handle it anymore.

He opened the drawer of his bedside chest and pulled out a letter that he had written earlier in the day and re-read it.

He looked back at the corner of the room. Again, nobody was there, yet the hair on his arms was standing on end.

It was dark outside when Ruairi regained consciousness. His head throbbed and his vision was slightly blurred. He walked the distance from St. Dunstan's to the Gainsborough house.

He was dizzy and light headed as he climbed up to General Gainsborough's balcony. The window was open and the breeze blew the curtain gently. Ruairi set his jaw and climbed through.

Gerry withdrew the pistol from the glove box of the car and held it a moment. He looked through the gate at the long, grass lined driveway and the grand house. He got out of the car and made his way down the driveway, conscious of every sound he made, every crackle of his footsteps. He stayed in the shadows, all the way up to the house. There were no lights on upstairs, but one burned strong on the first floor. Gerry was pretty sure it was in the kitchen.

He quietly climbed the front steps and put his bare hand on the doorknob. It turned easily and he found himself inside a large entrance way. He quickly walked towards the room with the light on, to see how many extra people he would have to deal with but there was nobody there. He was surprised that the General was on his own. He had anticipated that William would have secured protection. He scanned the different rooms on the first floor carefully, but again, saw nobody.

He climbed the stairs up to the second floor. He wanted to do the job and get out. Most of the doors were closed on the second floor but the one at the end of the hallway was open. Gerry raised the pistol and made his way towards it. He entered the room and saw the bed first.

General Gainsborough was slumped down on his pillows, with crimson spatters forming a gruesome halo around his head. Gerry flicked on the light to reveal the other figure in the far corner. Ruairi was sitting on a chair, head in his hands, a gun dangling from his fingertips.

The light must have been hard on his eyes and he blinked furiously when he raised his head. When his eyes finally adjusted they were void of life. The look sent a chill through Gerry.

"What the hell happened?" Gerry looked from Ruairi to the General to the gun and then back at the General.

"It was my job to finish," Ruairi said finally.

Gerry clenched his jaw and nodded. He walked over to Ruairi and took the gun from his hands. "Go spend the night with her. She'll never know it was you."

Ruairi shook his head blankly. "It won't matter," he said softly, leaning back and inhaling the smell of death.

Mairtin had trouble sleeping and so he wandered the house in the dark waiting for Ruairi and Gerry to come home. They arrived together. Ruairi walked straight past him and into the kitchen. Gerry lingered beside him, waiting for his brother to be out of earshot.

"He got to him first. I came in and the General was already dead," he informed Mairtin.

Mairtin nodded and sighed. "I knew he would do it. How is he?"

Gerry put his hands on his hips and scowled. "He's defeated. He thinks this is it for him."

Mairtin stared back towards the kitchen. "I have a bad feeling that it is."

Gerry glared at Mairtin. "Well, don't fecking tell him that! I can get Finn out on my own. We need to convince him not to go back to Ireland."

Mairtin shook his head. "Good luck."

"What about the girl? He wants to stay for her, surely." Gerry would marry Ruairi to any English girl if it meant keeping him alive.

"It's not about wanting to stay, Gerry, it's about wanting to live. He's sick of living with all of the dead."

"We all are."

"He wants to quit fighting."

"He can. He can stay here and get a real life like I did."

Mairtin looked down at the gun in Gerry's waistband. "Did you now?"

CHAPTER 27

Aisling found her brothers helping each other with their neckties. "I wish Ma was here," she said, reaching up and straightening Ruairi's.

Gerry nodded. "I spoke with her last night. She's not taking it well. Geraldine Reilly is going to sit with her today though, so that she's not alone."

Ruairi hadn't been able to think about his mother without crying. She had always sworn that she wouldn't survive burying a child. "She won't be alone for long anyways. We'll all be home in a few weeks."

Gerry held out his wrists for Aisling to do up the cufflinks. "You haven't changed your mind then?"

Ruairi checked himself in the mirror. "We're about to bury Thomas. I'm not going to let Finn suffer the same fate."

Gracie was trying to apply her make-up with shaking hands when Genevieve knocked on her bedroom door. She could see her mother in her dressing mirror.

"He's dead, isn't he?" Gracie asked.

Genevieve's face crumpled and her shoulders heaved. Gracie stood and ran to her mother, grief and guilt washing over her. Strong arms circled around both of them as Billy joined the embrace.

Rosaleen found Ruairi in his room, packing his few personal items in a canvas bag. He was dressed in a black suit.

"I spoke with Hanlon today. Georgiana is working on getting Karl released but the Club will remain closed for a good while." She lingered in the doorway.

Ruairi nodded. "Will he be out in time for the funeral?"

"I think so." She tapped on the doorframe.

Ruairi turned back to folding his trousers. "How's Billy?" he asked quietly.

Rosaleen tucked a stray hair back behind her ear. "Not very well, considering the circumstances," she paused, "I don't think he'll come to the funeral."

"I don't blame him." Ruairi turned back to her. "Will you be okay without him there?"

Rosaleen wrapped her arms around his waist. "I don't need anybody else when you are there."

It was the longest mile Ruairi had ever walked. The weight of his brother was heavy on his conscience; the weight of freedom was heavy on his soul.

Mick knelt in front of the casket, a leather bound book of poetry in his aged hands. Thomas had given it to him a few years earlier; the margins were full of his handwritten musings.

Mick was too practical for poetry. He didn't believe in the power of words. If words hadn't worked for Pádraig Pearse, they weren't going to work for him.

And so he laid the book on top of the coffin. The words would decay and be forever buried with the truth of who they were and what they believed in.

Ruairi looked around at those gathered at the grave. "These words are not my own. They are stolen from a poet, a friend, a countryman. They are the only words that are perfect enough to be spoken for my brother." He took a breath to calm his wavering voice. "To long a sacrifice can make a stone of the heart. O when may it suffice? This is Heaven's part, our part to murmur name upon name, as a mother names her child when sleep at last has come on limbs that had run wild. What is it but nightfall? No, no, not night but death; was it needless death afterall?"

As the last mourners walked away from the graveside, Rosaleen knelt down and placed a rose on the coffin. Ruairi turned around and walked back to her, kneeling down beside her and holding her to him as she cried.

Mairtin walked away from the grave quickly. His stomach was twisted and sore. He had spent the morning dry retching. This was one death too many for Mairtin Fitzgerald.

He lit a cigarette and leaned back against the cold stone gate of the cemetery. He closed his eyes and saw each and every one of their faces. They were there every time, unbidden. It had become an obsession of his, allowing the haunting to continue. It kept him focussed; it kept him raw; and so far, it had kept him alive.

He looked over at Ruairi, off in the distance, cradling another broken member of their fading family. Life would go on, just as it was now, without Thomas. But the thought of a life without Ruairi O'Neill shook Mairtin to the very core. Was there a way to change their destiny?

The cigarette was gone. He opened his eyes and found himself looking right at Gracie. Her eyes were different, cold. He recognized them. They were the same eyes that he saw every morning. They were angry eyes; eyes that had been betrayed by the world.

He reached out a hand to her, winding his fingers behind her neck. He saw the sudden fear that broke her face as he touched her but he pulled her towards him before she could put up a fight. He kissed her forehead roughly and let go of her just as quickly as he had grabbed her.

Nothing he would say would make a difference so he didn't say a word. He just walked away.

Ruairi knew he couldn't avoid her. She was standing at the cemetery entrance, intent on making him speak to her.

"Gracie, we said our goodbyes," he murmured.

"He's dead," she stated emotionlessly.

Ruairi swallowed and looked away. "I know."

She shook her head. "I didn't cry any tears over him. I cried them over you. I didn't believe that you would do it. I thought that if I let go, you would see that killing my father wasn't worth losing us. I thought that you would come back to me."

Ruairi's breathing was giving him away. "Don't, Gracie," he pleaded with her.

She stared up at him, the hurt shone through her eyes. "How could you do this to me? How could you hate more than you love?"

He felt the tears rolling down his face.

"You were right," she said, "I will never forgive you for that."

"I know," he said. Then he turned away. "Believe me, I know," he whispered as he walked back to his brother's grave.

They stayed by his grave all morning, drinking whiskey and reminiscing. Ruairi was the only one who abstained from the drink. He was silent and sober. Mairtin watched the death of Ruairi's eyes and took another shot.

Gracie lay in Billy's bed, shivering despite all of the blankets and the roaring fire. She heard the door open and saw her brother's figure cutting shadows across the walls.

He crawled in beside her and put his arms around her protectively. "You're like ice," he said.

"How could he do it?" she asked, her voice suggesting she was still in shock.

Billy rubbed her back. "I know that none of this makes sense to you but you have to understand how black and white this all is to Ruairi."

"To me it's just bloodstained." Her voice was very distant. "I told him that I would never forgive him. Those were the last words I said to him. I never told him that I still love him."

"Gracie, you are grieving. He knows that you still love him." Billy tried to comfort her.

"What if he doesn't?" She could barely breathe. She sobbed uncontrollably. "What if he dies thinking that I don't love him?"

Mairtin hauled his bags to the front door of the little blue house. Ruairi was sitting with Rosaleen on the porch swing. Kathleen sat between them.

"I just have something I have to take care of before we leave," Mairtin said, sticking a cigarette in his mouth and lighting it. "Can you take my bags for me?"

Ruairi nodded.

Mairtin walked his bags to the black Ford and placed them in the boot. When he turned and walked down the street, Ruairi noticed his hands weren't empty. He was swinging a crowbar as though it were a walking stick and whistling 'A Long Way To Tipperary'.

Mick stepped onto the porch and motioned for Ruairi to step aside with him. He had already said his goodbyes to his son but in his gut he knew that he would see Mairtin again. He had a different feeling about Ruairi.

"I'm not very good at these goodbyes," Ruairi began.

"Neither am I, Ruairi." Mick hesitated a moment and then clapped a firm hand on Ruairi's shoulder. "You be prepared for what they are going to throw at you."

"I won't just lie down, if that's what you're worried about," Ruairi assured him.

Mick's voice was low and grave. "You know that's not what I'm worried about."

Ruairi stepped forward and hugged Mick tight. When the embrace was over, Mick just stared at his feet, no longer able to look at the lad.

"You're one of my boys too," he mumbled. "Don't you forget that."

Ruairi stared out at the horizon. He nodded stiffly. He wasn't tough enough for moments like these.

Johnny Bexley looked up as the door to his study flew open. A masked man wielding a crowbar burst into the room. Johnny leapt out of his chair and cowered in the corner as the crowbar crashed through the desk in front of him.

"Who are you?" Johnny squealed in fear. "What do you want?"

"I'm a fecking Irishman," Mairtin roared.

Johnny threw up his hands in surrender. "Please don't kill me," his voice was weak and pitiful.

"I'm not here to kill you," Mairtin growled as he swung the crowbar again, this time smashing the windows on both sides of Johnny.

"Then why are you here?" Johnny cried, terrified. Glass was falling all around him.

Mairtin bared his teeth in an unpleasant snarl. "I'm here to teach you some respect."

Billy reached out his hand and shook Ruairi's hand one last time. It was the hardest thing he had ever had to do.

"I'm sorry for the way it had to end," Ruairi said.

"So am I," Billy said solemnly. "Take care of yourself."

Ruairi glanced at Rosaleen and then looked back at Billy. "You take care of her."

Billy nodded. "I will. I promise."

Ruairi cleared his throat. It was thick with emotion. "And take care of Gracie."

Billy met his eyes. "I will."

Rosaleen grabbed his hand as he strode by. He turned and caught sight of little Kathleen clutching her blanket to her face and he lost control of his emotions. Rosaleen pulled him to her and they both cried openly. Ruairi pulled away from her briefly to pick Kathleen up. The three of them held onto each other for a long time.

"I can't say goodbye to you." Rosaleen clung to his chest.

"Then don't," Ruairi whispered. "We've got eternity together anyway."

"I thought you said you weren't going to make it into heaven?" she sniffed, looking up at him.

"I won't. But right next to purgatory, they've got a little internment cell. It's for all of us Irishmen," Ruairi teased gently. He wanted to see her smile one last time.

She looked at Kathleen, who was still up in Ruairi's arms. "Give Uncle Ruairi a kiss now," she said gently.

Kathleen's big blue eyes looked into Ruairi's dark ones. "I love you, Ruairi."

Ruairi squeezed her tight. "Don't forget about me, my little faëry." He kissed her and tried to set her back down on the grass but she wouldn't let go of him. She began to whimper, softly at first but then her cries turned into screams as Rosaleen tried to pull her away.

Maggie stepped forward and untangled the little girl's hands from Ruairi's neck. She pulled the little girl into her arms and rocked her as she screamed.

Rosaleen put her hand up to Ruairi's cheek. His skin was wet with tears. She brought his face to hers and kissed him one last time.

"I love you, Róisín Dubh," he said one last time. He put his hand over his heart where the black rose was etched permanently.

Maggie asked Mairtin to pull up anchor and she went below deck to find Ruairi. He was alone in her room reading James Joyce. She crawled onto the bed beside him.

"Are you sure about this?" she asked, placing his book face down on the floor.

Ruairi rolled onto his side. "Aye."

Maggie closed her grassy eyes. When she reopened them, they were a dark emerald. She put her hand out and touched Ruairi's chest. Heat radiated from her hand, burning his skin. He grimaced.

She suddenly pulled her hand back and her eyes fluttered. The darkness drained out of them. She sighed and kissed his chest four times. He felt each touch as though it were a prophecy.

"I don't have the power to make you stay, do I?" she asked.

He reached out and brushed her delicate skin with his fingertips. She was human to the touch. "No," he finally answered.

General William Gainsborough was farewelled in an elegant and regal procession. Gracie watched as the casket was lowered into the ground. She had meant to cry but the tears wouldn't come. Afterwards, she wandered numb through the Gainsborough house as mourners paid their respects to the family. She heard the whispers, the lies and the accusations.

As the afternoon wore on, the wind blew in off of the harbour. Gracie was outside, standing near the embankment when a bugler stepped onto the verandah. He put his instrument to his lips and played 'The Last Post'.

Gracie closed her eyes and thought of Ruairi. Only then did her self-control disintegrate and her tears destroy her mask of propriety. She refused to find words to give life to her misery. Speaking them to any other living being would tear her perfectly unfulfilled love affair from the flawless realms of dreaming into the wretched world of reality. And it was only there, alone in this misery, this absolute despair, that her world was made beautiful.

She turned to Billy. "Get me a whiskey," she demanded softly.

Genevieve sat looking at the luggage that was piled in Valerie's foyer. "I'm surprised at how much I've accumulated in the last few years."

Mick watched her intently. "Are you sure you should be leaving now?"

Genevieve fidgeted with an earring. "I don't know what you mean."

"Gracie doesn't seem to be coping very well," Mick pointed out.

"I've begged her to come with us. There's nothing more that I can do."

"You could put the trip off," Mick suggested.

"Billy will take care of Gracie. I can't stay here right now," Genevieve began to tear up. "I have to go home."

Mick nodded. He leaned down and picked up the first trunk.

Ruairi spent most of the trip home in solitude. His notebook was his constant companion and he recorded every thought of her.

At night, Ruairi felt the darkness suffocating him. He had finally found something to live for that he didn't have to die for; but he couldn't possess it. The cost was too high. He had only his body and soul with which to pay and the time had come to offer it up. His eyes smouldered with the resentment and the bitterness of a man from whom everything else had been stolen.

Gracie slept through the days and was wide awake during the nights. She would often leave the house in the early evening to dine with Billy and Rosaleen but then she would slip away into the night, only to come home in the early hours of the morning smelling of bathtub gin and Canadian whiskey.

It was her penance to Ruairi; the only forgiveness she could offer now.

Before stumbling into the nearest speakeasy, she would wander the cemetery and as night fell, she would feel William's eyes on her.

This night was no different than the ones before. Gracie knelt by the freshly shovelled earth and inhaled the countryside. The red soil lay before her in a dark, still mass. It was dusk and the sky was cold and grey. Moments earlier it had been ablaze with colours but the night encroached and Gracie willed it to come. She wanted to feel the chill that would descend when the sun was gone. As if in deference to her thoughts, a cool breeze rustled the fabric of her dress and sent a shiver through her.

It was her way of healing, she told herself. It gave her the chance to ask the questions, say the words, and unburden her soul. But he refused her the answers. He was silent in his grave, mute in eternity.

She reached out and lightly traced the name that was etched into the marble stone. General William Gainsborough. It was cold beneath her fingertips. She withdrew her hand and tried to come up with some sensible way to end this guilt fuelled obsession; some final way of saying goodbye to a man that she loved and a man that she hated. She opened her mouth but there were no words. She pressed her lips together. The tears came sliding effortlessly down her cheeks. What more did she need than tears?

Across the yard, Moonshine Maggie appeared, the moon lighting her from behind. Gracie knew that she made for a lonely scene, and maybe a tad dramatic, here in the graveyard at night saying all the things that had gone unspoken in the last few days of William's life.

Tonight Maggie was ethereally beautiful, lean and graceful, with translucent skin and hair like burnt cinnamon. She was an illusion, too alive to be real amongst all of the dead. Her movements were slow and rhythmical, every footstep purposeful. She stopped and looked out at Gracie again, straining in the darkness to really see her. Then she blinked slowly. She fixed her eyes for a long moment. Then she began to move again and she crossed the yard even more slowly. When Maggie reached her, she removed her shawl and covered Gracie's shoulders, tucking the fabric into her arms.

"Thank-you," Gracie's words were barely audible. She was struck by her measure of kindness. She didn't know what to make of this angel whore.

Maggie sank to the ground beside her. She put a strong hand on her back and hushed her soothingly. Gracie felt strangely comforted, crying in the arms of the stranger.

"I know that he doesn't deserve this but . . . he was still my father."

"I know," Maggie said, nodding to herself while she looked around at the different statues and stones. "Everybody in here is somebody's somebody. They're laying here in God's acre while we are left to grieve. Heaven is reflected in their eyes and hell is reflected in ours."

Gracie felt very vulnerable when Maggie looked at her. Not uncomfortable, just transparent. "Philosophy is a bit lost on me right now."

She simply patted Gracie on the shoulder as she stood up. "Thomas would say that the right words are never lost on anybody."

Valerie dropped by the little blue house to see Gracie. She had moved in there to be closer to Billy.

"Would you like a cup of tea?" Gracie asked.

Valerie nodded and produced a book from her handbag. "I want you to read this."

"What is it?" Gracie asked. She looked at the author's name, Mary Wollstonecraft.

"I think it might get you thinking about the future; your future."

Gracie sighed and put the book on the counter top as she went back to fixing the tea. "I haven't thought about the future much."

"I know. It's time you start." Valerie stirred a sugar into her cup. "I want you to come to my house tomorrow morning at eight."

Gracie furrowed her brow. "That's quite early."

Valerie dropped her spoon on the saucer, making a sharp rattling noise. "Early or not, you will be there. You need to start living again, Gracie. You need to move on."

CHAPTER 28

R uairi laid his head back against the trunk of the tree. He was sprawled out on the ground, breathing in the scent of the earth. He and Maggie had found this place years ago. It was the perfect hideout, a clearing about a hundred yards square encircled by thick forestation.

They had built a hut in the middle of the clearing and had spent many nights in the safety of the grove. Maggie had made her own faëry ring here, burning a circle around the cabin by dancing for days in the same pattern. The grass had never regrown over her track.

He had missed this place. It held their memories, their triumphs, their sins . . . It held their spirits captive by the threads of time.

He thought about Rosaleen. She had planted a rose bush near the door. He looked at it now but the blooms were gone. Autumn was on its way and even the thorns were tucked up inside themselves to keep warm.

They would be safe here tonight, in the shadows of Cave Hill. And in the morning, they would re-join the ranks of Republicans, sworn to protect this maiden they called Ireland.

As the weeks passed, Gracie found herself back in Valerie's courtyard on a regular basis. It was her daytime diversion; her reason to get dressed in the morning. Spreading the feminist agenda gave her a reason to apply her make-up.

There had been a split in the community that had shocked even the most experienced socialites. Those that remained loyal to the traditional idea of island royalty continued to meet in the approved public places and the homes and gardens of old money. But there were a number of elitists that were growing bored with the same functions year after year who were more than happy to use the young Gainsborough girl's rebellion as an excuse to distance themselves from convention and instead cultivate new social outlets and engagements. This led them to Valerie Logan's door.

Gracie sat amongst the women who had gathered to hear Nellie McClung speak in Valerie's courtyard. She stirred her ice tea and listened attentively to the conversations going on around her. Gracie had become something of a figure head for Valerie's movement.

Norah sat beside her, occasionally patting her hand or giving her an encouraging glance. The conversation swelled around them. The girl on the other side of Gracie, a mousy brunette with a freckly complexion and a pot-belly, was regaling the surrounding women with a saucy anecdote from a recent rally.

Gracie felt hot. She removed the tweed jacket that she wore over her blouse. Her heart began to beat faster. She leaned forward and reached for her water glass. Her hand was trembling. Her breathing became shallow and rapid.

Rosaleen grabbed Maggie's hand. Maggie was already watching the girl. Nobody else had noticed yet.

"Why couldn't I forgive him?" Gracie interrupted, suddenly.

Fifty heads turned in her direction.

"He had warned me, from the beginning. He wasn't trying to hide who he was. He didn't lie to me. Not like everybody else."

Norah watched her friend with wide-eyes. "Gracie, honey, I think you need to lie down," she said softly.

But Gracie was on her feet now, her body trembling. She was warm, so warm and the room seemed to be getting smaller.

"Who am I to judge him? I mean," she put a clammy palm to her forehead, "I can't even imagine the life he has endured. Billy said the war changed him and you hear about all of those boys who went crazy."

Norah was trying to guide Gracie back into the house but Gracie kept spinning away from her.

"I convinced myself that I had tried to understand but did I really? Did I really try to understand or did I just try to change his mind?"

Maggie was walking towards her now, her eyes fixed on the young Gainsborough girl who was beginning to gasp.

Gracie looked up into Maggie's eyes as she approached. "I didn't want to hear the truth, did I?"

Maggie slowly shook her head and reached out to the girl. As their skin touched, Gracie collapsed into Maggie's arms.

Ruairi, Gerry, Mairtin and Denis O'Farrell, a seasoned veteran of gaol breaks, entered the grounds of St. Malachy's College the next morning two hours before dawn. Another man was positioned on Clifton Park Avenue and two more waited on the Antrim Road, acting as look outs.

Messages had been smuggled in and out of the gaol for more than two weeks now as the plans were slowly put into action. There were three other men that were going to escape with Finn. If everything went smoothly, all eleven men would end up back at St. Malachy's where three motorcars waited on the south eastern corner for an easy getaway.

Ruairi paced back and forth on the eastern side of the college. His breathing was slow and heavy. Mairtin could hear the nervousness in those breaths. He clamped a strong hand on Ruairi's wrist and dragged him back against the stone wall. "You're making me crazy," he growled.

Ruairi looked at his watch. Four more minutes until the explosion. Denis looked over at him and nodded. "It's going to work, Ruairi."

Gerry saw the strain in Ruairi's face. "You're going to make it through today, brother. Stop thinking what you're thinking."

Ruairi felt himself begin to sweat. He tore off his jacket, wrapping it into a tight ball. He felt for his gun. It was there. He was ready.

A blast detonated.

Ruairi worked on adrenaline. He made it to the gaol fence a good five feet ahead of the other lads. He shut off his mind and let his body feel for all of the next moves. He had been shot at twice already and Finn wasn't even through the second row of wire fencing. Ruairi felt the skin on his left hand rip open as the fence sprung back.

There was lots of noise, shouting and gunshots and water rushing out of a pipe that had been blown apart. Ruairi focussed on Finn's hand in front of him.

"It's grand to see you," Finn smiled up at him as a bullet ricocheted off the wall beside him.

"If we don't get moving, my face is going to be the last thing you see," Ruairi snapped.

They hadn't planned for such a quick mobilisation of the Royal Ulster Constabulary. Lorries full of officers from the Waring Street headquarters arrived at the gaol within minutes of the blasts. Ruairi could see the blockades set up on the Crumlin Road. He was sure the Antrim Road would have been sealed as well. The motorcars were now useless. Their only choice at this point was to scale the eastern perimeter and make a run for the Clifton Street Graveyard. They would then have to cross the Shankhill district before they would make it to the safe house on the lower Falls Road. Crossing the Protestant Shankhill district was the last thing Ruairi wanted to make these men do. But it was the only route left.

"Do you think it really matters if we all make it to the Falls now?" Gerry asked.

Denis licked his lips. "I think the best thing we can do, Ruairi, is run like hell and see who survives tomorrow."

Ruairi grimaced. He didn't want to leave any one of their fates to chance.

Mairtin grabbed him by the shoulders. "We are as good as dead if we stay here. We have to go and go now. Every one of us has done this before."

"And every one of us has turned up the next day," Denis reminded him.

Gracie opened her eyes and saw worried faces over top of hers. She heard herself whimpering and felt the wet tears on her cheeks.

"There you are, Love." Valerie came into focus. "You gave us quite a scare. Are you alright?"

Gracie tried to sit up but hands all over her body seemed to push her back down.

"You fainted, Gracie. It's best if you get up slowly." Rosaleen was beside her now, touching her forehead. "You were crying while you were unconscious. You must have been dreaming."

Gracie settled back into the pillows reluctantly. "It didn't feel like a dream," she whispered.

A pale face moved into view and Gracie felt her heart race as the red hair and green eyes and crimson fingernails came closer.

"It must have been a nightmare, Love," Maggie said, bending down close to kiss Gracie on the forehead.

Ruairi leaned his head back against the stone wall. "All right, boys," he said, forcing a brave tone. "Let's make a run for it. We'll scale the wall and head through the graveyard. Then split up and run for your lives. If you make it, meet at the Reilly's in Divis Street at noon tomorrow." Ruairi pulled a piece of paper out of his breast pocket, folded it and gave it to Finn. "If I don't show up there is a notebook under my bed at Ma's that I want sent to Gracie Gainsborough. Send this to Maggie. I want it buried in the ground at Thomas' gravesite."

Finn tried to shove the paper back at him. "Bury it yourself. You'll make it, you always do."

Ruairi shook his head. "They're after me, Finn, and they aren't going to stop until they get me."

Finn clenched his jaw. He didn't like the look in Ruairi's eyes. "You're the hero, Ruairi. This is just one more story we'll tell around the fires."

"I have to die to be a hero in this country."

Mairtin ran back to where Ruairi was crouched. "We've got about thirty officers coming through the western side of the building. They know we're here. This place will be surrounded in less than two minutes."

Ruairi nodded. "Let's go then."

Mairtin pulled Ruairi up to standing. They looked at each other one last time before Mairtin turned and scaled the wall. Ruairi and Gerry had their guns drawn to provide cover fire as their men dragged themselves over. Finn clenched his jaw. His nostrils flared as he held back the flow of tears that threatened when he looked at Ruairi. Ruairi reached over and smacked him roughly on the back. Finn nodded and ran without looking back.

When there were only the two of them left, Ruairi looked at Gerry. "Get your arse over it brother, I'll be right behind you."

Gerry grabbed Ruairi's collar and stared into his eyes. Then he pulled Ruairi in and hugged him roughly, his eyes stinging red. "You better be," he growled into Ruairi's ear. Then he turned his back and ran towards the wall.

The RUC began to fire on him. Ruairi answered back with all of the ammunition he had left. He cursed them for what they were doing.

Suddenly, the bullets started flying from behind him as well, and he turned and saw four or five officers coming through the blown up Crumlin walls. He tossed his gun and ran to the wall. He jumped, clawing with his fingers. He tried to get his boots to grip half way up. He lunged upwards as his left foot held and just as he pulled his upper body over the threshold he felt four bullets rip through his back. Unarmed and with his back to them, he slumped forward; half of his body in freedom, half of his body in no man's land. Ruairi gasped as the pain overwhelmed him. He could taste the blood in his mouth.

His body was dragged backwards, no one bothering to catch him as he fell. The officer's rolled him over and ferreted through his pockets for something to identify him with.

One of the officer's, pale and sweaty spoke up, "It's him. It's Ruairi O'Neill."

"How do you know?" another asked.

The man's voice caught and he hesitated to clear it, trying to mask the emotion that was choking him. "I served with him in France," he managed. Then he knelt down beside Ruairi's limp body and repositioned his arms and legs so that he looked less gruesome. "Bloody hell, Ruairi," he said softly, "you should have just stayed gone."

The next day at noon, the boys slowly gathered at Geraldine Reilly's. Every time the door opened and another body slipped in, Finn hoped it would be Ruairi's. But he had heard the gun fire and the yelling. He was sure they had gotten him.

His fears were confirmed when the next three people through the door were Mairtin Fitzgerald, Gerry O'Neill and Denis O'Farrell.

Gerry's eyes were red-rimmed and Mairtin's face was ashen. Denis looked terrible.

A head count established that everyone else had made it. They all stood, silent, waiting for the inevitable.

"Ruairi's dead," Denis O'Farrell began, through gritted teeth. "He was shot four times in the back while he scaled the wall. His body is at his mother's if you would like to pay your respects."

Finn's shoulders began to shake. They weren't supposed to cry, he kept telling himself. He turned and slammed his hand down on the kitchen bench. A few of the boys jumped at the sound.

Mairtin grimaced and walked back out the door and disappeared.

CHAPTER 29

Gerry went to his mother's house. He stood in her tiny parlour. Ruairi was laid out in a dark coloured casket in the middle of the room. Mrs. O'Neill was crocheting in the corner near the fireplace, her frail hands working furiously. He walked over and knelt in front of her, putting his head in her lap like he used to when he was a little boy. She stopped her crocheting and placed her hands gently on his head.

"I never had to worry about you," her voice was worn but velvety.

"That's because God doesn't want me," he choked out.

Ma O'Neill ran her fingers through her son's hair. "Well, take heart that the Devil doesn't want you either."

Rosaleen felt the blood drain from her as the words registered. Gerry's voice was far away on the line.

"Are you there, Rosaleen?" he asked finally.

She made a muffled noise but no words could come out.

"After the funeral, we're all coming back; Mairtin, Finn and Aisling too. Do you think you can hold yourself together until then? For Kathleen's sake?" Gerry was sick with fear that she would lock herself away.

Rosaleen felt the pain somewhere deep. A sob was ripped from her and then she was silent again.

"Rosaleen, I need you to answer me. Tell me that you aren't alone," he tried to be tough, demanding.

"Billy's here . . ." Rosaleen finally answered him.

Then there was a click on the line.

"Rosaleen?" he closed his eyes and prayed. But she was gone.

Mick hung up the telephone. He took one deep breath and then went to his closet. The new suits that Valerie had bought for him were lined up in front of him. He stared at them for quite a while, trying to decide which one was the blackest. He finally settled on one and slowly got dressed. He opened the top drawer of the box on the dressing table and chose the shiniest of the cufflinks.

He clutched the edges of the dressing table. He felt weak. He felt old. He leaned down and put his forehead on the cool polished wood. He breathed slowly and deliberately. He wouldn't cry. He knew this day was coming. He inhaled sharply and stood up straight.

He sat down on the edge of the bed and pulled on his socks and the pair of wingtip brogues that Genevieve had insisted that he buy to make him look dapper. He looked in the mirror. He was pretty sure he looked ridiculous.

He made his way down in the lift and out onto the Parisian street. He fidgeted with his jacket nervously as he made his way past outdoor cafés and patisseries. He didn't want a church. He was looking for his own type of salvation.

He sat down at the bar of a hotel. The bartender looked at him expectantly.

"Two Irish whiskey's," Mick ordered.

The drinks were set down in front of him. He drank one and said a prayer for the other.

Finn left Geraldine Reilly's out the back door and jogged down the alley towards St. Peter's Cathedral. He eased his aching body into a pew near the front and lowered his head for a long while. When he raised it, his face shimmered with tears. Thomas was dead. Ruairi was dead. For everything it had meant to him, Ireland was dead.

He reached into his pocket and pulled out the folded piece of paper that Ruairi had given him. He fingered it slowly and then finally opened it. His battered face blanched and he gasped for breath.

It wasn't long before the clicking of heels reverberated through the cathedral as the priest came running to quiet the young man in the pew who was screaming obscenities and tearing the catechism.

Mairtin walked over to the O'Neill house. He refused to duck in and out of alleys, instead he chose to walk, head held high through the streets. His eyes dared anyone to challenge him today.

He stood in front of the door and stared at the knob. By going inside, he would be acknowledging Ruairi's death. He would have to stare down at Ruairi, lying dead in some poor man's coffin. He thought of the pageantry that would have accompanied General Gainsborough's funeral.

He hesitated no longer. He walked through the door and straight into the parlour where Ruairi's body was laid out. He reached down and touched Ruairi's face. "Yeats was right; your sacrifice has made a stone of my heart."

He turned around and saw Aisling in the doorway, her face full of sorrow. He motioned for her to come to him. She fell into his chest and cried for her brother. Mairtin cried with her.

Billy found Rosaleen on the floor of the kitchen, cold and incoherent. He carried her to their bedroom and tucked her under mounds of blankets. She drifted in and out of consciousness but never said anything. She didn't need to. Billy knew the moment he had found her that Ruairi was gone.

When he told Gracie, she was already three fingers deep in her bottle of whiskey. He watched as the ghosts ran naked through her eyes. She was haunted now. Her tiny frame shivered from the eclipse.

He was surprised at how thin Gracie was when he picked her up. He could feel her shoulder blades protruding through the velvet wrap she had draped about herself. He hugged her closer as her weeping intensified into wrenching sobs. She clung to him with white knuckles and translucent fingers.

Billy hushed her gently and repeatedly but to no avail. She was intent on taking herself down.

Valerie let herself into the little blue house. She didn't want to be alone tonight and no amount of feminist brigade meetings were going to replace the need she had. She needed family.

She found Maggie in Kathleen's room, stroking the little girl's hair. Kathleen was curled in a tiny ball on the floor, her sheets and blankets a tangled mess strewn across the room.

"What's the matter, Love?" Valerie crooned, scooping her up and holding her close.

But Kathleen just sobbed, holding the teddy bear that Ruairi and Thomas had bought for her last Christmas.

Maggie looked up at Valerie with red eyes. "She heard me crying and she knew."

After Kathleen fell back asleep, Valerie tiptoed out of the bedroom. She was almost at the stairs when she saw the door to Gracie's room ajar. She poked her head in. The room was empty.

"Where's Gracie?" Valerie asked Billy. She found him wiping Rosaleen's face with a wet rag. She had been vomiting for the last hour.

Billy looked up. "She should be in her bedroom," he replied. He saw Maggie's face as she came in behind Valerie. "She's not there is she?"

Maggie shook her head no.

Billy jumped to his feet but Valerie stopped him. "You stay with Rosaleen," she directed. "We'll find her."

It wasn't long before word reached Gerry and Mairtin that Finn had gone crazy in St. Peter's. The priest gave Gerry a stern lecture about the boy's mental health while Mairtin dragged Finn out of the rectory and into a waiting motorcar.

"What the feck's gotten into you?" Mairtin turned a fiery eye on the sobbing lad. "You didn't even cry like this when yer own Ma died."

Finn took a shattered breath and clumsily fished the paper out of his breast pocket. Gerry took the paper and unfolded it.

"Bloody hell!" he spewed. "The feckin' bastard!"

Mairtin turned to face Gerry. "What is it?" he asked, concerned that the piece of paper had garnered that much of a reaction.

Gerry shoved the paper at Mairtin. "It's a feckin' suicide note . . . from General Gainsborough."

"But Ruairi said . . ." Mairtin stammered.

'Ruairi didn't say a damn thing other than it was his job to finish," Gerry's voice was strained.

"There's no way. There's no fecking way." Mairtin was shaking his head vehemently. "Ruairi killed the General. He had to have killed the General." It made sense that way, Mairtin thought angrily. He could accept it that way.

Finn took a deep breath. "He wanted the note buried in Thomas' grave. What does that tell you?"

Gerry shook his head in disbelief, his face cracked by shiny streams. "It tells me that my bloody brother thought that we could use one more Irish martyr."

Mairtin exhaled. He slid down and leaned his head back against the seat. He thought about everything that had happened in the last few months and closed his eyes. Ruairi had chosen to let Gracie believe that he had killed her father. He let them all believe that Thomas had been avenged.

Mairtin cleared his throat. "It doesn't change anything, I mean, not really." A smile softened his hard face. "The General's dead."

"But so is Ruairi," Finn choked out.

"And so is Thomas and so is Paddy Mulligan and Seamus O'Rourke and Michael Collins and Pádraig Pearse." Mairtin lit a cigarette. "We're the dying kind. Ruairi couldn't change that."

"And so we just leave it like that? We let the General go out a hero and Ruairi go out a criminal?" Finn was distraught.

Gerry slowly nodded. "We just leave it like that. It's what the boy wanted."

Maggie was the first to find her. She lay sprawled across the cobblestone floor of the cannery, distilled spirits ebbing and flowing around her as Maggie's footsteps splashed through the liquor pools.

"What have you done, Love?" Maggie cried in desperation as she reached down to feel Gracie's pulse. The girl was alive although she had cuts and bruises all over her body.

Gracie rolled herself up to an elbow and turned her swollen eyes up to Maggie. "So, I'm not dead then?"

Maggie wrapped her arms around the girl, wanting to both shake her and hug her at the same time. "No, you're not dead, you silly girl. What in heaven's name did you think you were doing, scaring the life out of us the way you did?" She looked around at the destruction that the tiny English girl had managed. Every barrel of whiskey was either completely smashed or bleeding alcohol. There was whiskey everywhere, the smell of it strong enough to get drunk off of.

"I wasn't going to let them have it all," Gracie whimpered angrily.

"Who, Love?" Maggie was confused.

"The angels; I'll never give them another damn thing. They took Ruairi; they can leave me the damn whiskey."

Maggie threw her wild red hair back and laughed. It was a hysterical laugh, full of sorrow and fear.

Ruairi's funeral took place in the rain. Gerry looked out at the sea of faces that filled the cemetery and knew that his brother was finally at peace.

The three boys took shovels and filled in his grave. *Never leave an open grave,* Ruairi had always said. Gerry knelt down and sprinkled one last handful of dirt over his brother. "It's always the best of us that they take," he whispered.

A bespectacled gentleman made his way to the front of the crowd. He was well known amongst Republicans not only for his eloquent words but his heart for the cause.

The man addressed the crowd. "I have been told that the only thing that Ruairi wanted written on his headstone was a line from one of my poems," the man paused, making eye contact with each of the Irish Republican Army Volunteers standing before him. "But I, being poor, have only my dreams;" his voice rang out. Stepping forward on top of the disturbed earth, the poet cleared his throat. "I have spread my dreams under your feet; Tread softly because you tread on my dreams."

That night, the pub didn't close. The drinks flowed and so did the stories. So did the tears.

THE LAST CHAPTER

Mairtin found himself in a strange position. Every fibre of his being wanted to stay in Ireland and continue the fight. But every night he saw her face, and every night she looked more fragile, paler somehow. He knew his fate had become entwined in hers.

The day before he left he sat beside the mound of dirt that was beginning to settle on Ruairi's grave. He had with him two shot glasses and one bottle of Irish whiskey. He poured Ruairi's first shot into the soil but after that, he drank for both of them. When the bottle was done, he patted the grave, cleared his throat and walked away. He had said what needed to be said.

Finnigan Murphy had no reason to stay. Ireland had failed him. Or he had failed her. He wasn't quite sure which. But either way, he was destined to say goodbye to the land that had been his muse.

He stood with Mairtin, Gerry, Aisling and Ma O'Neill as the green fields became more and more distant. They had dedicated their lives to Mother Ireland. "Do you think she'll miss us?" he asked.

Mairtin sucked heavily on his cigarette. "She doesn't even know our names," he said grimly.

They never spoke his name during the entire trip back. They couldn't bear it. But every night, each one of them met Ruairi in their dreams.

Gracie walked slowly towards the dock. For an entire month she had walked, every morning, down to the private docks to the exact mooring where she had first climbed aboard *The Phoenix*. She knew that soon, she would have to stop retracing her steps, stop clinging to every small routine that brought memories of him flooding back. But not today. Today she still needed him. Today she was still forgiving him.

The sky was a clear blue and the sun was already making its way up towards the top of the world. There was a gentle breeze blowing in off the water and Gracie closed her eyes to breathe in the salty air. She approached the dock and put one foot out on the wooden planks and then stopped abruptly.

There it was, bobbing lazily at the mooring. She ran towards it looking around wildly for him. She stood staring at it, breathing hard, tears streaming down her face. It wasn't him. She saw some bags tossed carelessly in the bow, none of them recognizable.

Her sadness changed to anger. *Who would be cruel enough to bring it out, in plain view, when I am still grieving?* she thought. *It should be locked away, nobody able to touch it, wash away what was left of Ruairi's fingerprints, footprints . . .*

She reached down and pulled off her shoes, dropping them on the dock and then she jumped down onto the boat deck. She leaned over the bags and started throwing them off into the water. They were light and floated easily.

"Och! What the hell do you think you're doing?" an Irish voice called out.

Gracie spun around and saw a young man running towards the boat from the opposite end of the dock.

"This is Ruairi's boat!" she screamed at him. "Keep off of it!"

The young man leapt onto the boat and straight over the far rail and into the water to save his bags. Gracie straightened up and watched him, shocked by his immediate reaction. One by one, he threw the wet bags back onto *The Phoenix* and then he swam over to the dock and pulled himself out. He rolled over onto his back and lay panting. When he caught his breath, he turned onto his side, propping his head on his hand and looking at her like she had four heads.

"Are ye mad?" he asked her calmly.

She gave him a dirty look. "I am not mad. What are you doing with this boat?" she asked crisply.

"A friend of mine gave it to me," he replied.

"Well it wasn't theirs to give!" She could hear her voice rising but she couldn't control it. "It belongs to," she stopped suddenly, "belonged to," she corrected herself slowly, a hard lump formed at the base of her throat and she couldn't go on.

The young man sat up and put his feet down onto the boat. He walked over to her and stood close to her, putting a hand on her arm. "It belonged to Ruairi. He told me to take care of a few things when he was gone."

Gracie stepped backwards, away from his touch. "You knew Ruairi?"

He crossed his arms understanding why she had moved away. "I'm Finn. You must be Gracie."

Gracie thought that she had no tears left to cry. But as soon as he said her name, she felt them, hot and salty, rolling down her cheeks. "Yes, I'm Gracie," she whispered.

It was all Finn could do to hold back his own tears. "Ruairi gave me something for you," he said reaching into one of the bags and fishing around. "I hope it's not soaked." As Finn pulled out the book, General Gainsborough's note slipped out and fell at Gracie's feet. She slowly bent to pick it up but Finn lunged at it, sweeping it away from her fingertips.

She looked at him with suspicious eyes. "What's that?" she asked.

He slid it into his bag. "Just a letter for Maggie," he replied, quickly. He would respect Ruairi's final wish.

Gracie reached for the notebook, her tears coming faster. She recognized it. It was the one he had been scribbling in at the café in Halifax. She turned it over and over in her hands.

Finn looked at her and swallowed hard. He wanted to tell her. He wanted her to know the truth.

"I still love him, you know," she said quietly, looking up. "I will always love him."

Finn bit his lip. "But you blame him for your father's death?"

"I did at first," she said simply.

"And now?" Finn asked.

"Now I'm alone," her voice was full of regret.

Finn nodded slowly. Maybe that was truth enough.

Moonshine Maggie looked around at what was left of her distillery. She twirled slowly, taking it all in. In her hand she held the General's suicide letter. She refused to bury the truth. It was too literal. She kissed it and placed it on one of the broken whiskey barrels. Her green eyes glinted as she struck the match. The corner of the page began to turn brown and then black as the flame singed the truth. She walked backwards, her eyes glowing pale.

"Our day will come," she whispered as the cannery exploded, "believe me."

Gracie waited until she was alone again on *The Phoenix*. She walked to the bow of the boat and settled down in the exact spot where she had lain that morning, so many weeks ago. She pulled her cardigan tightly around her. There were no sails to bed down in this time.

Gracie closed her eyes and took a deep breath. She opened the notebook. The first few pages were hastily scrawled notes that meant very little to her. She turned the page. *Gracie, I hope that these are worth cherishing,* he had written simply. She gasped. He had written her love letters.

He had given her his last words.

Drinking Grace

Evaporated Spirits
Dance all around
As the angels share whiskey
And the atmosphere drowns

I thought of you today
In the haze of what's become
You were blurred and unsteady
And you tasted like rum

I am drunk on your essence
Imprisoned by your love
But the angels they stole you
Took you high up above

So I age in this casket
And you dance all around
As the angels share whiskey
And my soul slowly drowns

ACKNOWLEGEMENTS

This word will never be enough but it is all that I can offer here so, thankyou.

To Matty for sticking with me through this journey. Your belief in me blows my mind.

To my Mama and my Daddy for showing me the measure of love and support; from you it has always been endless.

To Robyn, Sara, George, Melissa, Niamh, Carlin, Mandy & Joe for the phone calls, tweets, workouts, coffees, whiskeys and most of all, your friendship.

To Harry & Mick; you have become family & you will never know how much I needed that.

To Catherine Dean for your cover design and your enthusiasm for my dream; but mostly for your friendship. What were the chances that we would meet?

To Elizabeth Cowell, my editor, for teaching me so much about this process. Your notes and suggestions were invaluable.

To Margaret, Denis and Jim for your knowledge, hospitality and time. Thank-you, it has meant so much to me.

To LF for listening. It has made all of this possible.

To Gerry Buccini and Geoff Parker. I learned to love literature because of you.

To those of you, too numerous to name who have supported me with love and encouragement through these past six years; you know who you are.

To all of the writers, poets, politicians, teachers, historians and soldiers; thankyou for inspiring me to look further.

Finally, to Whiskey and Phoenix for never interrupting while I told you this story.

AUTHOR'S NOTE

I reland has played the role of my muse for many years now. This novel was born out of an intense passion for the artistic, mythological, historical and political landscapes that Ireland has cultivated. It was also born out of the desire to understand the humanity that lies beneath all of the rhetoric and propaganda of the last hundred years.

The historical events and personas that are referenced over the course of the novel have been fictionalized in their entirety. My intention in writing was not to give a history lesson but to tell a story. In doing so, I re-imagined the time instead of re-creating it. By placing fictional characters in historical situations such as the ambush involving Kevin Barry, I was forced to deviate from fact for the sake of the story. I have also taken artistic liberties in regards to such things as the reference of the phoenix which did not become a symbol of the IRA until 1969.

The introduction of the Irish myth concepts happened very early on in the writing. In my mind, Ruairi could not be fully embraced as an Irish hero if he did not abide by the law of the geis. I included Moonshine Maggie Monroe in honour of all of the wonderful traditional faëry stories that I was raised on. I did not feel that this novel would be complete without a touch of magic.

Slan,

SJ.

LITERARY ACKNOWLEDGEMENTS

I owe a great deal of debt to many writers, poets and historians whose work has inspired and laid the foundations for my novel. To the poets whose words have been quoted in the text, thankyou. No better words exist.

A Portrait of the Artist as a Young Man, James Joyce, B.W. Huebsch, 1916.

Aedh Wishes for the Cloths of Heaven, William Butler Yeats, The Wind Among the Reeds, 1899.

An Irish Heart, Dark Rosaleen, David McKee Wright, Angus & Robertson Limited, 1918.

Bootleggers and Baptists: The Education of a Regulatory Economist, Bruce Yandle, Regulation 7, no. 3, 1983.

British Voices: From the Irish War of Independence 1918-1921, William Sheehan, The Collins Press, 2007.

Dark Rosaleen, James Clarence Mangan.

De Valera: Long Fellow, Long Shadow, Tim Pat Coogan, Arrow, 1995.

Divorce in a Small Province: A History of Divorce on Prince Edward Island from 1833, Wendy Owen and J.M. Bumsted.

Easter, 1916, William Butler Yeats.

Guerilla Days in Ireland, Tom Barry, Anvil Books, 1993.

Kevin Barry (Traditional song), Author Unknown

Kevin Barry and His Time, Donal O'Donovan, Glendale Publishing Ltd, Dublin, 1989.

Michael Collins, Tim Pat Coogan, Arrow, 1991.

Mobsters & Rumrunners Of Canada: Crossing the Line, Gord Steinke, Folklore Publishing, 2003.

Molly Malone, Traditional song.

Myths & Legends of the Celtic Race, T.W. Rolleston, CRW Publishing Limited, London, 2004.

Rebels, The Irish Rising of 1916, Peter de Rosa, Random House, 1990.

Roísín Dubh, Traditional song, attributed to Antoine Ó Raifteiri, Translation by Pádraig Pearse.

Rum Row, Robert Carse, Flat Hammock Press, 2007.

Shakespeare Identified, Thomas J. Looney, Frederick A. Stokes Company, New York, 1920.

The Irish Civil War 1922-23, Peter Cottrell, Osprey, 2008.

The Black And Tans, Richard Bennett, Pen & Sword Military, 2010.

The Fox Industry of Prince Edward Island, Sarah Stresman, Sir Sanford Flemming College, 2006.

The Real McCoy, Frederic F. Van de Water, Flat Hammock Press, 2007.

Printed in Australia
AUOC011137061112
254324AU00002B/11/P